SCALES of SUN & STORM

✦ EMILY SCHNEIDER ✦

PRAISE FOR *SCALES OF ASH & SMOKE*

"…a masterful work of YA fantasy fiction which contains all the must-have ingredients for a thrilling read, from a compelling central pair of characters to a lavish and atmospheric setting filled with danger and intrigue." –Readers' Favorite

"Swoony, sweet romantasy meets elemental magic and an epic world of dragons in this unique story…"—Rachel L Schade, author of the Cursed Empire series

"The perfect series for fans of fantastical worlds, sweet romance, and magic! Schneider serves up a refreshingly unique take on dragons, a gripping love story that transcends deep-rooted enmity, and the palpable sense of hope that persists despite looming war. A tale not only worth reading, but celebrating!"— Natalia Macias Lucia, author of Girls of Salt and Sea

*"I. Am. Obsessed… The romantic tension between Kaida and Tarrin is just so well written (*internal squealing*), so if a (non-toxic) enemies-to-lovers trope compels you to pick it up, this book will deliver."* –Marissa Lete, author of Echoes

"My new favorite literary couple!" –Lucia Ferrara, editor

"The dragon story GOT should've had…Everything I could've ever wanted in a fantasy and didn't know I needed."—Amazon Review

"Wow, my heart is still racing. The flow of this book is outstanding. The characters are great. The plot is totally believable. I can't remember if I ate dinner. Very highly recommend."—Amazon Review

"Every detail was described to perfection."—Goodreads Review

PRAISE FOR *SCALES OF ICE & SHADOW*

"It was full of mind-blowing reveals, political intrigue, magic, love, and most of all, DRAGONS…You won't find anything else out there that's like it." –Amanda Chaperon, author of For the Boys

"This book contains everything I wanted in a sequel: tons of action…new characters and lore, and a fast-paced plot that kept me frantically flipping pages!"—Marissa Lete, author of Echoes

"I found it so hard to put this one down and could not wait to pick it back up again. Definitely had a book hangover after finishing."—Amazon Review

"This is the sequel you absolutely wanted and needed!"—Amazon Review

"This book was stunning. It now lives rent free in my mind… There are so many moments of pure wisdom and kindness woven into a story where it seemed like any hope at all should have been impossible. It was beautiful."—Goodreads Review

"I didn't think it was possible, but I loved the second book even more than the first book!"—Goodreads Review

DON'T MISS THE AWARD-WINNING FIRST
BOOK IN THE ASH & SMOKE SERIES:

SCALES OF ASH & SMOKE

FANTASY WINNER OF THE 2021 BEST
INDIE BOOK AWARD

 MAGIC KEEPERS PRESS

For information contact:
Magic Keepers Press, LLC
magickeeperspress.com

Hardcover: 978-1-7374957-7-2
Paperback: 978-1-7374957-6-5
Ebook: 978-1-7374957-8-9

First edition November 2022

Edited by Andrea Hurst
Copyedit and Proofreading by Lucia Ferrara
Cover Design by Damonza © 2022
Map by Nathan Vanderzee © 2022

For all those who have fought their way out of the darkness.
And for those who are still searching for the light.

PRONUNCIATION GUIDE

Characters:
Kaida: KYE-duh
Tarrin: TARE-in
Eklos: ECK-los
Lita: LEE-ta
Eldrin: EL-drin
Martik: MAR-tick
Roldan: ROLL-den
Aela: AY-luh
Alyaa: AL-yah
Rythos: RYE-those
Magus: MAH-goose
Gendon: GHEN-done
Kalev: KUH-lev
Maza: MA-zuh
Lena: LAY-nuh
Zaroch: ZAR-ock
Annion: ANN-i-on
Cassa: KASS-uh
Noam: NO-um

Locations:
Elysia: el-LIH-see-uh
Vernista: ver-NIH-stuh
Belharnt: BELL-harn-t
Shegora: sheh-GORE-uh
Mistwick: MIST-wick
Ilgathor: IL-ga-thor
Metta: MET-uh
Feltar: FELL-tar
Almyra: Al-MEER-uh
Other:
Cor unum: Core oo-num

ELYSIA

ELYSIA
ENDLESS SEA
Shegora
Metta
Zenduro Wastes
Sarphan
Absult
Zarkuse
Royal Palace
Cottage
Belharnt
BAYWOOD RIVER
BAYWOOD FOREST
ILGATHOR MOUNTAINS
Vernista
ENDLESS SEA
Port of Pyrn
Mount Sunder
PYRN
MYREWELL
END OF ELYSIA
Mistwick
N
W
E
S

PROLOGUE

Though the battle of Mount Sunder was over,
and terror reigned through every rise and set of the sun,
hope was not lost.
For out of the death of the human rebellion bloomed a rose.
It grew strong, larger, and brighter than any before it.
It had been granted the Ancient Magic that disappeared long ago,
dwindling like a flame until only an ember remained.
Though it was battered and beaten by the elements,
it blossomed and flourished,
unafraid to stand against the storm.
It took the violence in the wind,
the sorrow in the rain,
and the fury in the thunder,
and transformed it into a strength that could not be defeated.
The day the rose was plucked from its roots,
the earth stilled and watched,
through sun and storm,
as the horrors that saturated all of Elysia,
were finally brought to an end.

-Legend of the Ancient Magic

CHAPTER 1

TARRIN

I FORGOT WHAT THE sun felt like.

I forgot the golden warmth that seeped into your skin, or the bright light that caused the shadows to flee.

There was no light here. No sun, heat, or life. Only shadows and the kind of cold that burrowed into your skin like the biting teeth of a predator. I had long grown accustomed to the gnawing ache that had grown in my stomach after months of living on the brink of starvation.

Though truthfully, I had no idea if it had been months or weeks. Time was endless here. There was nothing to mark the passing of time. Nothing to indicate the time of day or how many minutes I had wasted away down here.

All I knew for certain was that I was dying. I grew nearer to the afterlife, felt death crawling closer, with every shuddering breath I took. I placed my palm against my stomach. My magic was cold and barren, thanks to the iron encircling my wrists. I was no longer able to feel the magic that enabled me to shift into my dragon form, and I was petrified that it was permanent.

I'd expected Eklos to use bluestone laced-chains since it was poison for shape-shifters. It destroyed the magic that allowed us to shift between forms, then killed the shifter. But Eklos said he had other plans for me. Those plans seemed to be a slower, more painful death.

Several of my fingernails had been pried off, bones broken then painfully mended only to crack and split again. Sticky blood coated my hands and arms, flaky old bits falling to the floor from the relentless itching.

I blew out a breath, wishing it would warm the cold-infested cell I was in.

A shiver wracked through me, transporting my mind back to Silverdew Valley, when Kaida had been only feet in front of me, when I had been so close to crossing into the safety of Shegora's borders, when those wicked claws had dug into my scales. Then it was only darkness.

And pain.

A picture of Kaida's face flashed behind my eyelids and a single tear spilled onto my cheek. Missing her was almost worse than the slow death I was enduring. I missed her smile, her taunts, even her sass. I missed the way she fit in my arms, the way hers always tightened around my waist, as if she couldn't bear to let go.

More burning tears poured from my eyes, the sudden heat sending another shiver through me.

Now all I had was the icy, numbing dark mixed with the prickling knife of anxiety.

I didn't know where I was. The dungeon Eklos was keeping me in could have been anywhere in Elysia. I knew I wasn't in the dungeons beneath the Royal Palace because Eklos had bragged about destroying them, and I couldn't be at Belharnt since Kaida destroyed it months ago.

I could only begin to guess, but I knew that if I was as well-hidden as Eklos constantly taunted, there was no way Kaida would find me. Our shifter bond was worse than silent. It felt like it had been shattered, all signs of her completely gone as if it had never existed. I had heard nothing from her since that last desperate

"I'm coming for you" that she sent through the bond after Rythos captured me. Her words were the only thing keeping me from succumbing to the dark pit my mind had become.

The thud of footsteps echoed outside my cell, and I fought against the dread that threatened to consume me.

He was coming.

How long would he torture me this time?

I had learned what kind of ruthless, merciless dragon Eklos was. Truthfully, I didn't know how much longer I could endure it. The endless pain wreaked havoc on my body, always, *always* getting worse when I didn't think it was possible to hurt more. My mind was so full of shadows it felt as though my thoughts were suffocating me. I was trying to be strong, to survive until someone could find me, *if* they found me, but every piece of me had withered like a dying plant infested with disease. I was a shriveled mess, and I had nothing left.

How Kaida ever survived seven years in Belharnt with him, I didn't think I would ever understand. It only revealed to me how strong and brave she truly was.

I wiped at the wetness on my cheeks, shoving the thoughts deep inside and forcing all emotion from my face. I wouldn't let Eklos see me afraid. He took pleasure from it, and even though my body was weak, I refused to give it to him.

The faint scent of carrion and smoke wafted between the bars.

"How's my favorite slave today?" a voice crooned in the dark.

I fought the urge to squirm and fight against the smoke encircling my neck. Fighting would only make it worse.

"I am no one's slave," I hissed, though my voice was hoarse, barely more than a whisper.

Eklos tutted. "And yet, here you are. In shackles, in a cell, forced to answer to me." A faint flicker flashed across the cell—his teeth as he spread his snout into a smile. "Sounds like a slave to me."

I swallowed down the painful lump in my throat, though my

mouth was completely dry. When was the last time I had been given water?

"What do you want?" I croaked out.

"Now, now. Is that any way to speak to the benevolent dragon bringing you food and water?" The clank of a metal tray hitting the ground echoed, and I was embarrassed by the way my body dove for it, desperate for any drop of water or morsel of food.

My hands landed on a stale biscuit and a small mug of water. I downed the liquid before stuffing the bread in my mouth. "Benevolent my tail," I couldn't help but mutter around a mouthful of food.

I felt the whoosh of air a second before claws collided with my stomach. The biscuit went flying out of my mouth and I collapsed to the ground, trying in vain to catch my breath.

"I'd take care what you say to the only thing keeping you alive," Eklos snarled.

"Why are you?" I retorted around a cough, unable to keep the question that had been burning in my mind at bay. "Why are you even bothering to keep me alive?"

Eklos simply laughed. "You're smarter than that, Prince. You know why."

A shaky breath escaped my lips.

Though my mind felt like it was swimming in dark waters, an explanation quickly surfaced.

I was the bait.

Kaida, stay away! I tried sending down the silent bond even though it did no good. I was the only one Rythos had been able to reach in Silverdew Valley, and he knew if he grabbed me, Kaida and Eldrin would come, just like Eldrin and I had come for Kaida in Belharnt.

"You truly expect them to find me here?"

"Of course, I do. I expect nothing less."

I yanked at my chains. "I don't even know where I am. How do you expect them to find me?"

I watched as his teeth flashed again. "You're in the tunnels beneath Vernista. In the new dungeon I had made just for you and those infernal shifters."

Dread pooled in my stomach. "Why would you tell me that?"

If he was revealing secrets now, he didn't expect me to be alive much longer.

Eklos chortled before sneering at me, his face close to my own. "Who are you going to tell? That iron is keeping your magic suppressed, including any bond you have with the girl. No one knows where you are unless I want them to. It's not as if telling you would give you an inch toward gaining your freedom." His dagger teeth gleamed again as he smiled, smoke pouring from his nostrils.

Pressure pushed against my insides as my heart doubled in tempo, just as it did every time Eklos reminded me how alone I was—how hidden. It had the darkness within me swelling like a wave, cresting higher and higher until it slammed over my mind, submerging me in its icy waters of despair and panic.

I squeezed my eyes closed, hoping that Eklos would miss the movement, knowing it would give away how afraid I truly was. I wished that I could control the fear-driven movements of my body, and I desperately tried to fight against it, but it was no use.

No one was meant to live through this.

And my hope was in vain.

"For all your attempts at bravery, your body betrays you," he drawled, his red eyes flaring brighter in the dark as he circled me. "It's too bad *she* isn't here to see you now. What would that abomination think seeing her once brave beloved on his knees before me, broken and dying?" He bent his snout so that his fiery lips were at my ear. "Too bad you won't be here to watch me kill her."

Anger flared in my gut but was immediately smothered by

icy despair as a thick collar of smoke slithered around my neck, squeezing tighter. White dots flashed across my vision in the dark. The scent of Eklos's carrion breath was behind me as he whispered, "Now, which part of you shall I break today?"

CHAPTER 2

KAIDA

MIDNIGHT SETTLED OVER Shegora and a blistering, bitter wind coated in icy pellets crashed against the windows in a soft roar. I watched as the ice drops pinged against the panes before settling into a tiny mountain of ice on the windowsill. Cold seeped through the glass, forcing its way through the cracks in the wooden walls.

"Layers. Need more layers," I muttered to myself as a shiver barreled through my body. Grabbing another pair of fleece leggings, I struggled to yank them over the pair I was already wearing, before shoving my arms into yet another sweater. After a moment of wrestling with the fabrics, I fastened my wool cloak around my neck. Three pairs of thick socks adorned my feet as I shoved them into the fur boots Gendon, the leader of Metta, had supplied before we trekked up the mountain.

When I deemed myself sufficiently covered, I tiptoed over to my door and peeked through the crack. The house we were staying in was quite small with only a main living space and one bedroom. My father and King Martik had given me the only bedroom, both choosing to sleep on the floor by the hearth. I could see Eldrin's human shape, bundled in blankets on one side of the fire; Martik's enormous body took up the corner on the other side. Sometimes

Z joined them at night, but other nights I wasn't sure where he stayed. I never bothered to ask.

Right now, I didn't see Z anywhere. Good. He wasn't going to stop me.

No one was.

Praying the wood floor remained silent, I crept through the house, a bundle of food I had stolen from the tiny kitchen slung over my shoulder. I made it to the door, putting my hand on the doorknob when a snuffling snort sounded, and I froze. I closed my eyes, begging the males to stay asleep. I risked a glance over my shoulder. Both my father's and Martik's eyes were firmly closed, and the King's body shook as he huffed out another snort. With a shake of my head and a silent farewell, I stepped over the threshold and shut the door behind me. I took off at a run through the village, the snow crunching beneath my footfalls.

The streets were quiet, not a single torch light in a window to be found as I passed tiny house after small hut. The people of Metta had repaired much of the damage done to Shegora, enough for it to be inhabitable as we had prepared to face Eklos. Even after the army disappeared shortly after Rythos took Tarrin, we remained in the mountain village, within the safety of the barrier just in case he or some other mercenary returned.

I hoped Gendon wouldn't take my leaving as an insult. I appreciated everything he had done for us. But it had been two months since Tarrin was taken, and all we had done was train with magic and swords while I tried not to rip my hair out. The thought had fiery wrath swirling in my gut. We had gone round in circles, Eldrin and Martik trying to convince me that it was too dangerous—and a trap—so we needed to wait until we had more information. But I had waited long enough. Tarrin wouldn't survive forever.

Over the past weeks, Gendon had occasional messengers that made the trek up the mountain to relay what was happening in the rest of Elysia, but they never had word of the Prince's whereabouts. Did anyone even know he was missing outside of those in Shegora?

I had *begged* my father, countless times, to go after Tarrin, but his only response was that it was too dangerous. I couldn't understand his unwillingness to help, especially when he and Tarrin had come to rescue me when I had been captured in Belharnt all those months ago.

The one and only time Eldrin had caved to my pleading, he sent three dragons to scout and find where they were keeping Tarrin, though he refused to let me go with them.

None of them returned.

After that, any talk of leaving the safety of Shegora to rescue my beloved was quickly shot down. A thick blanket of despair had covered the village in the wake of Tarrin's absence. King Martik kept saying that we needed to wait.

But wait for what?

If we didn't leave, we couldn't find him; couldn't rescue him. If we continued to sit here, throwing fire and swords around, but didn't plan to save the future King of Elysia…

Maybe they just didn't know how to help him. Maybe they felt there was nothing that could be done against Eklos and the might of his army. Maybe that despair was fogging their minds.

Either way, I couldn't take it any longer. Eldrin and Martik could stay here and keep throwing magic around all they wanted. Gendon would help them prepare for whatever plan they came up with. *If* they came up with one. They didn't need me to lead. Besides, how could I lead without Tarrin? How could I defeat Eklos without him?

No, they didn't need me.

But Tarrin did.

I'm coming, Tarrin, I called down the bond that had become as silent as the dead of night.

My inner beast thrashed against the silence, as it had done

every day for the last few weeks. She wanted out, wanted to avenge what was taken from me—from us.

He wasn't just my Prince, my beloved. He was my *cor unum*. Even my dragon form recognized how strong, how important that was.

The *cor unum* was the dragons' term for soulmates. Even if a dragon lived over a thousand years, they would still only have one mate—their one heart. Some lived their whole lives searching for their *cor unum*, while others ran away from it, afraid what such an attachment could mean in a world as cruel as Elysia. Some thought it was better to never find their one heart than to risk it being taken from them. But once a dragon did find them, it meant a life of love, a life of standing by each other's side regardless of what they faced. Most dragons in Elysia never found their *cor unum*.

But somehow, against all odds, Tarrin had found me.

And I would do whatever it took to find him now.

I made it all the way to the other side of the village, Silverdew Valley within my sights, when I finally heard the telltale crunch of footsteps following me. Choosing to ignore them, I pushed forward, bracing against the bite of winter as it fought its way under my layers. I wouldn't let anyone stop me.

These months without him by my side… I never wanted to experience it again.

Not only being separated from him but knowing what Eklos was doing to him. What he had done to me. A memory of being chained to that table in Belharnt filled my head; Eklos's hammer smashing my bones over and over.

My inner beast reared up inside me again, clawing to come out.

With a deep breath, I forced it back down, rubbing the hand that Eklos had shattered mere months ago. I didn't have time to deal with my beast *or* those memories now. I had to find Tarrin.

The invisible barrier that protected Shegora loomed in front of me. I let out a shaky breath, the air clouding in front of my face as I studied the valley. Could it truly have only been mere weeks since we raced across it—since Tarrin was taken from me? Though the winds had destroyed any sign of his footprints in the snow, I still knew exactly where they should have been—exactly where he was snatched by Rythos. Bile rose in my throat as anger made the fire in my core surge.

I took another breath, trying to calm the magic in my veins. I would need every bit of it to save Tarrin from whatever dungeon Eklos had thrown him into.

At the thought, my resolve solidified. This was it. I was leaving to rescue my love. After two months of intense physical training, both with magic and sword, I was the strongest I had ever been. I had to be to rescue him; for when I faced Eklos again.

I rubbed at my forehead, looking at the mountain peaks looming overhead. Only months ago, I had been a human slave forced to serve Eklos, and now I was *mutator formarum,* a shape-shifter with Ancient Magic supposedly strong enough to rid Elysia of his cruelty.

But it didn't matter what magic I had, not if Tarrin wasn't at my side.

My betrothed. The shape-shifter I had hated, who stood at my side even when I lashed out at him. He believed in me, no matter what, and even after all we had faced since fleeing Belharnt, he never let me give up hope.

Not only could I not face Eklos without him, but Tarrin didn't deserve whatever abuse he was enduring. He was worth fighting for—worth risking my life for.

I'm coming, Tarrin.

I glanced at my feet. As soon as I crossed to the other side of the barrier, any protection I had would disappear. I would journey into Silverdew Valley, and then down the mountain to whatever fate held for me. And I would be alone.

I closed my eyes against the hopelessness flaring in me and lifted my foot off the ground.

"And just where do you think you're going, little shifter?" a deep voice crooned in the dark.

I flinched before recognition set in, refusing to turn and face him. "Go back to sleep, Z."

He tsked. "Hmm. I don't think I can do that."

I spun on my heel, anger causing bright bursts of fire to flare into my palms. "Try to stop me."

Z let out a dark chuckle as if I hadn't just threatened him. "Oh, I wouldn't dream of it." He took a step closer, his dark-blue scales flashing in the moonlight. It was then I noticed the pack he carried over his own shoulder. "I intend to join you."

I rolled my eyes. "No. I'm doing this alone."

"After everything I've saved you from, you truly believe you can rescue that brat of a prince without my help?"

"I won't risk anyone else."

"That's not your decision, little shifter. I know how much he means to you, and I know nothing I could say would ever stop you. Therefore, I will accompany you, and ensure your safety. For Elysia, of course."

I narrowed my eyes. "Of course."

Z walked to my side, and I shoved down the sudden relief I felt. I couldn't tell him I was grateful for his help. He'd never let me hear the end of it.

"So, what's your plan?" He rubbed his scaled hands together with what looked like excitement in his eyes.

"Um…" I started, and Z cackled, though it was more of a rough barking noise.

"See, this is why I'm coming with you. You don't even have a plan."

"I was going to figure it out as I go," I snapped, a scowl on my face.

With another chuckle, Z gestured for me to cross the barrier. "How about we start by getting down the mountain and then we'll go from there?"

A shuddering breath billowed from my lips, and I searched his face for a moment. "All right."

With a strange smile twisting his snout, we took a step through the barrier and left Shegora behind.

℠

It took most of the night to cross Silverdew Valley, thanks to the deep snow, and my bones rattled beneath my layers of clothing. I was finally forced to shift back into dragon form just to stay warm, though it slowed me down thanks to the heavier weight.

We stood on a large outcropping of the mountain, and I crept to the edge to look down but could only see fluffy clouds. The air smelled of snow, promising yet another storm. I swallowed down the fear rising in my throat like needles. Z reached his long arms around my dragon stomach, securing a pack of food to the space between my wings.

He took a step back to study the bindings, before adjusting his own. "We should get going. More snow is coming, and it will only get worse as the day passes. Once we reach the base, it should lessen. We'll have to free-fall down the mountain until we can find enough air to glide on."

My stomach jumped into my throat. The last time I had done any sort of fall, Tarrin had been my safety net. He talked me through the movements through our bond, helping me every step of the way.

But Tarrin wasn't here, and I was alone.

"Wipe that look off your face," Z snapped. "You can do this." Any type of encouragement from Z was uncharacteristic of him, and I narrowed my eyes.

"Tuck in your wings and jump. Adjust your wingtips to guide

you in the direction you want to go. Just follow me. When you see me open my wings, copy my movements." I audibly gulped and Z barked out a laugh. "You'll be fine."

"Easy for you to say," I muttered.

Another gust of icy wind slammed into my scales, and I squinted against the onslaught as Z turned on his heel and dove off the cliff, the ends of his wings guiding him through the air rather than straight into the trees.

A sharp pang shot through my stomach. I shouldn't have to leave Shegora to rescue Tarrin. He should have been the one to make it to the village. My mind flitted back to my conversation with Jinna, the other slave girl who had served in The Den, after I found her in Mistwick. She had escaped from Eklos, but her brother's life had been the cost. Her freedom hadn't been worth it to her because Tal hadn't made it.

Don't go down that road. Tarrin will be all right.

I had to stay positive; be strong. If for no one else but him. I would soar to the ends of Elysia until I found even a sliver of our bond intact. I would find him, and I would get him out.

Whatever it took.

I took a breath and jumped after Z, tucking my wings into my back. My stomach immediately slid into my throat. I twitched the tips of my wings until they were angled slightly backward so that I fell with the slope of the mountain rather than crashing into it. Z was several hundred feet below me. I could feel in my bones that the air was too thin; no updraft or steady wind for the thick muscles and tendons in my wings to grab on to. It was just enough to keep us free-falling through the sky, and not into the trees.

After endless minutes, Z shouted up to me, "Get ready!" though the distance was great enough that I barely made out the words. Within seconds, he snapped his wings out in a mighty burst, his entire body shuddering as his descent slowed and he glided below me.

I counted down in my head like Tarrin had taught me so long ago.

One. I steadied my breathing, preparing to flex the muscles in my wings.

Two. Just a little farther. I forced my breathing to calm. I was mere feet away from where Z glided through the sky.

Three. My wings snapped open, and I couldn't hold back a roar as the cold wind barreled into my leathery skin. It had been a while since I had used my wings to fly and the sudden use of them was on the edge of painful. When I finally steadied myself, Z flapped his wings and headed south, in the direction of Vernista. The base of the mountain flew by beneath us though I saw no sign of Metta. Gendon must have still been using his magic to keep it hidden. With my dragon sight, I could see where the harsh winter landscape of the mountains ended in the distance and the slightly warmer, forested land that held Vernista began. I glanced behind only once to the towering mountain that had taken so much from me.

"You made that look easy," I said, as I arrived at his side. Snow was falling and whipping around us, but it was quieter down here. His eyes flickered with amusement as he turned his snout to look at me.

"It *was* easy," Z replied. "I told you you'd be fine."

I fixed him with a glare. "Why are you suddenly being so nice to me?"

Z smirked. "I'm always nice."

"Ha!" I barked. "Try again."

He chuckled but didn't respond right away. After several minutes without an answer, I assumed there wouldn't be one. That was typical Z. But then he cleared his throat.

"I lost someone once." His voice was barely audible over the wind, and I sidled in as close as I could without bumping his wings in order to hear him. "She was *mutator formarum*, like you." He paused, his eyes going distant. "She was to me what the Prince is to you."

A pang of understanding went through my stomach, my insides twisting as I felt a terrible ending lurking around the corner. We finally flew out of the snow and wind, and I took a breath of warmer air as the snow lessened, spikes of grass peeking up from beneath it.

He cleared the emotion from his throat. "She was killed by the Lone Dragon's beasts. I wasn't there when she needed me. I wasn't there when they cut her down and murdered her." Z turned his head and looked me dead in the eyes. "I have regretted it every day of my long life, and I will until my last breath."

I had no words to say as tears filled my own eyes.

"That is why I am helping you save your Prince. It's not only because you both are the last hope for Elysia's future. I've seen the way you look at each other. You have that rare, desperate, hope-filled love that can't be broken. I am old, Kaida, but you are not. You deserve a long, joyful life with Prince Tarrin. I know your past, what you've gone through. No one deserves happiness more than you do. So, I will do what it takes, even if it means laying down my life, so that you can have a life with Tarrin, and Elysia can stand a chance with its two greatest warriors, hand in hand."

A chill prickled over the skin beneath my scales, despite their warmth. I had no words to express my gratitude, or to accurately describe how much his words meant to me.

"Thank you, Z." I hoped those simple words told him how much I appreciated his help and his willingness to put his life at risk for this.

He nodded his head. "Anyway," he continued after a moment, "I have several safe houses that we can use while we search for the Prince. We should plan to travel at night and rest during the day."

I nodded my agreement, and we fell into a comfortable silence as we flew for a mind-numbingly long time. My thoughts spun in circles around Tarrin, creating terrifying scenarios. It was almost as exhausting as how long we had been in the air.

As we finally made it out of the woods bordering the Ilgathor Mountains, he announced, "Our first safe place is down there." He pointed to a cluster of trees with a wooden structure built into it.

The scales on my forehead bunched together. "A treehouse? That's where we'll be safe?" I asked, incredulous.

Z's snout twitched as if he were holding back a laugh. "Yes, there's magic imbued into the structure itself. Once we're inside, it will become invisible to any passersby."

At my look of confusion, he chuckled.

"It's a lost art of magic, and unfortunately, not many remain alive who remember it."

I raised a scaled eyebrow. "Just how old are you?"

Z huffed out a chuckle but said nothing. He back flapped his wings as he came in for a running landing. Though I was in the air, the ground rumbled beneath the weight of his steps. I followed his motions, though I was far less graceful. After hours of flying, I almost kneeled to kiss the grass and snow-mixed ground beneath my feet. Almost.

Z led the way toward the treehouse, before inspecting the area surrounding it.

"What are you looking for?" I asked. I craned my neck to look at the wooden structure somehow perched in the tree.

"Just making sure everything is intact. No one else should know about this place, but you can never be too careful."

When he was done, he nodded to himself before climbing the ladder in a nimble maneuver and popped inside. He poked his head out and gestured for me to come in. I struggled my way up the ladder, trying to pull my heavy body into the treehouse. I let out a sigh of relief as Z grabbed my clawed hand and yanked me the rest of the way before I collapsed on the floor.

Inside it was cozy, barely large enough for two dragons, just one simple room with a counter holding a wash basin against the far wall and a pair of cots along the right side. It was a pleasant temperature, not too hot or cold, for which I was thankful after weeks in the winter climate of the mountains.

"Make yourself at home," Z said, plunking his pack into a corner. He rummaged through the cabinets, pulling out some dried meat and fruit that I had no idea how long they'd been sitting there. I eyed it skeptically as he tried to give me a handful.

"We should save our packed food for traveling and eat what's here." At my hesitation, he added, "Don't worry, it's edible." His eyes flickered with amusement.

"Edible, maybe, but good?"

Z's stomach bounced slightly as he laughed. "Don't worry so much, Kaida. The magic of the treehouse keeps the food in perfect condition. Eat up and rest." Z shoved a mouthful of dried meat into his snout and then dropped his body onto one of the cots with a jarring crash. It was a wonder the bed could hold his enormous body. I took my time nibbling through the food, unwilling to admit that he was right. It *was* good.

When I finished eating, I shifted into human form and dropped onto the other cot, wrapping myself up in the musty-scented blanket. Z was already asleep, and I shook my head. Males. They could literally sleep anywhere.

I begged for sleep to come—for my body to get much-needed rest after the flight here. But every time I closed my eyes I saw Tarrin—his face full of terror as he faced whatever horrors Eklos was unleashing upon him. It made my stomach fill with acid, my limbs growing numb as I curled my knees into my chest and rocked myself against the anxious thoughts poisoning my mind until I finally slipped beneath the cold, brutal waters of a nightmarish sleep.

CHAPTER 3

ELDRIN

A THOUSAND YEARS OF life and I still hated winter. The days were short, darkness was ever present, and the cold crawled beneath my scales like an incessant plague. Even with the heat of my dragon body, it wasn't enough to keep the icy temperatures of Shegora at bay.

It was only midafternoon, but the sun was setting, painting a muted pastel ribbon in the sky. My breath clouded in front of me as I exhaled, the snow crunching beneath the weight of my scaled feet. The sound of nails being hammered, metal sawing into wood, and the swish of snow being moved around filled the air.

It had been this way for nearly two months.

Shortly after Tarrin was taken, Gendon had arrived at Shegora accompanied by a good number of dragons with supplies and weapons, ready to fight Eklos's army only to find that the army had disappeared. The only conclusion we could come to was that after Rythos captured the Prince, he used his magic to move the entire army somewhere else, perhaps biding their time until we tried to rescue him.

Or maybe Eklos had seen how treacherous the mountain was and how difficult a journey it would've been to get that army up to Shegora and decided to wait until we emerged. Either way, his movements and decisions were full of confidence. It didn't matter if we faced his army in Shegora or somewhere else. He knew he'd win.

So, instead of fighting a war, the dragons helped with continuing to rebuild the village. We didn't know if or when Eklos would return, but we would at least have places to sleep that protected us from the brutal winter elements of the mountain. Though Gendon, Martik, and I, along with Kaida and Z, had attempted to create some semblance of a plan to rescue Tarrin and defeat the army, we could never quite agree on a course of action.

We had no idea where Rythos took Tarrin, and I couldn't begin to guess where they might be keeping him. I agreed with Martik—there were too many variables, too many risks and unknowns. I couldn't bear the thought of Kaida, or anyone else, putting themselves in such danger when we simply didn't know what exactly we were up against.

A week after Tarrin was taken, I finally broke from Kaida's begging and asked Gendon to send three of his best scouts to see what information they could gather. They had orders to head toward Vernista and return within two weeks, regardless of whether they were successful or not.

Six weeks passed and none of them returned.

My stomach still sank at the thought. Had they been captured? Killed?

If Gendon's best couldn't survive, what hope did we have? Since then, any scouts that went out didn't dare go near that village. It limited our ability to learn anything useful, but it kept our dragons alive—though it made every plan we were able to come up with impossible to carry out.

That's why I refused to go after Tarrin now; why I wouldn't let Kaida go.

I didn't want to risk losing her, as selfish as that might be.

When I found Kaida's room empty that morning, my first

thought had been that Rythos had somehow gotten into Shegora and taken her like he had Tarrin, but then Martik told me that he saw her leave in the middle of the night, Z with her. I cringed at the memory of how I roared at him for not stopping her. We had fought so hard to get to the abandoned shape-shifter village. I knew Kaida wanted to rescue Tarrin, but after everything we all had endured and those scouts not returning…

I blew out a breath, forcing my mind back to Gendon. There was nothing I could do for my daughter now. We would continue getting the dragons ready for war. I eyed the beasts bustling back and forth through the snowy streets. Between Gendon and I, we had managed to train many of them in the art of battle.

Not that it currently did any good.

The army had vanished, leaving the foot of the mountain that held Shegora without a trace. Eklos had built up his pursuit to something truly terrifying, and then simply left.

It set all of us on edge knowing that if he could vanish an army in an instant, he could also cause them to reappear at any moment.

"Fancy seeing you here," a voice quipped behind me, and I turned to find Gendon.

"Same greeting, another day," I replied. I had taken to walking the streets at the same time each day, always running into the leader of Metta.

Gendon chuckled. "Yes, but on this day, I bring news."

"News? What have you heard?"

He began walking toward the center of the village where the small home Martik and I shared was located, and I fell into step beside him.

"Still no sign of Eklos or his army," he started, and I scoffed.

"That's hardly news. It's been that way for months."

Gendon narrowed his eyes. "You didn't let me finish."

I crossed my arms, the movement slightly awkward in dragon form.

"No sign of Eklos," he repeated, "but there have been rumors of the Remnant surfacing near the outskirts of Vernista."

"After two months of silence, they're coming out in the light of day?" I asked, a headache forming at the back of my skull. "Why?"

"My spies weren't sure, but they overheard mention of a hostage."

"Tarrin?" My voice sounded hopeful, even to my own ears.

"It's possible." He paused, scratching at the scales on his cheek. "I've also started to receive reports of occasional villages in the east going up in flames."

I blinked. "You think the army is destroying villages again?"

"They've remained silent and unseen for months, but it's the same signs as when they began doing it a few months ago. Scales know why they stopped, but if they're starting once more, that could mean that Eklos is getting ready to move. My spies won't get close enough to find out. I won't risk them after… last time."

Those three scouts that Gendon had sent first. Their loss hit him hard.

He was quiet for a moment before kicking at a pile of snow in the street. "That's not all I came to tell you."

"What else?"

"The elders of Metta have been meeting, and they have an offer for you."

The scales between my eyebrows bunched as I narrowed my eyes. I had asked no favors of them, nor had I been expecting any.

"I wasn't even aware they were meeting. What's the offer?"

Gendon exhaled a ring of smoke. "We would like to offer Metta as the center for your own army."

My snout popped open in surprise. "What?"

He nodded. "It is a difficult journey up the mountain to Shegora. While the dragons here were able to make the trek up, there are many more in Metta who wish to fight but cannot travel the distance."

The memory of us all trying to climb the mountain, of battling the cold and treacherous cliffs, flickered through my mind. It *was* a difficult climb. "What exactly are you saying, Gendon?"

"Metta has been a safe haven for centuries. While I don't relish the idea of giving that up, the greater good of Elysia is more important. Use Metta to train your own army. Use Metta when Eklos's army comes to call. Because you know it's only a matter of time."

I could barely keep the surprise and concern from my face. "But what about your homes? Your businesses? All the women and children and younglings? Your lives are there. I cannot ask you to give that up for death and pain."

Gendon was shaking his head before I even finished speaking. "You are not asking, we are offering. The elders have thought long and hard about this. We will move those who are too young, old, or who do not wish to fight, to another location. The entire village has agreed. Metta is yours and she's ready for war."

I put my snout in my hands, unable to hold back the emotion swimming in my eyes.

"Use this gift wisely. Raise an army to rival Eklos. Now that the distance is not so great, perhaps more will come to our aid."

I could only nod. There were no words to express the gratitude in my heart, or what this meant for the future. "Thank you."

Gendon grinned and clapped me on the shoulder. "Prepare to move out, Eldrin."

CHAPTER 4

EKLOS

THE HALLS OF the Royal Palace were dark, every torch unlit, allowing me to blend in with the shadows as I prowled down one after the other. Though the palace had been the hub for my army, it was silent now as every dragon had been dispatched either to villages across Elysia or to the camp being set up west of Vernista.

The quiet, the stillness, was not unwelcome as my claws echoed against the marble tiles beneath my feet, as I breathed in the stale air. After being surrounded by an army day after endless day, it was a blessed relief to finally be alone.

Though it was only so for a short while. For the haunting memories of the past mixed with the infuriating moments of the present were like daggers that had been thrust into my sides and never removed. After I had Rythos move the army, unsettling whatever meager forces those shape-shifters had conjured, I had him relocate the dragons into the Ilgathor Mountains where they were out of sight. They trained and forged enough weapons for an army twice their size. But after two months, they had become restless.

So, we moved back to Vernista, allowing small groups of dragons to leave and destroy human villages to quench their blood-lust while they waited for war. Stealing the Prince was a blow to the shifters, and rather than attacking while they maintained the advantage of location, I made their wounds fester by disappearing without a trace.

My cousin and the girl continued to evade me, but I still relished in the knowledge that I had the Prince within my grasp. He was wasting away in the cell beneath Vernista. I fully expected Eldrin and the girl to attempt to rescue him, but I had no intention of letting any of them get away alive. I had kept Tarrin alive, barely, and I felt immense pleasure at the sight of him wasting away day by day. It wouldn't take much now for him to simply pass into the afterlife. An extra day or two without water, letting his wounds fester, and he would be gone.

I smiled at the thought of ridding Elysia of that arrogant Prince while also making the girl suffer from losing him.

The paintings on the wall rattled as slow, thudding footsteps sounded down the hall, breaking me from my thoughts.

I wasn't afraid—I feared nothing. I was Regent Eklos of Elysia. I commanded an entire army of dragons, led the infamous Remnant of the Lone Dragon. The inhabitants of this world feared *me*. And yet, with the palace being empty, and those casual, measured footsteps coming in my direction, I still felt an ounce of trepidation.

"Who's there?" I demanded, studying the shadows to see who would emerge.

A dark chuckle sounded just before the huge, light-gray dragon appeared through the dark. "Don't know the sound of my footsteps yet, Master Eklos?" The dragon clicked his tongue. "You're slipping." Rythos's snout split into a wicked grin.

"Rythos," I growled, my muscles relaxing. "What are you doing here?"

"I come with a report."

Ah. Finally. I had commanded Rythos to remain on the mountain, to watch the shifter village so that I would know their every movement. Two months had passed, and there had been little to report. A smile crept over my snout. I waited, expecting him to continue, and let out a low snarl when he remained silent.

"Well, get on with it!"

The light-gray dragon gave a dark chuckle. "Eldrin remains in Shegora, though the girl escaped in the night and travels in search of the Prince. Another dragon accompanies her, but I didn't recognize him."

"What did he look like?"

Rythos looked at the ceiling, tapping his snout with a claw. "Oh, I don't know." His voice was full of dark humor. "Blue scales, wings, and a tail?"

It took everything within me to keep from lashing out, from hitting him, or pulling the fire whip from my side and letting the glass cut beneath his scales. I pushed the violent thoughts away. I had worked too hard to gain Rythos's trust, to ensure he was loyal to me alone. I wouldn't undo all those insufferable years by giving into my anger.

But still, who did he think he was that he could speak to me, the Regent of Elysia, in such a way?

I let a snarl slip through my lips. "I would be careful how you speak to me, dragon. Your life is a fragile thing."

Rythos, unaffected by my words, chortled. "As you wish, Master Eklos."

My words did nothing; imparted not even a drop of fear within him. Perhaps in my attempt to ensure his loyalty, I had been too lenient. But that was a battle for another time.

"Have you discovered what Eldrin's plans are?"

The dragon shook his head. "No, but there has been quite a bit of movement within the village. I think they're preparing to move."

My claws plinked against my scales as I thought it over. Where would they move to?

"Do you wish me to follow the girl?"

"No," I bit out with a violent shake of my head. "I want my cousin brought to me, at any cost. Stay up on the mountain and keep an eye on them."

Rythos nodded, turning to leave.

I let out another low growl. "I did not dismiss you, dragon."

He halted, looking over his shoulder. "Apologies, Master."

The way he said the words, almost disrespectfully, ate at me, but I forced the feeling away. For now.

"Stay on the mountain and if you see Eldrin leave, I want you to follow him. Find out where they're going."

"As you wish." Rythos waited a fraction of a second longer before turning on his heel, his wings held tight to his back.

"And," I called after him, forcing him to pause. "If opportunity presents itself for you to… capture my cousin… do it."

I chose my words carefully, knowing they would excite him, especially after what Eldrin did to him all those centuries ago, or rather what I had twisted Rythos's mind into believing he had done.

That signature grin, full of wicked delight, spread across his snout as he looked back at me, his wings flaring.

"It would be my pleasure."

CHAPTER 5

KAIDA

SNOW CLUNG TO the branches of the evergreen trees and stubbornly to the bottom of my boots. The cold oozed through the thick fabric, putting my toes in danger of frostbite. Winter had fully descended on Elysia, and with it, the fear that we would never find Tarrin. The snow covered the ground in thick blankets, even in the slightly warmer climates, hiding any trail that we might have found.

I had felt nothing through our shape-shifter bond over the last two months, save for that initial burst when I told him I was coming for him. In fact, the bond had been so silent that I feared it was irrevocably destroyed.

"You ready?" a voice said behind me, snapping me from my thoughts.

I turned to find Z, his scales like the deepest parts of the ocean, waiting in a copse of trees. He had the biggest sword I had ever seen strapped to his back between his wings. Though I had never witnessed a dragon wield a sword before, nor did I understand why a beast with magic would need one, it was a comforting sight.

"Yes," I said to Z, shifting back into dragon form. The sudden rush of heat as scales coated my skin made me exhale in relief. If it wasn't for the need for stealth that my human body could provide, I would constantly stay in this form simply to keep warm.

We had been traveling through Elysia for two weeks, sleeping in Z's safe houses when we could, and on piles of pine needles or in tiny caves to escape the bitter winds when we couldn't. As loathe as I was of the idea, we slowly made our way southeast in the direction of Vernista. I remained hidden while Z went into every village we encountered, asking if a dragon matching Rythos's description had been there, and if Tarrin was with him.

Thus far not a soul had seen them.

Where in the scales would they be hiding Tarrin?

"Still nothing?" Z asked me as I arrived at his side, and we made our way to a clearing where we could take off into the skies. The sun had finally set over the horizon, allowing us to travel faster under the cover of night.

I shook my head. "No. Not even a faint heartbeat. It's like he's gone; like the bond never even existed."

Z's eyes narrowed. "Don't go down that road, Kaida. We'll find him."

I met his gaze. "How do you know, Z? We've found no trace of him. Two weeks of searching has yielded nothing."

His eyes narrowed. "Eklos wouldn't go through the trouble of capturing the Prince simply to turn around and kill him. What would be the point?"

"To break me," I retorted before he even finished his question.

Z scratched at the scales on his head. "You've proven to him before that breaking you doesn't work. He took your mother from you and subjected you to seven years of terror in Belharnt, and still you stand here. Besides, I don't believe that his desire to hurt you is stronger than his desire to kill you. Killing the Prince would only hurt you. Capturing him to get to you so he can kill you is what he wants."

The air clouded in front of me as I exhaled. Z was right. This was likely all a trap. He would be waiting and ready if we ever managed to locate Tarrin.

"But what if Tarrin can't survive the torture Eklos puts him through?"

Z stopped in his tracks just as we entered a clearing, the stars illuminating the snow-covered field in front of us. "If there's one thing I've learned from Prince Tarrin in my time with you both, it's that he is more stubborn than anyone I've met in my long life. Tarrin is strong. He will be all right until we can find him."

"I think *all right* is subjective at this point," I muttered beneath my breath.

Z snorted and without another word, beat his wings and took off into the sky. The stars were bright, though the moon was only a tiny sliver overhead. We were in the sky for a handful of minutes when I noticed movement on the horizon. It was difficult to see, and at first, I thought perhaps I had imagined it. I blinked against the darkness, trying to focus my eyes.

I glanced at Z, but his attention was off to the left. I looked back and my stomach dropped to my feet. Impossibly closer, the distinct shape of a dragon was flying above the trees, headed directly for us.

"Z," I whisper-yelled, trying to keep our pursuer from knowing I saw him, but the wind drowned out my voice. I flew in closer, bumping my wing against his. He snapped his gaze to mine, annoyance contorting his face, but before he could say anything, I pointed toward the horizon.

Z's eyes widened for a fraction of a second before he shut off all emotion, and became the cold, calculated warrior I had come to know. Without a glance at me, expecting me to follow his lead, he tucked his wings into his side and dove for the trees.

Heart hammering in my chest, I copied his movements, aiming for a small gap between two trees. Thanks to training with Z, I had perfected the art of diving and landing in places a dragon shouldn't be able to fit. No longer did I lose control, opening my wings too late, and crashing into branches and tree trunks. Now, I spun at the perfect speed, training my eyes on a fixed point so I didn't become dizzy.

Only heartbeats before colliding with the treetops, I ripped open my wings, but this time I threw them above my head so that I fell feet first between the branches, adjusting my wings to keep me from crashing into the ground.

No sooner did my clawed feet touch the frozen snow, only a beat behind Z, before I heard the boom of an enormous figure land behind me, snow spraying against my back. I closed my eyes against the dread choking me before I turned around.

Part of me hoped the dragon hunting us was Rythos. I wanted to break him the way he broke me when he stole Tarrin away. I wanted to rip out each of his claws until he told me where my betrothed was. The beast within me was thrashing and begging to be given control, forcing flames into my palms. I swallowed hard, trying to calm the wrath swirling in my core. Ever since Tarrin was captured, my anger and need for revenge had only fueled my inner beast, making it harder to control, harder to tame. The monster in me wanted to raze Elysia to the ground until Tarrin was by my side again.

The fire fizzled as I realized the dragon standing across from us, chest heaving from the chase, wasn't Rythos. It was no one I recognized.

The Remnant had been surprisingly absent while we traveled. We had been able to move about Elysia easily, not once meeting a mercenary, even when we dared to enter the villages for supplies. Z had been highly suspicious, not understanding why we hadn't run into any enemies, but I was just thankful for a reprieve from running for our lives, however brief it may have been.

As smoke curled from the dragon's nostrils, his orange eyes, so similar to Rythos's, glowing in the starlight, I had a feeling that our reprieve had come to a swift end.

Z stepped forward, partially blocking me with his wings.

"What do you want?" he demanded.

"Your head on my wall," the dragon growled, voice like crunching gravel.

I couldn't suppress a snort and barely managed to stop from rolling my eyes. "So unoriginal."

Z gave a dark chuckle. "How unfortunate for you. You won't be getting it."

The dragon lunged for Z, fire erupting from his snout, but with a flick of his wrists, Z created two daggers made of ice and flung each one at the mercenary. The dragon easily deflected the first one, but the second was too quick to stop. It sliced into the scales beneath his left arm before shattering against the trunk of the tree behind him. Steaming blood seeped out of the cut, but it was only that. A cut.

Smoke seeped from the dragon's nostrils, and the smell of rotting corpses drifted across the space between us. The air thudded as the dragon thrust his wings behind him, soaring through the air to tackle Z.

But Z being… well, Z, the movement didn't faze him, didn't even *move* him. He simply used the dragon's momentum against him, grabbed onto his wings, and spun around before tossing him several feet away. The dragon landed with a crash in the snow, but I didn't miss Z's wince. He pressed a scaled palm to his side, and it came away with a streak of blood. Somehow the dragon had still managed to get a swipe at him.

I raised a scaled brow. "Are you losing your touch in your old age?" I taunted Z.

A low growl filtered between his teeth, and I swore I heard him harumph.

Z spun his claws in a circular motion before the snow around the mercenary's feet climbed above his ankles and then froze solid.

I couldn't help the giggle that bubbled out of me at the sight of him trying in vain to escape from Z's ice magic.

I probably should have been more concerned with winning this fight and escaping. But Z had proven his ability to protect me multiple times since I had met him. He was almost *too* good. It was a little annoying, though I appreciated his ability to stand face-to-face with an enemy and be entirely unafraid.

I scowled as he took another step in front of me, shielding me with his wings as if I were unable to defend myself.

He unsheathed the giant sword from his back and sauntered toward the dragon who was desperately trying to chip away the ice from his feet. "Any last words?" Z crooned, showing off his sword. This time I did roll my eyes.

"Bring him the girl. He will make you wealthy beyond your wildest dreams," the dragon spit, glancing over Z's shoulder at me.

Z pretended to study the carvings on the metal of his weapon. "Hmm, as tempting as that is…" Z paused and smirked at me over his shoulder. "I have no need for wealth or riches."

The dragon's orange eyes flared. "Then you're a foo—"

He never finished. With a mighty swing of his sword, Z sliced straight through the mercenary's neck, and I cringed as his head went flying before bouncing in the snow.

I pursed my scaled lips. "Tasteful."

Z wiped the blade through the snow to clean it, then sheathed the sword, turning to me with a smirk. "I know beheading is your favorite."

I chuckled. "Yes, why simply stab him through the heart when you can cut his head clean off?"

"That's the spirit." Z studied the dragon's body for a moment before bending down and ripping off something resting against his chest. The gold glinted in the starlight.

"What is it?" I called.

Z kept his back to me. "Amulet."

"Remnant?"

"A variation of it, I think."

I came up behind him to look over his shoulder. "What do you mean, a variation? There's only one Remnant of the Lone Dragon."

Z narrowed his eyes at me, clearly irritated. "I'm saying, it is similar, but not the same."

"Not the same in what way?"

When he didn't respond, I tried to grab it out of his claws, but he yanked it away.

"Are you ever not annoying?"

"Only when you're not withholding information from me."

Z rolled his eyes before handing it to me. "It's similar to the Remnant's amulet because of the sun, but it's different because there are two swords crossed in the middle."

I brought it closer to my face to study it. "What does it mean?"

"If I had to guess, I would say it's the symbol for Eklos's army."

"Why would they be different? Is the Remnant not the same as the army?"

"Based on the intel that my rebels were able to gather, the dragons of the Remnant are essentially the commanders of the army, though they all answer to Eklos."

I sighed. "So, what now then?"

Z peered up at the starlit sky, studying the constellations. "We keep traveling. Hopefully this is the last of the enemies tonight."

"But we don't even know where we're headed."

"Vernista is Eklos's pride and joy. That's where those scouts that never returned were headed. Where else would he be?" Without another word, Z took off into the sky.

"That's what I was afraid of," I muttered at his retreating figure.

I rubbed at the scales on my temple. The thought of going anywhere near Vernista ever again, let alone purposely trying to locate Eklos, was like a poison sucking the life out of my veins. The closer we got, the worse I felt.

But if getting near Eklos, and that village, meant finding Tarrin, I would endure it.

With a rough exhale through my nose, sending sparks into the frigid air, I took off into the night sky.

CHAPTER 6

KAIDA

"THE COTTAGE IS over there," I said, pointing to the faint outline of the roof through the trees.

It had been a long night of flying, my dragon teeth chattering away from the cold. I knew we would need to land soon, get out of the sky before the sun revealed us, so when I started to recognize some of the landmarks near the cottage, I figured it would be as good a place as any to rest for a few hours. The last time I had been there was when all of us were forced to split up to escape Eklos's mercenaries, before Tarrin and I met Z.

The first tendrils of a tangerine dawn crept over the horizon. Z beat his wings to zoom ahead, scouting the land below to make sure all was safe. When he finally peered back at me, he gave a single nod before dropping through the trees.

As soon as my scaled feet sank into the powdery snow, I shifted into human form, and stepped out of the trees into the clearing where the cottage was settled.

Everything within me went still.

The cottage had been a safe haven, where I had rested with Tarrin, where we had finally reunited with Eldrin and Martik after they escaped Eklos and the palace dungeons.

It was no longer a beautiful wooden structure.

Now, it was a burned husk.

The smell of singed wood and grass still lingered in the air, despite the snow smothering every surface.

Some of the wooden frame and beams, including one corner of the roof, were still intact, though clearly burned and no longer safe, but most of the structure was gone. It was an empty shell.

A dark, slimy feeling spread through me.

"I take it this is not what you were expecting," Z said beside me.

The magic in my core flared as anger leaked into my veins. "Eklos," I whispered. I should've known he would do this. When we escaped from his mercenaries before we traveled to Shegora, they would have found the abandoned cottage. It shouldn't have been a surprise to me. I should have expected it. But this was also the cottage that Eldrin had built for my mother. He had put thought and care into every piece of wood, every nail hammered. Pieces of my parents were imbedded into this cottage.

But now it was gone.

My fingers clenched into fists, and I shifted back into dragon form without thinking. The onslaught of heightened emotions had me doubling over. The fire in my gut swelled, thrashing around, trying to find a way out.

"Tamp it down, Kaida," Z murmured. "You control it. We're close enough now that if you lose it, you'll give away where we are to every single Remnant dragon from here to Vernista."

A whirlpool of hatred and fire swirled inside me. It spun faster and faster, pulling the human side of me down in it so that only the beast within me was left.

"*Tamp it down, Kaida,*" Z repeated through clenched teeth. His eyes were trained on me as I fought for control. My magic had been building inside me for weeks, growing in tandem with my fury. There had been no outlet, no enemies to fight in which I could release it. So, instead it built into a tidal wave that I was barely able to control anymore. If I released the magic fighting to free itself from my body, any dragon nearby would see it, likely *feel* it too. It would put not only my life in danger if I let go, but Z's as well. He had fought too hard to protect me. I couldn't repay him by revealing to Eklos's cronies where we were.

With a shuddering breath, full of sparks and embers, I forced the twister of fire inside me to cool, to calm, until it was manageable once more.

"That was faster than last time," Z remarked, watching me carefully. It wasn't the first time he had to help me reign in my magic.

When the fire finally simmered down to embers, I felt hollow. Empty.

Ignoring him, I turned my back on what used to be my family's cottage and walked back into the woods.

"Where are you going?" he asked.

"We can't stay here."

Z made an annoyed sound in the back of his throat. "Nonsense. There's no safer place. The Remnant will assume that we'll never stay here once we see that they've destroyed it. The beams look sturdy enough. There's only the one corner of the roof, but it's better than sleeping in the woods. At least if anyone approaches, we'll hear the creaking wood."

I shook my head, continuing into the trees.

"Have fun sleeping in the snow then," he called. I stopped in my tracks and peered over my shoulder.

There was no way that structure would hold the weight of a dragon. The moment he stepped on the charred porch, the thing would collapse into dust. I turned, crossing my arms to watch. I would laugh at Z as he was buried beneath the rubble of the cottage, and experience great pleasure at telling him "I told you so."

Except, when he stepped on the wood, it didn't crumble. It didn't disintegrate or come crashing to the ground. Ice crawled like millions of ants up the burned wood before solidifying over each beam and rafter. Z smirked at me, then rapped his claws on the ice to show it was solid. He headed to the corner of the cottage that still had a roof.

"Hmph," I huffed, irritated that I hadn't thought of that. I shifted back into human form, the lesser weight practically gliding across the snow until I reached the porch and walked inside.

Z was already situated in the corner, stoking the fire in the wood-burning stove that somehow survived the damage. Blessed heat spilled out of it, and I rushed to sit before it, holding my frozen hands up to the warmth.

"You need to learn to have a little faith, Kaida. I'm not as dumb as I appear."

I glanced at Z out of the corner of my eye. "I don't think you're dumb."

"Just dumb enough to risk going inside a crumbling cottage barely a breath away from falling over."

"Well, technically you did," I retorted.

He raised a scaled eyebrow. "The cottage is reinforced with thick ice. Only a great force crashing into it would bring it down now."

I waved a hand, dismissing his statement, knowing he was just patting himself on the back and rubbing it in my face.

"You did well, Kaida. Out there," Z commented, pointing his claws over his shoulder. "Controlling your magic. That was the fastest you've been able to calm yourself since we left Shegora."

I scoffed. "You call it control. I call it barely hanging on."

"I know that your magic isn't quite the same as the rest of us dragons," he began, staring at the gaping hole in the roof. "And I know that we don't yet fully understand what you're capable of. You have multiple abilities, with a strength and depth that far exceeds most dragons. And yet, you still struggle to remain in control."

"What's your point?"

Z pursed his scaled lips. "I know that your emotions often fuel your magic. When you get angry, your dragon responds." He threw his claws into the air when I opened my mouth to object. "Just hear me out."

I crossed my arms against my chest and fixed him with a glare.

"But… you fear your dragon too. If your emotions play such a large part in feeding your magic, it's no wonder you struggle for control when your mind is at war with itself."

"What do you mean?"

"You fear for Tarrin, but you also fear your inner beast. You look at your dragon form as separate from you, something to be controlled and dominated, rather than something to unite and work together with. If I were to guess, I believe that's why you're struggling for control so much. You can't conquer your magic when your mind is divided against itself."

"So, what? You're saying that all I have to do is *accept* my inner beast and I'll suddenly have complete control over my magic?" I asked, sarcasm coating my voice.

He scowled at my tone. "It's a theory, Kaida. It makes sense whether you want to admit it or not."

"If you say so." I didn't want to think about his theory. I didn't want him to be right. How could I do what he said? How could I unite with a bloodthirsty beast? My mind flashed back to the first life I took, the brown dragon who'd found us in Mistwick. I remembered the bloodlust, the thrill of the kill, and the look in Tarrin's eyes when I almost turned on him. That side of me couldn't come out again.

He opened his snout to say more but seemed to think better of whatever he had been about to say. Instead, he said, "We're close to Vernista now."

I nodded, keeping my eyes on the flames in the stove. Just the name sent tremors running through me. Only human slaves who had lived there would truly understand the pounding of my heart, the cold clammy sweat of my hands.

Z certainly could never understand.

It was a nightmare coming true, having to return there.

But equally as strong as the fear was the ever-present anger flooding my veins. My skin felt hot and prickly—like needles trying to pierce their way out.

The dragons that dwelled in Vernista were a special type of cruel. The thought of facing them once again… I wasn't sure if fear was the dominant emotion rushing through me or if it was my need for revenge—for them to experience all the pain they had put me through.

My hands clenched into fists on the floor. Despite it all, both the terror and the anger, I would face it all again to save Tarrin.

"Are you okay? With being this close to the village again?" Z's voice interrupted my swirling thoughts.

I forced those thoughts and feelings down deep inside me, where no one but my beast could reach.

"Would you be, Z?" I replied, my voice void of emotion. I stared into the flames once more. "If you spent your whole life abused in a village, would you relish the thought of going back there to face the beast that kept you in that state in the first place?"

He shifted closer but I didn't turn to him, and after a moment he settled back against the wall with a sigh. "I know this is difficult for you."

"You have no idea," I whispered.

Z went silent, and I lost myself in the sound of the crackling wood.

Come nightfall, we'd be leaving this place, likely for good, and heading to the one place outside of Belharnt that I hated most. I dropped my face into my hands. Maybe Z had a point. My fear for Tarrin, of Vernista, and my inner beast all battled in my mind for first place. I didn't know how to stop it or how to conquer it.

Ever since Tarrin rescued me from The Den and told me who I was—*what* I was—I had been afraid. I didn't want to be like *them*. So, I had been fighting against it, unwilling to allow myself to be a monster like the rest of the dragons.

But in fighting it, was I only harming myself? Perhaps my beast was just as desperate to help me as I was to defeat my enemies.

I rubbed at my face and settled into the corner to try to sleep.

I didn't know if Z was right, nor did I know how I would even begin to *accept* my inner beast.

I just hoped I could figure it out before it got us all killed.

CHAPTER 7

TARRIN

A COUGH WRACKED ITS way through my body, echoing endlessly between the stone walls and metal bars of the cell. Each swallow was like knives dragging down the inside of my throat. It had been days, though how many I couldn't begin to guess, since Eklos had last given me food, the stale biscuit and tiny cup of water doing nothing to ease the ever-present ache in my stomach.

I could feel it. If I didn't get water, and soon, I wouldn't last much longer in this dungeon. A heavy cloud of despair hung over me. It infused my blood with a sticky, poisonous panic that had my spirit withering away with each agonizing breath I took. My mind swam in dark waters, barely keeping above the surface; only a wave away from dragging me deep into its depths.

I couldn't lie—it was terrifying.

A faint rustle met my ears, but I dismissed it. There were rats and other pests crawling all over these dungeons. It was likely one of the vermin looking for scraps of food.

Me too, rat. Me too.

I put my face in my hands. I was talking to invisible rats now? I had been alone too long. Instinctively, I reached out for the shifter bond, begging for there to be some sign of Kaida.

It was quiet. Not even the faintest trickle of her heartbeat.

I should have been used to the silence after so long, but disappointment flooded me, my heart sinking to my feet.

Was she looking for me? As much as I wanted to escape this dungeon, I wanted Kaida to stay safe even more. This was all a trap to get her here, and I couldn't bear the thought of Eklos getting his hands on her yet again. Besides, even if she was coming after me, how would she ever find me here? My thoughts spun in a downward circle, faster and more violent with each one that passed.

The same rustling noise sounded again, this time louder and closer. My ears perked up. Something about it sounded… off.

Then the unmistakable sound of footsteps met my ears, and I froze. It couldn't be time for Eklos to pay me another visit. He hadn't yet sent anyone to tend to my injuries like he usually did.

I stood to my feet, though I could barely discern which direction the opening to the cell was. If I ever made it out of the dungeon, I wasn't sure if I'd ever be able to be in the complete darkness again. It bit away at my nerves, paranoia swarming my mind like a hive of bees.

The footsteps came to a stop—too light and faint to be Eklos or one of the Remnant.

Kaida?

I reached out through the bond again, but only a dark, empty void greeted me.

"Hello?" I whispered, cringing as the sound echoed far too loud.

There was no reply.

The clink and scrape of metal met my ears and I pushed to my feet. "Who's there?"

Again, silence was the only response.

"Reveal yourself," I demanded, trying to will some courage back into my fragile body, but my legs were trembling beneath my weight.

The darkness pressed in, my heart nearly jumping out of my chest when a voice spoke.

"Eat, Prince." It was a female's voice. It sounded unnaturally low, as if she were trying to deepen it to avoid being recognized.

"Who are you?" I asked, trying to take a step forward, but was forced to stop when the shackles held me in place. It was too dark to see anything but the faintest outline of a hooded figure.

"Eat," the stranger repeated before the soft scuff and scrape of running footsteps echoed like a whisper in the dungeon.

I felt the sudden absence like a kick to my stomach. She was gone.

I was alone again.

Taking a tentative step forward, as far as the shackles would allow, my fingers gingerly moved over the damp stone floor. Cold metal bit into my fingertips as I stumbled upon a tray. A frantic hunger overtook my body, and my hands scrambled for the food that laid upon it. A decent-sized hunk of bread, some cheese, and a handful of grapes felt like a king-sized feast, not to mention a pitcher of water that I immediately poured the entirety of its contents down my throat.

When every drop of water was gone, I was left panting, the burn of thirst momentarily quenched. I stuffed the bread into one cheek, and a chunk of cheese in the other, and barely held in a groan of delight.

As I chewed, my eyes wandered back toward the cell entrance, as if the cloaked female would suddenly reappear. I didn't know who the stranger was that had snuck me food. I wished she would have spoken up, revealed herself. Whoever she was, she must have known I was dying. Why else would she have risked her life like that?

Eat, Prince. The words replayed in my mind.

She knew who I was.

But according to Eklos, there were very few who knew I was

down here. Only the select beasts needed to draw Kaida here. But somehow this human knew who I was and put her life at risk to try to keep me alive.

The bread turned stale in my mouth.

The female had to be someone I knew.

But who?

It couldn't have been Kaida—she would've done everything possible to break me out of here. My darkness-addled brain spun in twisting circles as I tried to figure it out, and I clenched my teeth at the lack of answers I was able to come up with.

A shiver wracked through my body as another thought occurred to me. Could it have been my mother? But if it was, why wouldn't she have revealed herself? Why would she remain hidden beneath her hood and not help me find a way out of the dungeon? Surely my own mother wouldn't have left me here.

I didn't know for certain who the female was, but I did know that if Eklos found out that someone brought me food—if he scented it on me or found the stranger…

Neither one of us would make it out of these dungeons alive.

ଓ

Time ran together in the dark. The constant ache in my stomach was abated just a bit, thanks to the stranger who risked her life to bring me food. Though I certainly needed more food to make up for the endless number of days of starvation I had endured, for the moment I was one less step in the direction of the afterlife.

Would the female return? Would she bring more food? Or was that a one-time courtesy, and she wouldn't bother to risk herself again? I put my face in my palms, the shackles clinking against my skin. Though my stomach was already begging for more, I hoped the female wouldn't return. I couldn't stand the thought of someone else losing their life trying to help me.

I didn't want that blood on my hands.

Thudding footsteps clomped down the stairs in the distance, and the food in my stomach turned to acid. I had memorized that distinct noise; the way his scales scraped the floor with each step, his claws screeching against the walls as he dragged them across the damp stone.

Eklos was coming.

My heart sped up, the pounding echoing in my ears as he made his way to my cell. His steps were slow, measured, drawing out his approach simply to cause me distress.

I wished I could say it didn't work.

But that would've been a lie.

"How's my favorite prisoner?" A slimy, deep voice crooned in the darkness before his red eyes pierced through the black. Always the same question.

I didn't respond. I wouldn't give him the satisfaction. He took a step closer, and I couldn't stop the way my bones cringed away. My body had learned that his proximity meant pain.

"Not feeling particularly chatty today, Prince?" Another step closer.

Eklos sniffed the air, paused, then sniffed harder.

The food I ate turned to bile and worked its way up my throat.

He knew.

Red eyes were suddenly in my face, his claws around my neck as he lifted me off the ground. The shackles strained against my wrists.

"Is that... food I smell on you?"

I met his furious gaze but kept my lips firmly clamped together.

He gave me a violent shake, his claws biting into my skin. "Where did you get food?" Eklos demanded.

My lack of response only infuriated him more and he released me, sending me crashing to the ground in a gasping, painful heap. His foot collided with my ribs, and I couldn't hold back a cry as his claws pierced into my side.

"Roldan!" Eklos yelled and swift dragon feet echoed in the dungeon.

"Y-yes, sir?" Roldan appeared, barely visible in the dark, gasping for air. From what I could make out, he looked sicklier than the last time I had seen him, his scales faded and a limp accompanying his steps. Eldrin and my father had fought him and Barden before reaching Metta. Perhaps the injuries Roldan had sustained were greater than we knew.

"There's an intruder somewhere. Hunt them." Eklos's voice was icy death, leaving no room for argument. Roldan's snout opened and closed, wanting to ask a question, perhaps "How on earth am I supposed to find an intruder down here?" But he wisely kept his mouth shut, spun on his heel, and limped back the way he had come.

Eklos's red eyes turned back to me, sending a chill through my blood.

"You're going to wish whoever helped you never showed their face here."

My eyes widened as he stepped closer. I should've known. This whole time I had been more worried about what Eklos would do to the stranger who helped me, but I should've been more concerned about what he would do to *me*. Eating that food might have just cost me my life.

"Tell me who it was," he barked, and I felt that familiar sensation of Eklos's smoke running over my skin. It became more and more difficult to breathe and he tightened it into a noose around my neck.

"Tell me," Eklos roared, getting in my face as he lifted me off the floor once more.

"I don't know," I managed to gasp.

"Tell. Me. Who. It. Was."

Spots flashed across my vision, and my body begged for air. I opened my mouth to repeat that I didn't know who had helped me, but there was no sound. I tried to shake my head, but my body wouldn't move.

Unconsciousness lingered on the edges of my mind.

Eklos must have felt it for he released his smoke, and another cry of pain escaped my mouth as I slammed into the stone floor, my ankle giving a painful twist.

"That's all right," Eklos said after a moment. "I have ways of making you talk. If you refuse to tell me who helped you, I'll make sure you regret it."

Eklos turned on his heel and stalked for the door, leaving my bleeding and bruised body behind.

"I will find the intruder, and when I do, you will stand there silent and watch every second while I slaughter them."

CHAPTER 8

KAIDA

NIGHT DESCENDED AND I took to the skies with a lead weight in my gut. I slept in fitful bursts, unable to truly rest inside the dilapidated cottage. Z, however, snored away, making enough ruckus to keep the entire forest awake.

This was it. By dawn, we'd be arriving in Vernista, the very place I said I'd never return to. You'd think I'd have nightmares of Belharnt, but more often than not I dreamed of Vernista. Of the cold fear I would wake up with if I rose from bed even a second past dawn. The terrifying feeling of sprinting to The Den, knowing that I was running toward another day of abuse; another day where Eklos could kill me.

Vernista was synonymous with pain and death, and I wished with everything in me that I never had to set foot inside it ever again, but if it was where Eklos was keeping Tarrin, I would endure it. Tarrin was worth reliving my darkest days because he was the sun that pierced through the darkness. He helped me find myself after I had been lost so long in the pits of Eklos's enslavement.

I let out a shuddering breath, the cold biting beneath my scales. Though Vernista was often a warmer climate, the chill of winter had descended upon the area. The first torch lights of the houses came into view in the distance, and I fought the urge to turn around and fly back to safety.

Although, there was no place that was safe.

Not until the army was defeated.

Not until Eklos was dead.

Z's voice slid through the wind into my ears. "We should find a place to land and continue on foot. If we land in the middle of the village, it may cause a scene." A smirk split his snout and I couldn't hold back a chuckle. That it would.

I followed Z as he banked to the left, his head moving back and forth as he searched for a suitable place to land. Finally, he pointed to a small, wooded area next to the river and dove for it.

I landed only a second behind him, and my insides locked up. This was the exact area where Tarrin had led me the day he rescued me from The Den. It was the exact place I shifted into dragon form for the first time and saw my amethyst scales in the reflection of the water.

I hesitantly stepped to the edge of the river and peered over. Disappointment flooded through me when I saw the water was frozen. I couldn't see my reflection—though that was probably for the best. Part of me feared seeing the monster within that had been trying to claw its way out since Tarrin was taken. The monster that wanted to kill every beast from Shegora to Vernista in order to get him back.

I didn't want to be that monster. I didn't want the beast to have control. Z was always reminding me that I controlled my magic, my dragon side, but sometimes it didn't feel that way. Sometimes it seemed that I was at the mercy of the carnal nature of the dragon.

I blew out a breath, thankful that I didn't have to be scared of what I saw in the river, or even disappointed at what I *didn't* see. I shook my head. My mind was a mess. Without Tarrin to help me filter through my fear, I felt lost.

"You should shift," Z murmured, looking around to see if we were spotted. "Don't need the dragons scenting you before we even cross the village threshold."

With a nod, I pulled on the fire in my core, letting it fill my veins. It drove away the cold of winter with every inhale and exhale, building in power until a dull purple light flickered over my scales. It lasted only a moment and then I was back in my human body.

The degree of cold hit me like a fist to the gut. I hadn't realized how truly frigid winter had become in Elysia until I wore skin instead of scales.

"Come on," Z said. "Let's find shelter and figure out a plan. I'd rather not be caught unaware by Eklos's minions."

I nodded and followed him, careful to step in his footsteps so that I didn't leave a trail of my own. We reached the edge of the village, my teeth chattering painfully.

"You'll need to stop that racket if you want to remain undetected," Z remarked, glancing at me with amusement in his eyes.

I dismissed him with a wave of my hand. He chuckled before continuing to circle the west side of Vernista, searching for somewhere to hide. Maybe an abandoned hut or a slave's home that was currently empty.

"Do you see anything?" Z asked. "Anywhere suitable for us to rest?"

I scanned the houses and tiny huts, noticing which ones held the signs of slaves and which ones did not. On the very end on the left side there was a small house with a circle above the door, the silhouette of dragon claws holding shackles in the center. It was the slave crest. There was no sign of light inside and from the outside; it appeared empty. They were either working or dead. I pointed at it.

"You think I can fit inside there?" Z said, incredulous.

I shrugged. "Don't really have a choice, do you?" Without another word, I tiptoed to the front door of the slave's home.

The metal knob was icy, biting into my skin as I tried to turn it, but it didn't move an inch. Though it was pointless, I yanked on it, even going so far as kicking the door in hopes that it would swing open. It didn't. With an impatient huff, Z stepped forward, pointing a sharp claw at the metal. Ice spread like water across the surface, penetrating the keyhole until a distinct click sounded before the door popped open. I was going to have to ask him later how he did that later.

I hurried inside, searching through the dark, before lighting a small candle on the table, squinting against the sudden brightness to take a look around. The air was stale, like the house had been closed up too long. Fresh air poured through the doorway, and little balls of dust went rolling across the floor. There was a small table next to me, an armchair in the corner, and a counter with a wash basin and a few dishes in the other corner. Everything was covered in a thick layer of dust, indicating that the home was indeed vacant and must have been for some time. Perfect. We wouldn't have to worry about anyone coming home to find us.

I glanced over my shoulder to find Z contorting his body to fit through the door, before curling in on himself to avoid hitting the ceiling. He bumped into the table, spinning to try to get out of the way, before his tail smacked into the wooden chair, sending it clattering to the floor. He toppled over several more pieces of furniture before he finally settled into the corner, drawing himself up as small as he could.

I smirked at him. "Comfortable?"

"Shut up, Kaida," he said, though I could see his lips twitching, fighting a smile.

I huffed out a laugh. "Now what? We should be safe here for the time being, at least until someone picks up our scent outside." I glanced at the door that would do very little to keep out dragons. "Since we're at the end of the village, I'd say we have at least a day of safety here, but I wouldn't risk staying much longer than that."

Z nodded in agreement. "We need to look around the village, listen for any rumors of Tarrin or where he might be held."

"I can't go out there, Z. They'll recognize me immediately. My face is plastered all over Elysia."

"I know," he agreed. "It'll have to be me. It's been years since I've traveled to these parts, so there is minimal risk that anyone will know who I am."

My tired bones ached as I eased myself into the moth-eaten armchair. "So, what's your plan?"

"As much as I hate the thought, I'll need to be out in daylight if I have any hope of gaining information. I'll wait until dawn and then head into the village. Perhaps visit that tavern you mentioned? What was it called?"

A lump caught in my throat, and I swallowed hard, averting my eyes to stare at the floor. "The Den." An involuntary shiver shuddered through me.

"Right," he murmured, likely noticing my discomfort at the mere mention of the place. "I'll try to eavesdrop there while I eat breakfast. See if I can't learn anything helpful."

"And if that fails?" I asked.

Z scratched at his scaled cheek. "Is there a market in Vernista? Dragons selling wares whom I might be able to entice to spill information?"

I thought for a moment before nodding. "On the east side of the village. Humans were never allowed to buy or sell there, so I can't tell you what to expect."

He shrugged. "A market is a market, right?"

I squirmed in my chair. "I wouldn't expect this to be easy, Z. You're in Eklos's domain now. You could simply look at someone the wrong way, never mind whatever nonsense may spew from your lips, and the Remnant will be all over you."

Z rolled his eyes. "You have very little faith in me."

I snapped my gaze to his. "Or too much in Eklos."

He shook his head. "Kaida, I've been alive a long time. Eklos is not the first tyrant I've encountered, and he likely will not be the last. I know what I'm doing."

I filled my cheeks with air before blowing it out in a whoosh. "So, say the… tavern fails, and you learn nothing of substance at the market. What then?"

"I attack a Remnant dragon, of course," he said easily, shrugging his shoulders.

My mouth popped open. "You—*what?*"

Z chuckled. "The only option at that point will be to get the information right at the source. I'll find one of the Remnant, kick their tail, and make them reveal Tarrin's whereabouts."

"And why the scales do you think that would work?"

He clinked his claws against his scales. "I can be very persuasive."

"Sure, you can." I rolled my eyes.

"You dare not believe me, little shifter? How do you think I got to the position I'm in? Leader of the rebels, gaining their unswerving loyalty, and knowing where every enemy dragon is." His eyes flicked over me. "It's not simply my good looks and charm. I'm dangerous."

I snorted, mostly trying to downplay the threat beneath his words. The memory of Z shooting down the Remnant mercenaries that had attacked Tarrin and me with hardly any effort required, then convincing his rebels to travel all the way to Shegora to fight a battle that wasn't theirs to begin with… I supposed he had a point.

"All right. You're dangerous. Happy?"

His snout spread into a sneer. "Ecstatic."

I took a swig from my canteen, trying to rinse the bad taste from my mouth. I had confidence that Z could and would do what he said tomorrow. But I also knew Eklos. Eklos could outsmart him, landing Z either in the dungeon alongside Tarrin, or dead on the street. I closed my eyes against the mental image.

"Stop overthinking it, Kaida," Z said, interrupting my thoughts. "I'll be fine and back before you know it." He leaned his head against the wall and closed his eyes. "Get some rest. Tomorrow, we find your betrothed."

CHAPTER 9

KAIDA

ORNING CAME, THE sun already bright in the sky when I finally awoke. I couldn't recall a time when I had slept so late into the morning, especially not while in Vernista. My neck ached from the awkward position in which I slept curled up in the armchair. I glanced at the corner and immediately sat up. Z was gone.

I rubbed at my eyes. How long had he been gone? Did he leave moments ago, or had it been hours? I put my face into my hands, trying to breathe to calm my panicked thoughts.

What had he said? He'd leave at dawn… but I couldn't recall him saying when he'd be back. How long was too long? Would I have to go out and find him if he didn't return soon? Did Eklos's dragons already capture him? My head spun, feeling lightheaded and my thoughts quickly twisted downward. My breath came in erratic gasps and tears spilled onto my cheeks.

What was happening to me? I tried to slow my breathing, forcing myself to focus on the floor in front of me, instead of all the what ifs barreling through my mind. Instinctively, I reached for the shifter bond that linked me to Tarrin. Whenever I was upset, he was always there to calm me down. He could always sense what I was feeling; I never had to explain.

But the bond remained silent as always.

Swallowing my emotions down and tucking them deep inside me, I rose to my feet and stumbled across the small room to peek out the window, keeping myself hidden behind the curtain. The sun was bright on the white snow covering the ground, but from the angle of the window, I wasn't able to see if any dragons lurked on the street.

Releasing the fabric to cover the glass once more, I went to the wash basin in the corner and dunked my hands. The water was ice cold, but it was a pleasant shock to my scattered thoughts as I took palmfuls and splashed it on my face.

The barest hint of a knock sounded at the door, and I froze, water dripping back into the bowl like crashing boulders. I blindly reached for the towel on the counter and scrubbed it over my face. My ears strained to hear if anyone was outside the house, but everything was silent. Had I imagined it? I rubbed my eyes.

But then someone knocked again. It was barely there, as if whoever was outside was afraid of being heard. On silent feet, I walked to the door, wishing in vain that I could see through the wood. My mind flashed back to when we had hidden at Kalev's in Feltar. Kalev had knocked on the door, but when Tarrin opened it, a Remnant dragon killed Kalev and captured the both of us. I swallowed hard at the memory.

With a deep inhale, I held it in as I twisted the lock and opened the door a crack. I exhaled in relief, my breath pooling in the frigid winter air. It was a girl, perhaps a few years younger than me. Her eyes narrowed as she studied me before tears filled her eyes.

"You're not Maza," she whispered, burying her face in her hands.

My brows furrowed as I studied her before glancing around. It was broad daylight, and we could easily be spotted at any moment. "Come inside, quickly."

The girl glanced up with wide, red-brimmed eyes. When she

didn't move, I gently grabbed her arm and pulled her through the door. She didn't fight. I closed the door, making sure the lock was firmly in place before turning to face her.

"What's your name?"

The girl sniffled. "I should be asking *you* that. You're the one intruding."

"Is this your home?"

Her eyes were wide as she shook her head. "It's Maza's."

"Is Maza your mother?" I asked.

"No," she bit out. "Maza is my..." She paused, catching herself. "When I caught a glance of the curtain moving in the window, I thought..."

I fought the urge to smack myself on the forehead. That was a foolish mistake. "You saw the curtain move and thought Maza was home?" The girl nodded. "Where did Maza go?"

More tears spilled onto her cheeks. "I think she's dead." Her words were almost inaudible. Her tough facade broke, and she dissolved into sobs. Without thought, I reached forward and pulled her into my arms. Her body went limp, sagging against me, as my shirt grew damp from her tears.

I didn't know who this Maza was to her, but I did know that when my mother had been killed, all I had wanted was for someone to hold me while I cried. Someone to comfort me and tell me everything would be all right, even though in Elysia there was no such thing. I didn't know this girl, and I didn't know how to help her, but I could offer her this small comfort.

At last, she sniffled and pulled out of my arms. "Sorry," she mumbled.

"Don't apologize." I gestured for her to sit in the corner armchair while I took a seat in the creaky wooden chair at the table.

Her movements were slow, careful, as she perched on the edge of the cushion. Something about her seemed off, but I couldn't figure out why.

"What's your name?" I asked again.

She eyed me warily before sighing. "Lena."

"How old are you, Lena?"

"Fourteen."

I nodded in response. "I'm Kaida."

Lena's eyes widened for only a second before her brows lowered. "Why are you in Maza's house?"

"I needed a place to hide," I replied honestly. "When I saw there was no light in this home last night, I took a gamble that it was empty." I glanced around the room, then back at Lena. "Seems I was right."

She hesitated then nodded. "Maza is my older sister. She moved here after Momma…" Lena didn't finish, clenching her hands into fists. "I would come visit her here, but it's been weeks since I've seen her. I prayed that she wasn't…" She blew out a ragged breath. "I guess now I know."

"I'm sorry," I offered.

Her gaze turned piercing as she studied me and the *off* feeling from earlier crept back into my mind.

"You look kind of familiar," she said after a moment. My stomach fell to the floor, and I fought to keep my face neutral. Why had I told her my name? I wanted to put her at ease but didn't realize the danger I had just put myself in.

"I don't know why." I fought to keep my voice light and even. "We've never met before." Did she recognize me from the posters plastered across Elysia? The posters that depicted my face and a reward. Any slave that desired even one day of peace from their Master wouldn't hesitate to turn me in. Would Lena?

She squinted, and a calculating gleam entered her eyes as thoughts shifted in her head, trying to fit the pieces together. All signs of her earlier distress, of her tears, had disappeared. Lena's knuckles were white from how hard her fists were clenched.

A warning bell flared in my mind. Had she been… faking?

Was it all a ruse to get me to let my guard down and now she'd hand me over to the dragons?

I needed to get out of here.

"Anyway," I said suddenly, trying to distract her. "I won't be here long. Just until my friend returns. Then I'll be out of your sister's home."

Lena cocked her head, and the movement reminded me of an animal. "What friend?"

My gut filled with acid. "No one you'd know."

Lena's young face turned cold. "It wouldn't be the new dragon I saw prowling around the village, would it?"

Oh no.

"I don't know who you're talking about. I know nothing about a strange dragon." I fidgeted with my fingers and her eyes snapped to them before fixing back on mine. "My friend lives here."

"Hmm," she hummed. "If your friend lives in Vernista, why were you looking for a place to hide?"

My heart stuttered and she gave me a cruel smile. I fought the urge to burst to my feet and run out the door. I swallowed hard. Lena didn't even give me a chance to respond before speaking again.

"Here's what I think. I think you're that girl. The one all the dragons are searching for. The Prince's lover. The *shape-shifter*." Lena spit the last words like they were poison. She tapped her finger against her chin, thinking. "Hmm. Kai-da, was it?" She drew out the syllables of my name, each one like a nail being hammered into a coffin.

The blood drained from my face and the smile that spread over Lena's face was nothing short of feral. In that smile I knew the answer to all my fears. Lena would turn me in. There would be no hesitation. Whether she was doing it simply to save her own skin for another day, or because she had been corrupted by the evil of the dragons like the slave who had kidnapped me all those months ago when I was taken back to Belharnt.

"Here's what's going to happen," Lena said, her voice cold and sounding far older than her fourteen years. "I'm going to take you to my Master. You won't fight me. You'll come willingly. My Master will be quite pleased."

"Lena, don't do this." I knew it was useless to try to talk my way out of this. The ice in her eyes told me that her mind was made up. I was the reward that would keep a target from landing on her back. I was her next meal. I was clean water and perhaps a day off from labor.

Desperation corrupted just as much as hatred.

I shook my head, pleading with my eyes. "Please."

With a snarl, she lunged for me, but I leaped out of the way, running toward the door. My fingers landed on the cold metal of the doorknob before a cry escaped my lips as my hair was yanked backward, and I crashed to the floor.

"You will not escape!" Lena yelled. She jumped on top of me, landing a solid punch on my cheek. I grabbed at her arms, reached for her hands, but tears filled my vision, my panic making me see double, and I couldn't get her off me.

"Lena!" I screamed. "Stop!"

"You will not escape," she repeated, saying it over and over as if it were a chant.

With a surge of strength, I pushed her off me, and she crashed into the wooden legs of the table. I thought for a moment that I had knocked her unconscious, but she pushed off the ground and ran for me once again. I scrambled backward, getting to my knees, but not before she was on top of me again. A hot palm slapped across my face, black spots crowding my vision.

"Lena," I begged as she continued to hit and punch. I didn't want to hurt her, but if I let her continue, I wouldn't be walking out of this house. "Why are you doing this?" Tears streamed down my cheeks.

"The dragons," she spit, slapping my cheek once more. "They took *everything* from me. Momma, Maza, Da…" A strangled sob slipped from her lips, and she smacked me again.

My head hit the wooden floor with a thud and for a moment my vision went black. Hot blood dribbled from my nose.

"When I hand you over, it'll mean one more day that I get to live in spite of the dragons. Maybe they'll even reward me with extra food… or a day of peace." She gritted her teeth. Her hands held my wrists to the floor, splinters shoving their way into my skin.

"You think by turning me in to the dragons that they would ever give you any type of peace?" I snarled back. "They're *dragons*. They will never relent. They'd sooner suspect you of working with me and kill you than give you any type of reward."

She gave a violent shake of her head. "Your words are poison, shifter filth."

"Lena, what if I could make them pay for what they've done? What if I can get revenge?"

She paused, her grip loosening on my wrists just enough that I was able to shove her off me and push to my feet.

"What?" she whispered, her eyes wide and brimmed with tears.

"I'm going to defeat them, Lena. The dragons. All of them."

"You…" The girl appeared to consider my words but then a wall slammed behind her eyes, and her gaze grew cruel and distant. "No. Every word you say is a lie. You're coming with me to my Master. Right now."

She lunged for me with a scream, and I knew I had no choice. I pulled on the fire in my core, letting it fill my veins. I couldn't comfortably shift inside Maza's house, but I could summon my magic enough to disarm her.

"I'm sorry," I whispered before a burst of blue flames erupted from my palms. Her eyes widened before she flew across the room, hitting the wall. I expected that to be it, but as if it hadn't even hurt, she jumped back to her feet. She ran at me again. My hands filled with fire and lightning crackled down and around my fingers.

"Lena, don't make me do this," I warned.

She stopped mere feet from me. "You'd really hurt one of your own?" The hatred in her eyes was almost too much to bear.

I sighed. "Like you're doing to me?"

She shook her head. "You're not one of us. Look at you." Lena gestured to the magic in my hands. "*We* can't do that." She spit blood onto the floorboards. "You deserve this."

I shook my head. "Lena, this is what they want. They want us divided so we can't stand against them. Don't let them win."

She tossed her head violently side to side. "No. You won't get inside my head." She took another step closer. "And you will not escape."

As if it was in slow motion, she charged at me, and a regretful sigh flew out of my mouth. "So be it."

I released the magic building within me, and with a wave of my hands sent it spiraling toward the girl. It collided with her in a blinding flash, once again sending her flying through the house. She smashed into the wall with a dull thud before she fell to the ground in a heap. Everything went silent, my pulse pounding in my ears.

I waited, expecting Lena to jump to her feet and continue her attack. But she remained still. I carefully approached, not wanting to be caught off guard again.

Please don't be dead. The last thing I wanted was to kill a human girl. She was confused, hurt, and desperate. I couldn't hold this against her, no matter how badly I wanted to. I breathed a sigh of relief when I arrived at her side and saw her chest rising in a steady rhythm. She was still alive, just unconscious.

I needed to leave. I had to be gone before she awoke, preferably far from Vernista, for I imagined she would tell her Master that I was here. She had proven that she would do anything to save herself from the wrath of the dragons.

Tears filled my eyes as I donned my cloak and made to leave, casting one last glance at Lena, wishing it hadn't come to this. Wishing that a human hadn't turned against me.

CHAPTER 10

TARRIN

MY THROAT ACHED from all the screaming.

It had been days since the stranger brought me food. Days since the last drop of water splashed over my tongue. Days that I had endured extra special attention from Eklos.

And by that, of course, I meant torture.

How he managed to continuously come up with new ways to break me into a sobbing, screaming mess, I didn't know. I thought there were only a few ways to truly break a person.

I was wrong.

Once again, I caught myself wondering how Kaida managed to survive Belharnt for seven years in conditions like this. How had any of the humans survived such a thing?

Forced to sit in the dark and unable to do anything else, my mind whirled over ways to outlaw slavery in Elysia once I took the throne. *If* I ever took the throne. If there was even a throne at the end of all of this.

There had to be a better way. Metta proved there was. Some dragons would be angered by the law, but I wanted to believe that a greater majority would be glad to be rid of it.

Blood crusted my hands, arms, and feet, and somehow each of

my limbs were both numb and throbbing at the same time. Every time I moved, it sent shocks of pain throughout my body, so I had resolved to sit on the floor and move as little as possible.

My mind was in a haze, starting to doze off when a scuffing noise echoed through the dungeon. Every muscle locked tight, frozen like ice.

Acid swirled in my stomach, sending bile up my throat.

But then the scuffing noise sounded again, and it was eerily similar to when the female had brought me food so many days ago. Surely, she wouldn't risk it again. After sending Roldan to find the intruder, I assumed that she was caught since she never returned. The girl should have been scared away for good knowing there were dragons hunting her trail.

But sure enough, I just barely made out the flash of pale skin beneath a hood, carrying another metal tray.

I shook my head vehemently. "No."

"Shh." She had the audacity to shush me.

"No, I don't want it," I refused as loud as I dared. I didn't know how close the dragons were, but I couldn't afford to bring them down upon me. My heart picked up its pace. The intruder had to leave, and quickly, before one of them caught her and punished me. "Get out."

She simply shook her head, silently sliding the tray under the cell door. "I'm sorry I couldn't come sooner. I was throwing those infernal dragons off my scent."

"You need to leave."

"And you need to eat," she retorted.

"If I eat your food, Eklos will know, and it will not take much more for him to kill me."

Through the dark, it looked like the stranger flinched.

"Or is that what you want?"

"No, T—" she cut herself off, forgetting to make her voice lower. Her true voice sounded familiar, but with my addled mind

I couldn't put a face to it. She cleared her throat. "Prince, you need to eat. Eklos will not smell this food. It's safe and you need to eat it."

"Why should I?" I fought the urge to apologize for my rudeness. I hoped the stranger was only wanting to help, but I had been badly beaten the last time she *helped*, and there was no guarantee it wouldn't happen again. I didn't want to be rude, but I also didn't want to make a foolish mistake. "How do I know this isn't some trick of Ek—"

"Kaida is coming," she whispered, sending ice through my veins.

"What did you say?"

I heard her sigh before her fingers wrapped around the metal bars. "Kaida is on her way here."

I took a step closer, both fear and desperation warring for control over my body. "How do you know? Who are you?"

I could barely see her shake her head. "Eat, Prince. Get your strength up. You will need it."

I leaped toward the bars, jarring to a stop when the shackles held me in place, and clenching my teeth against the pain shooting through me from the sudden movement. "Where is she?" Tears filled my eyes. I wanted out of this cell, away from him and his abuse, but not if Kaida was the cost. A tremble settled into my bones.

I had never known that I could miss someone as much as I had missed Kaida since Rythos captured me. She was everything this world needed—even if she didn't see it. I had seen the beast within her. The utter devastation she could cause; the ruination that could follow her. It didn't scare me one bit. In fact, it only made me love her more. She hated the beast inside her, hated that it made her want to hurt and kill. She despised that all the things she couldn't stand about dragons were inside of her. But it only made me desire her more. Because she saw all the wrongs, all the pain that she *could* cause, and always chose to be better.

Kaida was the strongest person I knew. The strongest *dragon* I knew.

But I couldn't risk losing her.

"She can't come here," I whispered, my voice breaking. "Eklos will kill her."

I could barely make out the movement of her hood as he shook her head. "They know it's a trap, Prince. Kaida will not leave you here."

Hope swelled in my chest for the first time since Rythos's claws had wrapped around my arm, stealing me away. How long had I been in this dungeon? Weeks? *Months?*

If Kaida knew it was a trap, she'd be prepared, right?

"How long?" I said through clenched teeth.

"Soon. You must be ready," the female answered at last.

I opened my mouth to beg for more information, but she turned on her heel and fled from the dungeon.

03

When the familiar thundering footsteps came down the hallway again, the food the intruder brought was long gone, digesting happily in my stomach. Or, based on the nausea beginning to spin, perhaps not so happily. The freezing air of the dungeon swept over my skin, eliciting goosebumps.

Please, don't let him smell the food. Please let the intruder's words be true.

Eklos's footsteps crashed toward me painfully slow, one step for what seemed like ten of my heartbeats. I tried to look dejected, slumped against the wall on the floor, though fresh energy from the food poured through my body. It was a strange feeling after living on the brink of death for so long.

I glanced down at my hands. They were still covered in dried blood.

He never sent anyone to tend to my injuries.

He usually had a healer come fix what he broke so that he could start fresh each time he visited me, but he hadn't this time. What did that mean? Was he no longer going to mend what he broke or clean what he fouled? Would he just layer hurt upon hurt, blood over blood? I forced my breathing to stay calm though it hitched at the thought.

"Well, well, well," Eklos's voice crooned in the dark. "Little Prince finally woke up."

I tried and failed not to wince. During his last visit, I had passed out during one of his particularly heinous torture sessions, and when I woke, he was gone. I swallowed hard, shutting down the memories. I refused to look at him or even acknowledge that he had spoken.

Then he sniffed, and my stomach crashed into the deep depths of the earth.

But then he kept sniffing, turning his head every which way. Eventually his red eyes turned their focus on me.

"It seems the little mouse who was foolish enough to try to bring you food hasn't been back." His snout spread in a wicked grin. "Pity."

Relief was like warm ale sliding down my throat. *He can't smell the food. She was right!*

"Congratulations. You chased away a harmless human." I couldn't keep the words contained in my mouth.

Before I could blink, Eklos was in my face, gripping my cheeks between his claws. They dug in, moments from piercing the skin.

"No human is harmless," he spat, hot saliva landing on my face.

I didn't want to incriminate the stranger or reveal that she had returned so I remained silent, holding his gaze until, at last, he released me. He patted my cheek, though it felt much more akin to a slap.

"Anyway," he continued as if the whole interaction hadn't occurred. "Shall we begin where we left off?" A wicked-looking hammer appeared in one hand and a knife in the other.

My heart went from pounding to an absolute flurry of a storm. I couldn't take much more of his abuse. If I suffered any more torture, there was no guarantee I'd be walking out of here in one piece. I had to find a way to stall.

Eklos stalked closer, that dagger-toothed smile never leaving his face.

"Wait," I blurted, and his red eyes widened as if he couldn't believe I had uttered the word.

"Wait?" he half snarled, half growled.

I gave a sharp nod. "You never sent someone to tend to my injuries. Surely, you'd prefer a blank slate to work upon."

"It matters not to me, *Prince*, whether you're broken or whole. You end up the same either way."

My mind whirled, trying to sort through my wild thoughts to come up with some other way to stop him from swinging that hammer and crushing more of my bones, or carving away at my skin with the knife.

"But you'd prefer me to last longer, right? I'm in quite a bit of pain as it is," I said, referencing the pounding ache in the back of my head and the fractured bones I could feel over much of my body. "I imagine I won't last nearly as long when I'm already in such a state." I gestured to myself.

Eklos seemed to ponder this for a moment, scratching at his scales. Then he narrowed his eyes. "What game are you playing?"

I shook my head so hard it made me dizzy. "No game. Only thinking of you." It was a play at his pride, and I didn't know if he'd buy it. Eklos was many things, but stupid was not one of them.

I took advantage of his pause in attack. "Why are you doing this, Eklos?"

He was in my face faster than I could blink. "That's *Regent* or *Master* to you," he snarled. "You have not earned the right to call me by that name."

I raised my chin as much as I could. "I am no slave. I will not refer to you as though I am. I am the Prince of Elysia."

"You are the Prince of Nothing!"

I tried to fight it, but fear had been ground into my very bones, and I recoiled from his roar. The shackles jangled as I covered my ears with my hands and curled against the wall. He stalked over to me, his red eyes the only thing I could see in the darkness.

"Enough of this. I see I have been far too lenient with you." He began pacing in the small cell. I cringed as his spiked tail grew closer and closer to colliding with my legs.

"*Lenient?*" I breathed, disbelief coating my tone.

Eklos swung to face me. "The things I've done to you were *kind* compared to what I wished to do. But I had to keep you alive. If I destroyed you, there was less of a chance that *they* would come for you. Nobody wants to rescue a corpse."

Dread sparked like a flare in my gut. "So, you're telling me this wasn't your worst."

A dagger-filled grin crawled across his snout. "Oh no. You haven't seen my worst." He stalked closer. "But you will. My patience is coming to an end. Either the shifters are coming for you, or they've given up. I laid the trail perfectly, and if they haven't shown their ugly faces by now, it seems they may have abandoned you."

I shook my head, attempting to shut out his words; trying to recall what the stranger had said. *Kaida is coming for you.*

Tears welled in my eyes, and Eklos chortled, assuming it was because of his own words.

"Don't worry. When your time comes, I'll offer you a mercy

that very few get." He winked and my blood boiled beneath my skin. "I'll make it quick." He took another step closer.

"You still didn't answer my question," I gasped out, in one last desperate attempt to find out his motives while buying time.

"Nor do I intend to. Do you truly think I would be stupid enough to reveal all my plans to the likes of you?" He clucked his tongue. "I am no fool."

Smoke leaked from his nostrils and circled my neck. "And, because I'm no fool, I know you've been stalling." His red eyes burned into me. Before I could brace myself, his claws slammed into my face.

My head crashed into the stone wall, and I slumped to the ground.

Eklos raised his hammer for another strike.

CHAPTER 11

KAIDA

I RAN ALLEY TO alley, between each tiny slave home, trying to stay within the shadows as long as possible. I didn't know how long Lena would remain unconscious, but I could take no chances. I knew she'd alert the dragons to my presence in Vernista the moment she woke. I wanted to be angry with her, but I couldn't fully blame her. If our positions were reversed, I may have done the same thing.

The winter air nipped at my skin as I moved toward the center of the village, my breath clouding in front of my face with each frantic exhale. Thus far, there was no sign of Z. Had he found answers at The Den? Or had he attacked a Remnant dragon like he said, and was now lying dead somewhere, his body growing colder with each second that passed? I shook my head, dispelling the thought. Z would be fine. He knew what he was doing.

I hoped.

I thought about sneaking over to The Den to check if he was still there, but the thought of going back to that place felt like holding a pile of beetles and being forced to eat them. It put a creepy crawly feeling inside my stomach, making me nauseous. My hands were shaking, and not just from the cold.

But The Den had been the first part of the plan, and I didn't know where else to look for him. With a hard swallow, I steeled my shoulders and moved alley to alley, trying to stay hidden in broad daylight as I made my way to the tavern that had been such a great source of my suffering.

I passed the run-down bakery on the corner that had my stomach clenching into a tight knot every time I ran from my cave-home to serve Eklos. I passed the whipping post where Eklos would string up slaves and used his favorite whip made of glass and fire to punish them. Dried red stains littered the stones around it that no amount of rain could wash away.

I had been tied to that post. Many times.

So had my mother. Before she died.

Dragons in many sizes and colors bustled the streets of Vernista, making it a challenge to remain unnoticed as I searched for Z. I slipped into the darkness of another alleyway just as a brown dragon looked in my direction, and I pressed my back up against a stone wall, praying to the old forgotten gods that the dragon wouldn't smell my scent. Some may not recognize the shape-shifter scent, but I knew the very dragons hunting me would. After several earth-shattering heartbeats, the dragon turned away and continued down the road.

A shuddering breath leaked from my lips. My trembling limbs begged me to stop, to remain hidden in the shadows until Z found me. But I couldn't do that. There was no guarantee that he would find me, at least not before another dragon did. I was on borrowed time.

I reached the other edge of the village, waiting until the nearby dragons were looking away, and scurried across to the thin line of trees. The Den was just on the other side of them. I tried to see above the treetops, looking for those dreaded red steeples, but strangely, they weren't there. I pushed on, thankful that the darkness beneath the trees kept me somewhat hidden. When I finally crossed to the other side, I stopped dead in my tracks.

For where The Den once stood, the place I feared almost as much as Belharnt, the place where the dragons almost crushed me to death before Tarrin rescued me…

It was now a pile of cinders and ash.

The Den was gone. The red-steepled tavern where I had grown up, forced to serve the cruel dragons while being abused and ridiculed… It was gone.

There was no smoke, and the ashes drifted around in the slight winter breeze. The fire and destruction must have occurred some time ago. But what happened? Had it been attacked by Z's rebels or another enemy? Or had Eklos burned it down as some sort of punishment?

And if the tavern no longer stood… Where was Z? If he had found it destroyed, why hadn't he returned to the house?

What do I do now?

I couldn't go back to the slave house. I would be surprised if Lena wasn't already tearing through the village, searching for me, and alerting all the dragons that I was there. It was only a matter of time before Eklos received word.

There was no other place I could go.

My eyes caught sight of the winding trail that passed where The Den used to stand, continuing as far as the eye could see in the distance.

That was the path that Tarrin and I had walked down when he first rescued me. That path was the first I had walked in dragon scales. Hot tears burned my eyes at the memory. I missed Tarrin. It felt like my other half was missing without him by my side. He was the only thing that kept the darkness, the monster, at bay within me. I could feel it growing stronger, darker each day as the anger from Tarrin being taken from me continued to grow.

It was a toxic thing, poisoning the human in me, wanting her dead so that only the dragon remained.

I not only feared what would happen to Tarrin if I couldn't

find him, but I feared for myself as well. I didn't want to be a monster. Tears spilled onto my cheeks, burning against my skin in the winter air, and my breath shook with each exhale.

Instinctively, I reached for the bond that connected me and Tarrin.

Tarrin?

There was only silence.

Tarrin, I'm coming. Hold on.

I wished in vain that I could hear the faintest beat of his heart. Anything to let me know that he was still alive. But there was nothing

An eerie tingle washed over me, and I spun around. My eyes roved through the darkness between the trees, but my human eyes couldn't see anything. Still, that feeling remained, causing the hair on the back of my neck to stand on end. I couldn't escape the feeling that someone was out there. Someone was watching me.

There was nowhere for me to go or hide. I could try to run, but there was no use trying to outrun a dragon. I considered shifting into dragon form so I could at least defend myself, but I knew it would immediately give away who and what I was to whoever was out there. Yet while I had spent my time training on how to defend my human body with Z, I had little confidence in myself that I would be able to win against a dragon.

Feeling like I had no other choice, I drew on my magic, letting it fill my core. I was just about to shift when a cold hand slapped over my mouth and dragged me deeper into the trees.

CHAPTER 12

ELDRIN

THE SUN WAS high in the sky, though it did little to warm the icy air as our small company prepared to leave Shegora and travel down the mountain to Metta. The fact that Gendon gave Metta to us, freely offered for us to use it as our battle ground in the war against Eklos and the Remnant… It was a gift that brought tears to my eyes when I thought about it.

Countless families would be left without a home; left without their lives by the end of this. It hurt my heart to imagine, but Gendon was adamant that we use Metta. I wouldn't waste his gift.

"Are you ready to leave?" Gendon's voice rumbled as I opened the front door to the hut I had been staying in.

"Just about," I replied, turning to grab my two packs, belting one around my waist and the other between my wings.

"Good. The others are getting antsy."

I chuckled. "I imagine they want to be off this ice-encrusted snow globe of a mountain."

It had snowed nonstop for nearly a week now. The temperature continued to plummet, and we were all freezing, despite our scales.

Gendon let out a laugh of his own. "Don't you?"

I hesitated before nodding. Shegora used to be my home. I

had grown up there with Lita. That was where I had learned everything I knew about being a shape-shifter. I had discovered my magic there. Though I, too, was tired of the cold, it was hard to leave such a place behind. Especially not knowing if I would ever return.

With the battle against Eklos's army on the horizon, I found it a very good possibility that I may never set foot in this village again.

The small group of dragons and humans who had made the journey up the mountain were gathered in a circle at the edge of the village, including the King. Gendon was in the middle, shouting orders.

"Each human needs to pair up with a dragon. You will be secured onto their back for the flight down the mountain." Gendon spun in a slow circle as he looked each person and beast in the eye. "It won't be an easy journey, but hopefully you'll fair better than the one you had coming up." A twinkle flashed in his eyes. He was enjoying this a little too much.

Gendon's gaze snapped to me when I stepped up to the group.

"I'll lead us, Martik will stay in the middle, and you bring up the rear," he said, nodding to me. I gave a single nod back and he turned, heading into Silverdew Valley. I waited for the few humans to climb onto the contraption of ropes that would keep them secured on the dragons' backs. When they all crossed into the Valley, I looked back at Shegora, studying every single thing, from the shape of the homes, to the empty window boxes, to streets laden in snow. I pictured a younger version of Lita and me running around, using our wings to fling snow at the other.

An ache filled my stomach. There were such wonderful memories in this village.

That is, until the Lone Dragon destroyed them all.

I swallowed the lump rising in my throat as I turned my back on Shegora likely for the last time.

ଓଃ

We made it through Silverdew Valley with much less excitement than last time, when Rythos had attacked us and captured Tarrin. Even now, months later, my mind was still reeling from Rythos's sudden appearance. How had I forgotten him? Why had he grown to hate me so?

The villagers of Metta arrived on the cliff that would begin their free fall down the mountain. I could see the excitement in each of the dragons' eyes, and absolute fear in the humans'. I didn't blame them.

I stood behind the group and watched as, one by one, they fell over the edge. To the credit of the humans, not a single one of them screamed or cried out. Their fists bunched into the ropes and their eyes squeezed shut, but none made a sound.

I didn't know why Eklos thought humans were so weak. They were stronger than the dragons gave them credit for. More resilient too.

When the last of the dragons had fallen off the mountain, I walked to the edge and peered down. As far as the eye could see, it was sheer cliff face, with jagged edges cropping out here and there. Trees stuck out in some places, and I watched as each dragon expertly turned their wings to avoid each obstacle.

Icy wind stabbed at my scales, and I noticed more storm clouds forming. Another round of snow was on the way. We needed to make it to Metta before it hit, or we wouldn't be able to see well enough to make it down the mountain.

With a shuddering breath, I tucked my wings in tight and let myself fall over the edge. The wind tore at my body, building in pressure with each foot that I dropped. I unfurled my wings just enough to steer me around the trees and sharp crags of rock, picking up speed by the second.

I could have used my magic to jump to Metta, now that it had fully restored, but Gendon had specified that I take the rear of the group. I didn't know why he had placed me last, but I wouldn't question his decisions when he had led these villagers for decades. So, since I couldn't carry all these people with me, there would be no magic-jumping to Metta.

The storm clouds moved in fast, and though it wasn't even close to nightfall, they blocked the light so thoroughly it felt like night was descending over the mountain. The first of the snowflakes began to fall, whipping against my scales. Within heartbeats, it grew to a blizzard.

A large shape flashed out of the corner of my eye, but by the time I looked, there was nothing to see through the maelstrom of snow. I squinted, trying in vain to discover what it might have been, but I couldn't see anything. Surely, I hadn't passed the other dragons already. Even if they had slowed down, they were a great distance in front of me.

I turned my gaze forward, though anxiety curdled in my stomach.

A shadow moved in my peripheral vision once more and my head snapped to the left. There was nothing, only blowing snow.

If it were a member of Gendon's group, they wouldn't be hiding in the storm. They would have made themselves known. I thought about using my magic right then to jump but as soon as the thought crossed my mind, a huge figure barreled into me, knocking me off course. I spun through the air at a frightening speed, twirling countless times before I was able to open my wings. I frantically looked around for what had collided with me, but my eyes only met white snow and darkness.

I tucked my wings in tight, forcing my body faster. I needed to get to the bottom of the mountain. Cliffs and trees zoomed past me, sharp branches scratching against my scales as I flew too close.

I saw the shadow move again and I barely managed to roll out of the way. I heard a low growl as the thing passed over me. The sound was unmistakable. I looked up just in time to see a light-gray dragon suspended amongst the snow, nearly invisible except for his orange eyes.

Rythos.

Fear shot through my veins like a burning poison. I couldn't let him grab on to me. If he did, I would disappear just like Tarrin. I needed to jump. Yanking at my core of magic, I began to call on it when a voice spoke.

"Hello, Eldrin." The words cut through the wind, forcing a shiver through my scales. With a snarl, he reached for me, and I twisted to the side, his hands passing through the air my wings had just inhabited. His irritated growl echoed behind me as I tucked my wings once more and willed my body to dive faster.

Had Rythos been waiting on this mountain the entire time I was in Shegora? Did he leave Tarrin with Eklos and return, biding his time until I left the barrier of the village?

Rythos lunged for me again and I tucked my wings in and spun out of his reach, hitting the top of a pine tree. I held in a snarl, snapping my wings, trying to fall faster.

The snow was blustery and strong, whipping against my scales and mercilessly stabbing my eyes. I still hadn't fallen far enough to catch an updraft, though at this point it would do me little good. I didn't want to fight a dragon in the air. I had done it before, but it was infinitely more difficult. I glanced over my shoulder on instinct and found Rythos's hand only inches from me. I turned so my front faced him, drawing on my magic, and sending a ball of flame straight into his chest. It collided dead center and his roar filled the air.

I had to jump. I didn't have an option. I knew it went against Gendon's wishes, and it left the group exposed, but Rythos wasn't interested in the others. He only wanted me. I had to make it to Metta. At least with my feet firmly on the ground, I stood a better chance.

I inhaled, preparing the depths of my magic to fold me into the shadows. Rythos reached for me just as I snapped the magic out and vanished into the darkness. The searing wind disappeared, and my senses were smothered in black before a burst of light shot through my vision and my feet crashed into the snow.

Opening my eyes, I expected to see Metta in front of me, with Gendon and the other villagers touching down after their flight.

But it was not Metta that I stood in front of.

My magic dwindled into dust, my stomach falling through the earth as my brain fought to comprehend what I was seeing.

A dark chuckle sounded behind me as the sharp claws that I hadn't noticed encircling my arm peeled away.

"Welcome, Eldrin," Rythos's voice crooned. I looked around and all the fight and hope drained out of me. Countless dragons stood in a circle around us, their snouts split into violent sneers.

I was in the center of Eklos's army.

KAIDA

"SHH!" A VOICE hushed me as I opened my mouth to scream.

I couldn't see who spoke the words, but the voice was unmistakably familiar. So was the lemon pine scent of her skin.

"Lita?" The word was muffled against her palm.

"Quiet. I'm trying to get you to safety."

I pressed my lips together and she released me. The last time I had seen the Queen of Elysia, we were forced to split up at the cottage and continue to Shegora without her. The note she had sent Tarrin months ago said that she wasn't going to come to the mountain village because she felt her place was where Eklos was, trying to infiltrate his inner circle. I didn't expect to see her again, least of all *here*. How did she find me?

Her grip was firm on my arm as she dragged me through the trees before stopping next to one with an enormous trunk. She kneeled in the dirt and pushed a chunk of wood in, and a door opened at the base of the tree, just large enough for the both of us to fit through.

"What—"

Before I could finish speaking, she grabbed my hand and yanked, pushing me through the tree door. Darkness smothered me before Lita's hand wrapped around my bicep and pulled me forward.

"Where are we going?" I whispered, but she shook her head.

"Not here."

The tunnel was cold and damp, the dirt squishing beneath my boots. Each of our breaths echoed. Lita led me through turn after turn and I was thoroughly lost before we finally arrived in a cavern of sorts with torches spaced evenly along the wall. I blinked in the sudden brightness, my eyes watering.

When my vision finally adjusted, my mouth dropped open.

In the center of the room was a huge table, four unfamiliar dragons in varying shades of brown, blue, and green seated around it. Lita shuffled her feet across the dirt and took a seat next a fifth dragon that forced a scowl to my face.

It was Z.

"What the scales are you doing here?" I snapped at him.

It had been hours since he had left to scout Vernista for clues of Tarrin's whereabouts. If he had found secret tunnels, or Lita for that matter, he should have returned to retrieve me. I scowled at him, and he huffed a laugh.

"Nice to see you too, little shifter."

I let out an annoyed growl that sounded truly pathetic in human form. "Why didn't you return?"

"Because an unfamiliar dragon walking the streets of Vernista was drawing too much attention. Lita found me lurking about and brought me here." He shrugged. "I figured it was only a matter of time until you came looking for me."

I crossed my arms and fixed him with a glare. "I was attacked at the house."

The amusement slid off his face as his eyes roved over me, checking for injuries, though he didn't say anything.

"I'm fine, thanks for asking," I deadpanned.

"You look fine to me."

I opened my mouth to snap at him, but another voice interrupted.

"A dragon attacked you?" Lita asked, looking between the two of us.

I shook my head. "It was a human. A slave whose sister used to live at that house. She recognized me from the posters."

Lita shook her head and rubbed at her temple. "I was hoping to have more time before the village was alerted to your presence. It won't take the Remnant long to find another entrance to these tunnels. We need to move."

Narrowing my eyes, I studied the dragons around the table. "Who are they?" I pointed at the others.

Lita glanced at them before walking over to take a seat on Z's right. "Some of Eklos's disgruntled followers. I've swayed them to our side. They're going to help us defeat him."

Shaking my head, I took a step back and said, "Why would you bring me here?"

Why would she purposefully put me in danger by placing me in reach of Eklos's dragons? Even when dragons despised my former Master, none were brave enough to go against him. Though Eklos thought dragons were the superior race, he had no problem cutting down any beast that stood in his way. A picture flashed through my mind as I recalled him forcing me to watch his memories of killing his own father.

I stumbled another step backward, fighting the urge to run. These dragons would hand me over the first chance they got. I'd be surprised if Eklos didn't already know I was down here.

"Kaida," Lita said in a firm voice, trying to break through my fear smothered mind. "You have my word that these males will do no harm to you. I have spent these months infiltrating Eklos's inner circle. I've convinced them that there is a better way, a better world meant for Elysia. They want to fight for it."

One of the males at the table, a smaller dragon with scales

the color of rich green leaves in the height of summer, cleared his throat. "The human is right." He nodded. "We are tired of Eklos's tyranny and the hatred he spreads. It is draining and we no longer want any part of it." The dragon gestured to the others at the table. "We desire a different Elysia just as much as you."

My eyes narrowed. "Why now?" I snapped. "A thousand years of slavery, violence, and cruelty infesting Elysia, and you're just now standing up against it? Why?"

The dragons all exchanged looks with each other, but none spoke up. Then Z cleared his throat.

"It's been more than a millennium since someone has appeared with the Ancient Magic. It is the only thing powerful enough to defeat Eklos and his army. Without your magic, Kaida, there would be no hope. Together with the Prince and his World Weaver abilities, you two are unstoppable."

I scowled. "You mean to tell me that if I didn't have this magic, none of you would be here right now?"

The green dragon spoke up. "You need to understand, girl. Eklos is far too powerful, even for the entirety of Elysia's dragons to defeat. Xalerion was the most powerful dragon in Elysia's history, and his son killed him. As a Smoke Wielder, he can do the most terrible things. Poison us from the inside out while we suffocate, force us to experience our worst nightmares all within our own minds. You've seen what has happened to those who dare to defy him. You're the only one who has gone up against him, multiple times now, and lived to tell the tale."

I winced, trying to shut down the memories of fighting Eklos. They were nightmares I didn't want to relive.

"Why me?" I asked under my breath, not intending for anyone to actually answer. The burden of saving Elysia, and the crushing weight of their hope in me was too much, and without Tarrin at my side tempering my fear, I struggled to convince myself that I could win. Their faith in me felt misplaced.

"I don't believe any of us would be here if we didn't think you could win. Elysia is terrified of Eklos for a reason. We know you can defeat him," Z said, his eyes softening as if he could see the spinning thoughts in my mind. He gestured at the empty chair at the other end of the table. "Each of us will stand with you. Until the very end."

As if it were some kind of cue, Lita, along with each dragon at the table, stood to their feet and lowered to one knee. They clenched their right claws into a fist and brought it over their heart with heads bowed. The breath caught in my throat. It was the old sign of the human's failed rebellion a thousand years ago. Lita raised her head to meet my gaze, and pride shone like a beacon in her eyes. She nodded once, a small smile on her face.

Blowing out a breath, I slowly walked to the end of the table, taking the spot of authority across from Z. One by one, the dragons rose and faced me. A strange emotion flickered in Z's eyes, but he hid it away before I could determine what it was. He gave me a firm nod.

Sliding into the wooden chair, I waited as the others followed suit. For a moment no one spoke, and my heartbeat pounded in my ears. I looked each dragon in the eye before my gaze landed on Lita.

"First things first. Where's Tarrin?"

ᆼ

The tunnels were musty and ice cold as Z, Lita, and I made our way through the darkness. It felt like we'd been lost in the maze for days, but it had only been an hour at most.

"We're almost directly under where The Den once stood," Lita whispered, the sounds of each consonant hissing off the dirt walls. "Eklos had these dungeons built after he destroyed the ones beneath the palace. The cells are tiny, dirt-infested holes in the wall. Eklos keeps him bound in iron shackles." She paused to glance at me. "That's likely why there hasn't been anything through your bond in months."

"Is he all right?" I dared to ask.

She hesitated. "He's... alive. I've been trying to smuggle him food when I can. He's starving to death. I thought if I could provide him *something* to keep his body going until you arrived..." Lita sighed, exasperated. "The first time, Eklos smelled the food on Tarrin. He was punished for it, and I was nearly caught by the Remnant."

Bile rose in my throat. "Punished?"

Lita's wince was evident even in the dark of the tunnels. "Let's just say that was the only time I made that mistake."

Z's footsteps were quiet behind me, and I marveled for a moment over how silent such a large dragon could be.

"Does Tarrin know it was you?" I asked.

She shook her head. "I didn't reveal myself in case Eklos tortured him for information. I was trying to protect him, but it only ended up hurting him." Lita ran a hand over the top of her hair, the rest falling to her waist in a tight braid.

"We have to be careful," she whispered, holding her hand out to slow us. "We're getting close."

I reached out for the shifter bond between Tarrin and me, but there was only an empty, hollow feeling. I hoped that Lita was right, that it was only the iron dampening it, and not something like bluestone where it would destroy the bond, and his ability to shape-shift completely.

Though, bluestone seemed unlikely. I had been chained with it in Belharnt for only days and it almost killed me. It had been over two months and Tarrin was still breathing. I exhaled, reminding myself that Tarrin was alive. The relief was like water running down my throat after days without it.

"Why are these tunnels empty?" I whispered. "Shouldn't they be crawling with Eklos's dragons?"

Z's clawed hand brushed my shoulder. "We took care of it."

"*We?*"

"Did you really think we would attempt to infiltrate Vernista and the dungeons beneath them without help?"

At a stern look from Lita, we both fell silent, forcing my mind to quietly dwell on what Z meant. Were his rebels down here with us, unseen amongst the shadows, handling all of Eklos's guards?

Lita continued leading the way, with me in the middle and Z bringing up the rear. We were so close I could feel the heat emanating off his body.

"Was it really a wise decision for you to come?" I dared to ask a while later. I eyed his hunched over figure, pebbles raining down every now and then when his head skimmed the ceiling. "You barely fit down here."

His eyes let off a faint glow. "If Eklos can fit, so can I. I'm just your moral support." Z winked, bringing a scowl to my face which had his breath hissing in a quiet chuckle.

"It would have been less conspicuous if you had stayed behind." I turned forward again. "Not to mention easier for us to sneak in and out without a dragon getting in the way," I muttered beneath my breath.

Z scoffed, faking offense. "I'm not in your way. You two are the brains, I'm the muscle."

A bark of laughter erupted from my throat before I could stop it and I slapped a hand over my mouth, wishing I could rake the sound back into it. It was so loud it should've caused an earthquake. I cringed as Lita came to a halt, cocking her head, listening.

"Sorry," I whispered, and she waved her hand in dismissal, wanting me to be quiet.

Z's silent laughter taunted me, and he smashed his scaled lips together. At least the danger we were in wasn't dampening his usual annoying spirits.

The distant *plink* of water dropping into a puddle echoed

somewhere down the tunnel, but otherwise everything stayed silent. It was surprising that we were so close to the dungeons and yet we hadn't encountered any other dragons. How many rebels were hiding in the shadows?

Lita's steps slowed and Z's belly bumped into me. I bit my tongue to keep my snarky comment to myself and glared over my shoulder at him before running into Lita's back. Retreating, I waved my hands in apology, trying to stay silent. She put a finger to her lips and pointed down the passage.

My heart raced like a horse in my chest and my breaths puffed out in panicked gasps. This was it. After two entire months without Tarrin by my side, living with the fear that he was being tortured or killed, he was finally within my grasp. Hot tears welled in my eyes, but I bit my cheek to push them away. There wasn't time for emotions now. If we made it out of Vernista alive, I could cry all I wanted. For now, I had to be strong for Tarrin. He had lived through two months of hell. After surviving seven years in Belharnt, I knew it wasn't a question but a fact.

I exhaled, reaching for our bond once more. *We're almost there, Tarrin.* Only silence greeted me. I was counting down the seconds until I could feel our shape-shifter bond once more. It was much like having a limb cut off but trying to use it anyway.

"Almost there." Lita's voice was barely more than an exhale. She turned a corner and even through the dark I could see the unmistakable gleam of metal bars.

Tarrin!

I jolted forward, intending to run until I could find him, but Lita's hand landed on my chest, forcing me to stay put. She gave a single shake of her head. Not for the first time, I wished that she had retained the ability to speak through our bond. Though I knew Lita desperately missed her dragon form, I rarely ever thought twice about it. Lita was Lita, regardless of what form she took. But the ability to still speak mind-to-mind would have been useful.

She pointed at Z and spread her fingers in a gesture that meant she wanted him to stay before pointing at me, telling me to follow her. The scales around Z's eyes bunched. He didn't like the idea of staying behind. I tried to give him reassurance with a nod. He crossed his arms in an awkward human gesture and leaned against the wall.

"If anything goes wrong, shift into dragon form. I'll see the flash. I'll come for you." His words were whisper soft. The fact that this dragon, who owed me nothing, would be willing to risk his life for me, fight on my behalf… It had my eyes burning. I tried to give him a smile, but based on his deepening scowl, it ended up being more of a grimace. With an exhale, I turned back to Lita, and we tiptoed down the tunnel.

The darkness grew thicker the farther we walked, and I fought the urge to run up to the bars of each cell. After living so long with the uncertainty of Tarrin's fate, my patience was at an all-time low, especially now that I was mere feet away from seeing him again. I wanted to run, wanted to shout his name, but I could do none of it as I followed Lita through the never-ending dark.

The stretch of tunnel continued, on and on, grating on my dwindling patience. The darkness played tricks on my mind, forcing terrifying scenarios to play through my head. Pictures of Tarrin broken and bleeding on the floor, or missing limbs, or worst of all… that he was already dead, and Eklos left him in a cell to rot.

I closed my eyes, trying to shut down the images, and walked right into Lita's back. It was pitch black and I couldn't even see the annoyed scowl that I imagined was plastered on her face.

A wheezing cough sounded in the next cell and the tight leash I held on my restraint snapped. *Tarrin!* I sprang forward, ignoring Lita's hand as she tried to hold me back. The cold metal of the bars was like burning ice cutting into my palms. I felt Lita's body heat at my back before she let out a ragged breath. It took a lot longer for my eyes to pierce the darkness to see what was left of my beloved Tarrin.

He was slumped against the far wall, huge iron shackles encircling his wrists and ankles. No wonder I couldn't reach him through our bond. They made the bindings I was caged with in Belharnt seem tiny. Dried blood the color of dark rust coated much of his too-pale skin, and his clothes were hanging off him in rags. His dark hair was matted and caked with dried blood, sticking to the skin on his neck and face, which had grown so pale that it was tinged with blue beneath a short beard. All the muscle he had built through training before he was taken had been lost; his body reduced to mere skin and bones. I winced at the sharpness of his collar bones, the piercing angle of his cheek bones. A tear slipped down my cheek. Tarrin was dying.

Several of his fingers were bent at awkward angles and there was a wicked-looking cut on his temple that looked in desperate need of stitching. Tears filled my eyes knowing the more gruesome wounds would be in his mind and would take much longer to heal. If they healed at all.

"Tarrin?" I whispered as loud as I dared. He didn't move. Fear spiked through me like a thousand needles under my skin jamming their way out. "Tarrin?"

There was a stutter in his breathing before his head barely lifted off his shoulder, as he struggled to pry open his eyelids. It took him several seconds of blinking for his eyes to focus before they widened, fixed on my face.

"Kaida?" he breathed.

At the sound of his voice, every second, minute, and day apart from him rushed to the surface and I snapped, drawing on the entirety of my magic. I wrapped my hands around the metal bars of his cell, and flames coated my hands. I willed them to burn hot enough to melt the metal like it did to my shackles when I was chained in Belharnt. My magic blazed, changing in color and intensity until the metal began to droop between my hands, and I was able to pry them open. I pushed through them and was instantly at Tarrin's side.

"Kaida?" he repeated, blinking furiously as if trying to make sense of my sudden presence. His voice was so hoarse it was a wonder he could even speak. "Am I dead? Is this the afterlife?"

I choked back a sob at the question, cupping his face in my palms. "No, I'm here."

He squinted, studying my face as though I spoke a foreign language before clarity snapped over him.

"You have to leave—now," he coughed out. "It's a trap. Eklos—"

"Shh," I soothed. "We know. I'm getting you out of here."

I called flames into my palm, trying to melt his shackles like I had the metal bars but the moment I touched them, it sputtered out.

"*What?*" I gasped.

I tried again, but the flames remained just a flicker in my hands. They wouldn't grow hotter, wouldn't increase in intensity to free Tarrin from his chains.

"Hurry," Lita said, arriving at my side.

"I'm trying," I bit out. Why wasn't my magic working? I gripped the metal between my hands, an ache settling beneath my skin as they made contact with the iron. "Come on, come on," I muttered, forcing the magic in my core to swell.

I didn't come this far to be stopped by some measly shackles.

With a snarl, I shot every ounce of magic into the flames in my hands, smothering the iron until the shackles were forced to melt, careful to keep the fire from burning his skin. The metal dissolved, freeing Tarrin's wrists and ankles, and his eyes flared bright like green fire as his magic returned.

Pulling his arm around my shoulder, I helped him stand on shaking legs. How long had it been since he was able to stand—to *move?* He stared down at himself for several moments as if he couldn't figure out whether it was real life or a dream. Then, finally, his eyes met mine before he dragged me into his arms, wrapping them around me so tight that my lungs constricted. Twisted fingers tangled into my hair, gripping my neck.

Despite the cold of the tunnel, it was the first time in two months that I finally felt warm, like I could breathe.

"I thought I'd never see you again," he murmured, the words blurred as his lips pressed against my skin.

I held him tighter, unwilling to voice just how strong that same fear had lived in me.

"Ah, how sweet. Lovers reunited just in time to die together," a cruel voice crooned, and both of us stiffened. The heat of my magic that I had been stoking for hours in case we had to fight our way out instantly went cold. It was the voice of my nightmares. The voice of the beast that should not have made it out of Belharnt.

Fire flared as a torch was lit, a dark snout appearing out of the shadows, baring its teeth.

Eklos.

CHAPTER 14

ELDRIN

A CRUEL LAUGH BIT through the air behind me.

Dragons of every size and color surrounded me in a circle. The horns and spikes covering their spines and wings flashed in the sunlight that pierced through the camp. Though it was winter, the combination of the fires across the camp and the dragons' immense body heat kept the air at a slightly warmer temperature. A putrid stench permeated everything, likely from the dragons dropping their waste anywhere they pleased.

My gut sloshed and swirled as dread set in. Rythos laughed once more, opening his arms to gesture at the camp. "Welcome. We've been waiting for you."

I studied Rythos, then the dragons behind him. This wasn't good. There was no obvious way of escape, and my odds against so many were slim. They'd tear me to pieces before I even made it three feet into the air.

"What do you want?" I snapped, stalling for time.

Rythos rolled his eyes. "What do you think?"

"Well, get on with it then. Kill me."

The dragon burst out laughing, along with everyone within earshot. "Oh no, Eldrin. No. Eklos has special plans for you. By the end of it, you'll *wish* I had killed you in Silverdew Valley. That, I promise you."

I opened my mouth to speak but he nodded at the dragons behind me who then dug their claws into my arms. I heard the ring of a sword escaping its sheath just before the pommel smashed into my temple and everything went black.

ఆ

When I came to, I was tied to a pole dug into the ground in the center of an empty tent. The air was much colder in here, cut off from the heat of the fires and dragons. Night had fallen, forcing my eyes to adjust to the darkness. I could faintly hear the rumbling of the dragons outside, though it sounded like they were a good distance away.

I yanked at the restraints around my wrists, but they didn't budge. The cold bite of iron dug into my scales, cutting off access to my magic. The flap to the tent snapped open, momentarily blinding me as the sudden torch light burned my eyes.

"Look who finally decided to wake up," Rythos crooned. He put his snout up close to mine.

"Let me go, Rythos," I croaked.

For a heartbeat he blinked at me, seeming as though he may have been considering my plea. But then a cruel smile peeled back his snout. "No, I think not."

"Why are you doing this? I've done nothing to you."

"Nothing?" he snapped. "How quickly we forget, Eldrin. You don't remember our little conversation in the Valley?" He tapped his mouth as if he were trying to recall a memory. "Right before I took that Prince away from you?"

I grit my teeth. "I told you, Rythos. I didn't leave you, or forget you, on purpose. I had little choice in going to Shegora. You act as though I left you behind simply to hurt you."

A low growl escaped his lips. "I don't care what excuses come from your mouth, Eldrin. You're a liar. You broke your oath to me."

My scaled brows lowered. What oath? My memories of those early years before I manifested shifter abilities were fuzzy at best. I had no recollection of any promise I had made him. Not when I barely remembered *him*.

"What are you talking about, Rythos?" I tried, wanting him to explain what he meant.

"Don't pretend you don't remember the promise you made me as younglings. Don't pretend you didn't betray me."

"I have no idea what you're talking about!"

"Stop lying!" he growled. "You knew I had no family left. We were like brothers, yet you still left me behind." He panted as though the words had stolen the breath from his lungs. "But why, Eldrin?" His next words were soft. "Why did you break your oath? Did you truly believe you were better than me because you're a shape-shifter?"

"What?" I breathed. How could he think I would believe that about myself? Where did he even get such a thought?

Rythos steeled himself and cleared his throat. "It doesn't matter. Eklos will arrive shortly and then you'll be dead once and for all."

Fear perched on my shoulders and dug its talons beneath my scales. My mind spun through every possible plea. There was nothing my sluggish brain could come up with to convince him to let me go. I could see the hatred shining in his eyes. Still, I couldn't help myself from trying.

"Help us defeat Eklos. Once he's dead, all the riches will be yours for the taking."

The dragon guffawed. "You think I care one bit for riches? I may be a dragon, but I am no fool."

"Then what is it you desire, Rythos? Let me go and I'll help you get it."

His eyes narrowed and he put his snout mere inches from my own. "Liar."

I shook my head. "I'm not lying. Eklos's tyranny has gone on for long enough. There's a better Elysia that we could all experience. Let me go and we can create it together."

A spark lit his eyes, as if I had hit a nerve. I wished in vain that I could remember more of my youngling years when we had been close. Had we really been like brothers? How had he come to hate me so strongly?

"Why in the scales would I ever believe a word you say when all you've ever done is lie to me?"

"Rythos, it's been a thousand years. You're telling me you remember all those early years perfectly?"

"I remember everything!" he roared, and I couldn't help but cringe away. He paced across the tent, smoke billowing from his nostrils.

I tried a different angle. "Why are you helping Eklos? He's a vile beast who will only use and discard you."

He seemed to consider this before shaking his head. "No, Eldrin. You're the vile beast. Eklos will soon be High King and then all the filth in Elysia like *you* will be wiped away." He spat on the ground next to me.

High King? Was that what Eklos was planning? Destroy the Royal Family along with any who dared to stand in his way, and he'd rule over Elysia himself?

As if realizing the information he'd just revealed, Rythos scowled and marched up to me. "I care not what you have to say. The words you speak are only cruel lies meant to play with my mind."

"Rythos—"

"No!" he shouted, his chest heaving. "I won't listen to another word out of your mouth. Eklos has been nothing but loyal to me and I will not have you try to convince me otherwise." He turned on his heel and stomped toward the tent entrance. He paused and glanced over his shoulder but avoided my gaze.

"And when Eklos arrives at camp, you will die."

CHAPTER 15

KAIDA

EKLOS'S SNOUT SPLIT into the most terrifying grin I had ever seen. "Welcome home, slave. How nice of you to join us." He lifted his arms at his sides, gesturing to the dungeon that was now illuminated.

There were five cells, none of which were large enough for a full-sized dragon, with metal bars gleaming in the fire light. From what I could tell, the others were empty, but if we didn't escape these tunnels, they wouldn't be staying that way.

Suffocating smoke suddenly filled my lungs and vision. When it dissipated, Tarrin's grip on my arm loosened before a crunch echoed in the cell as he collapsed.

Eklos laughed, and I dropped to my knees, pressing my fingers to Tarrin's neck where I found his weak pulse.

"What did you do to him?" I demanded.

Eklos let out a dark chuckle. "Oh, don't you worry. He's still alive. For now." His red eyes turned on Lita. "So, you were the one sneaking in to bring him food. Lovely to see you *alive*."

Eklos hadn't seen her since he killed her dragon form last summer at the Beginnings Festival. Based on the way his snout twisted, he had no idea her human form had survived. His red eyes flared bright as more smoke leaked from his nostrils.

I pushed to my feet and stepped in front of her. "What did you do to Tarrin?" I repeated.

Eklos missed nothing, eyeing my position in front of the Queen before shrugging. "He's asleep."

I narrowed my eyes.

"If he were conscious, it would be too easy for you to escape," he drawled. "Now he's not, and now you'll stay." His snout split into daggers.

I gave a violent shake of my head. I had fought too long and hard to find Tarrin again. I suppressed the urge to look over my shoulder to see if Z was still watching from the shadows. I didn't know if Eklos was aware of the ice dragon, but I didn't want to give away our one advantage.

"It's truly a pity that the dear Prince is unconscious. I would have loved to brag to him about how right I was. You walked right into my trap just as I had told him you would." He sneered at me. "Now, tell me. Where is your father?"

I fixed him with a glare. "None of your business. And I'm afraid we won't be staying," I retorted.

Eklos's red eyes blazed. "Oh, I don't think you'll be going anywhere." He summoned flames to his claws and sent a ball of fire careening toward us.

Shielding both Lita and Tarrin, I drew on my magic, though it was difficult, like wading through mud, and managed to throw out a barrier of white flames before Eklos's attack could make contact.

Eklos clicked his tongue before sneering. "I see someone's been practicing."

My hands clenched into fists, and Z's words echoed through my head. *Shift and I'll come for you.*

I stepped out of Tarrin's cell, trusting that Lita would get him out of the dungeon, and inhaled through my nose, stoking the fire in my core once again. It only took a moment before purple lights flashed over my skin, the heat of my dragon form instantly warming my cold bones, and I was thankful that shifting forms had become as easy for me as breathing. When I opened my eyes again, I was face-to-face with Eklos.

His face contorted in disgust. "You think that will help you defeat me?"

"It worked in Belharnt," I retorted.

Eklos's eyes narrowed. "I'm going to kill you, slave. I'll kill everyone you hold dear, force you to watch, and then you will die."

I couldn't hold back a laugh, though his words weren't funny in the least. "Is that a promise?" I spit before I lunged after Eklos, forcing him back against the wall. My claws encircled his neck, and his red eyes flared for a moment before he swung his spiked tail and smashed the side of my head, sending me sprawling.

It took several seconds to clear the spots dancing in my vision, all the while the dragon of ash and smoke stalked closer, violence flashing like lightning in his eyes. He raised his tail once more, positioning it over my head. He bared his teeth and I saw the flash of spikes as he moved.

With a growl, I rolled away just as the spikes pummeled the ground where my head had been. I made to stand but a sharp burning sensation pierced my ankle, and I was forced back to the dirt, my head hitting the wall. A fire whip wrapped around my leg, the glass piercing between the scales as if they were made of paper.

With a yank, Eklos dragged me toward him, and I couldn't hold back a roar as the fire and glass cut deeper.

"Did you really think," he taunted, giving another pull, "that you could enter *my* domain, free your pathetic Prince, and escape with your lives?" Another yank at my leg. I was directly beneath him now. "Haven't you learned, *slave*? I cannot be defeated."

He let go of the fire whip and a steady stream of blood poured from my leg as the glass fell away. Eklos twirled his claws in the air, creating a fire spear from his magic. Before I could move, he stabbed the spear straight through my arm, pinning it to the dirt.

The roar that burst from my snout had pebbles raining from the ceiling.

Was this it? After everything, this was where I would die?

Eklos spun his claws again, creating another fire spear.

I dared a glance toward the cell, hoping that Lita had done what I expected—gotten out with Tarrin. Elysia needed him as their King. He had to survive. If my life was the price to free him, I would pay it.

I searched the darkness but didn't see any sign of them.

Another shocking burst of pain erupted in my gut, and my vision went dark before Eklos's sneering face came into focus. He had stabbed another spear of fire straight into my stomach. I was pinned to the ground. Blood coated my tongue. I tried to call upon my magic, any lick of fire or water to fight him off, but it sputtered out in my palms, and my core turned cold and empty.

Eklos laughed as my vision went in and out of focus.

"Was it worth it, girl?" he asked, bringing his face inches from mine. The heat of his magic as he created a third spear burned against my scales. "Trying to escape from me? All the death and pain you've caused. Was it worth it?" He twisted the spear in my gut farther into the ground beneath me.

I clenched my teeth against the pain, and hot tears burned against my scales.

"All the death and pain *I've* caused?" I panted, blood spilling from my lips. "You're the one murdering innocent people. You're the one forcing others to sacrifice their lives so that *you* can get what you want, Eklos."

"They know the cost of freeing this world from your kind of filth."

"You're destroying Elysia," I snarled.

"No, slave. I'm *saving* it."

Eklos's red eyes flared, and he lifted his last fire spear over my heart.

I tried to move, to roll away before he plunged it through my scales. I begged my magic to answer my call and save me, but nothing happened. I still hadn't figured out how to accept my inner beast… Was that why it wouldn't work?

The two fire spears in my arm and stomach held me firmly to the ground; my magic stayed silent.

I braced myself for the pain that would end my life. The heat of his magic grew closer, burning beneath scales and skin.

And then the heat was gone.

A deafening roar filled the tunnel as Z flew out of the darkness and collided with Eklos, sending him sprawling across the ground. The fire spears that had been plunged into my body sputtered and dissolved, and blood seeped from my stomach and arm.

For a moment I was frozen, blinking away the rest of the darkness swarming my vision before my eyes settled on the dragons as they fought with claws and magic.

Something akin to surprise flashed on Eklos's face, and he paused in his attack. "Well—"

"Alyaa, get Kaida out of here," Z snarled, interrupting Eklos, and sending daggers of ice flying toward his scales. Eklos shielded himself with smoke, but Z infused his magic with it, freezing it entirely before shattering it with a clench of his fist.

Alyaa?

The lavender-colored dragon that I had met months ago when Z saved Tarrin and me from those mercenaries suddenly appeared at my side. Her claws moved over my stomach and the pain flared before it simply… disappeared.

I glanced down and found a glowing purple patch spread across my wound, forcing the bleeding to stop and the pain to abate. She repeated the movement on my arm, and I stared in awe as another patch spread over it.

"What?" I breathed. Alyaa put her hands under my arms and

helped me to my feet. My head spun and I stumbled a few steps before she caught me.

"Steady," she murmured. "I'll explain later. Right now, Z's orders were to get you out of here alive."

My former Master let out a snarl that had rocks raining down in the tunnel and we both cringed, pushing up against the wall. A riotous painting of orange flames and blue ice crystals exploded. Eklos's flames burned white-hot, and the combination was like a bucket of paints being mixed and tossed over every inch of dirt surrounding them.

Z threw volleys of flames that were encased in ice toward Eklos, and I couldn't understand how the ice wasn't melting. Perhaps since they were both created by his magic, they fueled each other rather than destroying the other. I'd have to ask him later how he did it. If there was a later.

"T-Tarrin," I stuttered, searching the darkness for his unconscious body.

"He's safe," Alyaa said. "He and the Queen are heading for the safe house. We'll meet them there."

"But what about Z—"

"Kaida!" she snapped, cutting off my words. "We don't have time. Z will be fine."

Without another word, she pushed me forward, helping me hobble my way back into the darkness.

Eklos's roar of fury echoed behind us.

☙

We burst through the other end of the tunnel, the bright winter sun blinding me.

"Where are we?" I gasped, trying to catch my breath. The icy wind hammered against my scales, and Alyaa tugged me into the trees across from the tunnel.

"On the far western edge of the village."

I looked back, wondering if Z would make it out alive. "Z needs—" I started, turning around just as dozens of explosions erupted over Vernista. Enormous pillars of flame and smoke shot skyward, spreading out until the sky was consumed.

I looked at Alyaa in alarm and found a smirk on her snout.

"That was Z's idea," she said, nodding toward the destruction.

"W-what are you talking about?"

"Did you really think Z would risk going into Eklos's dungeons, facing that beast, without a plan to escape? He contacted us days ago and we've been waiting, preparing."

"What?"

"Come on, let's get to safety," she replied. "Then we'll talk." Alyaa headed deeper into the woods.

"What about Lita and Tarrin?"

"I imagine they've already arrived at the safe house."

Instead of elaborating, Alyaa picked up the pace and I struggled to keep up with her. Even though she had somehow stopped my injuries from killing me, I was weak from blood loss and trying to fend off Eklos. When she finally came to a stop, I was gasping for breath, and she bent down by the bottom of a tree, opening another secret door.

"More tunnels?" I asked, dread twisting my stomach. I had spent far too much of my life beneath the earth in the darkness. I didn't relish the thought of spending one more moment underground.

"No tunnels," Alyaa replied and gestured for me to head inside. "The Prince and the Queen should be inside. I've placed a few of our rebels in the woods to keep an eye on the house. You'll be safe here for now."

She eyed the patches still holding my stomach and arm together. "Have Lita tend to those. Once I leave, the magic will disappear."

"How?" I asked, unable to form more words.

"I'm a Mender," she explained with a shrug, as if I should already know what that meant. "I'm going to go check on Z. Get some rest." With a flap of her wings, she leaped above the trees and flew toward the columns of smoke in the distance.

"Kaida?" Lita's voice echoed through the hole in the tree.

I stumbled forward, trying to summon enough magic to shift back into human form. It took an enormous amount of focus, but my scales finally dissolved into skin and I all but fell through the hole into the safe house. Lita's arms came around me, saving me from crashing to the floor.

"You're hurt," she said, surprised.

My eyelids grew heavy, and I fought the urge to succumb to unconsciousness.

"What is this place?" The room was large, in the shape of a circle. A small kitchen area was off to the right, two doorways sat on the wall across from me, and a seating area was gathered on the left. Directly in front of me was a huge wooden table.

"One of Z's safe houses." She glanced at the door. "It was his idea to plant the explosives all over Vernista. We spent the morning directing his rebels where to plant them."

My eyebrows climbed my forehead. Was that why he hadn't returned when he found The Den destroyed? "Why would he do that?"

Lita walked to the kitchen area and washed her hands in the basin. "I believe his words were 'It's time for Eklos to experience having something important taken away from him.'"

Yes, that sounded like something Z would say. "But what about his fight with Eklos?"

Lita looked unconcerned. "That was part of the plan, too. We knew that Eklos would intercept us in the tunnels. I would have been surprised had he not. Once you shifted into dragon form, the countdown began on the fuses all over Vernista."

My eyes narrowed. "But how do we know he made it out?"

Lita stopped moving to stare at me, her hands on her hips. "Z is old, Kaida, even older than Eklos. I have full confidence that he somehow used the distraction of the explosions to escape Eklos's wrath."

I scowled at her scolding tone but decided to drop it. Tarrin was sprawled across the couch where Lita laid him down. His clothes were tattered and full of holes, and the stench wafting off him was almost unbearable. My legs wobbled as I walked over to him, pressing a hand against my stomach. The bleeding had slowed, thanks to whatever magic Alyaa had used, but it needed stitching. I kneeled next to his head, gently brushing the matted hair off his face.

The cut on his forehead was closed now, likely due to his magic returning after being freed from the iron shackles, but it would leave a nasty scar. Dirt was smeared all over his face, and dried blood was crusted in little drops under his nose. I let out a shuddering breath as I placed a hand over his heart and felt the solid beating under my palm. Tarrin was alive. After two months, I got him back. I kissed his cheek, wishing he would wake up so that I could hear his voice again.

Lita came over with a basin of water and some gauze. She cleaned, stitched, and wrapped my wounds before she began wiping the dirt and blood covering Tarrin's skin. I winced when she was forced to rebreak his fingers in order for them to heal correctly and I was thankful that for the moment he was unconscious. He had lived through enough pain.

As I watched her work and waited for my betrothed to wake, I made a silent promise to Tarrin. I would never let anyone take him away from me ever again. Through fire, storm, snow, or beast, nothing would ever touch him.

And for as long as I lived, and for as long as it took, I would make Eklos know the pain that he had forced me to endure the last two months; the pain he put me through for seven years in Belharnt.

Before this was all over, Eklos would feel the sting of such agony.

And then I was going to kill him.

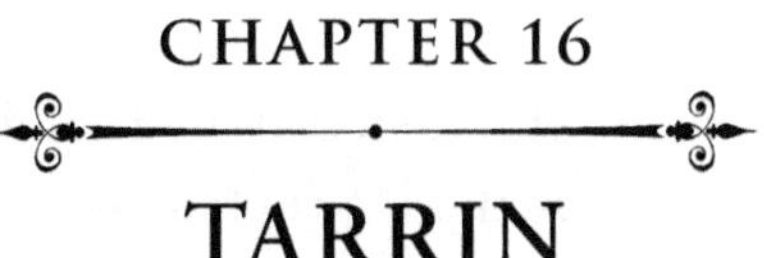

TARRIN

MY DREAMS WERE full of fire and ice as I fought against them, trying to pull myself out. I could hear Kaida's voice in the back of my mind, but I was unable to move. I couldn't make the dreams stop; couldn't get to her.

Eklos's voice swirled in and out along with other voices that I recognized but couldn't place. Fever plagued my body, even in unconsciousness, and I alternated between sweating and shaking. Why couldn't I wake from this dream?

I drifted in and out of consciousness, sometimes aware that there were things happening around me and to me, and other times I just drifted into the black of my mind. I didn't know how much time passed in this state, but the dark finally began to seep out like puss from an infected wound.

"He should be waking up soon," a garbled voice said in the distance.

The pain from my broken fingers and fractured ribs suddenly seared through the fog, sending sharp knife-like stabs through my body. It was enough to make my eyes pop open. After so long living in the dark of the dungeon, the single torch in the room felt like needles stabbing my eyes. I slammed them shut and they filled with tears against my will.

"Tarrin," Kaida said in alarm. "Oh, thank the scales. Tarrin." She cupped my face in her hands, her fingers ice cold against my skin.

"Kaida?" I croaked, my voice hoarse from the endless screams in the dark.

A sob ripped from her throat, and she carefully lifted my head and cradled it against her chest. I couldn't help but wince. Every part of me hurt. Missing nothing, Kaida lowered my head back into her lap, tears spilling onto her cheeks.

"Kaida?" I breathed, hardly able to accept that I was truly staring at her face-to-face and not in a dream. Her lips were like a flame touching my skin as she pressed them to my forehead. "What happened?"

A crease formed between her eyebrows. "You don't remember Rythos taking you?"

I tried to laugh but it turned into a choked cough. "N-no," I sputtered. "I remember that..." I don't think I'd ever forget the terror that flooded me the moment the dragon had grabbed my arm and Kaida disappeared in a swirl of darkness before I opened my eyes to see a smiling Eklos standing in front of me.

I shuddered, shoving the memory into a deep, dark place I could no longer reach. "I mean how am I here?"

Kaida's face relaxed, relief flooding her eyes. "We've been traveling for weeks trying to find you. We hadn't heard even a whisper as to where you might be." She glanced over in the corner. "Your mother found me in Vernista, and led Z and me—"

"Z?"

She arched an eyebrow. "Yes, he's been traveling with me, helping me track you down."

Jealousy flared inside me, scorching and bright like the sun. I knew I should be thankful that the dragon had accompanied her, kept her safe, risking his own life. But the thought of them alone together all this time… The state of mind I was in was not enabling me to think straight.

I swallowed hard, trying to tamp down the rising emotion in my throat, and focused on the other thing she had said. I cleared my throat. "Did you say my mother?"

On cue, my mother's face appeared behind Kaida.

"How are you feeling?" she asked.

"Confused."

Both her and Kaida gave a small chuckle.

"Lita led us through the tunnels to find you." Kaida glanced at my mother before she nodded. "She was the person bringing you food and water in the dungeon."

My gaze snapped her. "You?" I tried to sit up, but my head spun at the attempt, and I laid back down. "Why not just help me escape?"

Her eyes softened. "I wanted to more than anything, Tarrin. But I knew Kaida was on her way and I couldn't risk trying to get you out alone. I did what I could by bringing you water to keep you alive until she arrived."

Her words made sense, but I couldn't help the rising anger churning in my gut. I would have rather attempted to escape, and perhaps failed, then to be brought tiny morsels of food that ended up causing Eklos to beat me.

"Why didn't you tell me?" I asked, biting back the burning in my eyes.

"I didn't want to give you false hope. I knew that if I told you who I was, you'd expect me to get you out." She blew out a breath. "Tarrin, if there was any way I could've rescued you myself, I would have. Leaving you there was one of the hardest things I've ever done. Seeing you in that cell like that, knowing what Eklos was doing to you… There was no way I could rescue you by myself. I needed help."

"Hardest thing *you've* ever done?" I said, disbelief coating my voice. "Last I checked, it wasn't *you* who was held captive in Eklos's dungeons being tortured and growing closer toward death each day."

"Tarrin—"

"Hey," Kaida interrupted, putting a hand on my chest. "Enough, both of you. Regardless of the decisions that were made, all that matters now is that you are here, and you are safe."

Her words settled into me like a warm drink on a cold day, sinking into my muscles and forcing them to relax. I let out a shaky breath.

"How long…" I began but couldn't finish.

"Two months," Kaida answered, likely feeling the direction of my thoughts.

Though the shifter bond between us had returned, it still felt thin and stretched as if it might break at any moment. I wondered if my time in the dungeon had done irreparable damage to it.

"We're in the throes of winter now," another voice said before Z's snout came into view.

I couldn't keep the scowl from twisting my mouth.

Z huffed a quiet laugh. "Nice to see you too, little prince."

"Z?" Kaida breathed, before throwing herself across the room, hugging the dragon around the stomach. "Don't you ever do something like that again, do you hear me?"

Surprise lit Z's face and he glanced at me. I didn't even try to hide the anger on my face, or the jealousy flickering in my eyes. After months in the dark, I didn't have the strength to pretend her sign of affection toward another dragon didn't feel like a stab wound in my gut.

He gently wrapped his claws around her shoulders and pushed her back, and she returned to my side.

"How did you escape?" Kaida asked at the same time I said, "Why are you here?" I couldn't keep the irritation from my voice.

His eyes narrowed at me. "I've been keeping your betrothed safe. You can thank me anytime."

Kaida let out an exasperated breath. "Be quiet, Z. You two can antagonize each other once he's healed. I'm happy to see that Eklos didn't kill you but go clean your scales or something."

My heart swelled despite my rising anger from having Z in the room. With a *hmph,* Z stalked out of the room, through another doorway, and disappeared.

"Where are we?" I asked once he was gone.

"We're in one of Z's safe houses. His rebels are guarding the woods surrounding us," Lita said, handing me a mug of water.

"You're sure we can trust him?"

"Tarrin, I trust him with my life," Kaida said. "He's kept me safe and away from the Remnant while we searched for you. He's put his life at risk to help me find you. He took on Eklos so that we could escape the dungeon. Z has trained me and crossed Elysia to track you down. He isn't a threat, he's our friend."

I heard the passion for the dragon in her voice and I fought against the monster rearing its head inside me. A gross, bitter feeling leaked through my blood, and I struggled to keep it from filtering down the bond. The softening in her eyes told me I was failing miserably at it.

"Tarrin…" she whispered. "You have nothing to worry about." Her fingers brushed the hair off my forehead. I could hear the truth in her voice and feel it down the bond, but my mind spun in dizzying circles no matter what she said.

"Can you sit up?" Lita's voice interrupted my thoughts. She was standing next to me, a mug in her hand. "This should help with the pain."

I nodded and held my breath as I tried to sit up, Kaida holding me beneath my arms, lending me her strength. I bit back a groan as the ache in my ribs ripped through my abdomen. When I was upright and settled, sweat coated my forehead, and I exhaled a shuddering breath, trying to calm the pain that had flared from the movement. My fingers throbbed as I took the mug from my mother, and the hot tea scalded my tongue.

When I had taken a few sips, I cleared my throat. "How did we get out?"

My mother sat in the chair across from us. "Z planted explosives all over Vernista before we went into the tunnels."

My brows crawled up my forehead.

"Of course, as expected, Eklos was waiting for us when we arrived at your cell. Kaida held him off while I got you away from the dungeon, and then Z stepped in, allowing her to escape as well."

I eyed the doorway Z had disappeared through, before looking at Kaida. She had reddened bandages around her stomach and arm. "What happened?

Kaida looked down at herself, fidgeting with her fingers. "I picked a fight with Eklos and almost lost," she replied honestly. "If Z hadn't distracted him, I'd be dead. Alyaa, that lavender dragon in his group of rebels, helped me escape the tunnels."

My heart gave an agonizing lurch at the thought. "How did *he* survive a battle with Eklos?"

As if my words were a summons, Z walked back into the room. "It wasn't really a battle. I only had to keep his attention on me until my rebels saw all of you exit the tunnels. It was a simple game of which of us could dodge the other's magic until they set off the chain of explosives. I made sure to leave enough tunnels intact so that I could escape, and I barely managed to jump into a safer passage before the tunnel collapsed on top of Eklos."

Kaida's face twisted. "But Eklos survived?"

Z scoffed. "Of course, he did. It's Eklos. The only way to truly fell that beast is with a blade through his cold, blackened heart."

I snorted. "That's one thing we can agree on."

"Did he reveal any of his plans to you?" Z asked me.

"Z!" Kaida scolded. "He only just escaped. Now is not the time for those type of questions."

Z turned his haughty gaze on her. "On the contrary, little shifter. My rebels are out there risking their lives to keep you all safe. Eklos's army could be marching to our doorstep as we speak. I need to know that they're not risking themselves needlessly."

Kaida scowled. "Surely it can at least wait a few hours, Z."

"No, it can't."

"Enough," I said, rubbing at the headache pounding in my temple, biting my lip to hold in a cry of pain. My fingertips were still raw from when he peeled off the nails, the bones aching. Someone must have rebroken them, so they'd heal correctly. "Eklos told me nothing outside of his plan to trap you when you came to rescue me. I was simply bait in a long, drawn-out scheme."

"He expected you to die," my mother chimed in. "Based on what I had witnessed, he was confident that you would not leave that cell alive. I would have expected him to confide his plans to you knowing that you'd never be able to tell a soul."

I was shaking my head before she even finished speaking. "At first, I tried to pry information out of him. He never budged. As time passed and he withheld food and water, I grew weaker and the only thought I had was wondering if I would wake up the next time I fell asleep." I heard Kaida's intake of breath before she put her hand over mine.

I shook my head, trying to shove all the anger and terror back down in its place deep inside me where it couldn't reach the surface. "I learned nothing that would be helpful in defeating him," I said after a moment. I looked each of them in the eye, ending with Z. "Only that Eklos is the cruelest, most foul creature in all of Elysia, and if Kaida doesn't kill him, I will."

CHAPTER 17

EKLOS

I WATCHED FROM THE stairs to the palace as the dragons burned alive.

Six of them to be exact.

They had each been stationed throughout the tunnels as both spies and guards, meant to either stop that infernal girl from getting through or to at least warn me with enough time to properly prepare.

But they didn't.

They claimed dragons appeared from the shadows like demons, incapacitating them before they could alert me, but it was no excuse, and their inability to follow my orders had consequences.

They would die for failing me.

Why did everyone continue to fail me? Was it so much to ask for competency?

The dragons' roars as they burned was music to my ears.

Months of torturing the Prince, of planning and waiting in the dark for the girl and my cousin to show up so that I could finally rid this world of all three shifters... All of it was for nothing.

How did they best me?

And why was *he* there?

I hadn't seen him since... I shook my head, unable to recall.

He was supposed to be dead. If I had to factor him into their retaliation, into the war… It changed everything.

Anger had my magic flaring in my core, sending flames into my mouth and I bared my teeth.

If it weren't for him, the girl would be rotting on the dungeon floor by now.

How had I not sensed his group of so-called rebels lurking around Vernista?

"Rythos!" I snarled through the open doors of the palace, my voice echoing in the courtyard.

Only a heartbeat passed before his large light-gray figure appeared in the doorway. His eyes roved over the burning carcasses, but he said nothing.

"You called?"

I let out a low growl, baring my teeth. "Did you know the girl was so close to Vernista? Did you know those rebels had planned to destroy my village?" Whatever devices they had planted around the village, they had planned it well. Everything went up in flames, save for the few sections of slave homes.

Though Rythos had only arrived back from the army camp a short time ago, I had to ask—had to know if he was involved.

"How would I have known?" he replied, his tone bordering on disrespect. "I've been wrangling your army and watching that scales-forsaken mountain, remember?"

My tongue clicked in my mouth, and I waved a hand, dismissing his words. After everything, Rythos of all dragons wouldn't betray me. Not when he so desperately wanted my cousin dead as well. Not when I had twisted his memories of Eldrin so thoroughly.

After Eldrin had manifested his shifter abilities centuries ago, he was immediately taken to Shegora, a loathsome shape-shifter village in the north. I saw how broken and hurt Rythos had been in the wake of his absence. It had simply been too easy when Rythos joined the Remnant years later to twist his memories; to make him think Eldrin left on purpose—that he abandoned him because he thought he was superior to Rythos.

And Rythos had accepted it all as fact.

I smothered my internal glee at the thought.

Speaking of Eldrin…

I had been so focused on brutalizing that infernal Prince that my rage and need to kill my cousin had momentarily dimmed. Why hadn't he been with the girl?

"I want you to find where they're hiding. Leave no tree, rock, or speck of dirt unsearched," I ordered, returning my gaze to the burning dragons. They had all collapsed to the ground, utterly silent, but still the flames blazed on. The scent of burning scales, somehow so much worse than burning skin, filled the air, suffocating me.

"As you wish, Master." He turned and disappeared back into the palace.

I followed him inside, needing to escape the stench.

"Rythos," I called just as he disappeared around a shadowed corner.

He peeked his snout around the wall. "Yes?"

"Do you have anything to report from the mountain?"

A smirk twisted his snout. "I always have something to report, Master Eklos."

I rolled my eyes. I didn't have time for mind games today. I had played enough of them already.

"Get on with it," I snapped.

Rythos's eyes narrowed, his sharp teeth glinting as he bared them. "Just thought you'd like to know I captured Eldrin."

"Where?" I snarled, flames spitting from between my teeth.

His smile grew bigger.

"He awaits you at the army camp."

CHAPTER 18

KAIDA

IT WAS A long night.

Eventually, I had to force Z and Lita to quit questioning Tarrin so that he could rest. Sleep was the best thing to help his injured body heal, though, if I were honest, I was much more worried about the damage Eklos had done to his mind. His enhanced dragon healing would allow his wounds to heal quickly, but I feared it would do nothing against the nightmares.

A haunted look sat stubbornly on Tarrin's face every time I glanced his way. He hadn't yet divulged everything that Eklos had done to him, but I could see every vile, terrible thing that Tarrin endured just by looking in his eyes. My throat felt tight, thick with every sob I choked down, fighting the urge to wrap my arms around him and never let go. I knew firsthand the memories that haunted each waking moment that came after Eklos's torture; the draining fear that sucked every speck of life out of you.

It was a different kind of pain than broken bones or hunger. It felt much like I imagined burning alive would have felt. It blazed, scorching and endless, oblivious to your screams until you were nothing but an empty corpse. Though I had been free from my seven years in Belharnt for a year now, I still experienced the ghosts that plagued me in that dungeon. But I had grown up in slavery, and experiencing such heinous things was a normal part of a human's life.

Tarrin had grown up much differently. Though I didn't fault him for it, he had never truly faced hardships, and certainly not abuse like the humans did. I feared that this had irreparably broken his spirit.

He slept fitfully on the couch, and I had to wake him up countless times when he began screaming from nightmares. I slept on the floor in front of him, not wanting to leave his side.

Thankfully though, the tea that Lita had made for the pain seemed to be working well. His breathing was less labored, and he moved about a little less gingerly than before. Through the darkness of the room, broken up by the dying light of the fire in the hearth, I studied Tarrin's face. Even in sleep, his forehead was creased, his body curled in as tight a ball as his wounds would allow. It ripped my heart into ribbons. More than anything, I wished I could reach into his mind and take away the memories of the last two months. I didn't know if the Tarrin I had grown to love and admire would ever reach the surface again, or if I was destined to see the shell of a person Eklos had forced him to become.

"You can stop staring at me like I'm going to break into pieces," Tarrin's whisper cut through my thoughts, and my gaze snapped to his. "I'm all right."

"Are you?" I whispered back, unsure if I could believe him.

He hesitated for a moment before his head bobbed against the pillow and he dropped his hand over the edge of the couch. "I will be."

I ran my thumb over the back of his palm, not wanting to bump his healing fingers. "I missed you." Hot tears filled my eyes. "I was afraid I'd never see you again."

"I know," he croaked, as if the same fear had tormented him.

Tears spilled onto my cheeks, and I rose to my knees, pressing my lips against his, savoring the feeling that I never thought I'd experience again. His other hand cupped my cheek, his thumb sweetly wiping away the wetness left behind from my tears. He rested his forehead against mine. The crackling embers in the hearth filled the room with a relaxing melody.

"You should go back to sleep," I said at last, wishing that I could stay in his arms instead.

Tarrin simply nodded and laid his head back on the pillow, and I settled back down on my pile of blankets on the floor. I couldn't hold his hand without hurting him, so instead, I latched my fingers onto his wrist. After two months of living with the reality that there was a chance that my beloved no longer lived in the same world as me, I was unwilling to release my hold on him.

I was never letting him go again.

❧

Morning came far too quickly.

There was no sunlight inside the house, thanks to it being underground, but somehow I woke with the dawn, nevertheless. The fire had gone cold in the hours since Tarrin and I last spoke, and I sat up as silently as I could. Tarrin's chest heaved deeply, and for the first time all night, his face was smooth and at peace rather than creased with fear.

Withholding a groan as the stitches pulled on my own wounds, I pushed to my feet and carefully laid my blanket on top of him to make sure he stayed warm. He shifted slightly but didn't wake. I crossed to the hearth and carefully placed a couple of logs onto it and stoked it until a nice fire was blazing again. As blessed heat curled through the room, chasing away the cold of winter, I went to the kitchen area and filled a kettle full of water then hung it over the fire to boil.

There was no sign of Lita or Z and I hoped they were still sleeping as well. After the last few months, we all deserved a good night's rest. I placed a spoonful of lemon-mint tea leaves into a cup and managed to grab the kettle just before it began whistling. Pouring the water over the leaves, I let it steep for several minutes as I watched the flames flicker in the dark.

"Did you sleep?" Z's voice rumbled quietly, and I nearly dropped the cup in my hands.

I put a hand to my chest to calm my heart. "You startled me."

He continued to stare at me, expecting an answer to his question. Z knew that over the past couple of months sleep had become an elusive creature that I could never quite catch. He often had to wake me up from my own nightmares.

"A little," I admitted, fixing my eyes on the golden liquid in the cup.

Z nodded as if that's what he expected. "You should go back to bed. Rest as long as you can."

I shook my head, eyeing Tarrin's still figure on the couch. "I can't sleep."

His eyes narrowed. "Perhaps you should have Lita make you a sleeping tea."

I shrugged. "I'll be fine."

Z let out a sigh but didn't argue further. He knew it was a futile effort. "How is he?" he asked instead.

I sipped at the warm liquid as I struggled to find the right response. "I fear the Tarrin I love is no longer in him."

Z narrowed his eyes, his gaze moving between me and the sleeping male on the couch. "Why would you say that?"

"Eklos has a way of… breaking a person. I fear that the Tarrin I fell in love with is irreparably broken and has become someone I don't recognize."

"Has he given you a reason to believe so?"

I shook my head. "Not yet."

"Then put it out of your mind, little shifter. Even if your Tarrin has retreated into the safest parts of his mind, I am sure if anyone can get him to surface again, it's you."

Z's words brought fresh tears to my eyes, and I glanced at Tarrin's sleeping form. "I hope you're right."

"Of course, I am," he sassed. "I'm always right."

The sound that came out of my throat was somewhere between a laugh and a sob, and I put a hand over my mouth to hold it in.

"Do not be ashamed of your fear, Kaida. Though it often halts many, with you I've seen it push you to keep going. Accepting your fear but not bending to it or cowering before it is your strength. Don't forget that love is what makes that fear wilt and die. Love makes the fear we experience worth it."

I gaped at Z, unable to understand how such an ill-humored dragon had said something so profound and wise.

"What?" he said. "I'm capable of being deep."

A true laugh bubbled out of me this time. "You are many things, Z, but deep is usually not one of them."

He shrugged, though amusement flickered in his eyes. "Give him time, Kaida. I know your Tarrin is still in there."

I sipped at my tea, trying to cover the emotion bubbling up in my throat. "Thank you, Z."

"For what?" The scales on his forehead rose.

"Everything." I gestured to the room around me. "Training me, traveling with me, helping me, rescuing Tarrin, this place. All of it."

An emotion I couldn't quite place flickered in his eyes, and it was a moment before he spoke. "Little shifter, you will always have my help should you need it. I will be with you until my last breath."

CHAPTER 19

TARRIN

THOUGH I HAD a long way to go until I was fully healed, for the first time in two months I woke up with very little pain. My fingers still ached but it had been reduced to a dull throb, and the sharp pain that had plagued my ribs no longer hurt at all. Whatever was in the tea my mother had given me was helping.

I took a deep breath as my eyes flickered open to the dark room in Z's safe house. There was a fire crackling away in the hearth which illuminated all but the shadowed corners of the room. A light whispering noise was coming from the kitchen area, but my human eyes wouldn't adjust to find the source of it. I glanced to the floor, finding Kaida gone, her pile of blankets that she had slept on now covering me. My heart swelled for a moment before fear started to trickle in that she wasn't there.

"Kaida?" I croaked, my voice hoarse.

The whispering ceased.

"Tarrin?" She appeared behind the couch, her forehead creased in concern. She rushed around to sit next to me. "How are you feeling?"

How was I feeling? Like my mind was swimming in an abyss of black, the fear that Eklos was behind me, ready to torture me again like an incurable plague in my body. I wanted to say all of that, but instead I settled for, "Better." At least it was a partial truth.

I nodded to the corner where Z's figure loomed in the shadows. "What were you guys talking about?"

Kaida glanced back at Z and then met my gaze. "We're just trying to figure out what to do next. Elysia is crawling with Remnant mercenaries and there aren't many places left for us to go."

"Don't you think I should be involved in these discussions?" I snapped, unable to hold back the anger rising like a wave inside me. I knew I was being unreasonable, but my mind swam in darkness and I couldn't think clearly.

Her eyes softened. "Tarrin, you needed rest. Of course, we want you to be a part of whatever decision is made, but your healing is more important right now. I wasn't about to wake you when you were finally sleeping peacefully."

Though I knew she was right and was only protecting me, I couldn't bear the thought of them having secret conversations. I didn't like the way Z looked at her, or their new friendship that had cropped up in my absence.

"Next time, wake me," I bit out, and immediately regretted it when hurt flickered across her eyes. She pursed her lips before she nodded.

"She was only looking out for you," Z said in her defense as he stepped out of the shadows.

My restraint broke. "I didn't ask for your opinion, Z. When I want it, I'll ask. Otherwise, keep your snout shut and away from me."

"Tarrin!" Kaida breathed, her mouth gaping.

"It's fine," Z responded to Kaida, his voice neutral and void of emotion. "He's been through a lot. I'll go see if the rebels have anything to report."

Z left before either of us could respond.

Kaida's brows lowered as she turned to face me. "Tarrin, what was that?" she asked when the door snicked shut.

I ran a hand through my tangled hair, internally wincing at how dirty it was. "Nothing."

"That was certainly not nothing. Z has done nothing but put himself at risk to save *you*—"

"I don't like the way he looks at you," I interrupted. If I had been in dragon form, smoke would have been leaking in heavy streams from my nostrils.

She shook her head, her twisted face telling me I was being absurd. Perhaps I was.

My mind swam in an ocean of jealousy, and it clawed and reached for me, breaching over my head, trying to drag me down into its depths.

"I don't care how he looks at me—"

"He looks at you like he's in love with you!" I shouted before clamping a hand over my mouth.

Her eyes widened. "What?" Kaida put her hands on my shoulders and pushed. "I think you need more rest. You're clearly delusional." She felt my forehead, checking for fever.

"Kaida, no—"

"Look, Tarrin," she said, rubbing at her temple. "I know how terrible these months have been for you. No one understands more than me." She jabbed a finger into her chest. "But you're going to have to work through these emotions. I can feel you drowning in them through the bond. I know the fear that haunts you, I know the tricks and games your mind is playing on you." She huffed out a breath. "Tarrin, I love *you*. I don't care what your fear-addled brain thinks it sees between Z and me because there is nothing. He helped me rescue you, putting not only his life, but his rebels' lives at risk as well. He is our *friend*." She emphasized the word, driving the point into my brain like a hammer to a nail.

I knew she was right; knew it before I even snapped at her. Eklos had warped my mind and I was struggling to figure out what was reality and what was all in my head. Kaida rested her forehead against mine and for a moment we simply breathed each other in. It settled my mind and the swirling emotions that were trying to lash out.

"It's so dark in here," I whispered, and I knew she understood that I didn't mean the room. "How do I get out?"

Kaida planted a kiss on my lips before pulling back to stare in my eyes. "You fight it, Tarrin. With everything you have, you fight. You do not quit. You do not give up. Never yield to the fear. When it's dark, you find the light."

Her words felt impossible. "But I'm so tired."

She cupped my cheek with her palm. "I know, but you're not alone. The fight is difficult, but you never have to face it by yourself. Let us be your strength until you can bear it."

A tear burned its way down my cheek.

"The dark is only evident by the lack of light. Find the light and the darkness must flee."

"But what if there is no light to be found?"

Her grip tightened on my shoulder. "Then you make your own."

Kaida's words were a gift; a source of hope in the hell my mind had been living in. I took her face in my hands and pressed my lips to hers. She returned the kiss, leaning into me, her hands sliding around my neck. The kiss was fierce, full of all the love and fear we both had dealt with over the past two months. With every clash of our lips, we pushed back the darkness.

I was free, and we were together. That was all that mattered. I pulled her into my lap just as someone cleared their throat behind us. Kaida and I broke apart, glancing toward the source of the noise. My mother stood in the doorway.

"I've drawn a bath for you. I figured you might like to get cleaned up before we leave."

I nodded in thanks.

"Do you need help?" Kaida asked me, eyeing me as I struggled to stand from the couch. It took a minute; not being able to walk for so long had taken its toll on my muscles. Once I was firmly planted on my feet, I felt stronger than I had in months. Likely a combination of food and quality rest, along with the rapid dragon healing.

"No, I think I can manage."

Her hand hovered above my arm as I limped my way into the room that Lita indicated. When she was certain I wasn't about to collapse, she pulled back and let me continue on my own. Though I knew that I would need Kaida in the days ahead to help pull me out of this place my mind had retreated to, I appreciated the fact that she intuitively knew that walking into the bathing room and seeing to my basic needs by myself was what I needed in that moment.

I needed to know that I could do it.

I breathed out a shuddering breath, ignoring the pain that was slowly making its way to the surface as the tea began to wear off. As I undressed and settled myself into the copper tub full of steaming water, I forced my mind to focus.

Kaida was right.

I would not let the darkness win the fight for my mind.

I was Prince Tarrin of Elysia.

I would bow to nothing and no one. Not even the fear in my own mind.

CHAPTER 20

KAIDA

"WHAT DO YOU mean the Remnant has us surrounded?" I asked, my voice rising in pitch with each word.

Z's face was solemn. "Those who survived the fires in Vernista have been combing the countryside, searching for you. While they're not quite at our doorstep, my rebels say that they encircle us a few miles out."

I put my face in my hands. We hadn't even been in the safe house for a full day yet. We needed more time, both to figure out our next steps, and to let Tarrin's body heal before we were forced to travel.

"I don't think they know exactly where we are. We could risk staying and waiting it out," Z said after a moment.

I shook my head. "I won't put anyone else at risk if there isn't a need for it."

Tarrin sat next to me, his damp hair slicked back, his beard freshly shaved off. The black tunic and pants that Lita had found for him made his starved body look extra gaunt.

"Where are my father and Eldrin? Can we not go where they are?" Tarrin asked.

"We left them back in Shegora," Z explained.

Tarrin shivered. "I don't think I ever want to go back there."

"With any luck you won't have to."

"What do you mean?"

Z blew out a breath that smelled like ashes. "One of my rebels informed me that Eldrin and the King have moved back to Metta. Gendon has offered the town as a battleground should Eklos's army come calling again."

"Why would Gendon do that?" I asked. "Metta has stayed off Elysia's maps for centuries. They've built the only peaceful place in this world. Why would he give that up and risk having it destroyed?"

Z shrugged. "I only know what my rebels say. I suppose you'll have to ask him yourself when we travel north."

"How many more safe houses are there?" I asked. "And are they on the way to Metta? Or will we be sleeping in the elements once again?"

Z studied me, then Tarrin before he spoke. "I have two more places of refuge between here and the village in the north. I don't know if Eklos has learned of them yet, but they are worth a try."

"Well, then let's—"

Z's eyes widened a split second before the wood door to the entrance shattered into pieces and exploded through the room. I dove for Tarrin, taking us both to the ground. The clashing sounds of fighting and dragons roaring rippled in from outside. Smoke poured through the opening, filling the air with the scent of carrion.

My lungs protested the sudden lack of oxygen, forcing me to cough as I tried to pull Tarrin into another room. Where could we go?

"Is there another way out?" Tarrin shouted between hacking coughs.

Z's green eyes appeared through the smoke, putting his claws on each of our shoulders. "This way."

Smoke seeped into my lungs, and black swirling darkness smothered my eyes, forcing me to trust in Z's guidance as he led us through the doorway into the bathing room. The smoke was less dense there, so I was able to see him as he walked to the corner and pulled off the metal grate that was attached to the wall behind the tub.

"Hurry. This will lead you into the woods east of the Ilgathor Mountains."

"What about you?" I asked, eyeing the small opening in the wall, knowing it would not fit a dragon.

Z's eyes softened. "I will buy you time."

"Z, no—"

"Go. I'll be right behind you."

Taking a step forward, I grabbed his arm. "We can find another way."

"Quit arguing and get in that hole," he snapped, pushing me toward it.

Lita had already gone ahead. Tarrin was crouched in front of it, watching us through narrowed eyes.

Z let out a low growl, repeating, "Kaida, go."

The use of my name caught me off guard. He so seldom used it, opting for the nickname "little shifter" instead.

"Z—"

"Go!" he roared, before turning his back on me and running back through the door to face the onslaught of the Remnant streaming in through the door.

☙

Dirt crawled under my fingernails like little squirming bugs as we inched our way through the passage. It wasn't quite big enough to stand upright, forcing us to work our way through on hands and knees. It had only been half an hour or so, but my knees were already aching and bruised. Thanks to my quickened dragon healing, the wounds in my stomach and arm were much less painful, allowing me to move faster than I should have been able. Lita was a good distance down the tunnel, barely visible through the dark. I worried for Tarrin, hearing his occasional gasps and quiet curses as the pain in his body flared, knowing that it was difficult for him to be in the dark after months of blackness as his only company.

His labored breathing echoed off the dirt walls.

"Are you okay?" I dared to ask.

A grunt was his only answer.

"Do you think—"

"Z will be fine," he said, anticipating my thoughts. I forgot what it was like having someone know the swirls of thought and feeling constantly running through me. He knew me better than anyone. "If he made it out of the dungeon in Vernista after causing the earth to collapse, surely he will make it out of the safe house in one piece."

I cringed as the mental image of Z broken into pieces and left for the crows flashed through my mind.

"I'm sure he'll be right behind us."

"But we don't even know where his safe houses are. How are we supposed to find them without him?"

"We already discussed various hiding places last night while you were sleeping," Lita answered, suddenly right in front of us. She moved like a wraith, silent and unseen.

I studied her. "You seem to know a lot of Z's hiding spots."

"He made sure we were well equipped to travel on and stay safe, should anything happen to him."

What did she mean, exactly? Had Z known that we would be attacked?

My thoughts spun in circles as I tried to fit mismatching puzzle pieces together in my mind. By the time we saw a faint light at the end of the passage, I wasn't sure how much time had passed.

Only that my knees hurt something fierce, and Tarrin's breathing was raspy and labored.

"Almost there," I panted. Sweat painted his forehead and he nodded.

The light grew brighter as we reached the end, setting my eyes to watering. Lita stuck out a hand and motioned for us to wait inside the tunnel until she checked things out. I didn't particularly like the idea of her going out there alone, but my body ached so badly that I couldn't find it in me to argue.

A moment later, her face appeared at the entrance. "Come on, the safe house is close."

I helped Tarrin to his feet and put his arm around my shoulder for support. I wasn't sure how much his wounds were bothering him, but I was going to offer as much help as I could.

The last leg of the tunnel was uphill, and all three of us were breathless by the time we reached the exit. I squinted against the harsh sunlight, illuminating the landscape around us. Trees were sparse around the tunnel, but they thickened mere feet away, their branches crisscrossing through the air. The snow was thick and powdery, covering the ground like a fluffy blanket, and wisps of my breath seeped into the cold air.

Though I always dreaded when winter came as a child, I somehow found the scent of pine and ice coating the air to be a comforting smell. Perhaps because it wasn't the smell of smoke and ash that constantly accompanied Vernista.

Lita led the way farther into the woods. Tarrin's face was quite pale causing concern to sink deep into my stomach.

"What do you need?" I asked him, unsure of how to help him.

He ran a hand over the sheen of sweat on his forehead. "Need… safe house." Tarrin was still panting and gasping for air. Without another thought, I shifted into dragon form and wrapped my claws gently behind his back and under his legs and lifted him to my chest.

Though he was exhausted, a scowl crossed his face.

"I will never live this down if Z sees you carrying me."

I smirked. "It's a good thing he's not here then, isn't it?" I tried to swallow the sinking feeling as the words passed my lips.

Tarrin chuckled before resting his head against my scaled chest. "I never thought I'd see you again. The moment Rythos's claws wrapped around me, I thought for sure…"

"Hey," I said, keeping my voice soft. "I know." I pressed my eyes closed for a moment. I knew that feeling all too well. When that slave had stolen me away from the Royal Palace all those months ago and brought me back to Belharnt… When I had awoken to find myself chained in that room again…

My mind went to a lot of dark places then, ones that I didn't wish to drag from the depths I had buried them in.

He could lay all his thoughts bare for me if he wished, I would listen until I went deaf, but it did neither of us any good to dwell on those fears. We were free, together, and on our way back to our family. Tarrin nodded, hearing my unvoiced words through our bond. When I had first removed his shackles, the bond snapped back into place between us, though it still felt distant, difficult to hear him. But now, the more time that passed, it seemed to grow stronger, less stretched. As Tarrin healed and strengthened, so did the shifter bond.

We entered the thicker trees, and I immediately second-guessed my decision to shift into dragon form. The trunks grew close together, making it difficult to navigate my large body through them without banging my limbs into branches and trunks. The sun shifted overhead, casting the woods in long shadows as time passed, my legs wobbly from walking so long.

Lita slowed to let us catch up to her. "It's not far now. We'll be there soon."

Only minutes after she spoke the words, she came to a stop and pointed. We were facing a cluster of large boulder-like cliffs, numerous others scattered around the area. The one she indicated was hidden behind snow-covered ivy.

"I see nothing," I deadpanned, the words slipping through my lips before I could stop them. Lita scowled and I saw Tarrin bite his lip out of the corner of my eye, holding back a laugh.

"That's because it's *hidden,*" Lita sassed in return. "Wouldn't be much of a hiding place if it were clearly visible."

I wanted to sass back at her, but the fact that a spark of the old Lita, the Queen of Elysia, had surfaced for a moment had me keeping my sarcasm to myself. I didn't want her to retreat back inside the hard shell of anger and bitterness she had donned after her dragon side was killed.

Lita walked up to the ivy and began yanking on it, pulling it off to the side. When she was finished, I expected to find a hidden door, but it looked like a normal rock.

"I still see nothing." I set Tarrin on his feet, waiting until he was steady before I let go of him and shifted back into human form. The frigid cold bit through my layers, cutting through my skin.

Lita scowled at me before she pointed to a thin crack in the rock, hardly visible to my human eyes. Grabbing a tiny dagger from a sheath beneath her shirt, she slid it into the crack and dragged it up and down. Her mouth twisted to the side as she concentrated. It wasn't until I heard a distinct click that I realized she was picking a lock.

"How did you know to do that?" I asked.

She shrugged before slipping her fingers in the slit and pulling the rock door open. "Z told me."

I arched a brow. "Z sure told you a lot."

"He can be very helpful," she replied, adding, "When he wants to be," under her breath.

Stale air rushed out of the safe house, though it was blessedly warm. Wanting to get out of the cold, I grabbed Tarrin's hand

and pulled him inside. Lita closed the door behind us with a dull *thunk*. There was a rustling sound, followed by a muttered curse as she ran into furniture searching for a torch to light.

"Perhaps we should have left the door open until we found a torch," Tarrin suggested, and it was my turn to bite my cheek to hold in a laugh. A moment later fire flared in the hearth, illuminating Lita's scowling face.

Giant pieces of white cloth covered every chair, couch, and table in the room. Dust sat in a thick layer on the floor, the shape of our feet leaving imprints as we poked around the room. Tarrin ripped a cloth off the largest piece of furniture, uncovering a chartreuse green couch.

I couldn't suppress my snort. "Z sure has an interesting sense of decor." I pulled off the cloth on another piece and found a chair wrapped in a bright pink, fuzzy fabric. A laugh burst out of me.

Tarrin's eyes were wide, though the corners of his mouth twitched. "He may be good at many things, but decor is not one of them." A chuckle slipped through his lips.

"Feel better?"

He winked. "Infinitely."

With a roll of my eyes, I turned and began pulling the cloths from the rest of the furniture. They were all hideous, though they were in good shape. I plopped down onto the ugly green couch, pulling Tarrin with me, while Lita rummaged through the cabinets in the kitchen area.

"What are you looking for?" Tarrin asked her as he pulled me into his side, but I didn't miss his wince as my shoulder brushed his ribs.

"Z said there was food, but I have yet to find any." The doors banged as she shut each cabinet, her movements growing more frantic.

Tarrin studied her through narrowed eyes. "Is there a cellar?"

Lita's movements halted, her back heaving for a moment

before she stiffened, then headed through an archway into another room.

She's acting strange. The sound of hinges squealing before the bang of a door thudding met my ears.

Tarrin's brow furrowed. *Something must be bothering her.*

I answered Tarrin through our shifter bond. *She didn't even think to look in the cellar until you said something. That's unlike her.*

He nodded, his eyes still fixed on the archway.

A moment later Lita returned, carrying a sack of potatoes in one hand, and a basket of dried meats and vegetables in the other.

I opened my mouth, intending to offer my help, though my cooking skills were subpar, but she spoke before I could make a sound.

"Might as well rest up. We'll be here a while."

CHAPTER 21

ELDRIN

A DARK LAUGH RIPPED through my dreams, startling me awake.

I opened my eyes to the shadows of night, arms shackled in iron and connected to a wooden post. I was still in dragon form, but the ice in the winter winds whipped against me, buffeting my scales. They had taken the tent away, wanting me to suffer in the elements. A deep shiver ran through my body. I looked around, wondering if the laugh had only been in my dream.

Enormous tents as far as the eye could see circled around me, dragons moving amongst them despite the hour. There would be no escaping, even if I could somehow break my bonds.

The laugh echoed again from behind and I closed my eyes against the sinking feeling in my stomach. I knew that laugh. I'd know it anywhere.

"Well, well. What a pleasant surprise. Returning to my army and finding my *cousin* at the center of it." Eklos spat the word, steaming saliva landing on the ground next to me.

With a deep breath, I turned as best I could with the shackles and faced him, keeping my lips firmly shut. I would say nothing—give him no reason to harm me. If I was going to escape, I needed to remain unharmed, as much as it pained me to stay silent at his taunts.

"What? No slimy retort? No groveling for me to let you go?" His red eyes burned as they pierced my own.

I said nothing, though I refused to look away.

Eklos tutted. "That's too bad, Cousin. I do love our war of words."

His footsteps were slow as he circled me, like a predator sizing up its wounded prey.

"No matter," Eklos tsked. "I have a surprise for you. And I'm sure it will get that tongue moving." The grin that split his snout revealed a mouth full of daggers.

Eklos turned sideways, snapping his claws together before there was movement in the army followed by the sound of scraping footsteps. One of the dragons moved toward us, leading someone behind him. My heart jumped into my throat when I saw who it was, thick shackles made of rope around all four of his limbs.

It was Z.

His eyes met mine for a brief second, and my face began to twist in recognition, but at the slightest shake of his head, I smoothed it back into a neutral expression. Was I supposed to pretend I didn't know him?

"Not only are you pathetic dragons a nuisance," Eklos crooned at Z, "but now you're just becoming sloppy. It was child's play to track down the house that your so-called rebels were hiding in."

What had happened? How did Z of all dragons get captured?

He was supposedly the best of the rebels.

I tried to meet his eyes again, but he kept them firmly planted on the ground.

"Not a talkative bunch tonight, are we?" Eklos took a step closer to Z. "No matter. Words aren't the only way to get a point across."

Before I could register the threat, my cousin stepped forward, slamming his claws into the side of Z's face, knocking him sideways. He staggered, losing his balance, before falling onto his knees. Blood dripped between Z's teeth as he bared them at Eklos. Still, he said nothing.

Eklos kicked at his stomach twice more before Z fully collapsed onto the snow. His breath rattled in his chest; claws clenched into fists.

"Do you know who this beast is?" Eklos asked me. "Did you know this dragon used to work for me?" His eyes narrowed, watching my reaction closely.

It was an effort to keep the surprise off my face and keep my eyes from widening, or from glancing at Z's bleeding form on the ground.

"He used to be one of my prized mercenaries—the best in the Remnant. That is until he… *died.*" Eklos fixed Z with a glare.

At this, I couldn't keep a neutral expression.

"You work for the Remnant?" I growled, smoke leaking from my nostrils.

Suddenly, it all made sense. That's how he had helped Kaida and Tarrin evade Eklos's dragons when they traveled to Shegora. That's how he was able to defeat those mercenaries—how he knew how to fight and train my daughter and the Prince.

Had he been luring them toward Eklos this whole time?

Eklos tutted again, pleased that he had finally cracked through the tough armor I had tried to hide behind.

"He *did*, but alas, no longer. He was… how did you say it?" Eklos looked at Z, a sneer on his snout. "You were tired of all the killing? You grew too weak to stomach it any longer? Was that it, *Zaroch*?" He spit the name as though he couldn't bear to even utter the sound.

Zaroch? As in the infamous mercenary, Zaroch, who was known for his ruthlessness and bloodlust? I was a youngling the last time I had heard that name. How could he still be alive after all these years?

"You were slaughtering innocents," Z snapped, finally breaking his silence.

"You were ridding Elysia of the *humans*. They were not innocent. There is honor in following the orders you were given."

Z's scales lowered over his eyes. "There is no honor in murder."

At those words, Eklos slammed his claws into Z's face once more before leashing his throat in a collar of smoke. He pulled him close to his snout and Z's face contorted in a grimace.

"I should gut you right here." Flames seeped out from between Eklos's teeth. "Deserting the Remnant is punishable by death. And you've been deserting for a long time, Zaroch."

One moment, the frigid wind was blowing through the camp as Eklos held Z in his grip, and in the span of a blink, Z smashed his head into Eklos's before he swung his tail into him, knocking him onto his side. Eklos's control of the smoke wavered, and Z took advantage, creating a long, wicked dagger of ice, cutting the ropes around his wrists, and lunged for Eklos.

Why had the dragons only bound him in rope? Why would they not bind him with iron to suppress his magic? It didn't make sense. Unless… Did Eklos want this to happen?

Heart thrashing in my chest, I watched as he attacked my cousin. Was this it? Was this the moment that Eklos would finally breathe his last breath? Had someone finally bested him?

There was no hesitation, no mercy in Z's eyes as he plunged it into Eklos's scales, aiming for his heart.

Just as the ice slipped beneath his scales, Rythos slipped through the shadows and slammed the pommel of a sword into Z's temple. He instantly collapsed to the snow, unconscious.

My breath shuddered out of me, pooling in the cold air, and I couldn't hold in the curse that slipped through my lips. My stomach clenched as nausea spun within it. So close… Z had been so close to ending this war before it had truly started.

But once again, Eklos had won. I ran my claws over my face as my cousin spat on Z's unconscious body.

"Let that be a lesson to you, Eldrin. No matter what magic you have, what attack you try, I cannot be defeated," Eklos snarled, then pointed at the dark-blue dragon on the ground. "Chain him!"

Rythos and one of the other army dragons dragged Z a few feet away and shackled him, with iron this time, to another post.

Then, Eklos turned his burning gaze on me. "I tire of these games, Eldrin. My patience grows thinner by the day. Tell me where to find the girl and the Prince."

Find the Prince?

Despite the predicament I was in, elation swept over me as I realized Kaida must have succeeded. She had freed Tarrin… and Eklos had no idea where they were.

My muscles tightened against the threat, preparing for an attack as I spit, "Even if I knew where they were, I would never tell you."

Eklos narrowed his eyes as smoke began seeping from his nostrils. The ground trembled as he took a step closer. "I strongly suggest you reconsider your answer."

Heat flooded through my body, and my limbs shook at the menace in his voice, but I didn't back down.

"I would gladly give my life if it meant protecting my daughter and her betrothed."

"How noble," he mocked. "Too bad you didn't feel the same when I killed, oh, what was her name? Ae-la?" He drew out the syllables.

The blood drained from my face.

"If only you hadn't been a coward and left her maybe you would've been there the day I cleansed this world of her soul." A dagger-toothed smile spread on his snout and something inside me severed, that primal need to protect her, even though she was already dead, awakening.

I lunged for Eklos, entirely forgetting that I was in shackles, snapping my teeth at his throat before the iron bit into my wrists and yanked me backward. Eklos barked out a laugh that had the fire inside me flaring, though I couldn't access any magic.

"I'm impressed, Eldrin. I didn't think you had any more bite in you. Too many years of cowering and hiding." He bent down so his snout was level to where I was sprawled on the cold ground.

"But no, I won't kill you just yet. I won't reunite you with that pathetic slave. You don't deserve that. You see, first, I will capture your daughter and that infernal Prince, and then I will make her watch every single second as I torture you. As I kill you. Your death is coming but not yet."

My stomach swirled and fire rose in my throat though it was halted by the iron shackles. I forced myself to swallow, to shove down the fury at the thought of Eklos laying a claw on Aela, my *cor unum*. He goaded me and I took the bait. My breath shook as I exhaled. If I had any hope of escaping this camp, I needed to calm down.

I met his red gaze, unable to stop myself from saying, "You realize you could be done with these theatrics and end it all now."

Eklos's snout split into a smile so terrifying I swear my heart stopped beating before doubling in tempo. "But this is… so much more fun."

He gestured at Rythos behind me, and I saw the flash of metal out of the corner of my eye before something smashed into my head, and I fell into the dark.

⚃

A piece of icy rock hit my forehead and my eyes popped open.

Z was chained several feet from me, lying in a heap in the

snow, though his eyes were open, watching me. Blood coated the scales over his temple.

"Welcome back," he said.

My only reply was a grunt. The chains clinked as I lifted a hand to my head, rubbing at the spot Rythos had hit.

"What happened?"

A smirk twisted his lips, though there was nothing funny about our situation. "We picked a fight with Eklos and lost."

I snorted, sparks flying from my nostrils as I closed my eyes again. "Sounds about right." I pushed myself into a seated position, maneuvering my tail out of my way. "How long was I asleep?"

"Two days."

I rubbed at my aching skull. "You all right?"

"Never better," he retorted, pushing off the snow and leaning against the wooden post.

"What were you thinking?" I asked. Though I appreciated the nerve he had to try to stab my cousin, I had experienced firsthand that such efforts were usually futile.

"I saw an opening. I took it," Z said with a shrug.

"And look where it got you." Scorn coated my words, but I couldn't help it. Though Z had done nothing but help us and protect Kaida, it didn't sit right with me that he used to be a part of the Remnant. What if he never truly left? Was all this an elaborate ruse?

What if he had been working for Eklos this whole time, feeding him information?

"Stop it," Z snapped, his eyes narrowing as he studied me. "Stop that train of thought right now."

I squinted against the snow pelleting my face. "What are you talking about?"

He shook his head. "You're letting Eklos get inside your head." Fidgeting with the shackles on his arms, Z avoided my gaze. "He was telling the truth, but only partly."

I held my tongue and waited for him to continue, knowing I'd likely regret whatever words were ready to come out of my mouth.

"I worked for the Remnant… a very long time ago. I remember the days after Xalerion's death. The days of chaos and confusion when Eklos came to power and created the Remnant to carry on in his father's stead. I was one of his favorites." Z blew out a breath, rubbing at the side of his snout.

"I did his bidding for decades—centuries. I killed who he wanted me to kill; tortured who he wanted tortured. I never blinked twice at his orders—never questioned him either. At least… until I met her."

I blinked. "Her?"

Z gave a slow nod. "Cassa." He closed his eyes as he said her name.

"She was a shape-shifter," he explained. "I met her in the woods outside of Metta—though at the time, Metta didn't exist yet. I had been scouting the area, helping to plan the attack to destroy Shegora." He winced. "That was all the Remnant could talk about, destroying the shape-shifter village. I was supposed to scout the area, find a way up the mountain, and report back." Z blew out a shuddering breath. "I hadn't planned to meet her. She actually caught me, threatened to kill me." His snout spread in a wistful smile. "I think that's when I fell for her."

Z's eyes glistened, getting a faraway look in them as he recalled the memories.

"Cassa was… something else." He huffed out a laugh. "I knew the moment I met her that I couldn't go through with it—killing her or attacking Shegora. She was such a light in a dark period of my life. So, I left the Remnant behind."

Z pushed himself to his feet, dusting the snow aside. I stood too, wincing against the snow blowing into my face. The temperature had plummeted in the hours since Eklos had left, the wind buffeting us, throwing pellets of ice at every inch of me. I was immensely thankful for my scales, and even more grateful that I wasn't in my human form when Rythos captured me. If I wore skin instead of scales in this cold… I hated to imagine what state I'd be in.

"Cassa asked me to stay in the village with her, and I didn't even hesitate. I tried to warn her of the Remnant's plans to attack Shegora, but she either didn't believe me or wouldn't listen. Probably a bit of both. But months passed, no dragons arrived, and no one came to burn down the village.

"Something wasn't right, though. It was unlike Eklos to let such an opportunity go. I knew he was likely reeling from the loss of one of his greatest commanders, and the fact that I deserted wouldn't go unpunished. Wariness grew in the back of my mind like a monster until I could no longer control it. I begged Cassa to go with me, to leave Shegora behind and start a new life somewhere else. I didn't want Eklos getting anywhere near her."

I had never seen Z show such emotion, so my eyes widened when I saw the tears pooling in his own.

"We argued. I tried to sway her, to make her understand, but she wouldn't leave. Cassa said if there was truly an attack coming that she would stay and fight. She wouldn't abandon her kin."

Z's breath shook as he exhaled. "And then, she said the words that she knew I wouldn't be able to refute. Cassa said she didn't love me… could *never* love me."

He swallowed hard before he clenched his claws into fists and choked back down the emotion, stuffing it deep wherever he had kept it hidden all these years.

Z cleared his throat, his voice dropping low. "So, I left Cassa in Shegora—flew south until my wings could no longer carry me." He swiveled his eyes to mine, his gaze unrelenting. "And the Remnant destroyed the village, killing everyone I left behind."

A pit opened in my stomach, and I closed my eyes against the memories fighting to the front of my mind. I, too, had abandoned

Shegora. Though I had left with Lita and Martik long before we ever knew there was a threat, I still couldn't help but wonder what would have happened if we had stayed. Would we have been able to stop them? Or would we have perished along with all the other shifters?

"I'm sorry, Z." It was all I could say, all I could offer.

He sniffed. "The dead are dead, and nothing can change that. Does no good to dwell on it."

I studied him for a moment, taking in his hunched back and the claws he still held in tight fists.

"And yet, it still affects you."

"Our past creates us. Every breath we breathe, step we take, and decision we make all determines who we become. I would not be the dragon I am without my time in the Remnant, my relationship with Cassa, or even helping Kaida and the Prince."

"You don't regret being part of the Remnant?" I couldn't help but ask. It was unfathomable to me that a dragon who had been a part of such a terrible group of dragons could both leave it behind because he felt their actions were wrong but also not regret his time with them.

Z shook his head. "My only regret is taking the lives of innocent people who could not defend themselves. But even so, I wouldn't be who I am, with the knowledge and abilities I have now if it weren't for my years with them."

"If you were such an asset to Eklos all those years ago, how have you gone undetected for centuries? Why was there not more of a hunt for you?" I knew from experience that Eklos would have been desperate to either have his commander back or punish him for leaving in the first place.

For a brief second, Z's face twisted in an odd way, and he looked almost… sheepish. I had never seen such an expression on his face before.

He cleared his throat. "I faked my death and went into hiding."

He smirked at me. "The benefits of being well over a thousand years old—you learn how to hide well."

A laugh bubbled out of me. Wasn't that exactly what I had been doing all this time? Hiding from Eklos—refusing to fight?

A heavy sigh pooled in the cold air in front of me. "What do we do now?"

"We escape, of course."

I blinked. "Oh, yes. I'm sorry. Let me just crack open these iron chains and we can make a run for it." Rolling my eyes, I leaned my weight against the wooden post and crossed my arms. The human gesture felt awkward in dragon form.

"Another benefit to being old, Eldrin. You learn the depths of your magic, the depths of what you'll do to survive, and you get good at escaping places you shouldn't be."

With a wink, his hand flattened on the snow, drawing the ice from within it into a thin needle of ice.

My mouth dropped open. He had iron shackles. How was he able to use his magic when his ability should have been suppressed?

Z chuckled a humorless laugh. "Iron acts like a lock to our magic, shutting it down so we are unable to access it. But like any lock, it can be picked." A sly gleam entered his eyes. "This isn't the first time I've been chained in iron. I found the key to still using magic despite it long ago." He worked the ice needle inside the shackles.

"How?"

"Might I suggest, Eldrin, that we pause on the explanations until we're away from Eklos's camp and somewhere relatively safe?"

I scowled. I supposed he had a point.

"Fine. How do I break these?"

With a *click* and a *clunk,* Z's chains fell to the ground. The snow muffled the impact, but both of us still glanced around to make sure the dragons stayed in their tents surrounding us.

When no one came to investigate the noise, Z appeared in

front of me, fitting the ice needle into my own shackles. "It would take too much time to teach you." He glanced over his shoulder. "Time we currently don't have."

Within the span of three more breaths, my chains fell away and I rubbed at my arms.

"What now?" I whispered.

It was strange. Normally I was the one coming up with the plans, or doing the rescuing, but if it weren't for Z, I would have had no idea how to escape from my chains let alone the army camp.

If I were being honest, without Z I probably would have died here in Eklos's camp.

Z looked up at the sky. It was still a few hours until dawn, the moon bright overhead. Stars stretched across the sky like a giant sparkling spiderweb. For a moment, despite the urgency to escape, I couldn't help but admire the beauty in the night sky. How could there still be so much beauty in a world full of so much hurt?

"They have scouts in the air above the camp at all hours. We can't simply fly out of the center. We'll have to make it to those woods." He pointed to the trees a few miles away.

I eyed the distance from where we stood to the tree line. We wouldn't be able to make it there without one of the dragons spotting us. And even though Z and I could hold our own, it would hardly be a fight between us and an army of ruthless dragons.

"You ready?" Z whispered, his muscles visibly tightening, preparing to run.

It was then my magic flared to a blazing fire in my stomach. For the first time in weeks, a smile spread across my snout.

"I have a better idea."

Though my magic wouldn't be able to carry the both of us back to Metta, it would be able to get us outside of Eklos's camp.

With a smile still on my face, I gripped Z's arm and wrapped us in shadow.

KAIDA

IT HAD BEEN two days since the Remnant attacked the safe house, and every day that passed without knowing what had become of Z ate away at my nerves, causing a constant ache in my stomach that grew worse with every sunset that he didn't return. Lita didn't seem worried, and Tarrin was secretly glad he hadn't returned, though he'd never say those words out loud.

We didn't dare leave the safe house, not even to hunt for fresh food. While there had been a stock of dried meats and some vegetables in the cellar, it had been a very long time since any of us had eaten freshly cooked meat. My mouth salivated at the thought of venison or even a roasted squirrel.

You're not helping, Tarrin's voice drifted down our bond. I could feel his amusement and I glanced over my shoulder to find him smirking at me. He sat at the table, a piece of wood in one hand and a small dagger in the other. His fingers had healed, though I still caught him wincing at his ribs when he moved certain ways. I arched a brow in question.

What? I'm bored.

I couldn't suppress a snort. *We're running for our lives with an entire army searching for us and you're bored?*

Tarrin shrugged his shoulders, setting his focus back on the wood in his hand. *They haven't found us yet, which means they haven't figured out where we are. It's dreadfully dull when no one is chasing us.*

A giggle bubbled out of me, and a victorious grin spread across his face. It was a wonder Tarrin could even make jokes after what Eklos put him through, after all the dark thoughts I felt seeping through the bond. I expected to rescue a shell of the person I had come to love, and though he was much quieter than usual, he still seemed like the stubborn prince that he had always been.

Lita eyed us from her perch next to the hearth, though she remained silent. She had slipped into "motherly" duties very quickly, making sure we ate, bathed, slept, and cared for our remaining wounds.

It reminded me of the days of being around the Queen at the Royal Palace. Losing her dragon form had changed her, but this glimpse into the old version of her lifted my spirits. Based on the way Tarrin kept studying her, I think it was affecting him too.

Though the stubborn mother and son refused to talk about it.

I sighed, rubbing at my eye. Tarrin's nightmares ever since we rescued him were like a plague—relentless, unending, with no cure in sight. It made it all the worse that not only did he wake me by screaming each night, but I also had to live through the dreams haunting him through our bond.

Needless to say, neither of us had gotten much sleep since we escaped the dungeon, though thankfully, even with our meager food supplies, his cheeks were beginning to look a little less gaunt.

"You should rest," I mumbled through a yawn.

"You're one to talk, sleepyhead."

"You *both* should rest," Lita said, not taking her eyes off the fire. "We may need to leave at a moment's notice, and you need to be ready."

I squinted at her, but Tarrin spoke first.

"Do you know something we don't?"

Lita gave a shake of her head. "Just being cautious."

He studied her but didn't push it. His brows lowered as he continued to carve the wood in his hand, pulling his lower lip between his teeth. The movement made my core tighten, and memories of his lips on mine crashed through my head.

Tarrin's gaze snapped to mine as he felt the direction of my thoughts shift. The reflection of the fire flickered in his eyes, giving a realistic look to the heat now burning through me.

I swallowed hard. I was about to suggest that we risk going outside, to go for a walk or something so we could finally get the alone time we haven't been able to have since we rescued him, when Lita abruptly stood.

"I'm going to go scout around us—see if there's any sign of pursuers."

Tarrin gave her a funny look. "I thought you said we were supposed to stay inside."

She scoffed. "*You* need to stay inside. I said nothing about myself."

I opened my mouth to speak but she continued.

"I am the only one of us that is expendable, the only one who we can risk going out there to find out if we have enemies around us."

Lita slung a black cloak around her shoulders and pulled on a pair of fleece-lined boots.

"I'll be back soon." She glanced over her shoulder. "And if I'm not, then I suggest you run."

With that ominous warning, she climbed out the door, and disappeared into the dim light of the woods.

"That was… strange," I muttered.

Tarrin nodded. "Everything about her has been strange lately."

"Well, since she's gone, we could take advantage of being alone and—"

"Practice your magic," he interrupted, avoiding my eyes.

I fought to keep my expression from betraying the sudden spike of pain shooting through my stomach that had nothing to do with the stab wound that had all but healed. Because of our bond, I knew he understood the direction of my thoughts, but he purposely changed the subject and suggested we do something else.

Did he... not want me in that way anymore? Had Eklos broken that piece of him?

He cleared his throat. "I mean, now is as good a time as any, right? No one is around to get hurt if you lose control, and you need to practice that fancy magic of yours." Tarrin smirked but it didn't quite reach his eyes.

It was my turn to clear my throat, swallowing the lump that had lodged in it. "Yes. Sure."

I didn't bother to correct him or tell him that I had spent the last two months training with Z and Eldrin, strengthening my magic and learning to wield it. Or that, in his absence, my inner beast had been fighting against me, making it even more of a challenge to control it.

Tarrin's eyes softened, likely feeling my hurt despite the walls I tried to raise to keep it within myself. Before he could say anything, I pushed to my feet and kicked the small coffee table out of my way.

"What are we working on today?" I asked, trying, and failing, to keep my voice light.

Tarrin missed nothing. "Kaida—"

I turned my back to him, pretending to stoke the fire in the hearth as rejection reared its ugly head in me.

"I think we should practice more with water. I've been lucky so far, but—"

Warm hands slipped over my shoulders, turning me to face him, before holding my arms in a gentle squeeze. Tarrin's eyes moved as he studied me.

"What is it?"

I shook my head, forcing a fake smile onto my face, and tried to turn away. His fingers squeezed tighter, not letting me move.

"Kaida?"

"Nothing, Tarrin. Let's—"

And then his lips crashed into mine.

His arms wound around my waist, pulling me tight against him, his hands like little flames skimming up my back. Instead of it being painful, it set every inch of my skin aflame and had me gasping for air as our lips collided. My arms wound around his neck, pulling him closer—*needing* him closer.

His hand moved to cradle my cheek, deepening the kiss, catching my lower lip between his teeth. My hands tangled in his hair as his fingers skimmed the skin at the bottom of my shirt.

Tarrin pulled back slightly, his lips still brushing mine as he spoke. "Please, don't hide from me."

I shook my head, my cheeks growing warm in a way that had nothing to do with how he had made my skin feel feverish.

"Tell me."

"I just thought…"

Tarrin's thumbs stroked across my cheeks before tucking my hair behind my ears. He pecked a kiss against my lips.

I sighed. "I just thought that we could… W-we haven't had any alone time…" I stuttered out, my cheeks on fire. "But if you don't want to, that's—"

Tarrin pressed a finger against my lips before tipping my chin up so he could look in my eyes.

"Never think for a moment that I don't want you. Some days I want you so badly that I can't concentrate on anything else. Food tastes like dirt; sleep is only welcome if you're within my dreams. My fingers ache to touch you, my body begs for even a sliver of contact."

Tarrin pulled me closer, our chests touching, his fingers intertwining in my hair.

"You are my *cor unum*—my one heart. I always want you."

A hesitant smile stretched across my face, Tarrin's eyes glowing with a love I had never imagined before. It felt like the sun was revealing itself inside me after months of being under dark clouds and storms.

And knowing Tarrin, I knew he was trying to be practical—to make sure I was ready when the time came to face Eklos came. It was part of who he was—making sure I was prepared and protected.

But in this moment, I didn't want anything but him. I could face as many tomorrows as I needed to, slay all the giants in my path, and fight a dragon who wanted to kill me as long as I had these moments with him.

Moments that reminded us that we weren't alone—that we would face the future together, hand in hand. Moments that held all the beauty and wonder that this world had to offer. Moments where fear was pushed into a distant corner, and we could just be us—Kaida and Tarrin. Two sides of one heart.

My *cor unum*.

With a tug, I pulled Tarrin closer and let our lips talk in ways that words never could.

CHAPTER 23

ELDRIN

THE FOREST WAS so dark I could hardly tell the difference between it and the shadows that had brought us here. Z stood next to me and shivered as I let go of his arm.

"Let's not do that again," he whispered.

A chuckle escaped me before the reality of the situation hit me. We did it—we got away from Eklos's camp. I imagined we only had minutes before someone noticed our absence which meant we needed to move. Now.

"Sorry, Z. If you want to get far away from here, we'll have to do it again." I tried to peer through the trees, but the night was still too thick. "Let's start moving while my magic refills. I know I don't need to tell you to—"

"Be quiet," Z mimicked as I said the words.

With a roll of my eyes, we pushed through the trees, trying in vain to keep our large bodies quiet.

"How long until they notice—"

The sound of a horn in the distance silenced his words.

Z gave a tired sigh. "Well, I guess that answers that."

At an unspoken agreement, we took off running through the trees, our wings held in tight to our backs. It was nearly impossible to wedge our bodies stealthily through the fat tree trunks, and my body would be sore later from how many times I'd banged my limbs into them.

"Is it time for that shadow thing again?" Z panted, both curiosity and hesitation lacing his voice.

"The shadow thing?" I joked as we heard the first growls and shouts behind us.

He let out his own growl. "Yes, the shadow thing. The disappearing into a squeezing blackness that cuts off all your air before it kicks you in the lungs as the black recedes."

My eyes widened. "I can't say I've ever heard it described like that."

"Well, what do you call it then?" he said between gasping breaths, likely trying to distract us both from the sounds of pursuit behind us.

"I've never given it a name. It's always just been jumping from place to place."

Z's scowl flashed in the moonlight. "How unoriginal."

With a shrug, we dove deeper into the trees. With the physical exertion of running, my magic was refilling far too slow. I could jump, but we wouldn't make it very far.

"I'm still going to call it the shadow thing," Z muttered beneath his breath.

I huffed a laugh, the air clouding in front of my snout.

"Can we take to the air? It would certainly be faster than trying to maneuver our way through this forest."

Z glanced at the treetops, then behind us. While we couldn't yet see the dragons that were after us, we could certainly hear them.

"We'll be a much easier target in the sky. It's harder to fight in the air." Z narrowed his eyes at me.

"I have no doubt you can hold your own."

"Just because I can doesn't mean I want to."

"What part of this running for our lives do you think I want to continue with?" I couldn't keep the amusement out of my voice.

"Fair point."

We both glanced over our shoulders and in the distance through the trees we could see the first of the dragons' scales reflecting off the light of the moon.

"I think we've let them get close enough," I whispered. "Let's fly."

With a deep squat, I drew on all the power in my legs and thrust myself up through the treetops, flinging my wings wide to stay aloft before giving a mighty flap to get higher into the air. Z's movements were practiced, graceful, and he was flying on a steady stream of air before I had even cleared the trees.

"What took you so long?" Z yelled over the roar of the wind.

I rolled my eyes as he smirked and gestured for us to get higher. We barely made it a few feet when an arrow whizzed past my ear. I ducked just as another flew over my head.

The winter wind was like shards of ice jamming into my eyes as I turned to look behind me. What I saw chilled me to the bone.

It would have been one thing if the entire army were flying in the air after us, or even if Eklos himself was coming to exact his revenge.

But no.

Instead, my old friend Rythos soared through the air, gaining on us, fast. A group of five dragons remained behind him, their wings thudding as they kept themselves airborne. All of them held a crossbow, each aimed straight at Z and me.

"Faster!" I roared to Z, flapping my wings even harder to get away from the dragon. "Don't let him touch you!"

The memory of Rythos grabbing my arm as we descended from Shegora, trapping me as he brought me to Eklos's camp in an instant, flashed through my mind, panic flaring in my gut like an agitated beehive.

If he reached us, he'd either bring us back to our chains, or he'd take us directly to Eklos who'd waste no more time in slaughtering us.

Another arrow whizzed past my head.

"Look out!" Z's roar ripped through the air, and I barely managed to rotate, spinning to the left as Rythos reached for my arm.

"You're not where you should be," Rythos growled, reaching for me again.

I tucked in my wings, spinning once more to evade his reach. I knew we couldn't keep doing this. He was too fast, and my energy wouldn't last much longer if I had to evade him and stay in the sky. I couldn't fight him since any contact with him would send me right back to Eklos.

We had to jump. That was the only option—the only way Rythos couldn't follow. He wouldn't be able to find us, at least for a while.

My magic was our only chance to get away.

I reached deep inside, trying to see how much my magic had refilled.

I blew out a puff of hot air. Not enough. Nowhere near enough.

But it had to be—there was no other choice. Perhaps if I risked delving as deep as I could, tempting burn out, it would be enough.

Dodging Rythos's reach one more time, I banked, then flared my wings out as wide as they'd go and caught an updraft before flapping hard after Z.

"To me!" I shouted.

Z didn't hesitate even for a moment as he spun in the air and soared for me, even as Rythos closed the distance.

In the span of three breaths, Z's dark-blue body was at my side, and I grabbed onto his arm. I reached deep inside my pit of magic, deeper than I had ever pulled. It would take every last drop of magic to get us far enough away where Rythos couldn't follow.

Not for the first time, I envied his magic. While it was the same as mine, it didn't have the limitations that my own did.

Inhaling a deep breath, I drew my magic into every vein, until my blood burned like sparkling wine sliding down your throat. When I could no longer tell the difference between magic and blood, I yanked on it with a roar, wrapping it around Z and me. The shadows smothered us, and we were gone.

ơ3

I blinked against the sudden light of the moon.

Sand squished between my clawed toes, and it took me a moment longer to register the tiny granules that felt like cool velvet beneath my feet. The stars were bright overhead, not a cloud to cover their lights from flickering against our scales.

Z's snout swung every which way as he looked around, trying to pinpoint where I had brought us. The night air was cool, but not like the frigid winter air that dug its way under your scales, numbing your limbs. No, this was the one place in Elysia where winter couldn't touch. Whether it was through some sort of magic in the land or simply all the sand absorbing the heat from the sun that kept the air warmer, I wasn't sure.

But I knew that this was the one place Eklos would never dare to bring his army.

It was foolish for *us* to come here.

I heard Z mutter something unintelligible.

"What was that?"

Z swung to face me, his eyes narrowed. "Why would you bring us here? Are you trying to kill us?"

"Of course not," I snapped, crossing my dragon arms.

"This is the Zenduro Wastes! There's no water here—only heat, sand, and death."

I nodded, not denying his claim that this land was harsh and deadly. "And that's exactly why Eklos won't follow us here."

"You're a fool, Eldrin. Take us back to Metta."

I shook my head, tilting my snout to look at the night sky. I didn't even know how I managed such a distance. It was hundreds of miles, and I had never jumped so far, especially not while carrying another. My body was exhausted; even taking a deep breath was taxing.

"I can't do that, Z. My magic is used up. We'll have to stay here until it refills." Even as I said it, I felt the prickles beneath my skin telling me that I had used too much magic at once. I swayed on my feet.

His ocean-blue body, so close to the color of my own, kneeled and scooped a handful of sand into his palms. Z straightened and let the sand fall in a thin stream to the ground, the sound like hissing air, as he met my gaze.

"Stay where, exactly?" He flung the sand to his right and held his arms out at his sides. "In case you haven't noticed, Wastes indicates there's nothing here. Only desert. We have no shelter, no food or water, and as soon as the sun rises, we'll be baked alive. This is worse than winter."

While I could understand why he was upset, I had never seen Z lose his cool in such a way. He always had a plan for everything, always remained calm despite the chaos happening around him.

The whites of his eyes were wide, glowing in the light from the moon.

A stab of guilt pierced my stomach at his reaction, but there had been no other place to go. The Wastes were the one place that Eklos wouldn't be foolish enough to send Rythos or the army. It was too deadly to risk.

We needed to find shelter before the sun rose, rest until I replenished enough magic to jump back to Metta—or at least out of the desert.

Sand dunes loomed around us like tiny tan mountains; some small and some large enough to possibly provide some sort of shelter. I studied the biggest dune a short distance away… Yes, it might work.

"Come on, I've got an idea," I said to Z whose jaw snapped shut with an audible click.

I led us across the sand, our heavy bodies sinking deep as we trudged our way through. It was draining, having to fight against it, but I was immensely grateful that the sun wasn't in the sky, heating the sand to unbearable levels and burning through our scales.

"We can't just stumble through the Wastes, Eldrin."

"We're not."

Z scoffed but kept his mouth closed. When we arrived at the dune, which towered over us, I swung my tail at its base. The sensation was like hitting a wall of wood. I swiped again at the sand, forcing my tail between the granules until I could sweep it aside.

"What… are you doing?" Z drawled.

I snorted against the sand flying into my nostrils. "I'm finding us shelter."

I felt the heat of his stare burning into my back.

"You're what—digging a hole?"

I gave a curt nod, swinging my tail against the sand once more. "If we can dig it deep enough, we can rest out of the sun until dusk falls, then we can continue back toward Metta. Maybe by then my magic will have regenerated enough to get us out of the desert."

"And what exactly are we supposed to do about food? Water?"

I didn't have an answer for that, so I kept digging.

"This is madness," Z muttered before throwing his tail at the sand next to me.

If we could just carve out an area deep enough to block us from the worst of the sun's rays, then we could make it until night fell.

The first fingers of dawn stretched outward as the light from the stars began to wink out. By the time Z and I managed to dig a hole big enough for the two of us, the sun had peeked its head above the horizon, shades of red and purple swirling in the sky.

The only sound was our heavy breathing as we both collapsed into the hole that ended up being more of a sand cave. Even with our wings held in tight, we barely fit, forced to sit with our feet and shoulders touching. But at least we were out of the harsh sunlight that would have literally made our blood boil.

The Zenduro Wastes were utterly lethal. One did not survive here unless you outsmarted the sun.

Z blew out a breath as we settled in, rubbing at his temples with his claws. I dug my wings into the sand behind me, trying to give myself a little more room.

"Get some rest, Z. When the sun sets, we can start heading west."

He grumbled something unintelligible, snorting sparks from his nostrils, but I ignored him, shutting my eyes against the exhaustion settling through my body as the terror of escaping Rythos finally seeped from my limbs like air through a hole.

CHAPTER 24

EKLOS

MY CLAWS COLLIDED with Rythos's face, and he crashed into the snow.

The one dragon that hadn't failed me like all the others. The one dragon I thought I could count on to be just as ruthless and cunning as I was. I had spent years grooming him, using his hatred for Eldrin, deepening it, forcing it to fester like an untended wound. Rythos had shown such promise and skill.

And yet, just when he had my cousin within his grasp, at the very center of an entire army… Eldrin still managed to escape.

And now any sign of him was gone.

The thought sent a fresh wave of anger rolling through me and I slammed my claws into his face once more.

"S-stop," he stuttered, though the words were emotionless, not the pleading and begging I was used to from the other dragons.

"Stop? You want me to stop?" I growled, placing my claws around his throat, and squeezing. "You let them escape. You had one job to do—bring me Eldrin and keep him here—and yet you couldn't even accomplish that." I paused to blow noxious smoke into his face, taking pleasure when he coughed and gagged, unable to breathe. "I should kill you now."

Rythos gasped for air, and I considered following through for a moment before I loosened my hold, allowing him to spit out a wad of red saliva onto the ground.

"I didn't know about *him*," he wheezed. He was talking about Zaroch. "I didn't know he would be able to escape those chains. It shouldn't have been possible."

Fire filled my snout. "I have been hunting Eldrin for *centuries*. I've warned you before. He always manages to escape. Regardless of if Zaroch was there to help him or not, you should have stood guard over him. All night if you had to!" Rythos cringed away from the sparks falling off my tongue.

"Unless..." I drew the syllables out as I brought my snout close to his. "Unless you were working *with* Eldrin. Perhaps you conveniently left him alone so that he *could* escape." I tightened my hold on his neck once more. Rythos's eyes went wide.

"No," he coughed. "I want Eldrin dead just as much as you do. Why would I be working with him?"

In response, I put all my weight into squeezing his throat, his eyes bulging at the force of it. I should have killed Rythos centuries ago. But the temptation to use him as a weapon against my cousin was too strong. I still remembered when we were younglings, before Eldrin became an abomination, how he preferred Rythos's company to mine. I should have ended anyone who was once a friend of Eldrin's. But I didn't, and now I was paying for it. All those years twisting him into a beast that I could control was for naught.

I relished the feel of his throat being crushed beneath my claws, the way his scales bunched and overlapped as I tightened my grip. He was only moments from passing out.

I wanted to kill the dragon, but perhaps he could still prove useful. Even if he ended up betraying me and was lying about working with my cousin, at least I could count on nothing stopping him from finding Eldrin. Regardless of whose side he was truly on, he would lead me to him, perhaps even kill him for me, and then I'd be rid of them both.

Finally, I released him, and he crashed to the ground with a thud.

"And what are you going to do now, Rythos?" My voice was low, lethal.

It took several moments of coughing and gasping, the pitiful dragon trying to get enough oxygen into his lungs. My patience grew thin, and I turned to leave him bleeding in the snow.

"I'm going to find him," Rythos finally whispered, and I turned back to find his eyes on the ground, a fierce determination shining in them.

"What was that?"

"I'm going to find Eldrin," he snarled, releasing a plume of flame into the air.

I smiled, pointing at the sky.

"Then go."

CHAPTER 25

TARRIN

"HAPPY BIRTHDAY," I whispered, my lips skimming the shell of Kaida's ear as I brushed her hair behind it.

She was curled in a ball on the ugly green couch, buried beneath layers of blankets. I hated to wake her up, especially knowing how much my own nightmares had prevented her from sleep, but today was special.

Today, she turned eighteen.

After everything she had survived and lived through, today was a day to celebrate. There were countless times, before I even met her, that she could have died, and I never would have met my *cor unum*. Even now, with the Remnant searching for us, and an army on our tails, it was more important than ever to celebrate life—celebrate Kaida.

She brought sun to my life when there were only dark stormy clouds, laughter where anger had been, and compassion where a cold, calloused heart had once sat in my chest.

Elysia needed her… but I did too.

After months of torture with Eklos, being with her felt like I could finally breathe again. The darkness, the monster within me wasn't as strong or as violent.

Her arms stretched out from beneath the blanket, a small

smile twisting her lips as she rubbed at her eyes. "How'd you know it was my birthday?"

I smiled at the sound of her hoarse morning voice. "I have my ways."

Kaida tried to scowl but a yawn overtook it.

"Come on," I said, tugging the blankets off her. "I have a surprise for you."

Her body shivered as she tried to grasp hold of the blankets. "Let's pretend it's not my birthday and go back to sleep." She curled back into a ball, closing her eyes.

"You'd really take away my chance to surprise you on your birthday?" I teased, sticking my lower lip out in a pout.

Kaida peeked one eye open. "What surprise?"

"You'll just have to get up and see." I pulled away, giving her space to move.

With a groan and a scowl, she sat up on the couch, rubbing at her neck before she peeled herself off the cushions and staggered over to where I stood holding two cloaks.

Eyeing the fabric in my hands, she arched an eyebrow. "And what are we doing with those?"

"Going outside, of course," I replied, keeping my voice light as if it were the easiest answer in the world.

"Your mother hasn't returned. We don't know if it's safe."

"It's safe enough for this." I swung the cloak around her shoulders before donning mine, then grabbed her hand. "We won't be out there long." Popping the door open, I checked that the woods around us remained empty before I pulled her outside.

I led her up a narrow, rocky path that ended on top of the giant boulder that our safe house resided in. I had snuck out a few nights ago when sleep was elusive, and everyone else had been held in its depths. The boulder grew into a cliff that didn't really go anywhere, but simply overlooked the tops of the trees as far as the eye could see. You could faintly make out the mountains far in the distance, but there were no distinguishable landmarks to indicate where exactly in Elysia we were.

The midnight sky was lightening as dawn approached, sending spears of purple and orange into the blue expanse.

"Tarrin, what are we doing out here?" Kaida shivered against the frigid air, her breath pooling in front of her mouth.

"You'll see," I said, tugging her hand to hurry.

We stopped at the edge of the cliff just as the sun began to peek over the trees. Bright light burst forth, forcing us to squint against it. The land was bathed in golden light, driving the shadows of night away.

Though the winter sun was much weaker than it was during the summertime, I could still feel the strength it infused into my body as it hit my skin. Kaida let out a shaking breath, as if she, too, felt the relief flowing through her veins with the light.

I let go of her hand as she closed her eyes, letting her bask in the glory of the sun and moved behind her.

After a few moments, I said, "Kaida."

Her eyes were slow to open as she turned to face me.

I dropped to one knee, and she went preternaturally still.

"Kaida, my love," I began, unable to hold back my smile at her shocked expression. "There has been so much uncertainty swirling around us, but despite all of it, I have never been more certain of this: I love you, and I want to spend the remainder of my days, whether they be short or for eternity, with you."

Her eyes filled with tears as she covered her mouth.

I reached beneath my cloak, pulling out a crown made of branches, bright green leaves, and white snowflowers that I weaved together just for her. Dragons didn't have any symbol of marriage, and the humans never wore rings or bracelets or any indication of their marital status since they were always too poor to afford them. I knew she wouldn't expect a physical token of our love, but I had wanted to give her something, nevertheless.

I held it up in front of me. "Though our betrothal was arranged from the start, I want you to know that I choose this—choose you. Never doubt, Kaida, my feelings for you. You are my *cor unum*. My one heart. I don't ask this out of necessity or because it's a requirement, but simply because I love you."

I rose to my feet, settling the crown over her head. My throat grew tight at the sight of it—of her wearing a crown. My future Queen.

I swiped at her wet cheeks with my thumbs. "Kaida, my one heart… Will you marry me?"

Before a word left her mouth, she jumped into my arms and pressed her lips to mine. I chuckled against them.

"Is that a yes?" I murmured.

A laugh bubbled out of her, and I lowered her to her feet.

"I can think of no greater honor, Tarrin, than to be your wife."

My heart swelled in my chest. Despite it all—every heartbreak, every abuse, every danger lurking in the dark—it was all worth it. *She* was worth it.

I wrapped my arms around her waist, swinging her around. I wanted to scream from the treetops, yell to all of Elysia that she was mine, that I was going to marry her. But we still needed to be careful and cautious since we didn't know where the Remnant currently was. So, I kept my joy-filled shouts to myself, but held nothing back through the bond as I pressed a kiss to her lips.

We remained on the cliff enjoying the sun, and each other, and when enough time had passed to worry about being seen, I led her back down the path. She giggled as I held the door open for her and we disappeared back into the safe house.

ଔ

My mother returned an hour later, out of breath with a cut on the side of her forehead, steadily leaking blood.

"Mother?" I asked, shoving to my feet.

"Hurry," she breathed, all but running to the kitchen and shoving whatever food she could get her hands on into a sack. "They're coming. Hurry!"

"What's going on?" Kaida asked as I followed my mother's lead and began stuffing whatever we could carry into a second sack.

Her breaths were ragged, frantic as she kept moving throughout the safe house. "They must have picked up my trail in the woods."

"The Remnant? How many?" If there were only one or two dragons lurking out in the woods, perhaps we could still escape. But if it were more than that…

I squeezed my eyes shut, massaging my temple as I forced down my own panic, deep into the pit where my magic dwelled. That was the only place I'd allow it to live—in my core when it could fuel my magic instead of my mind where it would fog my decisions in fear.

Kaida grabbed our cloaks from a chair in the corner and brought one to me. "Where can we go?"

My mother shook her head, swinging her own cloak around her shoulders before heading for the door. "Z never gave specific directions for his last safe house. I have a general idea of where it is, but I'm not entirely sure of how to find it."

I felt a spike of Kaida's fear through our bond, ripping through me like an iron arrow through my wing. I internally cringed against the memory of those mercenaries attacking us so many months ago, before Z and his rebels saved us.

"So, we just keep running until we reach Metta?" Kaida asked, her voice trembling.

"We certainly can't stay here. The only option is to run. We'll find another place of shelter. The important thing now is getting out of here before those dragons try to burn us out." Mother extinguished the torch by the door and beckoned us to follow her outside.

I grabbed Kaida's clammy hand, giving it a reassuring squeeze before I pulled our hoods over our heads and fled the house.

Cß

We managed to escape without being seen; the dragons not yet finding the true location of the house, though we had been able to hear their crashing through the woods far in the distance. An hour passed and we finally slowed our pace, the three of us gasping for air.

Though the sun was high in the sky, the space beneath the canopy of trees was dark, broken up only by shafts of light peeking through the leaves at odd intervals. The winter snow hadn't made it to the ground of the forest, but the dirt was still freezing, the cold seeping through my leather boots.

"There's a stream over there," my mother whispered, breaking into my thoughts. "Let's fill our canteens and then we should take to the sky—get farther away from here. It's only a matter of time until they find our trail and catch up to us."

She led us on silent feet through the trees to the edge of a trickling stream. Even in the cold, the stream still burbled, making its way through sloughs of ice. Kaida and I kneeled by the edge, submerging our canteens into the water, the frigid temperature gnawing at my fingertips.

"Does Lita know what she's doing?" Kaida muttered to me under her breath. "We have nowhere to go that's outside of the Remnant's reach, other than Metta, but that's still at least a week of travel away."

I ran my wet hands through my hair. "Z isn't with us, so all we can do is try to make it to Metta."

Kaida narrowed her eyes, pressing her lips into a thin line, before she finally nodded. She took a long drink of water, shoved the canteen into her pack and, in a brief flash of purple, shifted into dragon form.

"I'll take the packs, you take Lita?"

I nodded, shifting into my scales, and biting back a groan as my body transformed after so long in human form. Then I secured our packs between her wings with some rope. It had been more than two months since I had used my wings to fly. I hoped that they were strong enough to carry us through the sky.

"Are you two ready?" my mother's voice said as she appeared through the trees like a wraith.

"Yes," I replied before bending down so she could climb between my wings. I could have carried her in my arms, but I needed them to be free just in case we met foes in the sky.

Kaida helped secure my mother with a tangle of ropes, so she didn't fall off.

"Ready?" she asked me.

A single nod was my only response before the two of us, in identical movements, jumped up through the trees, snapped our wings into the air and took off into the light of the sun.

CHAPTER 26

ELDRIN

THE HOTTEST, MOST miserable two days passed as Z and I made our way through the Zenduro Wastes.

We dug holes beneath dune after dune to escape the sun during the day, making our way across the scalding sand that took far too long to cool during the midnight hours. My mouth was so parched I was surprised my teeth hadn't dissolved into ash on my tongue. I had managed to find a single waternut melon—similar to a coconut but filled with water—buried beneath one of the dunes, but split between the two of us, it didn't go very far.

If we didn't get out of the desert soon…

I blew out a shaky breath to dispel the thoughts, wishing even a single tear would fill my eyes so that I could have something wet fall into my mouth.

Though our scales kept us from burning beneath the glare of the sun as we dug holes in the sand, it did nothing to prevent the skin beneath from growing hotter, more unbearable.

Legends told of dragons who used to make the Wastes their home, but after walking through it for two days, I couldn't understand how that would be possible. This climate was unrelenting, uninhabitable.

"How… much… farther?" Z panted, his shoulders and wings slumping.

The moon was high overhead, every granule of sand on the ground giving off an iridescent shimmer beneath the light.

"I don't know," I answered. I wasn't sure how far into the Wastes my magic had brought us, but it was far enough that I still couldn't locate the Ilgathor Mountains in the distance. The horizon was just a haze of heat and sand.

"I've survived… over a thousand years of battles, wars… ruthless beasts, and losing those I loved. But the one thing that will finally do me in is this sand-filled hell."

"That's the spirit, Z," I chided, and the enormous beast rolled his eyes.

The colors of our scales were similar, though his were just a shade lighter, a touch more iridescent in the light, like seeing a scaled fish swim deep in the ocean. We both blended into the night sky, though he fit in among the stars better than I did.

Z dropped on all fours and crawled to the closest dune and leaned against it, his wings tucked into his back.

"Has your magic refilled yet, Eldrin? I can't continue like this."

"You sure are whiny, oh mighty rebel," I drawled, trying to bring back the tough, hopeful dragon I knew him to be. I understood his despair, his sour attitude, but that would do nothing to help us get out of here. My wings dragged behind me as my legs slogged through the sand and I all but fell onto the ground next to him.

"Eldrin, I have been close to death many times, but all at the hands of other dragons. Never from the elements, from the relentless heat of the sun and the sinking sand that draws our feet deeper into its depths with each step." Z rubbed at the side of his snout. "The sun is supposed to be a source of strength for the dragons, but it's only killing us faster here. It's like a poison."

I pondered his words for a moment, the weight of them settling into me before something clicked into place in my mind.

"That's it, Z!" I cried, jumping to my feet and studying the stars. The faintest light sat on the horizon as the first flickers of dawn lit the sky.

"What are you talking about, old man?" Z said, his voice weary.

"The *sun*."

Z squinted at me. "It's a hot ball of orange death in the sky."

I couldn't hold back the grin that split my snout. "And it's our ticket out of here."

It was risky—not to mention against the laws of Elysia—but desperate times meant doing something drastic. And if that sand coating my mouth instead of saliva, and my stomach slowly eating itself from hunger weren't desperate, I wasn't sure what was.

Z let out an exasperated sigh and threw his claws into the air. "That's it. The desert has gotten to your head. We're going to die." He collapsed onto his side, draping his wings over himself.

"Don't you get it? The sun gives us strength. That strength fuels our magic."

"We've been in the desert—which is full of sun—for over two days, Eldrin, and you still don't have the magic to get us out of here. Explain that."

"Well," I drawled, "we haven't actually been *in* the sun. We've been hiding from it. But that's not my point." I stared at the sky, the midnight-blue of night brightening toward dawn with each minute that passed. "I'm assuming, since you're *old* that you've heard of the Current?"

Z narrowed his eyes at me calling him old.

"The King performs the Current every year on the Summer Solstice. He utilizes the power of the sun to strengthen the earth for the following year."

"Yes, yes, I know all this." Z pushed back into a seated position, fixing his gaze on me.

"It's against Elysia's laws for anyone to perform the Current but the King. It grants him enormous strength and magic he wouldn't normally have."

"But you're not the King and it's not the Summer Solstice."

I nodded. "You're right, but that might not matter in this case. I don't need the entirety of that power available on the Solstice. I only need enough to get us out of this desert."

Z pursed his lips, the expression comical on a dragon's snout. "Let's say I believe that'll work. Do you even know how to do that?"

I was silent for a few heartbeats as I forced my mind back centuries in the past, trying to recall the ancient words, the ritual to call upon the power of the sun.

"It's been a long time since I've spoken the old language. It may take me some time to remember the words."

The bright glow of the sun peeked its head over the horizon, bathing the Zenduro Wastes in early morning light.

"Well then I suggest you hurry up, old man," he responded, glaring at the sun.

I huffed out a breath at his response and closed my eyes. I had witnessed countless Currents over my lifetime, whether it was Martik or the previous King. But the old language predated even my time. Though it used to be the standard language in Elysia, it had been thousands of years since the old words passed from the memories of the dragons and humans. I had learned the words long ago, before Martik became King and was learning it himself, but it had been so long since I had even tried to recall them.

The heat of the sun gilded my scales, flashing blue lights onto the sand. While I wouldn't be performing the full ceremony, I still needed to draw on enough of the sun's power to fill my magic to jump us out of the desert. The problem was I didn't know exactly how much that was. And if I took too much—let it go on for too long—I risked losing myself. I had no tether, outside of Z, like Lita was to Martik. There was a chance I could lose myself in the power, in the darkness that corrupted dragon hearts with too much of it.

Inhaling deeply, I stepped out of the shadows of the dune and widened my stance in the sunlight. Lifting my arms into the air above my head, I closed my eyes. The heat of the desert sun was ravenous, searching for any way to get beneath my scales to the skin. I shoved the uncomfortable sensation of the sun aside and searched within myself for those ancient words.

With a deep breath, I took in the sunlight, and with each exhale I released it, letting the power flow in and out as it gathered strength. Minutes passed, the sun rising higher in the sky, my arms growing heavier by the second.

"What's taking so long?" Z muttered, and I squeezed my eyes tighter to shut out his voice. I couldn't let him ruin my concentration. I shook my head, trying to shut him up.

The words continued to evade me. Without the old language, I couldn't initiate the Current—couldn't grasp hold of the might of the power. Sure, the sun was giving me a bit more strength in my body, but it wasn't filling my magic.

And then… A memory of sitting at a table with Martik as he studied the ritual from a book surfaced in my mind. We had both read it, memorized each piece of the Current. As if the memory had unlocked my tongue, the words filled my mouth, my voice dropping to a low octave. I wasn't sure where they came from, only that they felt easy as breathing, as if they were waiting all along.

The heat of the sun changed, escalating from a painful burn to an all-consuming, powerful wave of heat as it filled my body. It started at my claws in the air. They grew unbearably warm before it moved down my body inch by inch. It filled the veins in my arms, seeping down like poison and I could feel each sliver of skin and blood that it heated as it moved. Next, it went into my shoulders before spreading wide into my wings. The heat was so intense my wings flared to the side, and I groaned against the burning spreading through the muscles and tendons.

It continued moving downward, through my chest, my heart racing and pounding against my skin, before it slid down through my stomach and legs, finally ending at my clawed feet in the sand.

I heard Z's sudden intake of breath, but kept my eyes closed. I couldn't break the connection—couldn't let him distract me.

In past Currents, the magic from the sun always caused the King to grow in size, becoming larger than any dragon in Elysia's history. It never lasted, of course, for once the ritual was broken and they snapped back into their body, they returned to their previous size.

Perhaps that was the uncomfortable stretching feeling spreading through my wings and limbs. I couldn't help but wonder if I opened my eyes if I would find myself towering over Z—over the desert.

One breath the heat was hot, burning, boiling beneath my skin and the next it suddenly turned into a frigid heat, and a different sort of burn began spreading in my blood—like being frozen alive from the inside out.

A darkness fell over my mind behind my closed eyes, suffocating and constricting. I lashed out against it, but felt its grip tighten as if the dark itself had talons that were digging into my mind.

What was happening? Was this the darkness that the King had to fight every year? Is this why Lita had always been his tether—his lifeline to bring him back from the dark? Power corrupted the hearts of the dragons, and the sun was pure, undiluted, raw power.

What had I done?

The darkness grew like a wave about to crash over me, ready to snuff out all light—all life—within me.

"Eldrin." I heard Z's voice in the background like a whisper being carried off into the wind. Then it disappeared as if he never spoke at all.

My body grew both heavy and weightless, and a terrible ripping pain, like being sliced open with a dagger, tore across my stomach. The power and my inner beast warred with each other as they both fought for dominance in my body. I could only stand there, my arms still extended to the sky, unable to move, unable to do *anything* as the dark terror of power and the inner light within me battled for control.

My thoughts scattered and I couldn't put any coherent ones together. I couldn't *think.*

Something grabbed my hand, ripping it from the air and the sensation was like being bathed in ice water.

"Eldrin!" a voice snapped, louder, closer.

I still couldn't get my body to move—get my voice to respond. The darkness clung to every inch of me, smothered my senses.

The heat of the sun roared inside my body, like a ravenous beast ready to devour me. The well of magic in my core was easily double the size it normally was, it bubbled over like a boiling cauldron.

If I could have formed the thought, and made my body obey my command, I would have recognized that I had enough magic to jump and end the Current now. Before it killed me.

But I couldn't think—couldn't make it stop. I had a strange sensation of being pulled away from my body.

I should have been alarmed, but all I could focus on was the darkness my mind had succumbed to, the ice burning through my veins.

"ELDRIN!"

The roar shattered the dark, like ice being cracked, exploding outward into tiny fragments. Light, bright and intense, seared through my eyelids as my mind snapped back into my body. Sand erupted beneath me as I crashed to the ground.

Slowly, so slowly, I pried my eyes open, squinting against the harsh light. My eyes watered against it.

Z stood next to me, panting hard, his wings drooping in the sand behind him. His gaze was fixed on the ground, but the moment it snapped to mine, absolute fear flickered within them.

"What in the scales was that?" he gasped out, unable to hold my gaze any longer. He dropped to his knees in the sand, before crawling back into the shadows of the dune.

I shook my head at his question, my tongue thick and heavy in my mouth, unable to form words.

Even if I could speak, I had no idea how to explain what just happened.

All the warnings I had ever been told in my long life flitted through my mind. They had all been right. There was a reason why only the King could perform the Current, why only one dragon in Elysia was granted such power, and even then, it was only for a short time until the ritual was over.

Every piece of me vibrated, shaking with the torrent of power flowing through my veins. This was the point where the King would deposit all the magic contained within him back into the earth to prosper all living things in a way that simple sunlight never could.

But I wasn't performing the entire Current, and a dragon's body wasn't made to contain such great power for an extended period of time. I had to release it—soon.

I tried to open my snout, move my tongue, but they still wouldn't cooperate. I had a feeling I wouldn't regain full control over my body, my senses, until I released this magic.

I looked at Z where he sat against the side of the sand dune. I barely managed to extend my claws to him, hoping he would understand what I needed.

We had to jump. Now.

Z studied my hand with wary eyes. Whatever he had witnessed while I battled in the dark power of the Current had truly terrified him.

I managed to wiggle my claws, not a full wave, beckoning him to take my hand. He hesitated for another second before finally reaching out, grasping it. His scales burned, so different from the icy fire beneath my own, and I suppressed a growl at the sudden flare of pain.

"Get us out of this scales-forsaken desert," Z breathed, so quiet I wondered if I had imagined it.

Reaching deep inside, like I had done countless times to jump, I gripped that special magic. It soared through my veins, reaching outward over my body, and I heard Z gasp next to me.

Shadows erupted like a cloud, enveloping the two of us in its arms.

And then we were gone.

CHAPTER 27

KAIDA

WE WERE UNDER attack.

An arrow whizzed past my ear, and I barely managed to bank to the left to avoid it. The packs, though light compared to carrying Lita, felt like enormous weights upon my back. A small black whip of shadow shot through the air, aimed for Tarrin, and he snapped his wings in, spinning to the side as his mother held on for dear life.

We had been in the air, soaring above the clouds to avoid being seen by the Remnant crawling the earth below, for a few hours before we started to see dark figures in the distance behind us. We had been hopeful they were just large birds, but that had been foolish thinking.

There was only one thing the winged shapes would be.

The Remnant of the Lone Dragon. It was always them.

Despite our frantic flying, trying to put more distance between us and them, they still managed to catch up to us. There were four of them, each different shades of green. Two held crossbows aimed for Tarrin and me and the others held a whip in one hand and giant chains in the other.

Dead or alive they wanted us; they were ready for either outcome.

I swallowed the lump of fear in my throat and watched as Tarrin banked once more to evade another string of arrows.

We have to get out of here! I yelled down our bond as I dodged another attack.

There's nowhere to go! They outnumber us and no matter how fast or far we fly, we cannot escape.

He was right, this didn't look good. There weren't many options—*any* options.

But I did not survive this long or come this far to be defeated now.

My inner beast perked up inside me, sensing the battle that loomed. Through narrowed eyes, it watched me, waiting to be summoned, waiting to be unleashed. As much as I despised the feeling of losing control, of that bloodlust that consumed me when I let my beast take over, I knew there was no chance of walking away from these dragons alive. Tarrin and I would die, and Lita would plummet to her death.

I remembered Z's words about how I had to stop fighting against my own mind and accept my inner beast. Once I united with her, and stopped fearing her, then nothing would be able to stop the force of my magic.

Flames sputtered in my palms as if my beast was giving me confirmation that she wouldn't yield to me. She wanted to work *with* me.

Another arrow whizzed past Tarrin, creating a shallow gash in his scales.

There was no other choice.

If he could survive two months in the dark, in his worst nightmares, I could face my own fear now.

I love you, Tarrin.

I felt his alarm flare through our shape-shifter bond.

Then I let go.

An image of my dragon form and human form locking hands

together appeared in my mind, and a sudden rush of magic burst through each of my limbs, as if I had never tapped into the full strength of my magic before.

Throwing my wings out and spreading them wide, I forced myself to a stop before I swung around to face the Remnant mercenaries. All four of them had sinister grins spread across their ugly snouts. The two dragons on either end had horns coming out of their cheeks, bending in toward their mouths. They were the ones holding the whips, the same fire whips that Eklos used to employ on his slaves. They had pieces of glass lining the length, and blue flames coating the rest.

I could deal with them last. My priority was to stop the two in the middle, each of varying shades of green leaves, and holding enormous crossbows aimed directly at my heart.

In the past, whenever my inner beast had taken control, I had retreated to a tiny area in my mind, letting my dragon reap destruction and death. This time, however, I wasn't forced back, nor did I cower like a fearful slave.

My beast stood next to me in my mind, gripping my hand in her claws, *wanting* me to join in the death she was about to unleash.

That bloodlust beckoned; my mouth watered.

These dragons would kill Lita—kill Tarrin.

An ear-shattering roar erupted from my mouth at the thought, fierce enough that it forced the four dragons to pause.

And that's all the time I needed.

For I was fire and lightning.

I was wrath and destruction.

I was *dragon*.

I intertwined myself with my inner beast, inhaling a mighty breath.

And then I exploded.

Lightning erupted from my claws, my wingtips, and my feet

as I flung my arms and wings wide. It seeped from my pores, my scales, flickering through the air as the clouds around me thickened, darkened.

The magic in my core was boiling, bubbling, and overflowing.

I was vaguely aware of Lita standing on Tarrin's back behind me, a bow in her hand as she notched an iron-tipped arrow of her own.

The clouds held onto my lightning, like a charged energy source I could draw from, and ether filled my nostrils. Sparks crackled in my veins, spitting out of my mouth as I let out a flame-filled growl.

The two dragons on the end held back as the two in the middle soared for me. I swirled my claws in the air, fire dancing between them as a fire spear formed. Gripping it between my scaled hands, I swung it at one of the dragon's heads just as he reached for me, sending him flying into the other. I adjusted my grip and made to stab at him while he remained disoriented, but he managed to duck, the spear cutting through the air just above his head.

Out of the corner of my eye, Tarrin flapped toward the other two dragons, Lita releasing arrow after carefully aimed arrow while she stood upon his back, ropes tightly coiled around her legs, keeping her from falling off. Her cloak drifted in the frigid air behind her, though her face remained obscured beneath her hood.

A clawed fist smashed into my face, sending me careening to the side. The dragon who hit me wasted no time, tackling me mid-air, both of us digging our claws into the other's scales.

"Give up," he snarled, digging in farther.

"You first," I growled in return, taking advantage of his momentary distraction to create a dagger of lightning and shoved it into his chest.

It wasn't the best place to hit, seeing as the scales over most of a dragon's body were like thick armor. There were only a few weak areas. If I had been able to, stabbing him under the arm would have dealt the most damage.

He roared against the sting of the dagger and moved to slam his tail into my chest, but I spun out of the way just in time. Free of the dragon's claws, I swung my wings down in a mighty arch, propelling my body upward.

Look out! Tarrin shouted down the bond just as an enormous arrow whipped past my head.

I glanced in his direction to find him engaged with one dragon while the other aimed its crossbow directly at me. Another arrow pierced the edge of my wing and I let out a pained bark before another dragon crashed into me. He grabbed hold of my arms and folded his wings into his back, forcing me toward the ground. We fell, faster and faster.

My wing was in too much pain to fight against the fall he had forced me into; his claws too tight on my arms to escape his grip. The dragon would only release me when I was too close to the earth—when my death was certain.

I tried—and failed—to flare my wings to slow my fall, groaning against the pain. Blood spiraled up into the air, but I couldn't take my eyes off the dragon. His yellow eyes burned with a fury that rivaled Eklos, and sparks flew from his mouth as he growled at me and tightened his hold.

Kaida! Tarrin yelled in my mind, but there was nothing he could do. He was locked into a battle of his own.

The ground grew closer, and fear clogged my thoughts, my mind refusing to think of a way out of this. Death loomed at the edges of my vision.

Use your magic! Tarrin cried, breaking through the fog that had settled over my brain.

As if his words unlocked the fear that had iced over my heart, I grabbed the lightning lingering in the clouds above us, channeled its enormous strength, before I unleashed it into the dragon with a roar that shook the earth below us.

Purple and white light flashed in a brilliant dance in front of my eyes, forcing me to slam them closed. There was a flash, followed by a pain-filled roar, then a flicker before everything went dark. The weight above me disappeared, and the faint feeling of rain plinked on my scales. I opened my eyes to find scales falling out of the sky as if the dragon had simply… exploded.

I flipped over to my stomach and eased my wings out to the sides, slowing my fall through gritted teeth as the pain in my wings had me seeing spots.

I didn't have time to think—to ponder the fact that my magic had literally disintegrated another being. Nor did I want to.

The other three dragons needed to be dealt with and, through our bond, I could feel that Tarrin's strength was flagging. He and Lita were still engaged with the two holding the whips, but the third dragon who had initially come after me was gone.

I scoured everywhere but saw no sign of him.

So, I raced for Tarrin.

Though I had used a fair bit of magic to incinerate the other dragon, my core still felt full, begging to be used. I wouldn't be able to get close enough to engage in a physical battle, nor would I win. Despite all the training I had done with Z, I still struggled against the strength of the male dragons in a physical fight.

My magic would have to be enough.

I allowed myself three breaths to figure out what to do.

One. I had multiple elements at my disposal. Fire, water, lightning.

Two. Water and lightning didn't mix well. My lightning was potent, but added *with* water?

Three. I didn't have time to second-guess myself as I rose an arm into the air, feeling the flicker of lightning encompassing my claws as I drew it from the clouds. I mentally pictured the scale

Noam had used to teach me to wield two magical abilities at once, as my other palm pulled on the water within the moisture-ridden clouds around me. Wings spread wide, a single strand of lightning linked my right hand to the sky, and a thin stream of water connected my other hand to the clouds.

On the fourth breath, I detonated.

Slapping my clawed hands together above my head, a deafening thunderclap rang through the air. Throwing my arms in front of me with as much strength as I could muster, I released the magic, sending two spears of intertwined water and lightning into the other two dragons. Tarrin dove out of the way just in time.

I squeezed my eyes against the intense flash of light, and the following clap of thunder was so loud, I instinctively covered my ears, wrapping my wings partially around me in defense. Wind battered against my scales as light flared and then everything stilled. My ears rang in the sudden silence.

Unfolding my wings, I looked at the destruction I had caused. Or should I say, lack thereof. For where the two green dragons had been… there was nothing.

Only scales plinking and falling through the sky. No sign of their bodies or souls.

Tarrin's snout gaped as he squinted at where he had fought the dragons.

"How—"

In the span of a single heartbeat, Tarrin's face transformed from pure awe to absolute terror as he looked at me. I didn't even have time to turn—or to register that I had momentarily forgotten about the last dragon.

Claws gouged into my wings, shredding through muscle and tendons and my roar of pain echoed between the clouds. The dragon snarled, clinging to my back, using his body weight to force me down through the air faster. My wings were unusable, and I could do nothing to stop my plummet toward the earth. I tried to summon my magic, but nothing would come. Even the flames in my mouth had disappeared at the intensity of the pain.

Kaida! Tarrin's voice shouted in my mind, and I was vaguely aware of thudding wings as he tried to reach us.

I twisted and thrashed, fighting against the dragon, trying to force his grip to loosen so I could get free, but his claws were like iron shackles.

"Let… me… go!" I growled. The ground grew closer, the tops of the trees visible now.

His only response was a snarl in my ear.

And then he gasped, his eyes widening before his grip fell away.

I turned to see the dragon flipping backward as he fell through the sky, an enormous iron arrow protruding from his heart. His eyes were wide, disbelieving, before the life left them, and his vibrant green scales faded to a muted color.

Lita stood tall on Tarrin's back, still holding her bow aloft as if she didn't trust that the dragon was truly dead.

I barely noticed that I was still free-falling through the air, my wings unable to hold my weight, as I watched the dragon crash to the ground, each of his limbs bent at odd angles.

Kaida! Tarrin shouted again, snapping me back into my body. Sharp, ripping pain ached through each of my wings, and thanks to the gaping tears the dragon had gouged in them, I couldn't slow my fall toward the earth.

Hang on! I'm coming! Tarrin's blue scales flashed in my periphery as he frantically flapped in my direction.

The leaves on the trees grew closer, more detailed, and I fought the urge to close my eyes against the death that was swiftly approaching. Branches stood up toward the sky like knives waiting to skewer me. The winter air was brutally cold against my face and scales as I plummeted faster and faster.

And then something hard and warm crashed into me, setting us spinning through the air.

"Kaida," Tarrin whispered, his voice hoarse.

He tried to tighten his grip on me, but his claws kept slipping. I was too heavy in dragon form for him to carry me much farther, and with Lita still on his back, I didn't know if he'd be able to handle the weight of two humans. Though humans comparatively didn't weigh much, dragons never carried passengers, so flying with us on his back would be a burden he wasn't used to.

"We have to land so I can look at your wings," he said against the wind. His clawed hands were like small fires beneath my arms as he banked and circled the forest below. Easing us through the tight trees, I suppressed a roar as I tucked in my wings to avoid snagging on branches.

As soon as my feet touched the dirt below, Tarrin released me, and I collapsed to the ground. The pain in my wings was all consuming; overwhelming. It sent a fog over my brain, making it impossible to think straight. My vision distorted, my eyes unable to focus in the dim light beneath the forest.

Lita was at my side in a heartbeat, Tarrin in his human form arriving only a second later. He kneeled at my side, putting his hand against my scaled cheek. Even his skin felt like an inferno.

I wanted to shift into human form, to wrap myself in his arms, to celebrate surviving more of Eklos's mercenaries, but the pain was too great. I wasn't even sure I could summon enough magic to shift.

"Hold still, Kaida. I'm going to take a look at your wings," Lita said, making her way around to my back.

Holding back a scream, I carefully stretched them out so that she could inspect the worst of the damage. I couldn't see what the dragon had done, but based on the pain, it must've been terrible.

Lita's fingers skimmed against them, and my teeth nearly bit through my tongue.

"It could be worse," she muttered, finally pulling her hand away. "He managed to make some good-sized tears in them, but he missed the major artery and tendons. They'll heal in a few days, and you'll be able to fly again. You got lucky."

I scowled. "I don't feel very lucky."

"Well, we could all be dead. So, there's that." Amusement danced in Tarrin's eyes, and despite the ache in my wings, I giggled before it turned into a full-on laugh. My stomach shook from the force of it.

Out of the corner of my eye, Lita looked at us like we had lost our minds.

Perhaps we had.

When I finally got myself back under control, I looked between the two of them, swiping the moisture from my eyes. "Now what?"

"Are you able to shift?" Tarrin asked, eyeing my wings again.

"I'm not sure," I replied, shaking my head. "I can try."

My core of magic contained only a flicker of fire, but I attempted to stoke it, trying to flare it enough to push the shifting magic through my veins. It was slow, seeping through me at a trickle rather than the usual deluge. It took several seconds, much longer than was usual, but finally I felt the familiar warmth spread through me before a dull flash of purple forced my eyes closed. I panted through my teeth as the pain from my wings transferred to my arms.

Thankfully my bones weren't broken, like Tarrin's had been after Z saved us from those mercenaries months ago, but there were still deep, bloody gashes along both, though they had already begun to heal. I let out a shuddering breath.

Lita made quick work of applying a salve to the gashes, then wrapping white bandages over them. "We should get moving," she said when she'd finished, glancing around the forest. "Just in case there were other dragons nearby who witnessed the battle in the sky. Not many could've missed the lightning storm you created."

With a nod of my head, I took hold of Tarrin's hand as he gently pulled me to my feet, letting me lean my weight against him.

"All right?" he whispered, his lips brushing against my ear.

I offered a nod and he smiled, his eyes dancing with mirth.

"You completely obliterated those dragons."

I cringed at his word choice.

"I've never seen anything like that. It was incredible."

"Yes, it was," Lita interrupted, and I met her gaze. "How'd you do it?"

I lifted a shoulder and gave a shake of my head. "Noam had started training me in using multiple elements at once, but we never got very far before we separated. I wasn't even sure if I could do it, but with my beast I just knew how." A pang of sadness pierced my heart at the thought of Noam. Training with him in Mistwick when he had told me about my Ancient Magic felt like years ago even though it had only been a few months.

I couldn't help but wonder where he was—where Eldrin had sent him off to.

Lita's eyes squinted as she studied me for another heartbeat before she turned away and continued through the forest.

"I sure wish we still had a shifter bond with her so we could know what she's thinking," I muttered to Tarrin.

He gave a small chuckle. "Even then, I never understood what she was thinking." Pulling me into his chest, he wrapped his arms around me. "I love you, Kaida." He planted a kiss on my lips. "In case we get attacked again, I wanted to tell you that."

I let out a laugh of my own. "Likewise." I kissed him once more, relishing the fact that we had just survived another attack and were still breathing, still able to hold one another.

After a few moments, I glanced at the sky through the foliage. "Where are we?"

"Based on the mountains in the distance, we're roughly four days from Metta," Lita answered.

The frigid temperature of the dirt beneath my boots seeped into the leather, freezing my toes. Tarrin wrapped my cloak tighter around me.

"What I wouldn't give for Rythos's ability to jump to other locations right now. We wouldn't even have to traipse through the woods in the cold," I said, frowning at the ground.

"Well, I could carry you so we can arrive sooner."

I narrowed my eyes. "And your mother, too? I don't think that would go well. You've never flown with two people on your back."

"I think I could handle it."

I opened my mouth to give a retort when the ground began to shake. It was faint at first but quickly intensified, forcing us both to our knees. The trees swayed and the fear that they might fall on us spiked in my mind. An earthquake? They were extremely rare in Elysia, only mentioned once or twice in the histories.

Even more concerning was the fact that the light from the sun started to dim.

And that's when I felt it. The same desperate need to get to that source of power that I had felt back at the Royal Palace when the Current had been performed during the Beginnings Festival, the uncontrollable need to find it… It gripped me and my legs moved of their own accord, taking off at a run.

The trees shook violently, many of them beginning to crack at their foundations, but I paid them no mind.

"Kaida!" Tarrin shouted behind me. "What are you doing?"

I kept running, my inner beast begging me to find that power, my magic purring in response.

But then scaled arms wrapped around me and I found myself above the trees. Tarrin had shifted into dragon form, Lita on his back as he carried me in his arms. Though we couldn't feel the quaking from the sky, the entire world, as far as we could see, was vibrating in a strange, chaotic dance.

"Let me go!" I yelled against the wind, squirming against his hold on me.

"Kaida, stop!" His grip tightened. "What's happening?" he asked his mother.

Lita shook her head. "Earthquakes don't happen in Elysia—not like this."

No sooner had she spoken when an enormous flash of light spiraled into a sphere far in the distance. It stretched and grew, growing even brighter, and the power in it thrummed through my blood.

Then suddenly, it vanished, the daylight remaining dimmer than it was before.

None of us spoke. The earth below us swayed for another heartbeat before everything stilled. And just like that, the desperate need to reach that power disappeared, leaving an empty, hollow feeling in my core. I stopped struggling and Tarrin's grip relaxed as he soared over the trees.

"Was that… the *Current*?" Tarrin breathed, his snout gaping.

"It's not the Solstice and that couldn't have been Martik," Lita remarked. "But there's no mistaking what that was." She looked over his shoulder at me. "What were you thinking?"

I scowled at her tone. "It called to me." It was the only way I could describe it.

"Explain," she demanded.

"Last summer, when I was at the palace and Martik performed the Current in Zarkuse, I felt it. I was overwhelmed with the sudden need to get to that power source. I couldn't control myself. I was halfway to Zarkuse before I could stop." I blew out a breath. "This felt exactly like that."

Lita looked in the direction the light had come from. "Like calls to like," she murmured.

"What?" Tarrin asked.

"Kaida's Ancient Magic is raw, it's the original magic. The Current is similar in that it is also raw; a magic that creates and fuels. It makes sense that she is drawn to it. Like calls to like. Her magic was drawn to that magic because they are essentially the same."

My mind felt foggy both from her explanation and the sudden loss of that power humming through the air.

"But one thing is for sure," she continued. "If there are other dragons outside of the King performing the Current, we may have an even bigger problem."

ELDRIN

THE SHADOWS WERE darker this time.

Usually when I jumped from place to place, they were smoke-like and wispy, like silk gliding over skin; the heat of the magic in my veins bearable and quick to dissipate.

But now, every part of me was burning. My blood was like tiny, heated needles prickling underneath my skin while my limbs grew heavy, sinking deep into the dirt. I couldn't breathe; couldn't get my lungs to expand.

The shadows clung to us, unwilling to relent their hold. It took all my concentration to force them away, and I swayed on my feet when they finally dissolved, my body weak after days in the desert without sustenance.

The sound of Z gasping for air broke through my thoughts and I glanced to my right to find him on all fours, his snout inches from the dirt. His eyes were squeezed shut and it looked like he was struggling to breathe.

"Z?" I asked, taking a tentative step toward him.

He muttered a curse. "I hate that shadow thing. That was worse than before."

"It was… different," I admitted.

It had worked though—done exactly what I had hoped. The

power from the sun gave me enough magic to jump both Z and me out of the desert, landing us in this forest. I hadn't intended to come specifically here, only to get as far from the Zenduro Wastes as I possibly could.

Thick woods surrounded us, even the snow unable to penetrate the foliage above, though the dirt was frozen beneath my clawed feet. The sudden change from the desert heat to brutal winter temperatures had a shiver wracking through me. I held up a hand, telling Z to stay put, and jumped into the air, grabbing onto the top of a tree to look around.

The Ilgathor Mountains stood tall and proud mere miles away.

I clenched my teeth to keep from gaping. Had the magic really enabled me to jump from the Wastes, hundreds of miles away to the west? I had never made such a jump, especially not while carrying someone else.

I let out a shaky breath as I dropped to the forest floor.

"I vote we never do that again," Z declared.

After the fire coursing through me, and the heavy strain of magic, I couldn't disagree with him.

"Where are we?" he asked, finally pushing to his feet and looking around.

"We're in the woods west of Vernista. Not far from the Ilgathor Mountains."

"That's… very far from the Wastes."

I nodded, noticing that Z wouldn't look at me, looking anywhere but at my face. It was clear he didn't enjoy the experience of the shadow thing, as he liked to call it, but my gut told me it went beyond that. His face after I had drawn on the power of the sun, after that enormous flash of light…

He hardly said anything to me as we pushed on through the woods in search of water we desperately needed after being in the desert.

"Is something wrong, Z?"

We had just escaped from the center of Eklos's army camp, ran for our lives only to end up in the Zenduro Wastes where we easily could have withered away from the elements, and now faced a long journey out of the forest, in search of somewhere safe.

Of course, something was wrong. *Everything* was wrong.

But this seemed different.

"Do you remember anything about what you did in the desert?" Z asked, his voice quiet.

I narrowed my eyes at him. "Yes. Kind of hard to forget that kind of power running through my veins."

Z blinked before turning away. "Try witnessing it from the outside."

My claws wrapped around his arm. "What's that supposed to mean? What's the problem here, Z?"

"Eldrin, whatever you were doing… it was turning the sun black!" He ripped his arm out of my grip. "The light was unbearable when you initiated the Current, but the longer you held it, a strange darkness began spreading across the sun like black ink. The heat was oppressive. The light was—" Z blew out a breath. "When I disrupted your connection, it was like a tether snapped and the black receded, causing the brightest flash of light I've ever seen in my life." He shook his large head, rubbing at the side of his snout.

"And the most terrifying part? You… *you* started turning black, Eldrin, like the sun. Your scales, they kept darkening with every second you remained connected. Your scales started to gap as your limbs expanded, and it looked like your body was either going to rip itself apart or explode."

The cold air stung against my teeth as my mouth hung open. "*What?*"

He shook his head. "I don't know what you did, but that was like no Current I've ever seen." Z leaned his body against a thick trunk, the tree swaying slightly under his weight. He fixed his gaze on the ground. "Your eyes… that was the worst part. Any sign of life left them… and the amethyst color—it was gone. Turned wholly black."

I blinked at him, trying to understand his words but it felt like my head was underwater. It had been an intense experience being connected to the sun's magic, every inch of me had been on fire, straining to the point of pain, but at no point had I noticed any of what Z mentioned. It was violent, but I hadn't felt like I was about to die.

"I didn't know what to do," he continued. "Trying to interrupt the ritual, to break your connection with that power, was the only thing I could think of. I was afraid you were destroying yourself."

I rubbed at my temple, pondering his words. "Is that why you've been acting strange, Z? You're waiting for me to turn evil or explode or something?"

"You didn't see your eyes, Eldrin. You became death incarnate. Like the worst beasts in this world. If that magic didn't kill you, I knew if I didn't stop you, you'd kill me."

Well, that certainly explained why the usually callous, hardened, brutal dragon was suddenly… cowering in my presence.

I sighed, giving him space. "I assure you, Z, I'm still me. I'm fine."

He eyed me warily. "For now. Who's to say it won't happen again?"

I shook my head, dismissing his words. "I'm *fine,* Z. It was only from being directly connected to the sun. The connection has been broken, and I didn't even retain any of it after making the jump here."

He eyed me skeptically. "You don't feel any different?"

"No, Z. The magic is gone." It was the truth. I was exhausted, yes, but I had retained nothing but my own magic, once again depleted. Even still, I had never heard of such a phenomenon—turning black while performing a Current. Maybe that's why the law had been enacted. Perhaps it was a physical manifestation of such power corrupting the hearts of dragons.

The dark ocean-blue dragon straightened, his chest puffing out. "Well. I guess I saved you from the darkness then."

I stared at him for a moment before I threw my head back and laughed, the sound deep and rumbling, the leaves vibrating on the branches near my head.

"Well done, Z," I laughed.

He narrowed his eyes at me. "You wouldn't be laughing if you had seen what I saw."

"Oh, I have no doubt. It likely would have made me wet myself." I eyed him.

He scrunched his snout, appalled. "I did *not* wet myself, old man. I've been alive even longer than you."

I waved my claws at him in dismissal. "I mean if you were *so scared* when I started turning black, it would have been perfectly understandable if you did have an accident." I split my lips in a grin.

If death could come by the hatred in someone's gaze, I would have keeled over into the dirt.

I chuckled. "Come now, Z. It's over. Let's keep moving. We need to get back to Metta before my cousin's mercenaries find us. We were impossible to find in the Wastes, but here... well, let's get going."

I turned, pulling my wings in tight to my back so I could fit through the narrower spaces in the trees. Z remained silent though I could feel his blood simmering, even from feet away. Just as the woods swallowed the both of us, I swore I heard him mutter:

"I did *not* wet myself."

TARRIN

WE CAMPED BENEATH the stars, our bones shaking as we braced ourselves against the frigid winter night. All three of our bedrolls were tucked together at the edge of a clearing, keeping us hidden from any dragons who might be flying overhead, but it also allowed us to see if anyone approached. The problem was, while the trees blocked most of the winds whipping the loose snow around, we still remained outside, and it was by far one of the coldest nights in Elysia I had ever experienced.

Kaida's icy fingers trembled in my hand as I tried to infuse warmth into her bones, but it didn't do much against the chattering of her teeth or the violent shaking of her body.

My mother, on my other side, wasn't shaking quite as much, but her back was still pressed tight against mine, looking for any bit of warmth she could find.

I thought about shifting into dragon form, generating more heat and therefore being able to offer more to them, but the trees in these woods were incredibly close together, and I didn't think I'd be able to fit within them in such a large form. Besides, the moonlight glinting off my scales would likely catch the eye of any dragons passing by.

"S-s-so c-c-c-cold," Kaida whispered through chattering teeth.

I wrapped my arm around her and pulled her tighter against my chest hoping that would help, but I was trembling against the cold just as much as she was. After the earthquake had stopped, I flew us all as far as my wings could carry the both of them, managing to cover a much greater distance than I had imagined possible, especially after so long being unable to use them in the dungeon. Eventually, I was forced to land and rest.

The memory of the sunlight dimming after that burst of light flared through the sky replayed in my mind. After witnessing my father perform the Current last summer, there was no mistaking that what we saw in the distance was exactly that. But how was that possible? If there were dragons taking in that much power, what did that mean for the coming battle? According to my father, the old language that was used during the ritual had passed away from Elysian knowledge long ago. Whoever performed it must have been very old to have known what to do and say. Could it have been Eklos? Would he be desperate enough for power to risk such a thing?

Dwelling on all the possibilities had my mind spinning in anxiety and I forced the thoughts away.

Though I never imagined I'd utter such words, I truly wished that Z were with us. If he were, he could have led us to another safe house, or perhaps he could have helped us avoid the battle with those four dragons. Then Kaida never would have been injured, and we could have been huddled by a hearth rather than in the frigid dirt.

But he wasn't with us, and we had no idea what had happened to him when we were forced to leave him behind at the safe house.

I was glad to be rid of him but I also… wasn't.

I bit my lip to hold in a sigh. According to my mother, we were roughly two days away from Metta. Two more days in this frozen tundra. Two more days of sleeping amongst the icy snow. Two more days of shivering, trying in vain to stay warm.

I glanced down at Kaida's arms in the faint light of the moon. They were wrapped tightly in bandages as the wounds from her wings healed. Though that dragon had dealt quite a bit of damage, they were healing quickly, much faster than even her dragon healing should've allowed. Another benefit to her Ancient Magic, perhaps?

Speaking of her magic, what she did to those mercenaries…

It still had my stomach curling in on itself; to see such raw, powerful magic not only being used, but being used by the kind-hearted, compassionate girl I loved. I would never be afraid of her, but part of me couldn't help but wonder how much more there was, and how much more she was capable of.

If she could obliterate two dragons just by combining two of her types of magic into a concentrated blow, then perhaps our chances against Eklos were better than we thought.

"You awake?" I whispered into her ear.

"I c-couldn't s-sleep even i-if I w-wanted to," she muttered.

"I know how to warm us up a little," I offered.

The moonlight reflected off her eyes as she snapped her gaze to mine.

I let out a soft chuckle. "Not what you're thinking." I poked her nose with my finger. It was cold as ice. "Since neither of us will be sleeping in this cold, let's head into the trees and see what else your magic can do."

Her eyes narrowed as she thought about it. "Isn't that risky?"

"We'll stay quiet and keep the flashy magic to a minimum." I winked at her, before easing to my feet.

My mother, likely having heard our plans, ignored our movement, and grabbed both of our bedrolls once we were on our feet and wrapped them around herself.

A gap opened up between the trees that was wide enough for the both of us to stand with a few feet between us. Summoning flames into my palms, I let out a sigh as the fire warmed my frozen fingers. Kaida must have seen the relief on my face because a heart-beat later she had her own white flames blossoming like a flower in her hands before it engulfed her entirely. I flinched, trying to reach her before she burned alive, but instead of a cry of pain she let out a groan.

"Why didn't we do this sooner?" she gasped.

I stared at her through wide eyes. She was completely covered in flames, but as I looked closer, the flames were only hovering above her skin, not touching it. Kaida was benefitting from the heat of her magic without hurting herself.

How?

Though I had good control over my own fire magic, I had never been able to cover myself like she currently was, not without burning my skin. At the thought, I touched the scarred skin over my cheek, wincing at the memory that resurfaced. Fire magic was not to be taken lightly, as even dragons could burn. My scars were hidden beneath the ilusai I cast so long ago, invisible even to myself, but I could still feel them.

"Why do you look so surprised?" Kaida asked, studying me through her white flames. "Can't you do this too?"

I lowered my hand, shaking my head. "No. I've never seen anyone do that. Not without burning themselves."

Kaida gaped at me before her teeth clicked as she shut her mouth. She glanced at my scars, her Ancient Magic allowing her to see past the illusion. "I… didn't know it was anything special. I just wanted to be warm, and my magic did it."

I arched a brow. "I wonder if you can extend that to another person or if it's limited to yourself?"

Her face grew pale behind the white flames.

"Why don't you try it?" I asked. "Try to cover me in flames."

Kaida gave a violent shake of her head. "No, Tarrin. I could hurt you. I couldn't live with myself if I accidentally—"

"I trust you," I interrupted. "Just try, love."

She hesitated for another moment, but then she blinked, seeming to steel herself, and clenched her hands into fists. She inhaled deeply before going still. The hairs on the back of my neck rose as Kaida slowly lifted her arms in front of her.

Then her eyes snapped open, lightning flashing within them, before she gave a simple gesture with her fingers and the white flames left her body, hurtling toward my own.

It was a feat of self-control to hold still, and not duck or dive out of the way. I told her I would trust her, so I dug my heels into the dirt and braced myself. The air grew hotter, more intense, with each inch it gained in my direction.

And then it was upon me.

Instinct opened my mouth to scream in pain, but I pressed my lips together as I realized it wasn't burning me. Like it did to Kaida, the flames simply hovered over my skin, offering me their warmth but leaving my skin untouched. A shaky laugh escaped through my lips.

I took a step toward her, expecting the flames to sputter out, but Kaida kept them burning, encompassing my body as I crossed the distance between us. I didn't stop when I stood in front of her, the corners of my lips twitching, as she stepped backward, matching each of my steps. There was no fear in her eyes; nothing but pride and love flickering in them between the flames smothering my vision.

I continued toward her, forcing her backward until her back met the trunk of a tree. A quiet gasp slipped through her lips at the surprise impact, and the fire surrounding me went out. A shiver ran through me as the winter air attacked my skin, but I pushed the cold from my mind, planting my hands on either side of her head, the rough ridges of the bark pressing into my palms. I leaned closer, relishing her body heat in the absence of the flames.

"You did it," I whispered, letting my lips graze the shell of her ear. "You're remarkable." Her cheeks reddened as I pulled back enough to see her face. I gave her the half smirk I knew she loved.

"See what happens when you push on, despite your fears?" I asked.

A soft smile bent her lips. "You were right," she muttered, fixing her gaze on my chest.

I leaned in closer, cocking my head. "I'm sorry, I didn't quite hear you. What was that?"

"You were right," she laughed, giving a playful shove at my shoulder.

I grinned before pressing my lips to hers, and stepped closer, wrapping my arms around her waist as hers tightened around my neck. The air pooled between our faces as our breaths grew quicker, until a loud crack close by broke us apart.

Kaida's head swung in the direction the noise had come. "What was that?"

I lifted a shoulder. "Probably just an animal." I leaned in to kiss her again.

She pressed a finger to my lips. "That wasn't an animal." Even in the dark, I could see her eyes roving through the woods, searching for possible enemies. Her palm rested on my chest, the heat of it like a fire burning through fabric and skin.

Kaida ducked beneath my arms and walked a few paces farther into the trees. Everything was silent save for the sounds of our breathing. Could one of Eklos's mercenaries have found us? Was it Rythos? My stomach sank at the thought.

"Kaida," I whispered, trying to keep her from going too far. If there was an enemy in the woods, we needed to leave, not search for them.

Another crack sounded, closer than before and I leaped after her. We needed to run. Had my mother heard the noise? Or was she still asleep beneath the stars?

The sound of rustling and twigs cracking grew louder, and I grabbed Kaida's wrist in my hand.

We need to go. We can't risk another fight.

She turned to look at me over her shoulder. A faint glow illuminated her eyes, similar to what happened when her inner beast took control. Did her dragon form sense danger? Was it trying to protect or shove her away so it could quench that bloodlust that Kaida mentioned so long ago?

She opened her mouth, to say what I didn't know, when a crack followed by a groan sounded mere yards away.

They were too close.

I tugged on Kaida's arm again, but her brow furrowed as she turned back toward the direction of the noise.

I don't think—she started to say down the shifter bond when a familiar voice crooned through the trees.

"Well, well, well. Isn't this a pleasant surprise."

My insides coiled tightly, though I wasn't sure if it was more from apprehension or annoyance.

"Look who we've found."

A dark, ocean-blue dragon emerged from the trees into a shaft of moonlight.

It was Z.

CHAPTER 30

ELDRIN

"LOOK WHO WE'VE found," Z crooned from several steps ahead of me.

My stomach dropped as I expected it to be a dragon mercenary, or even Eklos himself, but the tone of his voice wasn't fearful or apprehensive. It almost sounded… happy.

I quickened my steps to catch up to him, peeking around his shoulder.

Relief, like the first breath of air after being submerged under water for too long, flooded my veins at the sight of Kaida and Tarrin. Though my daughter's arms were wrapped in bandages, she appeared to be all right. I spied Lita standing in the background, staying within the shadows of the trunks.

The last time I had seen Kaida, it had been the night before she left Shegora to go after Tarrin. I glanced at the young Prince. I didn't know how long it had been since he was rescued, but dark circles sat stubbornly under his eyes, his cheeks and collarbone sharp beneath his skin. His clothes hung loosely on his body, and his arms and hands looked skeletal.

But he was alive. And so was my daughter.

Though I wasn't one for affection, I shifted into human form and rushed over to them, pulling each of them into my arms.

"I'm so glad to see you," I said into their ears before I pulled back to study my daughter's face. Weeks on the road had not been kind to her. Dirt was smeared over her forehead, her skin tight against her bones, though not as severe as Tarrin's.

"What are you doing here, Eldrin?" Kaida asked me.

I opened my mouth to answer when another voice interrupted me.

"While it's good to see you, little shifter, might I suggest we save the talking and noise-making until we're somewhere safe?" Z commented, his gaze roving back and forth between the three of us.

The comment brought Kaida's attention back to him, and she stilled.

"You're alive," she breathed.

My daughter stalked straight for Z, her footsteps crunching in the snow. When she stopped before him, a burning glare on her face, she shifted into dragon form, slapped Z across the face, then shifted back into human form, pointing a finger at him as she scolded, "Don't you *ever* do that again, Z."

The dragon froze, putting a scaled palm to his face. "Do what?" he barked in return.

"Decide to sacrifice yourself so that we could escape. You could've been killed!" She paused, breathing hard. "Eklos could have killed you!" Her voice cracked on the last words, angry tears spilling from her eyes.

Z's outraged face softened. "I would do it again in a heartbeat, little shifter, if it meant keeping you safe."

I felt an odd emotion surge down the shape-shifter bond, as Tarrin watched their exchange, accompanied by a new scent.

Where had I smelled it before? Were they... *cor unum*?

Well then. That explained the roar of jealousy coming through the bond.

"No, you wo—"

"How did you escape?" Tarrin interrupted. Kaida shot him

an angry look, but Z looked relieved that he had put a stop to whatever my daughter had been about to say.

Rather than the signature smirk I had come to associate with Z, instead, his snout twisted into a grimace.

"We can talk once we're safe. We need to get moving." He glanced at the sky which was beginning to lighten. Dawn was close. "We're still too far from Metta, but I have a place we can go until night falls again. We can talk more once we get there."

Without another word, Z turned, his wings held in tight as he pushed through the trees. Kaida and Tarrin glanced at each other, their silent thoughts passing down the bond, though they effectively shut me out. Linking hands, they followed Z, leaving me and Lita to bring up the rear. It was the first time I had seen her since we were forced to split up at the cottage before going to Shegora. I gestured for her to go first, as the sudden silence pressed in on us.

"Are you angry with me?" she asked after a moment.

"Angry? What for?" I asked, eyes widening.

She ran a hand over her hair, avoiding my stare. "For not coming to Shegora. For choosing to stay away when the battle with Eklos was looming."

I shook my head. "I don't blame you for following your gut, Lita. I know that if you truly felt that was the right decision it was for a reason, even if it was difficult to accept."

She glanced at me, something flashing in her eyes, before she nodded and continued through the woods.

The wind began to pick up overhead, rustling the leaves, creating enough noise to cover the crunches and cracks of our footsteps. The temperature dropped by the minute, and I was just about to ask Z how much farther when he veered off to the right, stopping at a wall of rock.

"Great," Kaida muttered. "Another house in a rock. Because those have been working out so well thus far." She rolled her eyes and crossed her arms as Z turned to scowl at her.

"I don't see you with a better idea, little shifter."

"Will we be attacked here too, forced to leave you behind again?" she spat, her hands clenched into fists.

"Kaida," I murmured. "You don't know what we've been through—what *he's* been through. Let's get inside and give him a chance to explain."

She held my gaze for another moment, before she snapped, "Fine."

Tarrin eyed the rock, rubbing his chin. "Do you just have magic rock houses all over Elysia?" he asked.

Z ran his claws over the door in an odd pattern before a loud click sounded and the door swung inward. He looked over a shoulder. "Living life as a rebel requires having hidden places to go if you're caught in the act of rebelling." With a wink, he led us inside.

Ψ

Night drew closer, though in a house with no windows, none of us knew the difference. Two couches and four oversized chairs littered the space, with a table near the cupboards, and a small table between all the furniture. The moment we had entered the house, the white cloths that had been covering everything were ripped off and each of us collapsed onto the cushions. Lita sat in an armchair closest to the fire, Kaida and Tarrin were sprawled across one couch, Z's enormous dragon form filling another, and I sat in human form opposite Lita.

"All right," Kaida declared. "We're inside, we're somewhat safe. Let's hear it. How did you escape?" She fixed those turquoise eyes, so much like Aela's, on me. "And why are *you* here?"

I huffed out a laugh, though nothing was very funny, glancing at Z, and he gestured for me to go first.

My silver hair slid through my fingers as I ran a hand through it. "Rythos caught me as I left Shegora."

Three sudden intakes of breath echoed between the rock walls.

"How?" Kaida asked.

"Gendon led a group of us out of Shegora, back to Metta to prepare for war." At her confused look I added, "The elders of Metta have offered the town up as a battleground for the war with Eklos. They know the journey to Shegora is too difficult for most to join us, so they offered us the village. His son, Phelix, will help move the elderly, children, and any who don't wish to fight away from the village, and those that remain are prepared to help us defeat the army. They want all of Elysia to prosper like Metta has, and if sacrificing all they've gained brings that about, then they're willing to do it."

"Wow," Tarrin said.

I nodded in agreement before continuing. "We hadn't seen any sign of enemies on the mountain, so we all left Shegora; I brought up the rear. I should have expected Rythos not to leave us alone. I should have anticipated that he would be hiding amongst the snow and pine trees. When I finally saw him, I tried to escape, tried to get to Metta, but he managed to grab my arm. That's all it took." I glanced at Tarrin, knowing he knew exactly what I meant. The Prince winced.

"Where did he take you?" Kaida asked, wringing her hands in her lap.

Z straightened on the couch. "To the center of Eklos's army. The same place I was brought after the Remnant captured me at the safe house."

"*What?*" Kaida and Tarrin said in unison.

He nodded. "After you three escaped through the tunnel, the house was overrun with Eklos's dragons. Even if I had tried to get away, there were simply too many of them. I surrendered, letting them take me rather than fighting to the death. Next thing I knew I was chained in the army's camp."

Tarrin stiffened. "What did he do to you?" he asked in a low voice.

Z adjusted his position on the couch, tucking his wings in tighter. "Outside of a little scuffle with Eklos, they left me chained in the cold winter air, and didn't touch me."

"That's hard to believe," Kaida replied. "Why would they capture you and leave you unharmed?"

Z shrugged, saying nothing more.

Suspicion flared in my mind as I studied the dragon while the words of Eklos came back to me. Z used to work for him; used to be part of the Remnant. Though Z was adamant that he left those ways long ago, was there a chance he was lying? Could he still be working for Eklos? Eklos had explained why he hadn't killed me yet, but didn't say anything about Z.

Kaida was right. It seemed too convenient—and very uncharacteristic of Eklos—to capture Z but not to torture or abuse him. I would have expected a rebel that defected to receive the worst Eklos had to offer.

I studied the dragon. His huge body was the epitome of relaxed, and the expression on his face almost looked… bored.

He had done nothing except help our cause, but could he be planning to betray us?

Our escape from the army camp had been too easy, especially when Eklos revealed his plan to torture me as a punishment for Kaida. There should have been someone watching us; someone around to make sure we didn't escape. But there had been no one and we made it farther than we should have before the alarms sounded. Did Eklos allow us to escape so Z could lead the army right to us?

"What did Eklos say when you were brought to the camp?" Kaida asked me.

I waved a hand. "The usual. 'I'm going to kill you all.' Nothing new." My nonchalance was meant to be humorous, but no one chuckled. No one smiled.

"Well, how did you escape?" Tarrin asked, tucking Kaida in tighter to his side.

"Z's magic," I replied, glancing at him.

"And then Eldrin foolishly jumped us to the Zenduro Wastes and then, even more foolishly, performed the Current to jump us back out." Z rolled his eyes when he finished speaking.

"That was you?" Tarrin asked, eyes wide.

"We would have died in the desert, and I wasn't sure how far into the Wastes my magic had initially brought us. The only way I could think of to gather enough power to get us out of there was to draw on the sun. Although…" I paused, casting a glance at Z. "It didn't feel like a normal Current."

Z snorted. "He almost killed himself and the sun."

The three other humans in the room gaped.

"Don't exaggerate, Z." I sighed, rubbing a hand over my face.

"You weren't watching as both you and the sun turned black, Eldrin. If I hadn't stopped you, you'd be dead and who knows what would have happened to the sun."

Lita cleared her throat. "There's more than one reason why it is against our laws for ordinary dragons to perform the Current, Eldrin. Though I've never seen it with my own eyes, my own father passed stories down to me, explaining what would happen." She looked to Z. "It's what you described. Since it was neither the Solstice nor performed with the power of the King of Elysia, the magic began a process of self-destruction. It would've killed Eldrin, and the sun would have been irreparably damaged."

Silence filled the room in the wake of her explanation.

"That was a dangerous chance you took," Lita remarked, her eyes narrowed on me.

"It was the only way."

Lita sighed. "Well, at least we know it was you and not someone dangerous like Eklos."

"Hey, I can be dangerous."

Her only response was a smirk.

Kaida's brow furrowed and changed the subject. "Wait, I thought you were chained up." She looked at Z. "You wouldn't have been able to use magic to escape."

Z huffed out an annoyed breath. "I'm old, that's how."

"How evasive of you, Z," Kaida drawled, and the dragon stiffened. "Tell us."

Z hesitated another moment before saying, "As you wish, little shifter."

A scowl twisted her lips, but she clenched her hands into fists and waited. When it failed to get a response, Z sighed and adjusted his position on the couch.

"Would you accept that I'm impervious to iron?"

She narrowed her eyes. "No, I would not."

Z rolled his eyes and muttered, "Of course not."

"Enough stalling," Tarrin said. "Out with it."

Z's snout spread into that signature smirk. "Fine. A long time ago I found a way to dig beneath the iron that nullified our magic to be able to use it. Like I told Eldrin at the camp, the iron substance is like a lock. All you need is a key to unlock it and the magic is usable."

"But how?" I demanded.

"When I told you I was old, Eldrin, I meant it. It's a forgotten magic, lost to history; not many remember it. Your magic essentially takes on the characteristics of the iron so that the iron can't tell the difference between your magic and itself. Then you can use it."

"Can you show us?" Kaida asked as she sat forward, her eyes bright.

Z shook his snout. "I'm afraid it would take far longer to teach and master than we have time for. Especially not before Eklos makes his final move."

She sank back into the couch and crossed her arms. "Then what do we do?"

"Not get captured and put in iron shackles?" Z offered in his usual sarcastic tone.

Anger flared through the shifter bond like something hot and slimy, but she tamped it down, her throat bobbing as she swallowed.

"You're as helpful as always, Z." Kaida pushed to her feet before stalking across the room to the small bathing room at the back of the house.

Z had the audacity to look surprised at her sudden departure. "Was it something I said?"

"You just can't be serious for one moment, can you?" Tarrin spat. "The entire time we've known you, you've been secretive, hiding things from us. Things that could help us win against Eklos. I'm starting to wonder if you're really on our side."

"Of course, I'm on your side, you foolish prince. We simply don't have the time before the army attacks to teach all of you what I know. Thousands of years of knowledge and magic practice cannot be condensed into a matter of days."

Tarrin's eyes widened.

"Yes, Prince. Days. That's all we have before war descends on Elysia."

"How do you know that?" I asked, sitting forward to lean my elbows on my knees.

The fire to my left was far too warm, though I noticed Lita curling even closer. Outside of her explanation about the Current, she had been strangely silent throughout the rest of our conversation.

"I overheard the Remnant speaking before they brought me to the camp. They were planning to move soon."

"Move where?" Tarrin asked.

Z lifted his claws into the air. "I didn't hear, though I imagine Rythos has reported that everyone left Shegora since he caught Eldrin. Whether he knows about Metta or not, I don't know, but

I imagine they have a general idea of where to strike. And now that Eldrin and I have escaped, I'm sure that will only hasten their movements."

"How many days?" I asked.

I tried not to be too suspicious of him, but the fact that Eklos had been discussing his plans somewhere where Z could hear, and that he was just mentioning it to us now didn't sit right with me.

"I don't know that either. If I had to guess, perhaps a little over a week?"

Tarrin blew out an exasperated breath.

My thoughts drifted to Noam who I had sent on a desperate mission before we had left Mistwick, chasing after a myth. My stomach sank at the realization that I likely sent him to his death. And even if he had succeeded, I didn't know how he would know when to return, when we would need him most.

Perhaps I should have simply been grateful that my only friend wouldn't be here for the upcoming battle.

"So, we have a week to make it to Metta and get the village ready," Tarrin summarized.

Z only nodded.

"What do we do then? Sit and wait for an army of dragons to arrive and slaughter us all?"

"No," Lita replied, meeting her son's gaze. "We prepare for war."

CHAPTER 31

KAIDA

THE ANGER WAS like a living thing, burning inside me. It was different from the fire that burned in my core. It was hotter, darker. Rather than feeding me, it drained me, and I felt both immensely heavy and incredibly light at the same time.

I sat in the copper bathtub tucked in the corner of the bathing room behind a white screen, watching tendrils of steam waft above the water. I had to clench my fists beneath the surface to keep my magic at bay—to keep it from lashing out and boiling me alive within. My head clanked against the back of the tub as I leaned back, staring at the ceiling.

I didn't know what it was, what was causing this darkness inside me.

Z had always gotten under my skin—that was nothing new. That couldn't be the cause now, so what was it? Why was I fighting this now? Why did my mind feel like I was swimming in black ink?

A knock sounded at the door and my entire body tensed. I barely stopped my magic from leaking out of my fingertips and turning the water to ice. I blew out a shaky breath. I had to get a better grip. Whatever this… thing was, it was causing my magic to act wild, making me lose control.

"Yes?" I croaked out, thankful that there was a screen blocking the tub.

"Kaida?" It was Lita. "May I come in for a moment?"

I hesitated for a heartbeat before I rose from the bathtub, quickly dried off, and wrapped myself in a silk robe that had been left on a shelf. When I was decent, I called for her to enter.

Lita's dark hair billowed in waves, nearly to her waist now, as she entered, peeking around the room until she found me. A tense smile spread across her lips, and she held her hands together in front of her.

"Feel a little better?" she asked, gesturing at the copper tub.

I nodded, furrowing my brows as I noticed her fidgeting with her fingers. Why did she seem nervous? The steam from the tub made the air sticky and I shifted uncomfortably as the silk of the robe stuck to my skin.

"Good." She leaned against the wall next to the door. "I wanted to…" She paused, rubbing at her forehead. "I'm sorry, Kaida. I should have been there."

At my confused expression she continued.

"I should have been there as you crossed Silverdew Valley. Perhaps if I had been there, Rythos wouldn't have gotten a hold of Tarrin. Instead of spending so much time tracking him down, you could have been preparing for the battle with Eklos."

I cocked my head. "I don't think you being there would have made a difference. That dragon would have attacked and gotten ahold of one of us, whether it was Tarrin or not. You made the decision to stay because you felt you were where you were supposed to be. If you hadn't been in Vernista, I couldn't have found him." I narrowed my eyes. "Besides, what do you think you would have done against Rythos?"

Lita rubbed at her forehead. "I don't know. Sometimes… it feels like all of this is some terrible dream; that if only I could wake up, I'd be a dragon again. Though months have passed, I still find myself forgetting that my dragon form is gone."

"Lita, you're one of the strongest people I know. Only the very best of us could choose to sacrifice ourselves for the sake of another, face down death, and still be able to laugh in its dark face."

She cocked her head as if she were considering my words.

"I can only imagine how difficult it must be, losing that part of you. Sometimes, at least lately, I wish I wasn't a shape-shifter. Though my life was harder as a human, it was much simpler." I crossed my arms. "Be grateful, Lita, that you have a second chance. You have the chance to fight back even after everything was taken from you. Not everyone gets that. Use your anger to fuel you, not hide away."

Lita arched a brow. "When did you get so wise? Your words sound like something I would have said long ago."

I shrugged. "Perhaps you rubbed off on me. In either case, stop focusing on all the things you can no longer do and instead look at what you've accomplished. You managed to infiltrate Eklos's inner circle and sway some of his dragons to our side. That is *not* nothing. You found a way to keep your son alive until we could rescue him. You've provided supplies and shelter when we had none. Do not underestimate your value or what you've given us. You may be Lita the human now, but you're still powerful."

She let out a slow, steady breath, considering. "Perhaps you're right."

"The bigger question is," I continued, staring her down, "why do you keep letting my father and Z dictate our actions? You were the Queen of Elysia, trained in strategy and ruler of this country. But instead, you stay silent, withdrawn. Why?"

Lita stilled, blinking at me as if she had never realized such a thing.

"You're still useful, Lita, even as a human. Don't let Eklos win by allowing yourself to withdraw into the darkness of your mind. He wants you to feel small and insignificant. But you were and still are meant for greatness. You are strong."

Even as I said the words, they clanged through me, having battled that similar darkness just moments ago. As if my words were a soothing tea, the burning in my veins settled, reducing to embers. Not gone, but manageable.

"Thank you, Kaida," Lita said after a moment. "As a human I felt I had nothing to offer, especially when preparing for a battle against dragons. But you've reminded me that strength isn't just physical, it's mental too. Eklos wins if I keep cowering as I have been. And you're right. I have centuries of knowledge and training. That is not nothing."

She straightened, pushing off the wall. "You have a strength, too, Kaida. One that I don't think you even realize you have. Don't be afraid of it. Don't hide from it."

Without another word, she left me in the steam and candle-light of the room.

附

My dreams that night were heavy, like swimming through mud. Brutal scenes of battles or growing up with Eklos when I was a child flashed through my mind, over and over, faster and faster, never staying in one place for long.

Until suddenly… it stopped.

I stood in the middle of Silverdew Valley, the snow gone, and in its place was vibrant, thick green grass. Warm, balmy air coated my skin, such a welcome change from the winter air. The sun was just beginning to rise over the mountains, casting the valley in a golden glow, and illuminating the silver dew that laid on each individual blade of grass.

I would have thought the sight was beautiful, perhaps would have wanted to lie down and welcome the thick blanket of grass beneath me, if it weren't for who stood across from me.

Light-gray scales glinted in the sunlight, casting rainbows over the ground. His eyes were closed, head tilted toward the sky and wings flared wide.

Rythos.

Why was he in my dream?

My fingers tensed, itching to grab for a weapon, wishing I had even a dagger strapped to my leg. But my pockets were empty, and my fingers brushed nothing but fabric.

"Don't bother," Rythos said, keeping his eyes closed. "You can't hurt me here even if you had a weapon."

I narrowed my eyes at him. "What are you talking about?"

His eyes snapped open, and his head cocked when he looked at me. "We're in a dream. This isn't real. Stab me all you like, but you can't kill me."

My hands clenched into fists. "Why are you here? Don't you bother me enough in real life?"

Rythos tsked. "You tell me."

"You have magic to infiltrate my dreams now?"

He rolled his orange eyes. "Don't be ridiculous. You created this dream. This was all your doing."

"You're lying."

His snout spread into a slow smile. "Am I? Don't you think if I had the power to haunt your dreams and torment you, I would have already done so? This is all you, shifter."

I rubbed at my forehead. Could this have been yet another manifestation of Ancient Magic? Or was Rythos lying, and this was just made up in my head?

Either way, neither of us could hurt the other, and for the first time since I had first seen him, Rythos truly seemed relaxed, basking in the sunlight, enjoying the warmth of the valley.

I plopped down into the grass, running my fingers through the soft blades. "So, where are you?" I asked, trying to see if he'd give me any information. If I was stuck in a dream with him, it might as well be a useful one.

The gray dragon rolled his eyes. "Do you think I'm stupid, shifter? I'm not telling you anything."

I grabbed a fistful of grass and yanked it, watching as pebbles of dirt sprinkled the ground. Rythos watched me through narrowed eyes, but kept his scaled lips closed.

"So…" I started, hoping he would start talking.

"You might as well end this dream, girl. I won't spill his secrets. I'm not going to betray Eklos."

I ran my hand across the tops of the grass again. "Why not? You know he'd betray *you* in a heartbeat."

The dragon shook his large head. "No, he wouldn't."

I scoffed. "Clearly you don't know him very well. That's the only thing in his blood: cruelty and betrayal."

Rythos turned his head, avoiding my stare. "I've been nothing but loyal to him. He would never turn his back on me."

"Scales, does he have you fooled. Don't you think that the moment you give him what he wants, the three of us shifters, you'll be cast off to the side? He'll no longer have a need for you."

"Your words are nothing but poison," he growled.

I sat up on my knees. "You could join us, Rythos," I said, ignoring his words. "Eklos is going to lose, and when he does, all of you, every dragon of the Remnant and the army will be killed. And he won't hesitate to take down whomever he can with him, especially if he thinks it will save his life. Join *us* instead. Help us. Tell us what you know, and we'll spare you when we meet in battle."

For a moment he seemed to consider it before he leaped toward me, wrapping his claws around my neck and squeezing. My lungs constricted and I gasped for air. How was he hurting me? It shouldn't have been possible.

"Do not try to turn me against Eklos," he spit, embers flying from his mouth and landing on my skin, forcing me to wince. "I will tell you nothing, and when I see you in Metta, I will kill you all."

His claws burrowed deep into my skin, and I could feel hot

blood running down my neck. My heartbeat thrashed in my ears as I coughed and fought for air, but Rythos only squeezed tighter. I scratched and clawed at him, but he didn't relent, his orange eyes burning with a fiery hatred.

My vision pulsed and I knew I was seconds away from losing consciousness… or whatever it was I'd lose when I was already asleep.

"Wake up!" Rythos snarled, slamming my head into the ground.

My eyes snapped open to a dark room, mighty coughs wracking through my throat as I fought to catch my breath.

"Kaida?" Tarrin's voice sounded from the doorway, though it was too dark to see him. I heard the faint sound of his footsteps as I continued to gasp for breath.

"Kaida? What is it?" Tarrin asked, rubbing the sleep from his eyes, and sitting on the edge of the bed.

"Rythos," I coughed out, my voice hoarse as if the dragon had truly been choking me.

Though I could barely make out his face in the dark, I could see his brow lower over his eyes, his hands clenching into fists in his lap.

"What about him?" he demanded.

It took another moment for my heart to slow, for the air filling my lungs to no longer be painful. I gingerly touched my neck, expecting to feel puncture holes from his claws or blood but there was nothing. It was smooth, like he had never touched me.

"Kaida?" Tarrin repeated, taking my hand between his. "What about Rythos?"

I blew out a shaky breath, realizing for the first time what he had revealed in that split moment of anger. I met Tarrin's gaze.

"They're headed for Metta."

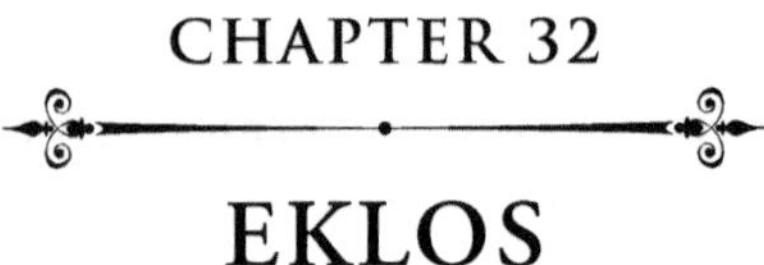

CHAPTER 32

EKLOS

"WHAT HAPPENED?" I barked, skewering Rythos with my eyes. He was seated in a cushioned chair in the middle of my tent, rubbing his claws over his temples as if he had a headache. I wished he would just leave me be.

I'd had enough of the other dragons complaining. The constant whining about the cold temperatures, many of the newer recruits wanting to return home… I quickly put an end to those fools. The army was not hurting for numbers, so I felt no remorse. If they weren't fully on board with our mission of ridding Elysia of the shifters and humans and wanted it enough to overcome the challenges of the winter weather, then I didn't want them, and they didn't deserve to see the future of this world. It also served as an example for those who foolishly considered defying me.

"She… the girl," Rythos hesitated, and I clenched my teeth against the urge to hit him.

Despite his previous failure, he had been a good spy thus far. After seeing his old friend again after hundreds of years, there had been the possibility of him turning against me; reuniting with Eldrin and joining him, even after I meticulously fueled his anger over Eldrin's betrayal as a youngling.

But seeing him again only fueled Rythos's anger and hatred more; poisoned him deeper than my lies ever could. So far, he had been more than willing to do my dirty work. It was only because of that fact that my hand was stayed, that I kept my claws clenched in fists, rather than pummeling into his face again.

"Spit it out. I don't have all day."

"The girl, she infiltrated my dream."

I bared my teeth. "How?"

"I don't know. I was hoping you would know and could tell me how to prevent it from happening again."

"Explain it to me," I demanded.

"I went to sleep, and everything was normal. And then a strange prickling sensation spread over me, and I opened my eyes, within the dream, and I was back in Silverdew Valley. The snow was gone, and the girl was standing next to me."

"What did she say?"

Rythos hesitated for a moment before shaking his head. "Nothing of importance. She didn't believe me that the dream wasn't my doing."

I arched a scaled eyebrow. The girl could control dreams?

Tucking my ash-colored wings into my back, I paced across the length of my tent, pondering how such a thing was possible. Dragons with the magic of Foresight often had dreams of the future, but never had I heard of them controlling dreams. If she were truly able to do such a thing, it complicated everything. She could communicate with anyone in Elysia, call for aid against my army, and I could do nothing to stop it.

Flames burned on my tongue. "And what, exactly, did *you* tell her in this dream?" I asked, voice low and lethal.

Rythos closed his eyes, and it was all the answer I needed. With a mighty thrust of my wings, I was in his face, my claws wrapped around his scaled throat despite my earlier reservations of doing so.

"What. Did. You. Tell. Her?" I yelled, smoke leaking from my nostrils. I squeezed tighter.

"I… didn't tell her… anything," he coughed out.

I narrowed my eyes. "You're telling me that in a dream where she had the control, she didn't get any information out of you?"

Rythos shook his large head as much as he was able to.

"After everything I've done for you," I spit, embers popping between my teeth. "I took you in when that infernal shifter left you all alone. You were an orphan. You had *nothing* until I took you under my wing. I gave you purpose and a place in the Remnant. And now you dare to lie to me?"

"I would never, Master Eklos." His eyes widened as I squeezed harder. "I didn't tell her anything. She spewed her usual poison, saying you'd betray me and that I should join them and—" He paused, and fear flickered in his eyes.

I fought to hold the fire inside me and not follow my instinct to burn the dragon alive.

"And what?" Blood seeped down his neck from where my claws dug under his scales.

"Metta," he whispered. "I told her we'd see them in Metta."

Everything inside me went preternaturally still, even my smoke curling back into itself, my inner fire banking and dimming.

The one thing we had on our side; the surprise of knowing about the village and knowing where to find them…

It was gone.

And then, as if my magic caught up to the severity of the position Rythos had put us in by revealing that information, I detonated, fire exploding out of me, burning everything to embers and ash.

CHAPTER 33

TARRIN

"WHAT DO YOU mean you had a dream with Rythos?" Eldrin asked, his amethyst eyes flaring wide.

Kaida shook her head. "I don't have any idea how I did it. He was adamant that it wasn't him doing it."

Eldrin, sitting in a chair by the hearth, looked at my mother, and arched a brow. "Did you ever have that ability with Foresight?"

Her lips pursed before she gave a shake of her head, her long dark-brown hair swaying with the movement. "I *had* dreams of the future, but I never *started* them, or linked minds with others."

I rubbed at my chin, the fire in the hearth making the room uncomfortably warm, especially with so many bodies shoved in a small space.

"And you're sure it was real—that you were truly talking to him?" Z asked Kaida, his eyes narrowed.

"I'm sure. It was real."

"It must be another manifestation of the Ancient Magic," Eldrin muttered.

My mother leaned back in her chair and crossed one leg over the other. "The only option now is to head for Metta—as fast as we can. We need to warn them. Whether Eklos just discovered the village and is making plans to attack or if the army is already on their way there remains to be seen, but we can delay no longer."

All of us, save for Kaida, blinked at her. It was the first time that she had really spoken up or offered input. My muscles loosened, and I noticed Eldrin's shoulders droop infinitesimally as if he felt the relief of having a piece of her come alive again.

But Kaida… She didn't seem surprised, but instead had a smug smile on her face, as if she expected my mother to finally emerge from wherever her mind had secluded to over the last few months.

"We should leave soon, before the sun rises, and take to the sky. We need to get as far as we can while the dark of night can still hide us," my mother added.

"And when dawn comes?" I asked.

Kaida adjusted her position on the couch next to me. "Then we'll move above the clouds, try to remain unseen. Lita's right, we don't have time to waste anymore. We need to make it to Metta and warn them before it's too late."

Z cleared his throat, watching her closely. "Well, then it's settled then. Everyone pack up and prepare to move out. We have about two hours until the sun breaks the horizon. Let's make them count."

ℛ

Before dawn could grace the sky, we left the safety of Z's rock house and fled as fast as we could for Metta. My mother rode on Eldrin's back, Z next to him, while Kaida flew with me. Though her wings were mostly healed, they were still tender enough to keep her from flying.

What if they beat us there? Kaida asked through our bond. *What if there's nothing left of Metta? We brought this upon them, Tarrin.*

I slid a mental hand down the bond, trying to soothe her.

It'll be all right. We'll get there in time.

We don't even know where the army is! What if they were almost to the village when Rythos said that?

I shook my head, flinging ice crystals from my eyelids as they condensed in the frigid air.

I don't think they've traveled there, love. I think that was truly a slip of Rythos's tongue. They may be headed in that direction, but I think we have enough time to get there and warn the village.

I felt her shudder through the bond, and I wished we weren't flying through the cold winter night so that I could wrap my arms around her. All I wanted to do was protect her. It was a deep, primal need within me. But more than needing me to protect her, I felt she needed me to remind her of how strong she was; how brave. That she was not the darkness inside her; that festers in all of us dragons.

So, I would keep reminding her; keep fighting *for* her and *with* her rather than tucking her away from all the dangers in Elysia, as much as a part of me wanted to.

I hope you're right, she replied.

Pink tendrils erupted on the horizon as the sun finally started to peek its face over the earth.

Let's glide up, get above the clouds, Eldrin's voice came down the bond.

My wings thudded in the air as I flapped in a few mighty thrusts to take us above the dense white puffs that would hopefully keep us hidden from Eklos's mercenaries… wherever they were. Fortunately, the clouds were dark and dense today, promising yet another storm.

Wouldn't that just be the cherry on top, to race for a village about to be destroyed by the might of Eklos, only to be slowed by a storm in the sky.

As if the thought had summoned it, lightning flickered in the distance, and I watched in unison as Z and Eldrin both slowed, waiting for me to catch up to them.

"It would not be wise to fly through a lightning storm!" Eldrin yelled against the wind.

"What choice do we have?" Z retorted. "We can't waste the time it would take for the storm to pass."

Something moved in the corner of my eye, and I turned to see Kaida no longer on my back but flapping next to me, wincing against her sore wings.

"Kaida, what are you doing? Your wings are still healing."

She shook her head. "We don't have time."

Lightning forked above us, and she turned her attention toward it.

And through the bond I could feel... something awaken in Kaida.

"I'll take care of it," she murmured, the sound almost lost in the roaring wind and with a great flap of her wings, she burst forward.

"Kaida! No!" I shouted.

"Where is she going?" Z demanded.

I shook my head, my tongue sticking to the roof of my mouth as I watched her amethyst form soar straight into the heart of the storm that had quickly formed into a writhing beast in front of us.

And then my heart turned to ice in my chest as Kaida stopped just before the darkest, thickest cloud, spinning faster and faster up into it, when a glowing purple streak of lightning struck the center of her body.

CHAPTER 34

KAIDA

THE LIGHTNING WAS hot.

Hotter than the forge-heated tools that Eklos used to torture me with.

Hotter than the fire whip that he employed on his disobedient slaves.

While I had never flown into the sun before, I imagined it was even hotter than that, too.

The moment it struck my scales, it forked through my blood, super heating it. I felt the power of the strike infuse with my own magic.

I didn't know exactly what it was that told me to go after the storm. It wasn't as if the force of it could speak to me, but something inside me told me to fly to the center and take the power of the lightning for myself.

Ancient Magic was powerful and strong, but was it strong enough to protect me from dying in a lightning storm? Was I flying toward my death in a foolish attempt at stopping my friends from being killed?

The moment the lightning touched me, those thoughts vanished, and the only thing running through my mind was the enormous strength, heat, and flood of power now running through my veins. It crackled between my claws, circling each of my fingers.

I wasn't sure what to do with it, but my inner beast seemed to as I circled my hands in front of me, encasing me in a ball of that white-hot lightning. Another flash, and I felt the impact as another bolt struck my shield, but it didn't penetrate. The thunder that followed was deafening.

The sleet picked up, pummeling my scales like tiny pebbles. It was so heavy that I could barely make out the three dragons behind me, keeping their distance. I studied their dark shapes. Could I expand the shield and cover the others to protect them like I did when I covered Tarrin in flames?

If not, we'd have to wait until it passed. We didn't have time for that.

With a flick of my claws, the lightning shield vanished, and I turned to fly back toward the others.

"I have an idea!" I shouted over the sleet that whipped through the air, fixing my gaze on Tarrin. "I think I can shield us until we fly out of the storm."

I swore I saw fear flickering in Eldrin's and Z's eyes before they both gained control of their expressions.

Tarrin's eyes narrowed before he gave a nod. Even if my father and Z were hesitant, I knew Tarrin trusted me—trusted that I wouldn't hurt him. That confidence alone had me unafraid of what I was about to do. The old Kaida would never have dared such a dangerous feat, but Tarrin's belief in me helped me conquer any fear trying to rise to the surface.

His turquoise wings flapped against the wind until he was as close to me as he could get. Z and Eldrin were slow to follow, but eventually all three of them created a half circle around me.

"Hold still," I commanded, turning my gaze to the dark clouds above us.

Doubt slithered through my mind like a poisonous worm.

Could I truly summon a shield of such power that encompassed our enormous bodies, and then hold it in place until we flew out of the storm? The possibility that I would lose control was great; so many things could go wrong. I looked to Tarrin once more and found his green eyes fixed on me, an emotion akin to pride flickering in them.

You can do this, he said through the bond.

Steeling my nerves with a mighty breath, I closed my eyes for a moment and felt that lightning return to my palms, a series of light shocks traveling up my arms. Feeling the magic in my core swell and spread, I called to the storm, bid the lightning to shield us, protect us, rather than harm us.

I heard several intakes of breath before Tarrin murmured down the bond.

Kaida, open your eyes.

My scaled lids were heavy as I slid them open, and I gasped against the sight. Purple and white streaks of lightning formed into an enormous ball that covered all of us, resembling a cage. Extreme heat emanated from the shield, like a hot summer day in Vernista—only worse. It stole the oxygen from my lungs. But that wasn't even what made me pause.

No.

It was the patterns.

Flowers made entirely of purple lightning, vines and branches and leaves, all intertwined among the streaks, as if the very essence of Elysia was forged by the storm into the shield I held around us. I expected to feel my magic draining from the force of it, but it remained steady, a constant give and take as the lightning both fueled my magic and reinforced the shield.

I could see the purple and white lights reflecting in Tarrin's eyes as he looked around us in wonder.

You're incredible, love, he said at last.

Z cleared his throat, breaking the moment. "Perhaps we

should start moving before the storm develops a mind of its own and decides we'd be better off dead and crispy."

With a roll of my eyes, I gestured forward with my claws, and we moved in tandem inside the cage, pushing on through the dark clouds. The shield did nothing to protect us from the sleet that slammed into our scales like tiny knives, nor from the winds that forced our wings to work harder. It didn't take long before we were all out of breath, but we pushed forward. We had to make it to the other side.

Because every storm had an end.

You just had to fight long enough to get there.

Lightning flashed through the sky above us, and I felt each jolt through my magic when it speared for us, hitting the shield, but it went no farther. Snow mixed in with the sleet as the temperature dropped.

I lost track of time as we flew, forcing myself not to cringe or flinch as bolt after bolt of lightning struck the shield. But never once did it penetrate.

"There!" Eldrin shouted, pointing with a claw toward the horizon. A sliver of sunlight broke through the clouds in the distance. With the end in sight, our energy renewed, and we all surged toward that light.

We forced our wings to the breaking point, flying as fast as the winds would allow. When the worst of the lightning was behind us, I released my hold on it, allowing the shield to dissipate. Freed from their cage, Z and Eldrin burst forward in a mighty flap and flew with everything they had to make it to the other side of the storm. Tarrin and I stayed close on their heels, and I sighed as the clouds finally disappeared, forcing me to blink against the bright sunlight. Though it was weaker in the winter, it still fused warmth into my bones, thawing my frozen limbs.

But then I looked at where we were, and my snout fell open.

The mountain that held Shegora loomed in the distance.

Somehow, despite battling the elements, we had crossed countless miles. I couldn't keep the surprise from my face. How long had I held onto that magic? While my wings were tired from flying so long, my magic still buzzed through my veins, not drained like it should have been after such extended use.

Relief filtered down the bond from both Tarrin and Eldrin as we beat our wings against the cold air, and finally descended toward Metta.

CHAPTER 35

TARRIN

DUSK WAS JUST beginning to fall over Metta, another snowstorm kicking up as we descended from the sky, whipping the landscape into a blur of white. Gendon must not have been using his Shielder magic to hide the village since torches lit up the streets as far as we could see. We landed where the forest met the path into town and forced our exhausted bodies forward.

A small boy with dark hair, bundled in a black fur cloak, ran past, catching sight of our group. His eyes widened before he gave a loud whoop, taking off into a sprint through the town.

"What was that about?" Kaida asked as she shifted into human form. I didn't miss the wince on her face or the way she rubbed her arms. Her wings may have been healing fast, but after flying for so long, they were bound to be sore.

I followed her lead, shifting from scales to skin just as a male voice crooned through the snow.

"Well, aren't you a sight for sore eyes."

Gendon's green scales materialized out of the white, his snout split into a wide smile. When he saw Eldrin, he rushed forward, placing his hand on his shoulder and squeezing. "When you didn't arrive here…" he trailed off. Gendon cleared his throat, releasing

Eldrin and looking at me. "I am immensely glad to see you alive and well, Your Highness. Come, we've been waiting for you." With a nod of his head, he led us in the direction of his cave-home.

Around us, Metta was a flurry of activity.

I opened my mouth to ask what was going on, but Gendon anticipated my question. "The people of Metta have been busy fortifying their homes and moving those too young or old to fight through the tunnels in the mountain to a safe location on the other side," he explained, gesturing with his hands to the dragons and humans rushing around despite the snow that was falling heavily. "We've been forging special swords and shields day and night to wield against the army, made of metals that will pierce through scales." In the distance, the forges were bright spots across the town, confirming his words.

I glanced around in surprise. I expected to see anxiety and trepidation throughout the village, but there almost appeared to be… excitement? The young ones who remained were in the streets, with wooden swords, having mock fights with each other. Though the circumstances were dire, not to mention on the verge of hopeless, it still brought a smile to my face to see such resilience, even amongst the children.

"King Martik has been invaluable in training the villagers, dragon and human alike, to prepare them for the battle ahead," Gendon added, as we arrived at his house, each of us staggering inside as though our legs could no longer hold our weight.

A turquoise dragon was seated in the living area, and he jumped to his feet the minute we entered.

"Tarrin?" my father breathed before his eyes shifted to Lita, and he sprang forward, scooping both of us into his arms. There was such energy in his movements, a light in his eyes that had been absent since my mother had first died last summer. Perhaps the time alone for him to recover and getting to work with the villagers had been good for him.

My father ran claws over my face and shoulders as if he couldn't believe I had escaped Eklos's clutches. Then he took turns greeting us before we all collapsed onto the couches and chairs littering the room. Kaida leaned into my side as though she could physically no longer hold herself up. I planted a kiss on her forehead, turning my attention back to Gendon and my father who both stood before the hearth facing us.

"I'm assuming, based on your preparations, that you know the army is on its way here," I said.

Gendon nodded. "My scouts reported that they were on the move a few days ago. The village has been doing everything they can to prepare. Eklos won't catch us by surprise. He might have the numbers, but a battle isn't won by only that."

"No, but they sure help," Z muttered beneath his breath, though we all heard it.

"Be that as it may," Gendon continued, ignoring Z, "everything has been prepared to the best of our ability. Trust that we will stand with you, until the last breaths leave our lungs." He glanced at Kaida and me. "By the looks of it, you all have had a difficult journey to return here. I suggest you get some rest. Leave everything else to us. If something happens, you'll be the first to know."

Kaida blew out a relieved breath, barely able to keep her eyes open. "Sleep… would be nice." I didn't know if she meant to say it out loud, but everyone huffed out a laugh in response.

I gave a nod. "Thank you, Gendon, for everything." Standing to my feet, I lifted Kaida into my arms and brought her to the bedroom, tucking her beneath the blankets of the bed.

She was asleep before I even had a chance to kiss her goodnight.

&

I stood on the rooftop balcony of Gendon's home the next morning, watching as the villagers prepared for the coming battle.

A cloudless blue sky sat over Metta, the winter sun finally making its appearance after days of clouds and storms.

It did wonders to lift the spirits of everyone in the village, including those in our group. Even Z, the perpetual grump that he was, appeared to be in a better mood.

And yet... I couldn't shake this feeling of dread that had settled over me sometime in the night.

"Tarrin?" Kaida's voice called from across the balcony. She strode toward me in a black leather outfit, the hilt of a sword peeking over her shoulder. Her cheeks were red, as if she had been training with Z or out in the cold for a while. The bandages were gone from her arms, only the faintest sign of a scar on each was all that was left of her injury.

The breeze whipped her long braid around, so much longer than it had been when I had first met her and brought her to the Royal Palace, sending wisps flying into her eyes. She had drawn light lines of kohl across her eyes, making her turquoise eyes big and bright. She was stunning and strong—no matter which form she took.

She arrived at my side and pecked a kiss on my cheek. "What are you doing up here?"

I studied her face, unable to make my lips move while I took in every feature as though it were the last time I would be able to do so. I couldn't imagine a life—a future— without her. I couldn't stand the thought of Elysia without her as its Queen; as *my* Queen.

Kaida was everything this world needed, and if we made it through this war with Eklos, I would make sure Elysia saw the brilliance that she was.

But looking at her now, a smirk twitching the corners of her lips as she waited for me to speak, I knew that waiting for that moment wasn't enough. This war could take everything from us.

It could take our family.

Our friends.

It could take us from each other.

The thought had my eyes burning and I closed them before the smooth feeling of Kaida's fingers drifted across my cheek as she cupped my face in her hand.

"What is it, Tarrin?"

I shook my head, holding her hand to my face. "We're finally here; finally in a position to fight Eklos—and win. And yet… All I can think about is how much we stand to lose. I can't…" A shaking breath rattled out from between my lips. "I can't stand the thought of losing any of these humans or dragons. But most of all I can't stomach the thought of losing *you*."

A full smile bloomed on her face, and I scowled. She wasn't supposed to smile at that—at the terrifying thought that kept haunting my nightmares. Kaida laughed at my expression.

"Aren't you always the one telling me not to think like that? To stay positive and keep hoping?"

My scowl deepened and Kaida chuckled again.

"I won't tell you that everything will be fine because I don't know if it will. I won't give you false hope, Tarrin. But I do know that we're stronger together than we are apart. Together we can face anything—even an army of dragons. We're not unprepared this time. Your father and Gendon have done tremendous work in getting Metta ready. Gendon's son, Phelix, is continually evacuating the young and old to limit casualties. There are many fighters, dragons and human alike, remaining; when the army comes, we won't face them alone. And… if it is our time to go to the afterlife, we'll face that together too."

I ran a hand through my hair, looking back out at Metta. "Now I remember why I always gave the pep talks," I muttered.

An absurd laugh bubbled out of Kaida's throat, and she dissolved into a contagious fit of laughter that had me chuckling along.

With a smile still on her face, she lifted her shoulders in a shrug. "I tried." There was no offense or sadness there. Her cold fingers laced through mine and the only thing on her face was… love.

"Whatever comes through that forest," she continued, her face sobering as she looked out past Metta, "we'll face it together. Until our last breaths, Tarrin, I will fight by your side."

I wrapped my hand around her hip and drew her to me so we were chest to chest. "And what if I want more?"

Kaida arched a brow. "More than fighting side by side?"

I nodded. "I had a thought."

A slow smile crept across her lips. "I'm listening."

∞

"Well, isn't this a lovely surprise," Gendon's voice boomed, his curled horns glinting in the torch light. He was perched in an over-sized chair near the hearth in the main living area, book in hand.

"To what do I owe this pleasure?" he asked as Kaida and I took seats on the couch across from him.

As the leader of Metta, he had been increasingly busy preparing the village for the upcoming battle, making sure those who would be joining us were adequately prepared. With all of that, we had hardly seen the dragon since we arrived the night before.

"We wanted to thank you," I began. "For offering up Metta. We know it wasn't an easy decision, and we want you to know how grateful we are for the sacrifice you all have made."

Gendon settled back in his chair, his scales moving on his throat as he swallowed. "All of Elysia deserves to prosper as Metta has. The elders of the village and I realize that Shegora is a difficult journey for any that desired to join you in fighting Eklos. There is no other place free of his reach outside of Metta." He paused, staring at the book in his lap with unseeing eyes. "I will admit, it is difficult to give up centuries of work building this village—to make it what it is. But the people and dragons of Metta have spoken, and this is their choice."

"We don't take it lightly," I replied, and cleared my throat. "We don't know what this battle will bring, but once it's all over, rebuilding Metta, and creating more villages like it, will be our first priority. You've given us hope, and we want to make sure to offer some in return."

Gendon's snout opened and closed, before he swallowed hard. "I do believe that the two of you will make wonderful rulers. I will be honored to serve you when this war is over."

I smiled, opening my mouth to offer my gratitude once more, when Kaida squirmed and changed the subject.

"Any news on the army?" Her eyes were wide, her fingers twitching within my grasp.

Gendon hesitated for a moment, looking between the two of us, his eyes glancing to our intertwined hands.

"My scouts have reported that the army is approaching."

Kaida's emotions froze like ice down the bond. It was frigid—dangerously cold.

"How long?" I asked him. I had hoped we'd have more time, that I'd get to spend as many moments as possible with her, keep training, give her a fighting chance. Give us *both* a fighting chance.

Once again, Gendon hesitated, his eyes fixing on the floor and staying there.

When the silence grew uncomfortable, Kaida let go of my hand and clenched hers into fists, taking a step forward.

"Gendon, how long until the army reaches Metta?" Her voice was stern, demanding. Just like a queen.

The leader of Metta let out a breath, smoke curling in front of his snout. "They'll be here in two days. By nightfall."

Kaida turned her head to look at me. There was fear flickering in her eyes, but even stronger than that, there was a fierce determination, a wild hope shining as strong as the sun that had filled Metta with joy today. I could see it in her eyes—we would fight until our last breaths, until we walked hand-in-hand into the afterlife.

We would not yield.

We would not give up.

We would fight with everything we had.

I took hold of her hand once more.

"In that case, there's one more thing I'd like to do before the war begins," I said to Gendon, squeezing Kaida's hand tighter.

Gendon studied us again, before looking me squarely in the eye, his snout spreading into a smile.

"What did you have in mind?"

CHAPTER 36

TARRIN

DEEP BENEATH GENDON'S home was a cavern of stars.

Or, at least, they looked like stars. Bright, glittering blue crystals lined the walls, the ceiling, and the black stones beneath my feet. There was no need for torchlight with the iridescent flickering filling the room. Though it was the dead of winter, the cavern was warm and comfortable, and the gentle silence set my anxious heart at ease.

This was it.

I was about to marry Kaida.

After everything we had been through and survived, it all led to this moment. A relationship that had started with mutual hatred but then bloomed into something so fierce and unexpected… There was no explanation other than it had all been fate.

There had been so many moments over the last several months, from rescuing her from Belharnt, to hiding in Mistwick, to flying all over Elysia, and evading the Remnant, where I knew this was what I wanted, that this was where we'd end up. But fear kept us running, forcing us to push it off.

But ever since she appeared in the dungeon beneath Vernista, fought against Eklos so I could escape, and then earlier when she walked across the balcony, a sword strapped to her back—that was it.

The person who held half of my heart and dared to protect it with everything she had…

I didn't want to waste another moment without her as my wife, my queen, my equal.

When I had asked Gendon to perform the ceremony—to marry Kaida and me—he had been ecstatic and overjoyed, as if it was the greatest honor we could've bestowed upon him. He told us about this room, appropriately called the Starlit Cavern, and offered for us to be married beneath the flickering stars of Metta.

"Are you ready?" he asked, giving my shoulder a gentle squeeze with his claws.

I smiled up at him in response. Gendon and I were at the far end of the room beneath a natural arch made entirely of the shimmering crystals. He towered above me as I stood in human form, wearing simple black clothes. We didn't have time for any special garments to be made for the ceremony, nor did we want to be anything but ourselves.

At least until my mother showed up at the entrance to the cavern, her arms full of fabric, footsteps echoing into the high ceiling as she approached.

Before coming to the cavern, we had gone to my mother, asking her to be the witness. I had asked her if we should tell my father, but she had explained how he was having a difficult time letting go—both of his son and his reign as King. While he didn't necessarily doubt that we would make good rulers, he didn't want to see his son inherit the stress and struggle of a kingdom at war.

In the end, we chose not to include him, or Eldrin, as he was helping the forges in a last desperate attempt to make more weapons before the army arrived. It was too important a task to take him away. Besides we didn't want to tell anyone else; just wanted it to be our secret for the time being. If we made it through the battle, we could shout it from the rooftops. But for now, my love and marriage to Kaida would remain a private affair.

My mother was supposed to be helping Kaida get cleaned up and ready, so my eyes widened when she strode across the cavern and handed me a… cloak?

"What is this?" I asked her. I held it up and a gasp slipped through my lips. The fabric itself was black and lightweight but stitched across the entirety of it… iridescent turquoise and amethyst dragon scales.

"I've known this moment would come for decades, Tarrin. I've had this ready and waiting ever since." With great care, she took the cloak from my hands and draped it over my shoulders, clasping it at my neck. Smoothing the fabric down, she continued, "It is tradition for the Kings of Elysia to wear a cape of scales with the colors of those to be married. It signifies the union and strength of the dragons as they become equals."

The title clanged through me. *King.* By us marrying, the crown would officially pass to us.

She took a step back to study me. Even in the blue light of the cavern, the cloak shimmered, reflecting the scales back onto the starlit walls.

"I started gathering the scales when you were just a youngling. I finished it right before you rescued Kaida from The Den and have been holding on to it ever since."

I gaped at her. "All this time…"

"I told you, Tarrin, that Kaida was special. I knew this moment would come." She planted a kiss on my forehead before turning to leave. "She's almost ready." My mother hurried from the room, calling over her shoulder, "Just wait until you see your bride."

Ↄ

Every word fled from my mind as Kaida stepped into the cavern.

Beautiful didn't do her justice. In fact, I didn't think there was a word in any language that would.

Her hair had been curled into long waves that fell to her waist, and her skin glowed beneath the crystal stars. A slight blush colored her cheeks, and a dark line of kohl lined each eyelid, making her eyes even more stunning. A crown of snowflowers adorned her head. But what really stole the breath from my lungs was the dress she wore.

It seemed my mother had thought of everything—or rather her Foresight did.

Kaida wore the perfect match to my cloak of scales.

Black fabric sat just off her shoulders ending in flowing sleeves, before hugging the curves of her waist, and falling to the floor in a train behind her. And covering the entirety of the dress? The same amethyst and turquoise scales that were carefully stitched to my cloak.

Kaida's entire being glittered and glowed beneath the starlight of the cavern.

How long had my mother been collecting scales? How long had she spent working on these garments?

Kaida smiled at me as she began to cross the distance between us, and my knees wobbled enough that Gendon reached out a clawed hand to steady me.

The familiar scent of lavender and cedar filled my nose as she arrived by my side, and it was all I could do not to sweep her into my arms and kiss her senseless.

Kaida's eyes widened when she noticed my cloak before glancing down at her own dress.

"My mother," I said in explanation and the smile that lit her face knocked the breath from my lungs.

You're breathtaking, my love.

Her cheek was warm as I skimmed my thumb across it, and I felt a pulse of affection filter down our bond.

"Are we ready?" Gendon murmured.

I was vaguely aware of my mother reentering the cavern and coming to stand off to my right.

I smiled at Kaida, taking her hands in mine before nodding for the leader of Metta to proceed with the ceremony.

"I am old," Gendon's booming voice announced, causing both Kaida and I to flinch before a giggle burbled out of her throat. I glanced up at him to find a smile on his face. "But," he continued, "I have never met two people, dragon or human, quite as in love as the two of you. I've never witnessed a love so fierce that a person would risk their life, their future, to keep the other safe. Never have I met a dragon or human who would go to war to protect the one they love."

Kaida squeezed my hands in hers.

"It is only through that desperate, sacrificial love that the evil in Elysia can be stopped; only through that love can healing truly begin. I am honored to stand here, uniting Prince Tarrin and Kaida of Elysia into a marriage, a union that will usher in a new era in this world."

There's no one else I'd rather be here with, my love. You are my everything.

Her eyes filled with tears. *I love you, Tarrin. You are even better than my dreams.*

"Prince Tarrin, do you take this beautiful female, this fierce dragon, as your wife, to love her endlessly, protect her at all costs, and care for her until the end of your time in this world?"

As the question settled into me, with all its weight and implications, I gazed into Kaida's eyes. She was beauty and strength, humility and kindness, and everything I never knew that I needed. There was no future without her in it. I would stand by her side no matter what, come death or victory, we would walk every day of what was to come together. And I would never cease loving her.

I squeezed Kaida's hands in mine.

"I do. For all my days, and every one in the next life, I do."

CHAPTER 37

KAIDA

"DO YOU TAKE Prince Tarrin, this strong, brave-hearted male as your husband, to love him endlessly, stand by his side through both pleasure and heartache, and care for him until the end of your time in this world?"

In the span of a blink, every fear I had buried deep flashed through my mind. Before all of this, I never wanted to be Queen. I never even imagined I'd get married. And yet, here I stood about to commit my life to Tarrin, to Elysia, until the end of my days.

Could I even do this? Could I be Queen of Elysia, rule by his side? Only months ago, I had been a slave under Eklos's thumb, facing a lifetime of abuse and torture.

But now I was to help Tarrin lead?

Every doubt, fear, and insecurity played through my mind as I looked at him. His hair hung in waves to his shoulders, his cloak shining around him, causing his face to glow. But the way his eyes were utterly transfixed on me, endless love flickering within them...

For him, I would do it. I would face it all.

Because love conquered all, even my fear.

Whatever the future held, as long as he was by my side, it was a future I could face.

I squeezed Tarrin's hand in return, a grin spreading across my face as tears spilled onto my cheeks.

"From here until the last breath leaves my lungs, I do."

ଔ

A fire crackled away in the hearth, casting a dim light through the room. Everything was quiet as the moon shone through the window; even the howling winter wind had gone silent. The click of the door echoed before Tarrin's arms wound around my waist.

"Hi, wife." He pressed a kiss to the shell of my ear.

I couldn't stop the smile from spreading across my face as my hands wound into his hair. "I like the sound of that."

His lips were hot on my forehead, and he hummed. "Me too."

With trembling fingers, I carefully unclasped the cloak around his neck, dropping it onto the edge of the bed, the scales plinking like gentle rainfall. The memory of comforting Tarrin all those months ago after his mother died, when he had asked me to stay with him, and the feeling of waking to our limbs tangled together flashed through my mind. So much had happened since then.

Tarrin pulled me back to him as if he couldn't stand any distance between us, even for a moment.

"Is this real life?" I whispered as he trailed kisses from my shoulder to my neck. "Are we really married? Are we really going to be King and Queen of Elysia?"

He stilled for a moment. "Technically, we already are."

"What?"

"Our marriage was the first part in the tradition of passing the crown. After the war, my parents will officially crown us in public, but unofficially… we're King and Queen."

My legs wobbled, and Tarrin's hands squeezed tighter against my waist.

"You have nothing to worry about," he reassured. "I'll be by your side every step of the way." He chuckled. "Have you already forgotten my vow?"

I pressed a kiss to the underside of his chin before shaking my head. "I'll never forget your vow, Tarrin."

He hummed again, returning his lips to the bare skin on my shoulders, sending a shiver through me. My fingers tangled in his hair as his mouth brushed the corner of my own, once, twice before he pulled back and I held in a groan.

"I meant it, Kaida, every word. I want forever with you, every second of what's left of it."

Reaching onto my toes, I pressed my lips to his, and his fingers skimmed down my arms, setting my skin on fire. I dropped my arms to his waist as his hands tangled in my hair, and a shiver ran through him as my thumbs grazed the skin at the edge of his shirt.

"Forever?" I whispered, looking at him from beneath my lashes.

His smile had my heart skipping a beat before he pressed his lips to mine.

"Forever, my love."

KAIDA

THE NEXT DAY was the coldest day in Elysia I had ever experienced.

But I expected nothing else—it was the Winter Solstice after all. Centuries ago, it used to be a day of celebration. A day to spend with loved ones, exchange gifts, and show gratitude. But those were only legends now. A proper Winter Solstice hadn't been celebrated since before Xalerion spread his poison through Elysia.

Now, it was simply the shortest day and longest night of the year, in the deepest depths of winter, bringing despair and sorrow instead of joy.

A violent shiver racked through my body as I rubbed my hands together in a vain attempt to infuse heat into them. In Vernista it never got so intensely cold, but here, it was the type that froze the snot inside your nostrils and crept beneath all your layers—no matter how many there were—and froze your skin until it went numb.

I was on the balcony of Gendon's home, in human form, training with Z one last time before the army reached Metta. We had been at it for an hour, practicing human against dragon, and I had lost all feeling in my limbs. Even Z appeared to be shivering despite the blanket of scales he wore.

"Perhaps we should take a break and warm up a little," I bit out through clenched teeth as I ducked beneath his wing.

"Nice try, little shifter. I don't think that excuse will work on the dragons in Eklos's army. They won't stop just because you're cold. You must fight on."

The air clouded in front of my face as I exhaled. "You really think I'm going to be battling many dragons? You know Eklos will come for me. My fight will be with him."

Z narrowed his eyes. "Or he'll send his dragons to wear you down so that when you finally face that snake, you're too exhausted to defeat him."

I rubbed a hand over my face, knowing he was right. Though Eklos's pride was enormous, he wouldn't miss the chance of weakening me before having to fight me himself. Any chance I had of winning this battle… he would make sure I had nothing left when I finally faced him.

Lost in thought, I missed Z's advance as he stepped forward, whipping his wing in my direction. I barely had time to register the burst of wind hitting my face before the hard skin of his wing slammed into my side, sending me sprawling across the coarse ground. My side ached something fierce and I gingerly touched it, wincing. There was no blood, so I swallowed my injured pride and pushed back onto my feet.

Amusement flickered in Z's eyes as he watched me limp forward to meet him again.

"You could have avoided that."

I rolled my eyes. "Spare me, Z."

The dark-blue dragon stared at me a moment longer, unmoving.

"What's wrong?" he asked at last.

I crossed my arms against the chill air. "I don't know what you're talking about."

He shook his snout. "You're not even trying. I know you're better than this." He paused to gesture at the ground where I had fallen. "I *trained* you better than that."

"Maybe I'm just not as strong a fighter as you thought, Z."

He took a step forward, smoke leaking from his nostrils. "That's a lie, Kaida, and you know it."

His use of my name caught me off guard, freezing my feet to the ground. Why was he so worked up over this?

"Z—"

He swiped his claws through the air. "No. I don't want to hear whatever pathetic excuse is about to come out of your mouth. This is *war*, Kaida. That means people are going to die. Humans and dragons both. Not all of us will make it to the other side of this. Eklos and his followers will take down as many with them as they can. You've fought against Eklos's tyranny your entire life, whether you knew it or not. Every day that you lived, that you rose from that bed, and went to The Den—you were fighting. You've faced down death and you've won."

Z rubbed at the back of his head, turning his eyes to look at the village below us. "You must fight, Kaida. With everything you have. Until there's nothing left." His eyes blazed as he fixed his gaze back on me. "For if you don't, when this storm is over, all that will remain is our ashes floating in the sunlight."

Before I could even open my mouth to speak, the door to the balcony squealed as it opened and Tarrin stepped through the doorway, his human formed bundled in a thick cloak.

When he saw our tense faces, he stopped in his tracks. "Everything all right?"

"Fine," Z snapped before stalking to the edge of the balcony and leaping off, flying into the snow-filled sky above.

Tarrin's emerald eyes turned to me. "What was that about?"

I shook my head, unable to put into words what he had just spoken—the sudden drive flaring through me like lightning. Z was right. I always felt as if I were running away from fights my whole life—being a coward. But I wasn't running. Every day that I rose from my bed and faced Eklos and the other dragons, I was fighting. Every day that I put up with the torture and abuse from them, those seven years in Belharnt. I didn't give up. I kept fighting. Continuing on, even when you had nothing left, wasn't running away. It was fighting.

I rubbed at my forehead, watching the dark-blue dragon disappear into the clouds. "Just Z knocking some sense into me."

Tarrin looked skeptical but kept his lips pressed together. I stepped closer and he wrapped an arm around me.

"The villagers are assembled outside. Gendon has been instructing them," Tarrin said. "Eklos's army was spotted not far away."

Alarm flared through me. "I thought we had another day. Nightfall tomorrow—that's what Gendon said."

His eyes, though full of concern, softened as his gaze met mine. "They moved much faster than Gendon's scouts anticipated. I suspect Rythos had a hand in that."

I glanced at the sun, already falling toward the horizon. So little sunlight in the winter—especially on the Winter Solstice. How were we supposed to win against an army of dragons in the dark?

He cleared his throat. "If you'd like to say something to the villagers," Tarrin said, interrupting my thoughts. "I think that might spark some hope into them."

"What could I possibly say?" My stomach churned at the thought.

Tarrin brushed the hair out of my eyes, gently tucking it behind my ear. "Remind them what we're fighting for, love. Eklos's army appears large and undefeatable. Perhaps you should offer a different perspective." He planted a kiss on my forehead, his lips hot against my cold skin.

My fingers tightened on his arms. "Shouldn't you be the one to speak to everyone? Or your father?"

He gazed at me tenderly. "Remember our conversation in the mountains? *You* give them hope. They've heard of your abuse as a slave, your torture in Belharnt, the loss of your mother. Despite everything, you're still willing to stand up and fight for a better future. You're a leader even if you don't know it." My favorite smirk twitched his lips. "Besides, you know as well as I do that my father has no say anymore. He could speak but it would do nothing." He winked at me, and my cheeks blazed.

"When are you going to tell—"

"Soon. I'll tell him soon."

I arched a brow. Why was he waiting to tell his father?

He laced his fingers with mine and tugged me toward the balcony door. "Come on. You can do this."

My heart hammered against my chest with every hurried step we made toward the courtyard outside Gendon's home. When we arrived at the door, as far as I could see, humans and dragons were huddled together in the cold, waiting. The bright greens, blues, and yellows of the dragons' scales reflected off the snow beneath them, creating a symphony of colors despite the dreary winter day. A soft murmuring echoed against the side of the mountain, but everything went silent as we stepped into view.

Gendon had just finished speaking moments before we arrived and stepped to the side, his claws clasped in front of him. He gave us a nod, gesturing at the crowd.

I gulped and Tarrin let out a quiet laugh before clearing his throat.

"People and dragons of Metta," Tarrin called. His voice was deep, resonant; made for this. I couldn't help the swell of pride that had my magic awakening within me.

"In just a short number of hours, death will come knocking on our doorsteps."

I nudged him and whispered, "That's your version of a pep talk?"

He nudged me back, a smile on his face.

"You have so graciously sacrificed your homes, your peace, your *lives* to fight against an army that you could very easily choose to hide from. The fact that you are giving up the one solace in Elysia, the one true place of freedom, to help us bring about a new age in this world—a better one—is not lost on us. Your sacrifice is beyond anything we could have ever hoped for or dreamed of."

Tarrin took a small step backward, putting his hand on the small of my back. His palm burned through my shirt. His fingers contracted in a reassuring squeeze and then… he waited.

What could I say to them? This wasn't their fight, not really. They had managed to figure out how to cohabitate peacefully and now they stood to lose it all.

I opened my mouth, willing my voice not to tremble. "I have spent my entire life enslaved by the dragons." I paused, my hands shaking at my sides. "I have been abused, tortured, and on the brink of death too many times to count." Tarrin gave me another squeeze. He was with me—no matter what.

"I hated the dragons. Every single one—whether they had personally hurt me or not. I believed they were all despicable creatures, and each night I went to bed and each morning I woke up wishing all of them would just… be gone." I stopped speaking, my chin trembling as the horrible memories came rushing back, but I forced myself to continue.

"That is until one day when a shape-shifter rescued me from the claws of Eklos and showed me that not all dragons were cruel. There were those who could be kind and compassionate. There were dragons who didn't relish in the pain of the humans, who didn't desire to hurt them. Prince Tarrin saved my life from my dragon Master, offering me a new chance at life. At hope. And now I want to give that same hope to the rest of Elysia."

I saw a few nodding heads and that spurred me to keep going.

"I've seen what Eklos does—he's no respecter of persons. He is cruel to both humans and dragons and won't hesitate to slaughter anyone in his way. He must be stopped if we have any hope of Elysia prospering. You have built something so beautiful; something I previously had thought was impossible. All of Elysia deserves to experience what you have, but that can't happen unless Eklos is defeated."

More nodding heads and I felt Tarrin's pride swell down the bond.

"I don't ask for your sacrifice lightly, nor had I ever expected it. Words cannot express how grateful I am that you all are willing to fight for the freedom of Elysia, for the end of Eklos's cruel tyranny." Tears pooled in my eyes, and I bit the inside of my cheek to keep them from spilling over.

"I am proud to stand with such brave humans and dragons. It takes true bravery to experience the beauty of Metta and be willing to give it up so that others could have it. For the rest of my life, I will not forget this." I grabbed Tarrin's hand. "*We* will not forget this. We stand by your side, as equals, and we will fight with you," I declared. "We will fight *for* you."

Before anyone could react, a voice filled the air.

"And who are you to speak to all of them like this? Who are you to lead?" Martik's booming voice reverberated, his turquoise eyes blazing as he stepped out of the shadows of another doorway. There wasn't anger or bitterness on his face, something more along the lines of curiosity.

He had never questioned Tarrin or me in such a way before, and the fact that he was doing so now, publicly, had a weight settling in my gut. Sweat coated my palms, and I opened my mouth, to say what I wasn't sure, but Tarrin's voice echoed over the crowd.

"Do *not* speak to your Queen like that."

A weighted silence fell over the gathered villagers, many of them looking at each other with raised eyebrows or gaping mouths, and Martik stilled.

"What did you call her?" His voice rumbled.

"Kaida is your Queen."

Tarrin's father narrowed his eyes, taking a step forward. "I never took you for a liar, Son."

"I'm not lying, Father." He hesitated a moment before speaking louder so everyone gathered could hear. "We were married last night. Gendon performed the ceremony. Mother was the witness. The official coronation will take place once this war is over, but nevertheless, Kaida is now the Queen of Elysia." Tarrin drew himself up to his full height, looking at his father. "And I am the King."

Martik was silent, though I was sure he could hear my pulse thrashing in my ears as I waited for him to respond. I expected him to lash out in anger, but instead, his shoulders slumped, and his eyes softened.

Was he… *relieved?*

Though Eklos had tricked Martik into signing over power to him, I had never stopped thinking of him as the King.

I thought that Martik would be angry that we went behind his back, that we didn't include him in the decision or the ceremony. I had asked whether we should invite him, but Lita had said it would take longer to convince him than we had time for. I had assumed that meant Martik wouldn't approve of our marriage, at least at that moment in time.

But looking at him now, there was definite relief on his face.

And then, to my astonishment, the former King of Elysia got down on one knee, bowing before Tarrin and me. Everyone in Metta followed suit, and at the same time hundreds of voices murmured, "Long live the King and Queen."

CHAPTER 39

EKLOS

THE COLD CLUNG to my scales like frozen daggers inching their way beneath them until every part of me was numb.

I had forgotten how much I despised war, especially in the winter. It had been years—centuries—since I had fought such a battle, back when Xalerion was still alive, forcing me to lead each attack. But now I would finally succeed where the Lone Dragon had failed. My father let his brother, Bakari, escape his claws, allowing his union with Faryn to lead to the birth of Eldrin, further spreading the shifter filth into the world. Eldrin, too, desecrated the dragon line by mating with a human slave, resulting in yet another abomination. After centuries of hunting them down, I was finally about to eliminate them all. Smoke escaped my snout despite the snow swirling in the air.

The army surrounding me was silent, save for the subtle rumble of their footsteps over the snow. We would be at the village where the shape-shifters were hiding in a matter of hours. When Rythos had come to me, explaining what Metta was, how humans and dragons lived together as *equals*, I had fought the urge to immediately raze the place to the ground. Such a place, such a concept, was as abominable as the shifters themselves. I was all too happy to march on Shegora to burn it down, once and for all, but a place like this so-called Metta… it needed to be destroyed.

It was just another thing I'd take away from them by the end. Before I took their lives.

"Master Eklos," a voice came from behind me, and I turned, letting out a low growl when my wings bumped into dragons that dared to stand too close. They scurried farther away, revealing Rythos stalking toward me.

"What is it?"

"The village is ahead."

"What of it?" I snapped. This infernal beast was getting on my nerves.

Rythos narrowed his eyes. "The army has been walking for days. Perhaps this would be a good chance to stop and rest before heading into a battle with exhausted dragons."

Instinct had me lashing out a leash of smoke at him, encircling his throat like a collar. Fire flared in my core, thawing my frozen limbs. Ice cracked off the edges of my wings as I threw them out to the side.

"Who are you to be making such decisions, or even to have such thoughts?" I snarled.

The gray dragon coughed and clawed at the smoke but to no avail. "I'm… only… thinking of you."

I squeezed harder and Rythos's eyes bulged. "It sounds more like you're trying to overthrow me."

"No," he spluttered, his orange eyes flaring, his claws digging into his neck as he fought to free himself. "A tired… army…" he wheezed, "would only give the… shifters an advantage."

His words were like a key to a lock, snapping open and dousing my anger with ice. The fire in my core dulled to a simmer, and I released my hold on the smoke collar. Rythos fell to the ground, huge shuddering breaths working through his body as he fought to get air into his lungs.

Losing patience with the sound of his wheezing, I let out a tree-shaking roar. It was the ultimate signal to tell the army to pause their movements. Usually the Remnant dragons, my commanders in the army, gave them enough notice that such a signal wasn't necessary. But I didn't have time for them to spread the word.

We would stop. They would rest.

And then we would destroy the village of Metta.

"Master," Rythos coughed out from the ground.

I spun halfway back to him, eyeing his pathetic figure in the snow.

"I am losing patience with you," I snapped. "You are quickly losing your usefulness. I suggest you remedy that before I cast you out and you're forced to face those shifters by yourself."

An emotion flickered in his eyes as he recoiled, but I didn't care enough to examine it further. Without another word, I turned my back on him and stalked through the tired dragons toward my tent rising at the center of the army.

CHAPTER 40

ELDRIN

ARRIED. MY DAUGHTER was married.

And she hadn't told me.

I supposed I could understand why she hadn't felt the need to include me in such a decision or invite me as a witness alongside Lita. I had spent all day and night in the forges of Metta, helping to procure as many swords, shields, and arrows as possible. There was no telling what Eklos's army would have in their arsenal, so we needed to be ready.

I understood her not wanting to pull me away from it, and though she was my daughter, Kaida and I hadn't grown terribly close over the past few months. Whether that was just from the stress of being hunted by the Remnant, or simply the fact that she was a grown woman now who didn't need a father figure, I wasn't sure. But I couldn't stop the pang of regret that kept poking into my stomach, especially when she would call me by my name instead of Father.

But even more shocking than Tarrin announcing they were married was the news that they were King and Queen.

My *daughter*.

The Queen of Elysia.

My eyes burned as I watched Kaida engage with the villagers

of Metta. Both humans and dragons were lined up far in the distance, waiting for their turn to speak to them. We should have been getting ready, making sure all the preparations were made for when the army arrived, but the people seemed to need this—to embrace their new rulers; ones that gave them a hope for a better world.

Perhaps that was all the fuel they needed to head into battle with peace and fervor. Kaida's speech had been brilliant, infusing even my old heart with fire.

In a flash of purple, Kaida shifted into dragon form so she could speak with a pair of dragons face-to-face.

My breath trembled in the cold air as I let out a sigh. Aela would have been so proud of her.

As much as I missed her, I was thankful that my love was no longer here. Not for this. War was no place for a human, let alone those who couldn't defend themselves against the dragons. At least Gendon and Martik had been preparing these people, but if she were here, I wouldn't risk her life for anything.

She deserved springtime and sunshine, warmth, and to roll through a field of wildflowers. Not death, rage, and destruction.

I shook my head, turning away to go check on something—anything—to keep my hands and mind busy until my cousin arrived.

Though the villagers of Metta offered us a chance of victory, it was only that. A chance. I didn't know the final number of Eklos's army, but I had a feeling it was more than we had, and they were all powerful dragons, driven by hatred.

I walked down the snow-covered path toward the forge, intending to check and make sure all the weapons we had made were ready and accounted for. With the crunching of snow beneath my feet, my mind spun over the last few months, to our time in Mistwick, then running for our lives.

To Noam, whom I'd sent on a mission, one that likely ended

in his death. Even if he managed to do as I said, what were the chances that he would even return in time? It's not like I had any way to contact him.

It was a small happiness knowing that my greatest friend wouldn't be here to die at the hands of Eklos and his dragons. Like Kaida, he was born into slavery and endured the loss of his family. From witnessing his parents' beheadings to watching his sister murdered as punishment for trying to escape, he deserved an escape from further death and destruction. At least in sending him after a legend I had protected him in some capacity.

But still… if I could just find a way to reach him, figure out where he was, or if he had succeeded.

I nearly walked into a wooden pole as my mind drifted, flashing back to when Kaida had that dream—a dream where she spoke to Rythos.

She claimed she hadn't known she was linking their dreams together; that she had no idea how to do such a thing again.

But could she link *my* dreams with Noam's or pull the both of us into her own? Could she use her magic so I could speak to him?

I stopped and looked over my shoulder at Kaida down the road, back in human form, walking hand-in-hand with Tarrin into Gendon's home. Turning on my heel, I abandoned my trip to the forge and headed for my daughter.

She may not be able to get me in contact with Noam, but it was worth a shot. Our victory might depend on him.

☙

"You want me to what?" Kaida exclaimed. "Eldrin, I have no idea how I even started a dream with Rythos. How in the scales do you expect me to be able to create a dream between two people apart from me?"

I ran a hand through my silver hair. Kaida, Tarrin, and I all stood in the main entry of Gendon's home. Tarrin was leaning against the wall, arms crossed, watching his… wife, I supposed, carefully.

I shook my head. "Then don't do it apart from you. Pull the two of us into your own dream."

"Eldrin, you're missing the point. I don't know how to recreate such a dream. It was a fluke with Rythos. Even if it *was* me who linked our minds in sleep, it was unintentional."

Kaida waved a hand, gesturing into the main room where a smattering of couches and chairs sat around the hearth. She plopped down on one of the couches, Tarrin settling beside her.

I knelt in front of her, holding her hands between my own. "Kaida, this is important. This could mean the difference between winning and dying in this battle with Eklos."

Her brows lowered over her eyes. "Just where did you send Noam?"

"I sent him after a myth, and that's all you need to know."

I didn't want to tell her. I didn't want to sow false hope when in a matter of hours, we could all lose everything.

So, instead of being honest, I tried to pull on her heart strings. "Let me say goodbye to my greatest friend."

Her eyes softened, and after a moment she laid her hand upon mine. "I can't promise you it'll work, Eldrin. I don't know what I'm doing." She looked at Tarrin before she faced me again. "But I'll try."

☙

Waiting for Kaida to fall asleep was like waiting for rain in a drought. Though, if I didn't fall asleep soon too, I might miss my only chance to speak with Noam.

I laid down on the floor next to the couch Kaida was sprawled on. Her breathing was still shallow, so she wasn't asleep yet, but I could see it on her face, in her body language. She was exhausted. We all were. Tarrin was watching us from the chair on the other side, but with his heavy eyes, it wouldn't be long before he was pulled into the land of dreams too.

Closing my eyes was difficult, even though they burned with a need for sleep. There had been so much to accomplish since we arrived back in Metta, and not a lot of time for things like food and sleep. My hands clenched into fists over my stomach. I needed to relax. I would never fall asleep if I couldn't force my muscles to loosen, my brain to stop spinning over scenarios that hadn't happened yet.

I forced myself to inhale slowly, letting it seep through my lips like steam from a teapot. The seconds turned into minutes, and I didn't know how much time passed before I heard the steady, deep breaths of Kaida finally entering the dream world.

I fought against the panic that flared in my stomach at not being able to fall asleep. *That* certainly wouldn't help. Focusing on my feet first, and working my way up toward my neck, I relaxed each muscle, until my body felt like jelly on the carpet. I didn't know how long I lay there, or how long it took for me to finally fall asleep, but the next thing I knew, I opened my eyes, and I was standing in Silverdew Valley at the height of autumn.

The grass was a vibrant green beneath my feet, with orange, yellow, and red wildflowers painting the valley floor. The air had that crisp scent that only came when the warm summer days transitioned to the cool fall nights. The last time I had stood in this valley, I had been knee-deep in snow, the cold seeping beneath my scales like a disease. That was also where Rythos had taken Tarrin away from us.

A shiver went through me at the memory.

Kaida stood several feet away, the grass swaying around her bare feet, a pale-yellow dress adorning her body. Her eyes were still closed, but the faintest smile was plastered on her face, as if she were truly at peace.

If I was here with her, did that mean it worked?

"Kaida?" I called, and the sound seemed to echo between the mountain peaks. She didn't move or respond for a moment, just tipped her head up into the wind, the autumn breeze a pleasantly warm one, like catching sun rays in your hands.

When she finally opened her eyes, they were no longer turquoise, but silver. It reminded me of Lita's.

"Kaida?" I asked.

"It seems it worked," she remarked. Her brow furrowed as she looked around us. "Why do these dreams take place here? Last time it was summer when I spoke with Rythos."

Excited that she managed to pull me into her dream, I didn't respond to her question, but asked instead, "Can you pull Noam in?"

Her silver eyes snapped to mine. "For being a thousand years old, Eldrin, you are enormously impatient."

A startled laugh bubbled out of me.

"Just give me a moment," she whispered, closing her eyes once more.

I didn't know how long it might take her, and it had been such a long time since I had felt grass rather than snow, that I dropped to my knees, running my hands over the silky green blades, bending over to sniff the wildflowers. The scent was like walking through a garden of lilies covered in cinnamon. It was a strange smell, to be sure, but distinctly autumn.

I sighed. Winter in this part of Elysia was brutal enough, let alone when you're forced to take on an army of dragons amidst the worst of it.

"Eldrin?" a voice called, and I froze. That was not Kaida's voice.

I jumped to my feet, spinning on my heel, as I turned to find Noam standing several feet away. He was looking at himself, then the valley with wide eyes and a gaping mouth.

"Noam," I breathed, before breaking into a run and enveloping him in a hug. "She did it!" I exclaimed, glancing at Kaida. Her eyes were still closed, her face scrunched as if it was the only way to concentrate enough to keep us both here.

I needed to hurry.

"How is this possible?" Noam asked, looking around the valley with his mouth hanging open.

I chuckled. "Kaida has discovered a new ability. One that allows her to enter the dreams of others or link them together."

Noam's mouth opened further. "A Dream Weaver?"

"It's a real ability?" I asked.

Slowly, Noam nodded his head. "It's a rare gift, in the same vein as Foresight, though not every person with Foresight can weave dreams. Even I have only heard but a few instances of such a magic." He caught sight of Kaida off to the side and rubbed at his chin. "But it would make sense for someone with the Ancient Magic to have such a gift."

"It does?"

He turned to study her in earnest. "The Ancient Magic was the first magic in all of Elysia. Within it, every magic you know of now, and even those you've never heard of, were encompassed in it. Throughout the stories passed down through my ancestors, when the Ancient Magic would manifest after the Magus were killed, it was never whole or complete like it once was. In my lifetime, I've never met a Dream Weaver."

"Can you tell me how it works so I can help her?" I asked. "We likely don't have much time." One look at Kaida's face, furrowed even more than a few moments ago had me grabbing my friend's shoulders, a sudden sense of urgency flaring deep inside me. "Rythos was in her last dream, and he tried to hurt her."

"Rythos?"

I mentally smacked my forehead. Noam had no idea about the dragon who had taken Tarrin in Silverdew Valley, nor did I have time to explain it all.

"He's… on Eklos's side," I said after a moment. It didn't feel right saying he was our enemy or that he was evil. I didn't remember much about him, but something told me he wasn't truly our enemy, even if he acted like one.

Noam looked thoughtful, tapping his chin. "I know next to nothing about Dream Weaver abilities. I wouldn't even know where to start." He paused, his brows lowering as he studied my face. "Perhaps fate linked their dreams together so that you could learn information you wouldn't otherwise have? Or for a deeper purpose? The Ancient Magic manifests in odd ways so I'm not certain." He paused. "What's wrong, Eldrin? Why am *I* here?"

"Where are you?" I asked in return.

Noam arched a brow. "I'm on my boat. Where else would I be?"

A panicked laugh slipped through my lips. "On your boat?"

He nodded. "You sent me away, remember?"

My eyes went wide. Why was he acting so nonchalant about this? I knew Noam liked to joke around, but now was not the time to be cryptic.

I squeezed my fingers into his shoulders. "Noam, have you succeeded? Have you found it?"

He cocked his head. "Remind me what I was supposed to do again?" A cruel smile twisted his lips.

Something wasn't right. My stomach flipped before it sank to my feet.

"Noam?" I whispered, the last of my hope cracking like glass. If he hadn't found what I sent him after…

And then I watched in horror as my friend, with his bright eyes and graying hair, cracked straight down the center of his body, like a shot of lightning, before he erupted into sparks. I squeezed my eyes shut against the bright light, and it took several seconds to clear the black spots from my vision before I could see again.

I wished I hadn't opened my eyes.

Because where Noam had disintegrated, Rythos now stood.

And he was grinning.

The dragon tsked, shaking his head. "Eldrin, Eldrin, Eldrin. Have you learned nothing?"

"What have you done?" The words were a hoarse whisper, barely audible.

Rythos chortled and I took an automatic step backward.

One glance at my daughter and I knew this wasn't what she intended. Her face was twisted in pain, as if the magic she was using, or the fact that Rythos had infiltrated another dream, was causing her physical agony.

The grass crunched beneath the dragon's feet, and I snapped my attention back to him.

"So, tell me, old friend. What did you send the dear human to find?"

My breath lodged in my throat. Had that even truly been Noam? Or was it Rythos the whole time? And why was he in Kaida's dream again?

"As if I would tell you," I spit. "Why are you here?"

He lifted his claws into the air. "As if I know. One minute, I'm asleep in Eklos's camp," he stopped to sneer at me before continuing. "And the next, I'm standing here talking to you."

"Was that you the entire time, or was I really talking to Noam?"

Rythos bared his teeth in a dagger-filled smile. "I don't know, were you?"

The hope I had felt at finally being able to talk to Noam, to find out if he had succeeded at the mission I gave him, wilted and died.

I couldn't handle his cryptic answers; couldn't handle the way my heart felt like it was squeezing in my chest while my stomach simultaneously wanted to eradicate everything I had eaten in the past twenty-four hours.

I willed my breaths to slow, my heart to calm, and fixed my gaze on the gray dragon.

"Why are you working for Eklos?" I tried, knowing Kaida had already attempted to sway him to our side in their first dream encounter. "You know he will kill you at the first chance he gets. Eventually he will see you as competition, and he'll slaughter you just like he did to his father."

I expected him to get angry, to shut down such a suggestion and deny it; defending Eklos like he had when Kaida asked before.

But this time he hesitated before speaking. "You too, Eldrin? Did your daughter not tell you she already tried this?" He scoffed, and turned his back to me, staring at the mountain surrounding us.

"Ah," I said after a moment, studying his strange reaction. "I see he's already begun to doubt you. Maybe even turn on you."

Rythos snarled, spinning to face me. "You have no idea what you're talking about."

"Don't I? He's my cousin. I've become well-versed in his mannerisms and actions over the past millennia. If he hasn't started to doubt you yet, he will soon. That, I can promise you."

Something strange flickered in his eyes and he avoided my gaze.

If Eklos was beginning to tire of him, perhaps now was our opportunity to get him to work with *us* instead.

"Come on, Rythos. This angry, vengeful person is not who you are."

The growl that erupted from his mouth echoed between the mountain peaks, and a hush fell over the valley in response.

"How would you know, old man? You abandoned me the moment you became a shifter. You didn't even remember me. If I'm as evil as you claim, it is all because of you."

"I never claimed you were evil."

Rythos rolled his eyes. "You might as well have."

I shook my head, my silver hair falling from its binding and gathering on my shoulders. "No, you're not evil. *Eklos* is evil, cruel, merciless. That is not what you are." I paused to let the words sink in, hoping it might break through to him.

"I think those are the words of an old man who is desperate for more dragons to fight on his side. Someone who would say anything, even stooping to flattery."

"Think what you want, Rythos, but I know I wouldn't have befriended someone with a cruel heart. You must've been kind, despite the world we live in. Eklos took the hurt that you experienced when I went to Shegora and turned it into something hard and bitter, that he could use at his leisure.

"But that's the thing, Rythos. He treats you like a pawn; something expendable. But you're not. The real Rythos that you've buried somewhere inside you wasn't afraid to do what was right. He was brave and honorable. Those would have been the first qualities Eklos eradicated from you, likely by the cruelest means necessary." I didn't miss his wince. "And you simply let him. Because an evil master was easier to face than the hurt in your heart."

"I don't want your sappy words," he snarled. "I don't want to hear what you think I was or am. I am Rythos, a member of the Remnant of the Lone Dragon, and the next time I see you, you will die. By my hand."

As if it were him, and not Kaida controlling the dream, he turned his back on me, wings flared wide, and took off into the sky.

I blinked and I was back on the floor in Gendon's home, Kaida's piercing turquoise gaze inches above my own.

"What just happened?" she whispered.

Tarrin rubbed his eyes at the sound of her voice as he squinted in the dim light of the room.

I gave a shake of my head, unable to understand what just happened.

"I swear it was Noam I pulled into the dream, Eldrin. I don't know how Rythos was there."

"Rythos?" Tarrin asked, leaning forward. "He was in your dream again?"

She gave a solemn nod and pulled herself back onto the couch. I was slow to sit up before I moved closer to the fire. My limbs felt like ice, as if that conversation with Rythos had seeped all the heat from my body.

"I could hear everything you were saying, but it was so hard to keep two of you inside the dream that it took every bit of concentration I could muster. When Rythos appeared instead of Noam, I tried to get him back, but either my magic is weak, or the dragon has more to do with these dreams than he let on. It makes no sense."

I held my hands out toward the flames. "I don't know if it was Rythos or simply fate having a hand in all this, but I still have no idea if Noam has accomplished what I sent him to do, or if he understood it was time to return."

Kaida narrowed her eyes. "Are you going to tell us where you sent him?"

I looked over my shoulder and gave a small smile. "No."

She arched a brow. "I could command you to tell me."

I couldn't hold back a chuckle. "You could, *Your Majesty*," I teased. "But you won't. Besides, it's better if you don't know, daughter. Perhaps your hope will stay intact a little bit longer."

TARRIN

NIGHT FELL AND with it a brutal winter wind that picked up the snow and turned the landscape into a tundra of white. Minutes ago, Gendon's scouts had arrived with new information, and we all squeezed into the main entry of his home, waiting, while they conferred in the corner. The hissing of their quiet voices set my nerves on edge.

Finally, Gendon straightened, dismissing the scouts, and turned to face us. Too many emotions flickered across his face far too quickly, and I couldn't pinpoint whether it was fear, anxiety, despair, or determination on the leader of Metta's face. After another moment, he cleared his throat.

"The enemy army is less than an hour away. They appear to have stopped their advance, though we aren't able to tell why or for how long."

I glanced at Kaida. Whether they halted for a practical reason or not, we both knew that Eklos wouldn't miss a chance to push all our nerves to the breaking point.

"What do we do in the meantime?" Kaida asked, her gaze moving to each person in the room. "Should we have everyone move out to their positions for battle?"

Z shook his head. "No. The cold is unbearable for more than a few minutes. If they're not here yet, then we'll keep everyone warm for as long as possible. This is the kind of cold that you don't mess around with. I'm sure there will be casualties on both sides simply from the elements." He turned his blue snout and stared at Kaida for a moment before fixing his eyes on the ground. "I'll head out and make sure everyone is ready to move at a moment's notice," Z declared. "Everyone should get some rest… while you can."

Kaida opened her mouth to say something, but Z was out the front door before anyone could protest.

"He's right, we won't last long if we're all falling asleep with weapons in our hands," my mother agreed. She turned to face us. "Go, we'll wake you if anything changes."

I wanted to stay, to help the others plan and prepare. The fact that the army was so close, that *war* was almost at our doorstep… My nerves felt prickly, like needles stabbing beneath my skin.

But seeing the circles under Kaida's eyes, and the way she swayed on her feet, I didn't argue. Putting my arm around her shoulders, I led her toward our room. Before I even had the door closed, she collapsed on the bed, kicked off her boots and was asleep in seconds, exhausted from the magic used with Eldrin and Rythos. I let out a quiet chuckle and removed my own shoes and shirt and crawled beside her, settling the blanket around us.

The sounds of people and dragons crunching through the snow outside seemed unbearably loud, keeping my mind from tuning out all the worries spinning through it. I let out a frustrated breath, wishing I could fall asleep as easily as she had. Wrapping an arm around Kaida's waist, I pulled her closer, hoping that if nothing else, her scent would soothe my anxiety enough to rest.

After months of sitting in Eklos's dungeon, being in a dark room still made me uneasy. The moment I closed my eyes, the walls pressed in on me, and my heart squeezed in my chest. A ringing noise mixed with the pounding of my pulse echoed in my ears, and my lungs constricted, forcing the air out of my body. I started gasping, trying to get any amount of air down my throat.

I couldn't breathe.

I couldn't bre—

"Tarrin?"

Everything stopped. The ceiling stopped descending over the bed, blessed cool air rushing into my lungs.

"Tarrin?" Kaida repeated, cupping my scarred cheek in her palm. "What's wrong?" Concern filtered down the bond.

"The dark…" I croaked out and understanding flashed across her face.

Her arms drew me against her, wrapping around me and holding me as tight as she could.

"You don't have to explain," she offered, and I bit my tongue to keep my tears away.

I needed to be strong for her—*wanted* to be strong for her. Even after everything we had been through, it was difficult being vulnerable or letting her see that I was still struggling, that I couldn't even handle laying in the darkness beside her.

"I'm here," Kaida whispered, her breath tickling my lips. "I'm not leaving. I'm here."

I closed my eyes, letting her voice soothe me as I rested my forehead against hers. After countless minutes, the dark suffocating feeling retreated, relinquishing its hold on my mind.

A shaking breath escaped my lips as I relaxed into Kaida's arms.

"Better?" she murmured.

A small smile twitched my lips, despite the panic I had felt moments ago.

"You chased the darkness away," I whispered in reply.

She pecked a kiss on my cheek. "And I'll do it every day, Tarrin. I'll help you fight your demons until the day you can fight them yourself."

My heart squeezed in my chest again, but this time it wasn't from panic and fear. Kaida's words were exactly what I needed, whether she knew it or not. And sometimes just knowing that there was someone fighting for you when you no longer had the strength to… that made all the difference.

"That's what you did for me when you saved me from Eklos, and now I'm going to do the same for you." Her eyes were wide in the dark.

"I love you." It was all my choked voice could manage.

Wrapping her arms around my neck, she pulled my lips to hers. "I love you, husband."

"Mmm. I like the sound of that."

The thought of this potentially being the last day I had to live with Kaida had me squeezing my arms tighter around her, our legs tangling beneath the covers.

"You should try to sleep. We'll be fighting for our lives in just a few hours." The sudden sadness in her voice cracked through my heart.

After living a life in slavery, a life full of abuse and surviving the most heinous things someone could do to another, I hated the thought of her in battle. I hated that she was even a part of this war. After everything she had been through, if anyone deserved to sail away and live at peace for the remainder of their life, it was Kaida. I would do everything in my power to protect her, but I was only one person. Love couldn't wield a physical sword or win in a fight.

The reality was that I would fight to my very last breath to protect her, and though we had trained hard, and often, the fact remained: Eklos had more numbers. There was a terribly high likelihood that one or both of us would not be walking away from this war. The thought made my eyes burn.

I grabbed the hand that was touching my cheek, kissing it gently before holding it to my chest. "If these are my last moments with you, my love, I'm not wasting a single one."

CB

A knock sounded at the door sometime later, rousing me from sleep. At first, I thought I had dreamed it, and I closed my eyes once more and wiggled closer to Kaida. The warmth of her skin seeped into me, and my body relaxed.

Another knock echoed, and my eyes snapped open. Not a dream. My limbs felt both leaden as I pulled myself away from Kaida, and rolled out of the bed, the chill air causing bumps to rise on my bare chest. Pulling a shirt over my head, my feet made quiet smacking noises, and I barely registered the first lights of dawn peeking through the window as I padded across to the door and cracked it open.

My mother stood on the other side, a black cloak covering her small frame, the hood barely concealing her silver eyes. I could just make out an expression I had never seen on her face in my life. And it was her next words that made me recognize it as absolute terror.

"Eklos is here."

CHAPTER 42

KAIDA

O N THE OUTSKIRTS of Metta, where the forest met
the village, stood Eklos with Rythos at his side.

I wished I could say that seeing him after so many
months of training and getting stronger made me feel brave in
the presence of my former Master. I wished I could say that my
stomach didn't swirl with bile or that my hands remained warm
and dry.

But that would've been a lie.

Seeing his ash-gray scales and those red eyes still had every
nightmare flashing before my eyes, every brutal day and haunting
night in Belharnt replaying in my mind. Sweat slicked my palms
inside my gloves, and I gripped the hilt of my sword tighter within
its sheath, my heart quickening to a painful tempo. I refused to
cower before him, and though I approached him in human form,
I wouldn't let him see my fear. Eklos would never get another piece
of my fear again.

What do you suppose he wants? Tarrin asked. He walked next to
me, in human form, staying as close as possible.

Z's footsteps, large as they were, were silent behind us. My
father, Martik, and Lita had opted to stay in Metta, rather than

joining us to speak to Eklos. They would wait for the signal from Z before telling the villagers to attack.

Nothing good. He'll likely tell us to turn ourselves over in exchange for leaving Metta alone.

Tarrin tensed beside me. *Would he?*

I fought the urge to shake my head. *No. Eklos has no honor. He is a liar and a coward. He can say he'll spare Metta all he wants, but now that he's seen it, he'll never let such a place exist. Not in his Elysia. Even if we gave ourselves over, everyone here would die.*

"Well, well," Eklos crooned. "I see these months on the run haven't been kind to you, slave. You look tired."

My lips flattened into a line as I fought to keep my expression neutral. I would not let him get to me; goad me.

"What? Not happy to see your Master?" he asked, spreading his arms and wings wide. Rythos took a step back to avoid being hit by the spikes on his wings.

"You're no longer my Master, Eklos. No one owns me anymore."

A growling laugh came out of him like a cough. "What a fool you are, human. I owned you every day of your life, I own you even now, and will continue to do so until the day you die. Every human is *mine.*"

It was my turn to laugh, the beast inside me peeking an eye open. The magic in my core started to awaken, filling me with each inhale I took. I didn't silence the beast, didn't hide it away or cower at the thought of it. Instead, I let it show, let that glowing power fill my eyes, let the lightning rim my hands, my head. If I had been able to see my reflection, I knew I would have seen a circlet of lightning and flames intertwining with each other, surrounding my head like a crown.

"No one owns me," I repeated, willing my power to strengthen and flare.

Eklos's expression was wrath incarnate. All the hatred in his black soul flashed in his eyes as he watched me take another step toward him. A step that was full of power, full of confidence, and void of fear.

Dark, noxious smoke billowed from his snout as a low snarl spilled off his tongue.

"I will kill you, slave. And I will enjoy it."

Tarrin stepped up behind me, placing a hand on my shoulder. It wasn't as much a protective gesture as it was his way of telling me that he was with me; by my side no matter what.

"I'd like to see you try," Tarrin replied, a crown of flames hovering above his head. I took his hand from my shoulder and intertwined our fingers before turning my gaze back on the dragon of my nightmares.

"What have you done?" Eklos demanded, glancing back and forth between our faces, our crowns, with absolute horror and disgust twisting his snout.

"It's over, Eklos," I declared. "Take your army and leave and we'll spare your life."

Sparks shot out of his nostrils as he snorted. "Spare *my* life? Just who do you think you are, slave?"

It probably would have been better to try to defuse things, to try to talk Eklos out of this war, but there would be no point. Eklos had made up his mind a thousand years ago, and his heart had only grown harder, colder, throughout the years. He was set on having this war, and nothing I said or tried to negotiate with would change his mind.

So, instead, I let a grin spread across my face, allowing my inner beast to show a little more.

"You're standing before the new King and Queen of Elysia. I suggest you tread carefully, Eklos," Tarrin spoke up, standing shoulder to shoulder with me. "Or better yet, *kneel.*"

"I would rather die!" Eklos's voice snarled so loud the leaves on the trees behind him trembled.

"Good," I snapped. "Because you will."

My former Master flared his wings out as wide as they could go. "Enough of this. Turn yourselves over to me and I will end this battle before it begins."

See? I bragged to Tarrin. *Told you he would say that.*

I felt his amusement through our bond, but his focus remained on Eklos.

"I know you think humans are stupid, Eklos, but surely you can't think that I would ever believe you."

He chortled, shaking his snout. "You're just like your pathetic mother. She could never keep her mouth shut."

I snapped at the mention of my mother, lunging at the monster who had brutally executed her in front of me. He hated the human race for killing his mother in a rebellion, yet he took mine from me. Before I could get close to him, Tarrin grabbed me around the waist, holding me back.

"Not now," he whispered in my ear.

I struggled in his arms. *He must die, Tarrin. Let me go.*

Don't do it out of anger or revenge, Kaida. That's not the way to make things right.

I fought against the tears burning my eyes.

The dragon let out another laugh, turning to look at Rythos. "See? They're all the same. Hateful, vengeful, murderous creatures."

Though Rythos gave the barest of nods, for the first time, I noticed something different on his face. With all our previous encounters, there had been no hesitation, no questioning of his Master's actions or the orders that Eklos had given him. But now...

Something flickered in his eyes, a slight downturn to his scaled lips that had me wondering if he was finally questioning Eklos, whether he was wrong; if he was realizing that he was expendable and Eklos wouldn't hesitate to kill him.

When he met my gaze, it wasn't cold, or full of hatred. I couldn't pinpoint the feeling in his expression, but I knew in that moment that I had gotten in his head when we shared that first dream. When I told him Eklos wouldn't hesitate to betray him, Rythos had been adamant that such a thing could never happen. But watching him now, and the way he kept looking at the ash-colored dragon… I had gotten under his skin.

The question now was, would Rythos turn against Eklos? Would he help *us*?

I was sure he knew information that would give us an advantage in battle. Perhaps what Eklos's plans were, or his strategy to get his hands on us shifters. Would he give that information up?

Eklos tried a new tactic. "You're truly willing to sacrifice this entire village just to keep yourself out of my hands for a few hours longer? Are you really such a coward?"

I huffed a laugh. "Nice try, Eklos."

He opened his snout to utter a retort, but I held up a hand wreathed in lightning.

"A coward wouldn't come to negotiate with you to protect those in this village. A coward wouldn't do everything in their power to protect those they love. A coward, Eklos, wouldn't be willing to sacrifice their life so that all of Elysia could prosper when you are finally dead."

His snout opened and closed, his red eyes wide, as if he couldn't believe I had spoken such words.

"Go back to your army, Eklos. I'll see you in battle." I turned my back on my former Master, though it went against every instinct inside me, and began walking toward the village.

"Kill her, Rythos," Eklos demanded.

My body stiffened, preparing for an attack, but nothing came.

I glanced back over my shoulder, expecting to see the gray dragon stomping toward me, fire in his palms, but indecision warred on his face. His orange eyes were wide as he looked back and forth between Eklos and me.

When Eklos finally realized that Rythos wasn't moving, he

smacked his claws across his snout, sending him careening backward into the snow.

"You stupid fool. I'll do it myself." Eklos's eyes burned like hot coals as he lunged for me.

Tarrin's grip on my arm tightened as he tensed for the attack, ready to throw me behind him. But in the blink of an eye, Z was suddenly there, wrapping his claws around Eklos's arm, preventing his claws from touching me.

"You will not lay a finger on my Queen," Z growled, his voice more menacing than I had ever heard it.

My heart swelled at his words. Z had a complicated past, one that we were still uncovering, but the fact that he was willing to risk himself against a dragon like Eklos simply to protect me filled my heart with gratitude.

Eklos's eyes burned into Z's. "Playing the hero, Zaroch? What a shame. All that potential wasted."

"You will destroy Elysia, Eklos. Your vision for the future will bring nothing but death and destruction. End this now before it's too late."

Eklos ripped his arm out of Z's claws and let out a crude laugh. "It's funny watching you try to be a good male when we both know who you really are." His red eyes snapped to me and Tarrin. "I wonder, do they know the full extent of the monster you are, Zaroch? Or are they blindly accepting a demon into their ranks?"

It was an effort to keep my expression neutral. While Z had confided bits about his past to me in the weeks we traveled searching for Tarrin, he had never been entirely forthcoming. He never quite let me in all the way. There were large gaps in his past that I didn't know about, but apparently Eklos did.

But Z had proven himself time and time again that he was on our side—that he would fight for us. No matter what Eklos said, I would trust him. I wouldn't let that wicked dragon come between one of our greatest allies.

But at Z's silence, Eklos crooned, "Ah, I see you haven't told them." His snout split into a grin of knives. "Pity. I'm sure they would be much more hesitant to have you stand behind them if they knew how many people you have stabbed in the back."

Z growled. "That's behind me, Eklos. I'm not that dragon anymore."

Eklos tsked. "I'm sure they would like to know all the humans you've killed. All the battles you yourself have led. All the heinous, disgusting things you've done."

Though there was no mental bond between Z and me, I knew him well enough to recognize that his tough, calm facade was cracking. Eklos was getting under his scales, attacking at the most vulnerable parts of him. And while Eklos's words surprised me and Z and I needed to talk about this, I wouldn't let Eklos take anyone else from me.

"I know everything about him," I lied, defending him. "You're wasting your breath. Go back to your army. We're done here."

I waited for him to say something else, but my declaration that I knew about Z's past must have thrown Eklos off. Seconds passed as he glared between the three of us. I counted to ten in my head, timing them with my breaths, forcing them to slow down.

By the time I reached ten, Eklos still hadn't moved. Wanting to be away from him, the control I had over my fear and trembling beginning to waver, I turned on my heel to stomp back to Metta, calling over my shoulder:

"I'll see you at war, Eklos."

CHAPTER 43

KAIDA

"START TALKING, Z. Or should I call you *Zaroch*?"

Z's snout contorted into a wince. "Please don't call me that. I haven't been that dragon for a long time."

We were back in Gendon's home, close to the fire in the hearth, trying to infuse warmth into our bones after standing in the cold.

I swiped at the wisps of hair that had escaped its tie as they fell in front of my eyes. "I defended you, Z. You've been our friend, but I know there are things you haven't told us. So, start talking."

Z shook his head. "Eklos is rounding up his army to attack. Is now really the best time, little shifter? We should be readying our own people."

I held up a hand to stop him when he made for the door. "No, Z. We need to know that we can trust you. *I* need to know that I can trust you. We're about to face Eklos, and I need to know that you won't be there with a dagger to stab into my back when I'm about to kill him."

He rubbed at his temple with a clawed finger. "Is that really what you think of me, Kaida? After everything we've been through, after all I've helped you with and sacrificed, you think I would turn you over to Eklos? Or kill you myself?" He turned away from me, exasperated.

"Don't turn this back on me, Z. You haven't been honest with us. Just tell us what Eklos was talking about. Why is that so difficult?"

"Because I'm ashamed of my past!" he yelled, and I couldn't fight the flinch as I took a step backward. His breath was shaky as he lowered his snout to his palms.

"You don't understand, little shifter." The sadness that entered his voice was heart wrenching. "The types of things you were subjected to under Eklos… the torture and the abuse… I was forced to mete that out on thousands of innocents. No—I wasn't forced. I *enjoyed* it. I liked seeing the humans in pain. I relished their fear. I did Eklos's dirty deeds with a grin and a wicked heart. I helped him scout out villages to burn, hunt down shape-shifters, and I loved it all."

"Then what changed?" I asked in a quiet voice.

"Cassa changed everything." Z closed his eyes for a moment. "She was like you, *mutator formarum.*" He looked at me, willing me to understand. "I was ordered to kill her as part of Eklos's plans to destroy Shegora. But… she changed everything. She took this dragon's cruel, wicked heart and breathed life into it for the first time in centuries. I knew I couldn't do Eklos's bidding anymore. I couldn't look at Cassa in her human form, with the most beautiful long blonde hair you've ever seen, like rays of sunshine, and scales a brilliant orange like Flamaria, and turn around and kill hundreds of other humans."

Z shook his snout side to side as though the memories were causing him physical pain. "Cassa was everything I could never be. I could never go back to the life of a Remnant *slave.*" His eyes glistened as he met my gaze. "She brought this monstrous heart of stone to life."

The ticking of the clock on the mantle was the only sound in the room. Z had told me, so many weeks ago when we were trying to rescue Tarrin, about someone he had met, and loved, that I reminded him of. She had forced him to leave her, but Z had never gone into detail like this.

"Why didn't you tell me, Z?"

He narrowed his eyes. "Do you think I enjoy reliving these memories? I despise the dragon I used to be. I would rather die than be forced to do all the horrible things Eklos made me do again. Ever since Cassa was murdered, I've been trying to figure out who I am; what I want to be. Zaroch died when she did. Z has just been trying to find out who he is since then."

"That was hundreds of years ago," Tarrin commented. It wasn't meant to be mean, more a statement of curiosity, but based on the glare Z was giving him, it had hit a nerve.

"Imagine losing Kaida," he bit back. "Do you think you could continue living as if nothing had changed? That you wouldn't feel like a part of you had died with her?"

Tarrin's mouth went slack as he thought about it, and his eyes held nothing but sadness as he looked at me and finally understood a piece of Z.

I wished I had the time to be more compassionate, but with Eklos mere miles away with an army that wanted nothing but our deaths, there wasn't time.

"I'm sorry that you lost Cassa, Z, but I need to know. Are you going to betray us to Eklos? Can we trust you?"

Hurt flickered in his eyes. "After everything—"

"It's a simple question, Z. Please don't make this more difficult than it already is. Are you planning to betray us to Eklos?"

Z rose to his feet, tucking in his wings to keep them from banging into the walls. He crossed the distance between us, lowering himself down to the floor so he could kneel before me. Extending a scaled palm, he waited.

I hesitated for only a heartbeat before I placed my hand on top of his scales. Z curled his claws up, so they were just barely touching my skin.

"Kaida, when I vowed to protect you all those months ago, I meant every word. I see much of Cassa's spirit inside you. It's a spirit that desires peace and prosperity in a world of hatred and fear. She had a vision for it, just like you." Z paused, his gaze flickering to Tarrin before looking back at me.

"Your vision for the future is what Elysia needs. I am sorry that I wasn't honest about my past, but I promise you now, with King Tarrin as my witness, I will not betray you to Eklos and the Remnant."

My heartbeat pounding in my ears was the only sound as his words settled.

"I vow to protect you, to fight alongside you. Until my last breath." Z bowed his head over our clasped hands. "My Queen."

CHAPTER 44

TARRIN

HOURS LATER, NIGHT descended over Metta, and with it the first horn sounded, ripping Kaida and me from each other's arms.

The army had arrived.

From the window of our room, I could see the orange light of flames in the distance, spreading quickly.

My heart thrashed in my chest, and I swallowed the lump rising in my throat. This was it. The battle we had been expecting, anticipating for months. It was time to kill or be killed.

I rubbed a hand over my face as I stared out the window. I needed to get dressed, needed to move, to defend this village, but my feet were glued to the cold floor.

"Tarrin?" Kaida's voice said in my ear, and I flinched. Her fingers curled around my arm, her eyes softening. "We need to go."

I nodded but still I couldn't move, couldn't get my feet to go toward my battle clothes piled on the chair across the room. My mind was full of fog, thoughts made entirely of panic and fear swirling as black shadows amidst the white. We'd trained for this. We were as prepared as we could be.

But my fear was a monster of a different sort, one that had my feet cemented to the ground, my limbs unable to move.

Before I could protest, Kaida pulled me out of my perch by the window, grabbed my clothes and thrust them into my hand. I was reminded of when my mother had died and she had stayed to comfort me, helping me undress and get into bed. The same softness was in her eyes now, but also a hardness that I had yet to witness from her.

"Tarrin, we need to go. Metta is counting on us." She pressed a hand to my scarred cheek.

Whether she intended them to or not, her words cleared my muddled mind like a strong wind forcing the fog away. I threw my shirt on, followed by my pants and boots, lacing them tight up to my knees. Grabbing the light metal armor that the blacksmiths of Metta had forged for Kaida and me, I tossed it over my head, letting her lace up the back so it was snug around my chest. When I had done the same for her, we both stilled, taking in each other's faces.

A sad smile tilted her lips like she knew this would be the last time we'd be together.

My heart wrenched at the thought. No matter what, Kaida had to live; continue on and help Elysia to prosper.

I cupped her cheeks in my hands and pressed my lips to hers. "From now until the afterlife, I will fight for you and beside you, Kaida. If this is the last moment I have with you, know that I am eternally grateful that I met you, that I had the chance to love you." I paused to wipe the tears streaming down her cheeks. "I see you, my love, and your inner beast doesn't scare me. Your heart is *good*. Don't forget that. I love you, Kaida."

She wrapped her arms around my neck and placed a bruising kiss on my lips before she pulled back and gave me the most beautiful smile I had ever seen.

"I love you." She ran her fingertips over my scarred cheek.

"My husband." She paused, tears spilling down her cheeks as her fingers fell away and she squeezed my hand. "My King."

og

Sleet fell from the heavens, pelting our skin like tiny needles.

Though it had only taken minutes to get outside, the fighting was already in full force. Through the dark, the dragons emerged from the shadows like demons and charged for Metta. Some took off into the sky, crossbows in hand, ready to shoot down anyone in their path.

Z and Eldrin were at the front of the battle, meeting the foes with magic and the longest swords I had ever seen in my life. Z's rebels were close behind, and the villagers of Metta remained in the back, ready to fight anyone who made it through the front ranks. The clanging of steel and the metallic scent of blood smothered my senses, and it was an effort to push my feet toward the battle.

Before we left the steps in front of Gendon's home, I took hold of Kaida's hand, holding it as if my life depended on it.

"We're in this together," I said, keeping my eyes on the fighting at the end of the road.

Unwavering affection flickered in her eyes, and I squeezed her fingers in mine. Turning to face the mass of dragons gathered in front of us, hatred lit up their eyes, even in the darkest part of night, their torches flickering in the sleet that pelted into my skin. I let out a breath as Kaida and I shifted into dragon form simultaneously and released a white-hot volley of flames into the air, the signal for all of Metta to charge into battle.

Hand in hand, Kaida and I took to the skies. I glanced at my betrothed, the shape-shifter—the human—I never knew I could love so much, watching her eyes light up with nothing but fierce love.

She nodded. "Together."

၀၃

The wind battered against us in the sky, making it feel like we were constantly slamming into a wall of stone. The dragons were endless, no matter which way I turned, they filled the skies, the ground, with claws and wings and fire. The sleet coated everything in a layer of ice and the humans on the ground below struggled to stay on their feet as they fought for their lives against the dragons.

No matter which direction I looked, beasts and humans battled, sword against magic. Blood coated the snow and my heart ached for the people of Metta. This wasn't a fair fight—it never had been. I didn't know if we had been foolishly optimistic or simply naive.

A yellow dragon moved in my periphery, and I barely managed to duck in time before fire whizzed past my face. I twisted, thrusting my hands in front of me as I met another surge of fire with my own. The dragon grew agitated as I thwarted every advance he tried to make.

"Give it up," he spit. "You're going to die anyway. I'll do you a favor and make it painless for you." His snout split into a terrifying smile full of brown teeth, and I fought down a shiver.

In one swift motion, I reached behind me, grabbed the sword between my wings and swiped at the dragon in a downward motion. Everything stilled within me as sword met scales and sliced clean through the dragon's neck. It thumped to the ground, followed by his lifeless body, smearing the snow in dark-red blood.

I didn't know where to look—at the yellow dragon head, void of life on the ground, or at the wickedly sharp sword shaking in my hand, coated in blood.

Dragon scales were a type of armor in itself, nearly impossible to cut through. The villagers had worked day and night to forge weapons with a special metal that would easily cut beneath scales, but I never imagined it would be so *effortless*.

I didn't have time to remain shocked, or to keep staring at it before another dragon leaped at me. I exhaled, my breath hot in the air, and jumped back into the fight.

Eklos's army was never-ending. Just when I cut down one dragon, there were three more to take its place.

Even though I was in dragon form, I gripped the hilt of a sword in my claws. It was less draining on my magic to infuse flame into a physical weapon than to maintain a weapon entirely of fire.

Adjusting my grip on the hilt, I called on the fire still simmering away in my core, coating the blade in white flames. Another yellow dragon made an appearance, letting out a barking laugh before he lunged through the air, swiping at my wings with his claws.

That had been a favorite tactic of theirs. Attack our wings first so that we were forced to the ground where they could finish us off. I had watched countless dragons plummet to the earth, some who remained fighting below, and others who didn't survive the fall.

I snapped my wings into my back just as the dragon's claws met icy air, and dove behind him, slicing my sword through the center of his wing as I came up behind him. The resulting roar was full of agony, and no longer able to keep himself aloft, he fell through snow and ice, and crashed into the snowy earth below. I didn't wait to see if he survived.

Kaida fought a green dragon in the distance. I wasn't sure when we became separated, having fought side-by-side as long as we were able, but eventually the dragons drove us apart.

The clashing of weapons, the screams of humans, and the growling of dragons were a symphony of pain echoing off the side of the mountain. Half of Metta was on fire despite the sleet pouring down upon it in droves.

The night was dark—darker than it should have been. I

looked to the sky, searching for the moon, for any light to guide us through this endless battle, but even behind the cloud cover, the moon was absent. I scoffed to myself. Even the moon had forsaken us this night. I shook my head, taking in the carnage below; the dragons falling from the sky.

No matter how many we felled, there were always more. Eklos's army was too great—they had too many. And worse than their numbers were their hate-filled, vengeful hearts. It drove them. Fueled them.

For hours we battled in the dark and the cold and the snow, entirely in defense. There had been no opportunity for us to advance against them. They were too well trained.

Something had to change but I was out of ideas. My brain was a muddled mess. Exhaustion was setting in beneath my scales, my limbs weighing hundreds of pounds as my wings struggled to keep me in the sky. I didn't know what would be worse, to remain in the sky or take my chances on the ground.

Kaida! I called down the bond. Where she went, I went. If she desired to stay in the sky, I would follow her no matter what, even if my body begged for a reprieve.

Yes, my love? Though she was locked in a fight, her words through the bond were full of amusement. A small smile tilted my scaled lips.

Do you—

Another dragon lunged for me from behind, digging his claws into my shoulders as he latched himself onto my back.

No! I had to get him off. If he ruined my wings, that was it. I couldn't fly, couldn't protect Kaida.

I thrashed, panic swirling through my core as I fought to get him off.

Tarrin! Kaida shouted, but it sounded far away. Everything narrowed to that moment.

The tips of the dragon's claws met the top of my wing and I braced myself, unable to throw his enormous body off me.

I didn't know what to do. My mind stalled, frozen in panic.

One more heartbeat and I knew my wings would be shredded, the muscles turned into ribbons. I closed my eyes, unable to do anything but accept it.

And then suddenly the weight of the dragon was gone.

Ragged breaths tore through my throat as I gasped for air, embers shooting from my snout, steaming as they met the falling snow.

"Are you okay?" Kaida yelled over the din of the battle, and I spun to find her behind me, the dragon that had been on my back now in pieces on the ground, a sword coated in blood in her hand.

I swallowed the heat in my throat. "I'm okay."

Her eyes softened when she looked at me, and I knew she could feel the panic and despair seeping through my body. It was a poison without a cure, infecting every piece of me.

Let's go down to the ground, Tarrin. Our wings need a break.

I gave a grateful nod, following her down to the earth. Dragons flew past on every side of us, but none of them touched us.

With a crunch, our feet landed in the snow. Eldrin and Z fought next to each other, both of their blue forms nearly invisible in the dark of night. Their movements were in sync, as if they were born for war, born for killing. I glanced behind me and found my father and mother, dragon beside human, fighting with everything they had to keep more dragons from entering Metta and destroying it. My mother's face was red, sweat sliding down her temple, but she didn't waver—not once. She met every blow the dragons dealt with grace and strength and even with numerous cuts across her body, her clothes torn, she didn't relent.

I blew out a shaky breath. If my mother—a human in a war of dragons—could fight fearlessly, then I would silence my inner voice of fear and push on. Kaida panted next to me, exhausted as I was.

It was even more chaotic on the ground.

The dragons were more concentrated here and the clang of swords hitting scales was even louder, hammering into my ears.

"There are so many," Kaida said, and I could hear the despair within her voice.

I gripped her claws in my own. "We can't give up."

She arched the scales above one eye. "Who said anything about giving up?" She lifted her snout in the air in defiance. "I'm simply making an observation."

I couldn't help but chuckle. Even now, she was still defying Eklos, still standing despite the fear coursing through our veins.

I kissed the back of her hand before I turned to face the dragons fighting around us. "Shall we, my Queen?"

Kaida's eyes began to glow with that otherworldly power that shone when her inner beast was about to be unleashed.

"It would be a pleasure, my King."

CHAPTER 45

ELDRIN

I COULDN'T CATCH MY breath.

It was hot and sharp, like freshly forged knives slicing up the inside of my throat.

It had been years—centuries—since I had last fought in a battle, though if I were honest, I had never fought in one like this.

Everywhere I looked was death and destruction. The humans weren't faring well, and against the might of Eklos's well-trained dragons, the dragons of Metta were barely hanging on.

Thankfully, Z's rebels remained strong, unrelenting, not wavering even amidst the snow, sleet, and darkness smothering the earth. They met each burst of magic, each crossbow and sword, as if they were made for nothing else in the world but to fight. For each villager that was cut down, a rebel stepped up and took their place.

My heart ached as it pulsed beneath my skin as I watched the destruction of Metta. Half the village was in flames, and I couldn't help but wonder whose houses were floating to the sky, who would return to charred earth instead of their homes. That was… if the people would even be able to return.

Z loomed off to my right, his ice-infused sword swinging and arcing through the air, turning dragon parts to ice before shattering them into pieces as he sliced into them. It was a sight to see, Z in battle. It was like war ran through his veins. The sword wasn't just a weapon but an extension of his arm. The way he used magic and sword in tandem was mesmerizing.

I could understand—watching him—why Eklos would be so desperate to have Z in his ranks. Not only was he a great fighter, but he seemed to be keeping his mind straight while doing it. That was the thing with dragons—they tended to lose themselves in the bloodlust. It was some primal thing deep inside of all of us. Those who weren't strong enough to fight against that utter need to kill, lost themselves to it, unable to think clearly or to stop.

Though Z was hyper-focused as he cut down anyone in his path, his eyes were clear, even in the dark. He wasn't a beast out of control, but a dragon made for battle and strategy.

Though Tarrin had a rough relationship with him, I found myself incredibly grateful to have Z on our side.

Sucking down a deep breath of icy air, I followed his motions and launched into the fight next to him, infusing fire with my blade that was the perfect twin to his sword of ice.

My mind went blank as I sliced and parried and stabbed at the enemies around me. The motions flowed through my body, my muscles acting from memory.

For a moment, I had a reprieve and looked around for Eklos.

I lost track of him in the battle, and I had no idea where that coward was hiding. Was he even fighting or was he forcing everyone else to die on his behalf?

A sharp pain cut through my swirling thoughts.

I looked down to find a small blade thrust beneath my left arm.

With a growl, I ripped the blade from my scales and chucked it as hard as I could back at the dragon, a small smile twisting my snout as it sunk deep into the scales over his heart.

Eklos must have also had special weapons made for such

a dagger to cut beneath a dragon's scales like they were butter. Normal steel weapons couldn't do that, and the process to strengthen the steel to the point of penetrating scales took much time and experience.

The dragon's eyes widened as he looked down at the hilt sticking out of his chest. Tiny embers popped out of his mouth as he opened it to say something but before a word was spoken, he crashed backward to the ground, his scales fading as the life left his body.

Pressing a hand to the injury beneath my arm, I winced as my scales came away bloody. It wasn't a fatal wound, but it was enough to cause pain and be a distraction.

I glanced over my shoulder, back to where Lita and Martik were fighting. Even in the dark, I could see the exhaustion on Lita's face, her cheeks and nose red from the cold, the air clouding around her with each gasping breath. We had been at war for hours. How was she still standing, let alone fighting?

Even from the distance, I could see the tremble in her arms as she lifted her sword into the air, swinging at any beast that happened too close. Martik was doing his best to fend off the dragons around her, but he was only one against many.

Fire filled my core as I drew on my magic and jumped over to the two of them.

Lita's brow arched when I appeared next to her, her eyes instantly moving to the blood dripping down my scales.

"You're hurt," she deadpanned.

"How observant of you," I replied, wiping sweat from my scales. How I was sweating in such horrendous cold, I had no idea. "You need a break," I said, hoping she wouldn't take it as an insult to her strength or human body. "Can you clean the wound before it gets worse?"

Martik responded for her. "Go Lita, I can hold them until you return."

Lita looked like she wanted to argue, but exhaustion took control and her shoulders sagged, her feet dragging through the snow as she worked through those still fighting and headed toward Gendon's home. Heat smothered me as I entered, feeling much too hot after being in the cold for so long.

"How'd you get hurt?" she asked as she went to the little chest in the corner of the foyer and rummaged through it.

"Wasn't paying attention to my surroundings. They have weapons that can cut through scales too. Thankfully, it didn't go too deep."

Lita found some towels and bandages and walked over to me, settling us into the two chairs against the wall.

"I've heard stories of war my entire life. My father used to tell me what Xalerion's battles were like, and how he never wanted to see another like it for as long as he lived." She pressed an alcohol-soaked cloth to the wound, and I grunted against the pain. "I was prepared for war, Eldrin, but I wasn't prepared for *this.*"

"What do you mean?" I asked to keep her talking to distract me from the needle she was using to pull the skin beneath my scales together so the bleeding would cease.

"I knew that war meant killing. But this… this is mindless slaughter. The dragons don't even seem bothered or remorseful at all. I was prepared for death, but not like this."

I winced as she finished the stitching. "Do you—"

A pain-filled roar shattered the air, heartbreakingly loud and Lita and I both stilled as recognition settled into us.

"Martik," she breathed.

We raced back into the sleet-drenched night.

CHAPTER 46

KAIDA

BLOOD AND SCALES and body parts littered the snow. The sleet had stopped for the moment, but the temperature had been dropping steadily over the past hour, and every piece of me was both numb and shivering. It was late in the night, or early in the morning, depending on which way you looked at it, but dawn was still a ways off, and I was tired of fighting in the dark. There were too many shadows for the dragons to hide in; too many humans fighting that couldn't see through the darkness.

Though, by now, a large portion of Metta was ablaze, illuminating the battlefield around me. Bile swirled in my stomach, and I forced myself to stop looking around. Eklos's army was relentless. Just when I thought we had made a dent in their numbers, or that we had pushed them back and had earned a momentary reprieve, a fresh resurgence poured out of the trees, as if they had been waiting for exactly that moment.

I swung my sword with trembling arms at the arm of a blue dragon, my inner beast relishing when it connected with flesh and the dragon let out a growl of pain. In a nimble maneuver that I wasn't even aware I could make, I spun on my feet, smacking my tail into the dragon, knocking him to the ground. Before he could move, I thrust the sword through his chest, stopping his heart with a quick stab.

My beast smiled, begging to be released, but I held on, not wanting to fully lose myself. I might have to kill to survive this war, but I didn't want to be a monster about it. Besides, I had to save the strength of my magic, my beast, for that final battle against Eklos.

An enormous, pain-filled roar filled the air and everyone surrounding me, even the army, froze as they stopped to search for the source. Something was different about this sound and every human and beast recognized it.

I spun to find Tarrin bounding across the snow toward his father who was now lying in the snow, clutching his chest.

It was Martik who had been wounded, shattering the night with his roar.

The battle continued to rage on, but everything within me went silent.

Z and his rebels remained at the front, locked in a fierce battle. Even across the field Z met my eyes and remorse flickered within his. Was Martik… dead? With a series of whistles, Z and a few of his rebels fell back, closer to where the former King had fallen, and he gave me a nod as if to say that they would protect us while we took care of Martik.

"Kaida!" Tarrin shouted, and the sound of war slammed back into my ears. My feet moved beneath me on instinct. The ground rumbled as I ran as fast I could in dragon form, falling to my knees next to Tarrin, tucking my wings into my back so I could get closer.

Martik's wings were crumpled beneath him as he lay there gasping, blood leaking from a large wound in his chest. His snout was contorted in pain, his eyes squeezed shut.

Tarrin's claws hovered over his father, visibly shaking.

"Tell me what to do," he demanded. "How do I fix this?"

I wasn't sure if he was asking me or Martik.

The former King shook his head. "I don't think this is a wound one can heal from, Tarrin." His voice was hoarse, rattling, as if there was blood in his lungs. He coughed, forcing more blood to spill from the hole in his chest.

"I need to tell you something, Tarrin. Something important."

Tarrin shifted into human form, likely trying to mute the overwhelming emotions coming down the bond. Tears spilled onto his red cheeks, his nose pink from the cold. Placing his hand on the wound, Tarrin tried to stop the blood from leaking out, but it was no use. It spilled between his fingers.

He shook his head. "No, you're going to make it, Father. I don't want to hear it. Whatever it is can wait until you're healed."

The sound of running footsteps sounded behind me and I glanced over my shoulder to find Lita and Eldrin sprinting for us. They both crashed to their knees in the snow on the other side of him, Lita running her hands over Martik's scales.

"This is important, Tarrin. I need you to know…" He looked at Lita. "I need you both to know."

"What is it?" she asked, cupping his snout with a hand.

"I haven't… I can't…" The words stalled on Martik's tongue, and both Lita and Tarrin were struggling to keep their emotions from taking over.

"Father, perhaps you shouldn't speak. Let's move you inside where we can—"

"No!" Martik's voice echoed among those gathered in a lose circle around us, and we all flinched in unison.

A growl ripped through the air behind me, and I turned just in time to see Z stop an enemy dragon from slicing through my back. With a practiced maneuver, he beheaded the dragon before moving back to his place among the rebels. Anxiety pierced into me like talons. If we stayed in the open like this for much longer, we'd be killed.

"There's a secret I've kept… buried." A cough wracked through his body. "One I tried so hard to keep silent for centuries… until I was convinced I could no longer access it."

The four of us all exchanged glances.

"Martik, what are you talking about?" Lita asked, her brow furrowed low over her eyes.

"I wanted to protect you at all costs," he rasped, though blood continued to pour through Tarrin's hand as he pushed against it. "I buried it, suppressed it, so that there would be no backlash or outrage. I did it to protect you both."

"Father, what is it?"

"I'm—"

But before he could finish, Martik's eyes widened as he gasped, his turquoise scales instantly fading to gray as the light left his eyes.

Soul-sucking silence filled the area as the four of us held our breath, every sound of war filtering away until it was just a faint noise in the distance.

Our shifter bond went still, and it reminded me of when Tarrin's mother had died—before he started screaming. To his credit, Tarrin didn't scream, though tears cascaded down his cheeks as he gently shook his father's body, trying to infuse life back into it. Lita's chin trembled as she stared at her dead husband.

What had he been trying to tell us? What secret had he kept for so long?

I couldn't escape the feeling that it was vitally important.

"Lita," my voice shaking with grief. "What was he trying to tell us?"

She shook her head, her chin trembling, lips pressing into a thin line.

"Eldrin? Do you know?" I pressed.

My father shook his head, his mouth still wide open as he stared at his friend.

I opened my mouth, to say what I didn't know, when Z

appeared at my side, and the sounds of battle rushed into my skull once more. I fought the urge to cover my ears.

"I'm sorry," he panted, looking each of us in the eye. The sword he held rested in the snow, dripping thick drops of red onto the ground. "Perhaps we should move him into the house where his body can rest peacefully." He winced, likely expecting his words to come across offensive.

My insides were numb, and not just from the bitter cold. It felt like Z had taken his magic and infused it within my bones— my heart. If I all but twitched a finger, I would shatter into a million shards of ice.

Gendon appeared out of the crowd of villagers, his eyes shining with extraordinary grief as he beheld his old friend.

"I'll help you move him," he offered to Eldrin who then nodded and knelt before the former King.

Arrows and dragons flew overhead, but everything narrowed to this moment—watching Martik's lifeless body being carried away. Lita and Tarrin were silent as he was lifted off the ground, their hands that had been resting on his scales falling to the snow with a crunch. Rather than watching him move toward Gendon's home, they stared off in the distance in different directions.

I put my hand on Tarrin's shoulder. "Tarrin?" I didn't know what to say to him; didn't know what to offer. That hopeless feeling I had felt when his mother had died flared strong within me.

He had already lost so much. How much more would we all lose before this was over?

We needed to return to the battle, to defeat Eklos once and for all, but I couldn't move and instead rested my head on his shoulder, wrapping my arms around him. I faintly registered Z's rebels still fighting off the dragons around us when I felt a strange surge in the crowd around us before I heard multiple intakes of breath.

I lifted my gaze to where Eldrin and Gendon both held Martik's body, just outside the cave-home.

That was when I saw him.

A strange man stood in the doorway, with short gray hair, and a long face, somewhere around Eldrin's age in human form. He held a blanket tightly around him, his bare feet and legs peeking out from underneath, and his eyes were wide in disbelief. I studied him, trying to place why he seemed familiar though I had never seen him before. When I took in his eyes, I let out a gasp of my own.

Tears flooded my eyes as I pointed, telling Tarrin to look.

Lita was on her feet in moments, sprinting for the door.

Z, Gendon, and Eldrin looked horribly confused.

But I couldn't fight the smile as I took in those familiar turquoise eyes, the same no matter what body they were attached too.

Tarrin's mouth hung open as Lita threw herself into the man's arms.

A soft sob escaped me as I said, "Tarrin, your father was a shape-shifter."

CHAPTER 47

TARRIN

MY FATHER… WAS a shape-shifter?

How had I never known? Why would he have kept such a secret from me—from us?

He said he had kept it hidden to keep us safe. Safe from what? We were already shifters. There was nothing to protect. And if he had been a shape-shifter this entire time, my entire life, how had he made all those decisions that hurt humans? The memory of him sentencing the humans in Absult to the fire chamber replayed through my mind. I knew he had to go along with the whims of the Council, but surely, if he were half-human himself, he would've fought a little harder, tried to protect them.

But instead, he continued to allow the enslavement and mistreatment of slaves.

Anger swelled in me like a tide, momentarily smothering my relief that he was alive.

Not only that, but how had he suppressed that part of him for so long? Even after months on the run with Kaida and Eldrin, not shifting or using that part of my abilities, had taken its toll. It drove me crazy being unable to shift or release that magic.

How had my father gone my entire life without shifting? Had

it been decades? Centuries? He said he thought it might be gone forever, just before his dragon form moved into the afterlife.

But there was no denying the man I was staring at as my mother sobbed in his arms was my father. Though he no longer had dragon features, his eyes flashed with that familiar cunning as he took in his surroundings; the same downturn of his mouth as his mind churned, though it was with lips instead of scales.

My body shook from head to toe, but whether it was from the cold or the fact that I had just watched my father die and come back to life, I wasn't entirely sure.

Was fate playing a cruel joke on us? Or was this an incredible mercy that we had been granted? My emotions were a mess, running all over each other, making it feel like my brain was being kicked repeatedly. Even back in human form, it was still too much. I couldn't process it all. Did I cry out of grief because my father's dragon form no longer lived? Or did I laugh and weep tears of joy because of this incredible secret he had kept that meant he had another chance at life?

Cold fingers interlaced between my own and I could barely turn my head to look at Kaida. Wide, turquoise eyes flitted back and forth over my face. My feet were held to the ground by invisible fingers of ice, and I couldn't move.

I looked over my shoulder at the carnage of the battlefield, at the humans and dragons still battling away, Z's rebels in a half circle around Gendon's home to protect us as we tried to make sense of my father being a shape-shifter. As I watched, their protective circle quickly shrank as they were forced to take step after step backward. Though the rebels fought well, the sheer numbers of the army were simply too much. We only had minutes left before we'd be forced to join back in the fight.

A strange feeling crept over me, like being covered in needles, and the hair on the back of my neck stood on end. Nerves bundled in my stomach in a tight, twisting ball. My eyes roved back and forth over the fighting dragons, but I didn't see anything that would warrant such a feeling.

Then a brief flash flickered, like light hitting metal, and my body tensed.

"Tarrin?" Kaida said at my side. "What—"

"Look out!" I yelled, tackling Kaida to the ground. I cradled Kaida's neck and back as we fell to the snow, cushioning the impact as much as I could.

Then three things happened in quick succession.

The distinct snap of a crossbow sounded in the distance.

Metal whistled through the air before a wet crunch echoed.

Then an ear-shattering scream rent the air.

I held tight to Kaida, expecting to feel the pierce of an arrow burrowing into my skin.

"No," the whisper slipped from her lips, hot on my ear as she craned her neck to see what had happened—who had been hit.

Lifting my head, my limbs grew even colder though it should have been impossible after hours in the brutal winter temperatures. A massive iron arrow protruded from Gendon's chest—just to the left of where my father and mother stood. His eyes were wide as he stared down at himself, his snout open in disbelief. Humans and dragons were scrambling around, some looking for medical supplies while others were merely frantic, holding off the press of army dragons that surged forward.

Z was instantly at his side, carefully supporting his weight as he helped the dragon lower to the ground. Blood started leaking from between Gendon's teeth.

I pulled myself off Kaida, helping her up before we both sprinted across the snow to the dragon's side. His breathing was labored, and his scales had already begun to fade, as if they knew it was only a matter of moments until his heart stopped beating.

Kaida kneeled next to him, carefully placing her hands around the arrow still stuck in his chest.

Why had the army targeted Gendon? Surely it would have made more strategic sense to take out Kaida or me, or even Z.

But why Gendon?

Unless…

He had been standing very close to my parents. Had whoever shot the arrow meant to hit them instead?

"Hang on, Gendon. A healer is coming," Kaida whispered.

A sad smile twitched on his scaled lips as he looked at her.

"Queen Kaida," he began, and she flinched at the title. "It is my honor to die fighting by your side. I know you will make things right. I am thankful to have been able to give you all I have, to support you when it mattered most." He stopped speaking as a wet cough erupted from his snout.

"Shh," she murmured. "Don't talk like that. We'll get you help. Just hold on a little longer."

Gendon gave an imperceptible shake of his head. "I am honored to have fought with you, my Queen." His claws searched for her hand, and she gripped his massive hand in both of hers. Tears poured down her cheeks, steaming in the cold. "I believe in your better world, and if anyone can do that for Elysia, I know it's you." Another cough shuddered through his body.

"Now, go," he ordered, his voice fading. "Go make them pay for what they have done."

As soon as the words left his mouth, so did the light in his eyes. The last of the air in his lungs seeped out of his snout, his green scales fading to the color of ash.

Though we were in human form, a surge of wrath and fury soared down the bond. It was terrifying but also somewhat awe-inducing to feel that inner beast of hers thrashing to be unleashed—to end the bloodshed before anyone else could die.

With tears still sliding down her red cheeks, Kaida stood to her feet, blood coating her hands. Her feet pivoted beneath her as she turned to face the army, many of the dragons stopping their attacks to sneer at her. They thought they had won.

She looked back down at Gendon's lifeless body and said in a low voice, "Don't worry, Gendon. I intend to."

Like the Queen she was, Kaida lifted her chin in defiance and stalked toward the battlefield. In a brief flash of purple, she was back in dragon form, letting out a stream of white-hot flames in the air.

"Eklos! Come face me, you vile beast!"

Kaida's scream had everyone's movements slowing before coming to a stop. The soft hiss of snow hitting the ground was all that could be heard as she stood there, waiting. There was no sign of Eklos.

Shifting back into dragon form, I moved to stand by her side, eyeing each dragon as they first sized her up, then me. Z and Eldrin followed, remaining a few steps behind us. I didn't see my mother as I glanced over my shoulder. Had she stayed back to look over Gendon and my father?

An invisible line ran between us and the army as they raised their weapons and aimed at us.

I pulled the long sword from the sheath between my wings, the hilt groaning as I tightened my frozen claws around it.

"Eklos!" Kaida shouted again. "Face me, you coward!"

Still the enemy dragons didn't move, didn't part to let the dragon of ash and smoke through their ranks. There was no sign of him. My eyes roved among the dragons, searching for that familiar pair of red eyes.

"Let's end this!"

I could hear the anger, fear, and desperate need to end this war combining in her voice. It made my heart ache. She had carried it with her for months, and we had already lost so much; lost people that hadn't deserved to die. Kalev flashed through my mind. The former captain of the King's Guard had rescued us in

Feltar, protected us, and was murdered for it. Now, the same had happened to Gendon. Not to mention the countless humans and dragons that laid face down in the snow around us, their souls already released into the afterlife.

When would this end? Even if we had turned ourselves over to Eklos, nothing would have prevented him from wiping Metta from the face of Elysia.

A ripple went through the army, and my head snapped toward the right flank. And there he was, like a demon emerging from the smoke and shadows of the night. Eklos materialized, slowly making his way down the barren snow left empty between us. His matte black horns and ash-colored scales were almost invisible in the dark, his glowing red eyes making my stomach drop as he grew closer.

"Nice of you to show your face," Kaida snapped. Reaching behind her head, she pulled out the two swords that were strapped between her wings, brandishing them in front of her.

Eklos laughed, causing the dragons around him to chuckle uncertainly.

"And just what are you going to do with those, girl?" He eyed her swords as if they were nothing but twigs. "Put those down before you hurt yourself."

Anger swelled inside me, and if it wasn't for the mental hand Kaida pressed to my mind down the bond, I would have lunged for him right then.

Let me handle him, she said in my mind. *This is no one else's fight but mine.*

"Send your minions away, Eklos. This is between you and me."

Eklos scoffed, sparks flying from his snout. "On the contrary, girl. This is between all dragons and humans. And *you*," he spit, shaking his head side to side. "You're the worst of them all."

Kaida bared her teeth in a terrifying smile. "Come and get me then."

His red eyes smoldered. "As you wish."

Eklos ripped the crossbow from one of his dragon's hands and aimed it directly at Eldrin. Before any of us could blink, let alone move, the trigger clicked, and an arrow soared for the midnight-blue dragon.

"No!" Kaida screamed, throwing her arms out in front of her.

Her eyes flickered with the purple color of lightning, and suddenly the arrow stopped mid-air. Kaida held both of her scaled palms up toward the sky, and a cocoon of blue flames slid over our small group. I could feel the heat, though it didn't burn, and offered a pleasant reprieve from the winter air. The arrow was incinerated instantly, mere inches from Eldrin's chest.

Eklos's face went from a smug smile, to shock, to absolute fury, his teeth flashing as he snarled.

"I said," Kaida bit out through clenched teeth, her head slowly turning to look at him like a predator about to pounce on its prey. Her eyes were blazing. "This is between you and me. Touch my family again and you will die."

The shield of blue flames remained around us as she stepped through, the fire parting around her body, leaving her unharmed. She lowered her swords to her sides, one hand holding a sword smothered in flames, and in the other a sword wreathed in lightning.

The snow crunched beneath her feet as she took one slow, taunting step at a time toward Eklos. His eyes tracked every step before he let out a wicked snarl and leaped into the air, taking off into the dark of night.

Kaida didn't hesitate for a moment before she leaped after him, flames and lightning soaring through the sky.

And then the army attacked.

CHAPTER 48

ELDRIN

MY MIND WAS a mess of grief, fear, and desperation as pure chaos broke out in Metta.

Slash. Cut. Stab. Duck. Swipe.

I lost myself in the movements of the fight, barely even having a heartbeat to breathe before the army had attacked. I lost track of where Tarrin and Z had gone, and only the vague flashes of lightning in the sky told me where my daughter was fighting.

My heart begged for me to leap into the sky after her, to help her defeat my cousin, but the onslaught of the enemy dragons was too much. It was like a tidal wave of claws, fire, and steel flooding and consuming anything that dared to stand against it.

How did it even come to this? It should be *me* fighting Eklos in the sky. I had so many chances over the last millennium to fight him, to kill him, but I could never bring myself to do it. I wasn't sure if it was because at the heart of it all he was family, or if I was simply just a coward.

Either way, I was now stuck fighting on the ground while my daughter fought for her life against one of the vilest dragons to ever walk Elysia.

A dragon swung at my head, forcing me to duck for the umpteenth time. The movement brought my eyes back to Gendon's house and my throat grew thick even as I spun on my heel, slamming my tail into the dragon's chest before stabbing my sword through his gut.

Gendon was dead. The most selfless dragon I had ever met, who had sacrificed the village he had built from the ground up, the dragon who had helped us, healed us… He was gone because of my cousin.

And then there was Martik. He had died, only to reveal that he had been a shape-shifter. How had I never known? Why would he have kept such a secret from me? From Lita?

I wanted to be angry with him for lying to me for centuries, but I was so incredibly relieved that he wasn't dead, that perhaps Lita and him would have another chance at life *together*, that the anger faded to the background. There would be time for us to talk—for him to explain things after the war.

Or, at least I hoped there would be.

Another dragon came from behind me, latching on to my back, his claws digging in between my scales. Panic should have been my first response, but my limbs were so cold and numb, my body heavy with exhaustion, my *mind* consumed with every emotion imaginable that I was slow to do anything at all.

I felt the moment the dragon's claws skimmed against my wings, knew that I'd never be able to fly again after he was finished tearing through them. But I couldn't make myself move. The only thing I could do was fall backward, trying to squish him with my own bodyweight.

The slam didn't work as I had hoped, and aside from a grunt from the dragon, he simply wrapped his long arms around my neck and started to squeeze. Dots flashed in my vision as I gasped for air. I thrashed and wriggled, clawing at his arms, but to no avail. My eyes slipped shut, as my tired body began to accept that death was creeping in, when a wet, sickening crunch sounded right in my ear, hot liquid splashing onto my snout. The arms around my neck slackened in an instant and I rolled away, coughing, trying to get air into my lungs.

"Looks like you could use some help," Z's voice remarked. I glanced over my shoulder and found him standing there, his long sword through the skull of the dragon that had been choking me.

"I had it covered," I said, my voice a choked rasp.

A smirk lit Z's face. "It's been a long night."

I coughed out a laugh. "That's the understatement of the year."

"We've lost many."

I could only nod, unable to look at all the dead bodies surrounding us. The first streaks of dawn speared up from the horizon.

We had fought all night long, and yet the army still pressed against us. I cringed to think of what daylight would illuminate—what we'd find left of Metta and its villagers.

"We can't keep going, Eldrin. We can't win like this."

The words were a knife to my gut. I had known it from the start. We simply didn't have the numbers to sustain a battle and win in the end.

A blue dragon appeared behind Z, his mouth opened wide, ready to bite down on his shoulder. Without a second thought, I thrust my sword through the air, feeling immense satisfaction as it slipped through his open mouth, cutting straight through his skull. He fell back to the ground with a thud.

Z's eyes were dull, bored as he looked at the dead dragon then back at me.

"Now you're just showing off," he muttered.

Embers shot from my nose as I snorted before engaging with yet another dragon.

Chaos reigned around us, the clanging of steel and the growl of beasts deafening in my ears.

It was visible—the exhaustion and defeat—in every person fighting against the army. Swords were just a little slower, the dragons' reactions a split second too delayed. Z was right. If something didn't change—and soon—there would be no one left to stop Eklos. We'd all be dead.

But what could be done? I didn't have the ability to summon people out of thin air to fight on our behalf, and the longer the battle continued, the more the dead bodies piled up in the snow.

I closed my eyes for a heartbeat, despite the war raging around me.

How did we keep fighting when there was no hope? How did we keep fighting when we were out of strength, and there was no one to help us?

Time slowed as I watched the army dragons cut, slash, and strike against humans and dragons alike. Their muted cries and roars of pain sounded far away, echoing before they stopped altogether.

Despair was a poison spreading through my body, weakening my knees to the point where I crashed into the snow, my head hung in defeat.

"What are you doing?" Z snapped, and it was a struggle to pry my eyes open to look at him. He was a few yards away, his chest heaving from killing the dragon on the ground in front of him. His green eyes were bright with fury.

A fog of hopelessness smothered my mind, and I sank farther into the snow, unable to make my limbs move.

A low snarl ripped from his throat as he stalked toward me. "Get up, Eldrin." He smacked my snout with the side of his blade.

I couldn't even look at him in surprise or anger. I just wanted the fighting to end. An impatient snarled ripped from his lips, and he summoned ice to his palms before shooting it at me.

His ice spread over my body, forcing my legs to straighten, pushing me onto my feet. The ice fortified my shaking limbs, helping me to remain upright though every part of me begged for sleep.

"I said, *get up,*" he bit out. "You've come too far to quit now.

This is not where you yield, Eldrin. You. Keep. Fighting. The battle is not lost yet."

I blew out a breath as his magic released me, every part of my exhausted body trembling with fatigue.

A horn sounded in the distance, followed by an unearthly chorus of roars, cleaving my head in two. My stomach sank. That couldn't possibly be more reinforcements coming to Eklos's aid.

But then the roars sounded once more, and all at once, the battle halted, every single body, both human and dragon, freezing where they stood. I looked to the south, in the opposite direction that the army had come from.

In the distance, barely visible as dawn spread its fingers through the sky were massive-winged shapes, hundreds of them, flapping toward us. At the very front flew a dragon with scales white as the snow, with horns that sprouted from the center of his head like tree branches. It took more than a moment for my exhaustion-riddled brain to comprehend that Eklos was screaming.

But he wasn't screaming in triumph.

He was screaming in fury.

"Stop them! Shoot them from the sky! Kill them all!" he shouted, repeating the commands over and over to the dragons on the ground below him, his battle with Kaida momentarily pausing.

If those dragons weren't part of the Remnant's forces, who were they?

I studied the approaching hoard and saw the figure of a man riding upon the white dragon's back. I blinked, unable to comprehend what I was seeing. And as I looked even closer, I saw hundreds of humans, each riding on the backs of the dragons.

With renewed hope and energy pumping through my body, I pushed off my legs and took off into the sky after them.

Who is it? Tarrin yelled down the bond as he engaged in battle with another dragon.

They're here to help! I shouted over the din. I still couldn't believe what I was seeing—w*ho* I was seeing. *Tell everyone to reform the lines and to hold them!*

Who are they, Eldrin? Tarrin's voice came down the bond once more.

Unable to contain it any longer, a roar of victory erupted from my snout.

My old friend Noam has saved us all!

CHAPTER 49

KAIDA

EVERY RAVAGING BREATH that ripped from my throat was a combination of icy daggers and whips of flames.

I couldn't breathe—couldn't get enough air into my lungs. The cold ripped it away, sending it tumbling through the air in thick cloudy waves, as my lungs sputtered to get even the smallest amount of oxygen.

The moment the horn had sounded, and the symphony of dragon roars split the dawn, Eklos had taken off for his army screaming at them—as if I was the last thing he cared about in all of Elysia.

I was back on the ground, the snow crunching beneath my feet, and I ducked as a dragon clawed at my head, snapping me back to reality. My arms were heavy, but I gripped the swords in my hands tighter and lunged for the dragon's weak spot beneath their arm. Caught off guard by my speed, the dragon didn't have time to deflect before I shoved a sword beneath his scales, pushing it up into his chest.

I yanked it free as he fell with a ground-shaking thud in front of me.

My father's words rippled into me again. Noam was here? How?

Eldrin soared through the sky as it quickly lightened to a red-kissed hue as the sun began its ascent over the horizon.

My favorite scent in the world, night air and blue cypress, filled my senses and I spun to find Tarrin behind me, gasping for air. When I had taken off after Eklos, I had lost track of him in the fray. There were bloodied scales on much of his body, but thankfully, based on the scent, none of it seemed to be his.

"Noam is here," he said, his eyes fixed on the dragons soaring for us.

"How?" I couldn't understand it, my exhaustion-addled mind unable to riddle it out.

Shadows passed over me and I glanced up, seeing an endless number of dragons racing toward Eklos's army. Some dropped to the ground, shaking the earth, beginning to fight the dragons, while others remained in the air, swooping in and out as they shot dragons with their crossbows or sliced through their bodies with enormous swords.

All at once the screaming of humans dying turned to the pain-filled growls of the army as the new band of dragons slaughtered through them. I watched as both Z's rebels and the villagers of Metta fought with renewed vigor, sensing a tide turning in the battle.

A white dragon was suspended high in the air, conversing with my father.

Without a second thought, I pushed myself off the ground, soaring for them. The sun had peeked its head halfway over the horizon, illuminating the gruesome snow below, but I didn't see it. I saw nothing but Noam's beaming face as he clung to the white dragon's back.

"Kaida!" Noam whooped when he caught sight of me.

Tears sprang to my eyes. "Noam," I croaked. "I've never been so happy to see your face."

His eyes softened, his grin turning to a kind smile. "Likewise, my dear."

"What are you doing here?" Tarrin said, coming up behind me.

Noam's gaze flicked to his, but Eldrin responded first.

"I sent him away from Mistwick all those months ago to find help."

Tarrin narrowed his eyes. "To find help?" He looked around at the dragons fighting below. "Who are they?"

Noam's face brightened and patted the white dragon's scales beneath him. "This is Annion. He is the leader of Almyra." He paused for dramatic effect, glancing between the two of us, mischief twinkling in his eyes. "Almyra is an island south of Elysia… an island of shape-shifters."

"An island of shape-shifters?" I exclaimed at the same time Tarrin yelled, "There's actually a land outside Elysia?"

Annion laughed, his voice a deep rumble that reminded me of Gendon. A pang shot through my heart at the thought of him. I shoved it down deep inside, locked tight in a place full of other horrors that I'd have to examine and deal with at some point. But not now.

"There are many lands outside of this one, Young King," Annion said. "Worlds that have other creatures, other races, much more than what you've seen in Elysia."

I looked to Eldrin, whose face was nowhere near surprised enough.

"Did you know, Eldrin?" I asked him.

"I've heard rumors over the centuries that there might be other lands beyond ours, but I have never left to find out for myself." He paused, his wings thudding behind him. "I had hoped that there would be others that Noam would find that might be willing to aid us in this war. That's why I sent him away. He sailed far to the south." My father looked at Noam. "He may have just saved us all."

A distant shouting pulled my attention away, to a young girl with brown hair, frantically waving from the back of a blue dragon.

"Kaida!" she shouted against the wind, a grin plastered on her face. My snout fell open as I gazed upon the dragons still arriving, countless humans riding them, coming to our aid.

"How…"

"I docked in Mistwick before heading here. I tried to recruit as many like-minded people as I could; humans that might be willing to fight alongside the dragons for their freedom," Noam explained, before pointing at the girl. "Jinna was the first to volunteer."

Tears pooled in my eyes, spilling over onto my scales. I waved back at her, watching her soar toward the ground and the awaiting army, sword in hand.

Noam looked smug before he sobered, looking at me. "We'll buy you time, Kaida. There are hundreds here, ready to fight." He pulled a long, wrapped bundle from behind his back. "This is for you."

With careful claws, I unwrapped the cloth from the item, a small gasp escaping my lips. It was a long sword with beautiful etchings along the metal. It was in a language I couldn't read.

"The writing is the legend of the Ancient Magic, etched in the old language." He pointed to the handle where a lion's head sat on each end of the guard. "The lions stand for bravery." He tapped the top of the pommel where a large amethyst sat shining in the light of dawn. "The amethyst symbolizes strength and peace in chaos." He cleared his throat.

"This sword has been passed down through the generations of my family. It's yours now," Noam explained, a wistful smile on his face. The generations of his family… Noam was descended from the Order of the Magus, the humans who first shared the Ancient Magic with the dragons. He was also a direct descendant of Silas and Vitea, two of the humans who fought against the Lone Dragon in the Battle of Mount Sunder.

I opened my mouth to speak but no words would come. He just smiled.

"We'll take care of the army. Go take care of Eklos."

I didn't have the words to express how grateful I was not only for Noam risking his life to find us help, to bring us hope, but that humans who didn't even know us, and an island full of shape-shifters, of *strangers*, would be willing to risk their lives to come help us defeat the vilest dragons in Elysia. Dragons were normally selfish beasts; they perverted the Magus's gift of the Ancient Magic and tried to wipe out the humans to be the sole keepers of it.

But watching these dragons, the morning sky full of vibrant colors, as they soared around, cutting and killing anyone in their way—protecting us, protecting the humans below—it was a piece of that better world that I had always dreamed of.

It was within our grasp.

The only thing that stood in the way of it now was Eklos.

My eyes searched the sky, scouring for the dragon of ash and smoke. When I finally found him, he was hidden behind a group of dragons on the ground, letting them fight on his behalf. Fire stoked in my core, my inner beast thrashing and begging once more to be released. I had been saving it, all the magic, all the wrath of my dragon for this moment.

Eklos would pay for all he had done; all he had taken from me... from all of us.

I looked to Tarrin, feeling that heat swell within me.

"Together?" I asked.

His snout split into a smirk, and I could easily see the human-ness in it.

Perhaps we all had a bit of monster in us, but it was our choice whether to yield to it.

Tarrin's eyes softened as he looked at me, and I could see all the words he didn't say as he said, "Together. Always, my love."

CHAPTER 50

KAIDA

THE WIND SHIFTED directions, pushing my wings, my body, faster as I soared toward the cowardly dragon on the ground. It was as though nature itself wanted to see him dead and was aiding my flight to reach him.

Eklos poked his nose over the snowbank he was hiding behind and began growling and barking orders for the dragons to surround him, to create a cocoon of bodies so that I wouldn't be able to reach him. He didn't even bother to fight alongside them.

What a fool.

The ground rumbled as I landed hard in the snow, flaring my wings to the side as I stared down the thirteen dragons surrounding Eklos. Varying shades of red, black, and orange eyes met mine, some surprisingly flickering with fear, though most were just full of hatred.

Tarrin landed behind me, spraying snow in every direction.

I stared down each of the dragons surrounding Eklos, noticing the amulet with the dragon inside the sun that each wore around their necks. So, they weren't simply dragons in the army, but members of the Remnant... Eklos's commanders.

I bared my teeth and said with deadly calm, "Move."

A familiar brown dragon began to laugh, and a moment later

everyone else joined in. He stepped forward and I realized it was Roldan, the dragon that had conspired against Martik, that had attacked him and my father in the forest, and that had planned to kill Tarrin.

"Give it up, girl. You won't be reaching Master Eklos."

My insides simmered as the magic in my core swelled, growing and coursing through each of my veins. My scales vibrated on my body, and I no longer noticed the winter air. I was made of fire.

I let a bit of magic leak out of my claws, holding a ball of flames in each hand at my sides.

"Move," I repeated, not breaking eye contact with Roldan.

His only response was to widen his stance, still chuckling, though it was tinged with a bit of uncertainty.

"Get out of the way, Roldan," Tarrin commanded, standing at my side. "You won't win this. Leave now while you can."

All the Remnant dragons burst out laughing, turning their snouts to look at each other.

"You hear that, males? The little prince thinks he can defeat us." His eyes fixed on Tarrin.

Tarrin straightened, extending to his full height, glaring at the brown dragon. "That's *King* to you." His voice was lethal, full of dominance.

For the briefest moment, Roldan looked like he second guessed his decision, as if the news of him now being King was an absolute shock, and he realized the grave error he had made, but then Roldan wiped the emotion from his face, a smooth, cruel smirk twisting his snout.

"Oh, my," he crooned. "Did you hear him, my fellow dragons? You stand before a King now." The words were scathing, mocking. "Well, you heard the male. Bow before your King."

The brown dragon dropped onto his knee before using the movement to push off the ground and lunged at Tarrin.

But Tarrin was expecting it and put his claws out to slow Roldan's momentum.

"Go, Kaida!" Tarrin growled, never taking his eyes off the Councilman. "I'll take care of him."

And then my husband was gone, fighting Roldan with everything he had.

I turned my attention back to the twelve dragons in front of me, separating me from Eklos.

"I suggest you move," I warned, staring each one down.

Movement at the end of the line caught my attention. A rich-green colored dragon shifted his stance, staring straight at me. Why did he look familiar? Then movement on the other end had my eyes narrowing. He looked familiar too.

That was when I realized who they were, along with two others hidden amongst the Remnant.

Those dragons that Lita had swayed to help us rather than Eklos? They were standing in line. They, too, wore the Remnant amulet. Were they undercover, ready to help me defeat them? Or had they been lying all along, and now I'd have to face them as well?

My question was answered as all four of them moved in tandem, drawing their swords and attacking the dragons next to them, narrowing my focus to just four instead of twelve.

My inner beast smiled, welcoming the challenge of cutting down these Remnant dragons—of ridding Elysia of their evil.

I lifted my claws to the sky, flames and lightning wreathing between them as I crooned, "Fine, have it your way."

And I unleashed my fury on the Remnant.

CHAPTER 51

TARRIN

I DUCKED JUST AS Roldan swung his tail at my head. In a smooth step, slide, and twist, I whipped the sword from the sheath on my back, and sliced through the air, expecting it to make contact with his body.

The air whistled at the force as it met nothing, and I fought to keep from falling forward from the momentum.

"Is that your best?" he drawled. "I expected more from a King." His dagger teeth glinted in the light of dawn.

"If I killed you outright, I wouldn't be able to tell stories one day of how I fought and rid this world of you," I spit back, satisfied when his eyes glowed hotter, and he pushed back harder.

Out of the corner of my eye, flames and lightning soared through the air. That primal beast within me demanded that I go to her aid, protect her no matter the cost, but I silenced it, knowing that this was how I could best do that.

A sudden pain spiked through my arm as Roldan's dagger penetrated beneath the scales on my arm. I hissed, blowing a mouthful of fire directly at his face. He ducked just in time, the flames soaring over his head.

The cut was deep, blood pouring steadily from it, but it could've been worse.

Roldan sneered. "Did the little prince get hurt?"

With a violent snarl, I lunged for him, swinging my sword for his neck. Once again, the dragon dodged out of the way.

"My, my. How clumsy. For a *King* I expected…" He paused, gesturing at me. "Well, more."

His cruel words had me launching forward, momentarily forgetting all the training I had endured, blinded by my anger. After months in the dark, wondering if I'd ever see the light of day again; being tortured, screaming in the shadows for hours on end…

I wanted Roldan to feel a piece of that.

We met blade to blade, the metal ringing in my ears as they crashed together, sliding apart, and meeting again. His eyes flashed, a wicked smile on his snout as he slowly wore me down.

A roar in the distance cut through my bloodlust.

Kaida.

My eyes snapped to where she battled the Remnant dragons.

The distraction cost me as Roldan slammed his blade into mine, sending me sprawling backward. My tail collided with the icy snow, shooting pain up my back. I tried to scramble away, to get far enough that I could get back on my feet, but the brown dragon advanced too quickly. My limbs slipped and slid around as I fought to gain traction.

"I hope you enjoyed your short reign, King Tarrin. I wished I could say I'll miss you but… I won't."

With fury in his eyes, and loathing in his heart, Roldan lifted his sword to the sky, swinging it down in an arch toward my head. Frozen, I could do nothing as the blade inched toward my face.

The metal flashed but the impact never came. A dragon, green like the trees in a summer forest, tackled Roldan around the waist, sending them crashing and rolling through the snow.

Recognition snapped through me, and it was everything I could do not to stand there gaping at the new arrival.

The green dragon got Roldan beneath him and slammed his

clawed fist into the Councilman's face over and over, his body inching deeper into the snow. When he stopped, Roldan lay there, groaning, unable to move.

The green dragon pried himself off the ground, unafraid to turn his back on the enemy.

I stepped forward. "Master Alathar?" My words were tentative, hope-filled.

The last time I had seen my old tutor was the day before I saved Kaida from The Den, at our last training session when he said he would be going away for a while.

"What are you doing here?" I asked in a whisper.

His scaled lips spread into a smile. "I'm here to help, of course."

"But how—"

Alathar held up a clawed hand. "I told you that I was going away for a while, but I was not honest with you about the reason why, and for that I apologize. But I was sworn to secrecy."

"Secrecy? What are you talking about?" The words sputtered out of me before I threw a glance at Roldan to make sure he was still on the ground.

"I was sent away, Young King."

His use of the title surprised me. How did he know already? No one outside of those gathered before the war should've known.

Questions bounced in my head, but our time was limited, so I only asked, "What do you mean?"

Alathar glanced over my shoulder at Roldan who was beginning to stir. When he met my gaze, he said, "I was sent away, to prepare Almyra for war."

"What?"

How could he have been sent on such a mission? No one even knew that Almyra existed, let alone that there were shape-shifters there that could help us fight Eklos's army.

"Sent by whom?"

Master Alathar hesitated for a moment. "Your mother."

Spots flashed in my vision at his words. "My mother?"

She had known about Almyra and the shape-shifters? How? We were always taught that Elysia was the only land in the world. We *were* the world. Sure, there had always been rumors of what might lay beyond the shores of this continent, but no one had ever returned when they dared to leave, so no one knew for certain.

How had she known to send my tutor all the way there?

"What do you mean my mother?" Though I was happy to see him, at the moment I wished to throttle him for giving such vague answers that only prompted more questions.

None of this made any sense.

A snarl ripped through the air behind me and Alathar's eyes widened before he pushed me to the side in time to miss Roldan's claws gouging into my wings.

I turned to face the Councilman, muttering, "Don't think this gets you out of answering my questions."

Alathar chuckled. "I wouldn't dare to think so."

When it had been only me against Roldan, we were evenly matched. It was a struggle to outthink and outmaneuver the beast, but with my old tutor by my side, the very dragon who taught me to fight, trained me in magic… well. Roldan didn't stand a chance.

Master Alathar assumed his typical battle stance, widening his legs, one slightly behind the other, one arm across his chest, the other above his head. Water pooled over the scales covering his hands.

I called on every memory, every second of training that Alathar had instilled in me, only strengthened by that of both Z and Noam.

Fire flared in my hands and, in unison, our steps and arm movements identical, the two of us attacked Roldan.

The Councilman fought, tried to stand his own against both of us, but we were too strong for him. It was only a few minutes before I managed to strike him down, and Alathar swooped in with the fatal blow to his heart. A part of me wanted to be saddened by his death, but that part was crushed by relief.

"All right. He's dead," I announced. I needed answers. "Explain."

Alathar gestured at all the other dragons fighting around us. The air was filled with the cacophony of battle.

"Shouldn't we help first? There's still a war to be won."

I shook my head. "It can wait for a moment. I need to know."

A deep smoke-laced sigh came out of my tutor. "You know about your mother's gift?" It was both a question and a statement.

And that's when everything clicked.

"Foresight," I whispered and Alathar nodded.

"Many years ago, Young King, your mother had a vision of this very war. Her rare gift of Foresight granted her the knowledge that Eklos would create an army, that he would attack you all here, in Metta. That you would be King by the time the battle began. Her vision showed her of an island hundreds of miles south of Elysia. An island that held countless shape-shifters. A human with graying hair would come to the island looking for help and that was my signal to move the shifters I had prepared back to Elysia."

Noam. My mother must have seen him through her Foresight.

Alathar paused, his wings drooping behind him. There was a weight on his shoulders, the burden my mother had given him by sending him to prepare Almyra, a burden that was not over.

"Lita knew that Eklos's forces would be mighty, and if we had any hope of defeating them, we needed more numbers—more strength. So, she came to me, explained about her vision, about everything she had seen. She wasn't sure, you see, if Almyra was even real. Though her Foresight visions had never led her astray before, there was no record, no knowledge of such a place, so she had nothing to go on but a dream."

"Why didn't you tell me?" I was trying not to be offended. He was only my tutor, it wasn't like he was a best friend with whom

I shared everything. But still… if war had been coming, if my mother had known about it as long as he claimed… why had no one said anything?

"It wasn't my place." Alathar's gaze was bright as he watched me process his words. My mind flashed back to the time after my mother had died, when my father first told me of her gift. He had said that she knew everything that was to happen, and every decision she had made was because of what the future held in store.

All along she knew. She knew about Almyra and the shifters, about Noam, about this *war*.

I only wished my mother, my friend, had shared the burden with me; let me shoulder the load with her. Perhaps I wouldn't have fought her so hard about finding Kaida or acted more like a king and less like a spoiled prince.

I sighed. None of that mattered now.

The battle still raged around us, and Kaida's lightning was in the distance, fighting the last Remnant dragons before she could finally face Eklos.

"Master Alathar…" I began, my voice trailing off.

He slowly turned to face me. "Yes, my King?"

His words had me straightening, reminding me of the strength and power I now possessed. But still… I had to know.

"Do we win?"

His scaled lips twitched, eyes shining in the light from the sun, but he said nothing before he leaped off the ground and took to the skies, letting out a barrage of flames, signaling the final wave of dragons now arriving above Metta to descend and wipe Eklos's army from the face of Elysia.

CHAPTER 52

ELDRIN

I FOUGHT ON THE ground, Annion on my left, and Noam on my right. Enemies surrounded us, but between the fresh surge of new dragons, and the sudden hope flaring in my heart, it felt as though the battle had just started.

Renewed strength soared through my bones as the sun continued to rise in the sky, and I even managed to joke with Noam.

"That's six now. How many are you at?"

Noam's face twisted into a scowl. "Not fair, Eldrin. You're bigger than me."

I cocked my head to the side as I sliced into another dragon.

"Seven," I announced with a haughty voice.

Noam rolled his eyes, though he thrust his sword beneath the arm of another dragon, directing it up into his heart. The dragon fell with a thud in the snow.

"Three," he spit out, though I could see the corners of his lips twitching, fighting a smile.

Annion chuckled, blood glinting on his white scales as he beheaded the green dragon in front of him. "Perhaps we should focus more on winning this battle than on comparing number of kills."

"Where's the fun in that?" Noam and I said in unison which set us laughing, though we continued fighting those in front of us.

In my peripheral, I could see Kaida's signature purple lightning splitting through the air as she fought through dragon after dragon, trying to get to Eklos.

Noam noticed my gaze. "Should we help her?"

I considered it for a moment. I would love to get my hands on my cousin, to finally rid the world of him. But at the same time, I knew that Kaida had to be the one to fight him. After being enslaved by him her whole life, being tortured and abused like all the other humans in Elysia… It needed to be her. She needed that closure. If things started to look bad, I'd step in. I wouldn't let my daughter die. But I had confidence in her, and I believed she could defeat him.

I eyed the dragons she was fighting through, one by one each of them falling to the ground in a heap of scales. Her lightning was doing all the work for her, lashing and striking, dealing fatal blow after fatal blow as she continued to fight with a flame-wreathed sword in each hand.

"If you think you can assist her, I imagine she'd be grateful for the help," I said in response to his question. I didn't like the idea of putting Noam in Eklos's path, but my friend was well-trained and smart. He would be all right.

"As you wish, Eldrin the Great. But this counts as double the number of yours."

I let out a chuckle, remembering his old nickname for me. He had told me once that it was because I never enslaved him, never harmed him like the other dragons—that I was greater than the rest of them.

"Only if you're careful, old friend."

In the span of five heartbeats, I grabbed his arm and jumped us to a safe place close to Kaida. With a squeeze of my hand on his shoulder, I thanked him silently, then returned to the field, continuing to fight side by side with Annion.

ɞ

The sun rose steadily through the sky, and while it did a great deal to help my exhausted body, it also lent its strength to the enemy.

A mighty roar sounded, and I looked up to see a green dragon leading in another large group of dragons. They descended over the army like a withering disease, cutting down dragons left and right, somehow knowing exactly who was friend and who was foe.

I breathed a sigh of relief, though I still engaged with the dragon in front of me. He swung at my chest with a spiked tail, and I bounced backward, renewed strength keeping my steps light. Spinning on a heel, I stayed low to the ground and used the slick ice-covered snow to give me momentum and kicked the dragon's feet out from under him. The maneuver was one I had adapted from the human's fighting stances, and it was one of my favorites. The dragon's eyes widened before he crashed to the ground and Annion came in with a finishing blow to the head.

"Thanks," I said, breathless.

A smirk on his white scales was his only response as he dove back into battle.

I took a moment to look around at the battlefield.

There was blood everywhere, coating everything. Before Noam arrived with help, there had been more dead humans in the snow than Eklos's dragons.

But now... the enemy littered the snow, as numerous as the ashes beneath a fire.

After months of wondering if we'd be able to defeat them, if we would have enough numbers, victory was finally in our sight. The numbers were on our side and our chance of winning grew with every second that passed. We had been fighting for hours, from the time night fell to well past sunrise, and for a while, I thought we were going to die.

There had been no visible hope of winning.

But that's when it mattered most—to keep fighting when you didn't see hope. Maybe that made the oncoming victory even sweeter.

Annion continued slashing at the dragons around him, their enormous bodies dwindling with each second that passed. Time slowed as I watched him turn in my direction, his eyes widening, flickering to something behind me. I only had time to turn around, to face whatever threat was there, not even able to lift a weapon to defend myself.

A huge orange dragon with black eyes loomed over me, and I instinctively raised my arms in front of my snout as he swung his sword. Pain erupted in my body, blinding and sending burning lights across my vision. I crashed to the snow.

Hot blood coated my scales from where the dragon's sword had cut deep into my arms, skimming my chest as I fell. I growled in agony as I fought to push myself back up, but it was no use. My snout bounced off the snow as my body collapsed once more.

The orange dragon laughed. "Eklos will be pleased," he growled, prowling closer. "He might not be able to end you himself, but at least you will meet an end." He lifted the sword, blade pointed down.

I needed to move, needed to defend myself—do *something*. But my body wouldn't respond. I could do nothing but watch as he plunged the blade straight into the center of my chest.

Fiery, blinding pain erupted through me, stealing the breath from my lungs. My vision went dark before the sun light was blinding again. The frigid air evaded me as I gasped for breath, looking down at the gaping hole in my chest. The dragon's snout spread in a pleased smile, standing over me as my blood spilled into the snow. He raised his sword once more.

I could do nothing but close my eyes and wait for the afterlife to find me.

A muffled thud sounded but nothing happened.

I hesitantly opened my eyes and found the orange dragon bleeding out on the ground, a light-gray dragon standing over him, bloodied blade in hand.

"Rythos?" I croaked out. Pain coated every nerve, every thought and I fought against the haze smothering my mind.

"Get up, Eldrin," Rythos responded, his voice weary.

I tried, I really did, but the wound in my chest and the deep cuts on my arms were too much, too painful.

"I can't," I whispered.

"You have to get up, Eldrin." There was a faint note of panic in his voice.

"I'm not going to fight you, Rythos. Just kill me and be done with it." I laid my head back down in the snow with a wet crunching noise.

Rythos let out an exasperated grunt before he was suddenly next to me, touching my arm, then my chest. I roared in agony as hot, knife-like pain shot through them, but then it stopped. The sudden absence of pain had me gasping down air as if I hadn't taken a breath in hours.

Surprised, I glanced down and noticed glowing blue patches on my arms.

"You're... you're a Mender?" I gasped out. Like Foresight and Dream Weavers, Menders were extremely rare. I had never met one in my thousand years of life, only hearing stories passed down through generations of dragons. They had a combination of healing and mending abilities that allowed them to take the pain out of an injury, or in my case, hold my wounds together long enough to get proper help.

"It'll hold you together until the battle is over," he explained, ignoring my revelation. "Now, get up."

The pleading in his voice was so surprising that my feet moved beneath me, and I pushed to my feet with a groan.

"You should have just left me for dead."

His gray scales shimmered in the sunlight, giving off an iridescent glow.

"Why are you helping me? Ever since Silverdew Valley, you've sworn you were going to kill me." I spread my arms out, the wound in my chest twinging. "Now's your chance."

Fire flared in his palms as he stared me down. "Is that what you want, Eldrin?"

"I've made a lot of mistakes in my lifetime, Rythos, but being your friend all those centuries ago wasn't one of them." I paused as his glare grew more intense. "I won't fight you. I won't kill you."

He took a step toward me, sending flames to cover the blade of his sword. "You would let me cut you down, right here, and you would do nothing to stop me?"

The air clouded in front of my face as I exhaled. My body was so cold, so tired.

"You were my friend, Rythos. No matter what you've done or been a part of, I won't hurt you. I know there's a good heart somewhere inside of you. You just got lost along the way."

Rythos stilled.

Then he stalked toward me, gripped my neck in his claws and lifted his sword to my scales.

"Fight me, Eldrin," he growled, a desperate look entering his eyes. His claws squeezed tighter around my neck.

"I won't."

"He wants me to kill you." His words came out as a frantic whisper. "I can't kill you if you won't even fight back."

Tears burned my eyes. "Do what you have to, old friend. If you think this is what's right, for you *and* Elysia, then do it. Be done with it." I closed my eyes, waiting for the bite of the blade into my neck.

Screams and growls and metal clanging against metal filled the air, but my ears felt like they were stuffed with cotton. My legs trembled beneath me, begging for a reprieve from both the fighting and the cold.

And then the sting of his claws digging into my scales disappeared, along with the cold metal beneath my snout.

Rythos staggered back as if I had dealt a physical blow. "You never did leave on purpose, did you?" His voice was so quiet I could barely hear him over the din of battle. "You never thought you were better than me—than any of us. Did you?"

Cold pooled in front of me as I exhaled. "No, Rythos. I didn't."

He held my gaze for several moments despite the chaos around us. Then finally he gave a slight nod and took another step back.

"You were right, Eldrin." His breath shuddered out into the cold air. "Eklos has corrupted the dragons, and the world he would bring about would be utter destruction." He dropped his sword into the snow. "I won't kill you."

The scales on my forehead bunched as I arched a brow. "You're betraying Eklos?"

His eyes were firm, utterly serious as he met my gaze. "He betrayed me a long time ago, the moment he poisoned me against you."

I wanted to say more, to understand why my old friend who had grown to hate me so much, suddenly had such a change of heart. But he reached his arm out, grabbed my shoulder and blackness surrounded me, squeezing the air from my lungs.

Then I opened my eyes and ice filled my core as I watched lightning fork through the air, connecting with one of the Remnant before he went limp and fell to the ground with a thud, steam rising off his body.

I was several feet away from Kaida as she took on the last two Remnant dragons. Noam was crouched behind a snowbank on the opposite side. Why had Rythos brought me over here? Kaida was holding her own; she didn't need my help.

I turned my head, intending to ask him, but Rythos had disappeared once again.

CHAPTER 53

KAIDA

ONE BY ONE the Remnant fell.

They were no match for my magic. It sought them out like a writhing snake looking for a victim to inject with its venom before it devoured them whole. Only two remained, the rest were in faded piles of scales in the snow. I lost track of the four dragons that had been helping me. They were either dead or went to help fight the rest of the army.

Lifting my claws to the sky, I felt a surge in my core as I called the lightning to me, pulling it straight from the clouds before I swept my arms down in an arch, slamming the burning, purple streaks into the dragon on the left. He didn't stand a chance; didn't even move before he was burned alive from the inside out, crashing to the ground in a steaming heap.

A smile split across my snout. One more dragon.

"Last chance," I growled.

There was movement in my periphery, but I didn't pay it any mind. All I could see—could focus on—were the red eyes hiding behind the dragon in front of me.

Eklos was a coward. Standing there, watching me slaughter each of his commanders, each of the Remnant that he had spent centuries preparing for this moment. He didn't even bother fighting for them or defending them. He just cowered behind them, waiting to see if I could defeat all of them before I came for him, likely waiting for me to wear myself down before I faced him.

Even if I didn't relish the thought of taking lives, simply by the fact that Eklos wouldn't defend his own, showed that he had no mercy in his black, hardened soul. Even if I wanted to spare him, which I didn't, even if he begged, pleaded, for me to let him go, he would only betray that second chance. If Elysia had any chance of prospering, Eklos could no longer be a part of it.

With a flame-covered sword in one hand, and a lightning-wreathed sword in the other, I called on every bit of training that both Noam and Z had forced into my brain and attacked the last remaining Remnant dragon.

My weapons were extensions of my arms, slicing, moving, cutting through cold and scales. The dragon let out a plume of fire, and I crossed my swords in front of my face, flaring my magic, watching with glee as it consumed his attack.

"Finish her!" Eklos roared at his minion and the dragon stiffened, losing focus for a split second—a second that allowed me to uncross both swords, slashing through his neck.

Before Eklos's command had even finished echoing on the battlefield, the dragon's head bounced into the snow, his body collapsing next to it.

A wicked smile spread across my snout.

There was no one else in my way.

Now, I would finally end this war with Eklos and we could start building a better future for Elysia.

A low snarl ripped from between his teeth.

"You won't win, slave. Give it up now, and I'll spare you."

A short laugh barked out of me. "You wouldn't spare the life of a bug, let alone the life of a shape-shifter. Call off your army, Eklos," I demanded, willing my teeth not to chatter as the wind cut beneath my scales. "This is between us." Lightning wreathed my fingers, bouncing lights over the snow as it reflected off my scales.

He clucked his tongue. "I am neither kind nor merciful, you stupid human. Everyone here is guilty of helping *your kind*." Sparks flew from his nostrils as he spat the words. "All will suffer. All will face my wrath."

I swung my swords toward the ground where blood, both dragon and human, coated the snow. "Don't you think there's been enough bloodshed?"

A blood-chilling laugh burbled out of his throat, and his eyes grew brighter, like living flames.

"It will never be enough." Eklos's voice was slimy, like wading through a muck-filled swamp, feeling the algae rub against my skin.

I tightened my grip on the hilts of my sword, sending my magic spiraling around them. "Let's finish this."

His red eyes burned like bright embers as his scaled lips spread into a grin of knives.

I lunged toward my former Master with a roar that shook the stars.

He swung at me, and I barely managed to sidestep, stumbling to regain my balance. When I spun to face him, I expected him to be there with another attack, ready to pierce my scales.

Instead, what I saw made my veins turn to ice, my blood growing cold.

Eklos, with his scales of ash and smoke, and those bright red eyes, loomed a few feet away with a fire whip in each hand.

The same fire whip that he used to punish slaves.

The same fire whip he had used on me countless times.

The same fire whip that had killed my mother.

Despite being in dragon form, my human instincts took over and I retreated a step. Then another.

My heart thrashed in my chest, my breathing erratic. I couldn't get enough oxygen into my lungs. Black spots dotted my vision, and I was forced to retreat another step. Sweat spread over my scales despite the cold temperature.

Eklos took a taunting step forward, snapping the whip at his side.

"What's the matter, slave?" he crooned, his red eyes burning with hatred.

I shook my head, my tongue heavy and mouth utterly dry. My mind wouldn't operate—wouldn't form coherent thoughts.

Only the memory of the whip biting into my skin, flaying it into pieces, the fiery burn afterward filled my head.

Panic consumed every thought, and I was suddenly desperate to get away from here—from Eklos.

As if he could tell the effect he was having on me, he grinned wider, cracking the whip again. It sounded like the snap that had my mother's head separating from her body, thudding to the ground.

I squeezed my eyes against the memory. My knees wobbled, legs trembling, and I fought against the need to fall to my knees.

And then a warm, scaled palm encircled my arm, and every horrible thought and memory halted. I turned to find Tarrin next to me.

Breathe, he said in a calm voice down the bond. *Don't let those memories—let Eklos—have this kind of power over you, my love. You are stronger than your past, stronger than your pain. Breathe.*

The dam holding my lungs closed fractured before it burst, a flood of oxygen coming into my lungs and I gasped, the spots disappearing from my eyes.

Good, Tarrin said, rubbing his scaled fingers in a soothing motion on my arm. *Eklos only has the power over you that you give him. You came here to finish this war. You are strong, Kaida. Let's show him.*

Warmth licked up my limbs, flaring out from my core, thawing all the ice that had encased my body. Smoke leaked from my nostrils, and I exhaled, bursts of flames sliding between my teeth.

Tarrin was right. Eklos had no power over me any longer.

And now, I would make sure he never had power over anyone else ever again.

I took a step forward, enjoying the sight as Eklos's eyes widened.

Pulling myself up to my full height, I smiled as I united with my beast, letting her have control, and a roar ripped from my throat as I leaped after Eklos, swords blazing in my hands.

CHAPTER 54

KAIDA

EKLOS DIDN'T MISS a beat.

I didn't think it was possible to parry a sword with a whip, but somehow, he managed, the collision sending white sparks flying. His snout was so close to mine that I could smell the carrion on his breath, feel the heat of the flames in his mouth.

He pushed back, forcing us apart and the momentum had me spinning on my heels.

"Kaida!" Tarrin roared, and I yanked my sword up just in time to deflect his whip. It coiled around my blade, and I gave a mighty pull, but it remained firmly in his grasp.

The heat of the fire whip grew closer to my face as Eklos pushed harder, his eyes like living flames.

And then the weight was gone, and a series of snarls filtered into my ears before I realized that Tarrin had tackled Eklos, both scratching and clawing at each other. Eklos's wings were pinned beneath him, and an idea formed in my mind, forcing me to move.

Flaring the flames on my sword, I took advantage of the distraction and shoved the blade into his wings, over and over, severing muscle, tendon, and bone. There would be no escape for him.

His roar was so deafeningly loud that I fell backward, covering my sensitive dragon ears. Before I could react, Tarrin's body was soaring through the air, and hit the snow with a crunch.

"Tarrin!" I screamed, but then Eklos was on his feet, bleeding wings drooping behind him as he stepped between us.

His claws circled my throat, digging into my neck. I coughed, desperately ripping at his scales, trying to get him to release me, but he only squeezed harder, baring his teeth. My claws dug through the snow as I searched for my sword, but it was just out of reach.

Then, a mighty pain-filled growl ripped through Eklos's teeth that had the pine needles on the trees shaking off their branches, forcing him to release his hold on me. Blessed air streamed into my body, and I coughed violently, searching for what had hurt Eklos.

That's when every inch of me locked up.

Noam stood behind Eklos, both hands gripping the hilt of his sword as he plunged it deeper into the dragon's back.

The shock was evident on Eklos's face as he stared at the sharp tip poking through his chest. He stumbled backward, which had Noam scrambling out to the side to keep from being trampled. My lungs spasmed, trying to get air back into them as I coughed, struggling to get my vision to focus. I couldn't even bask in the glory of Eklos being wounded, to see him backing away from me for once, because as Noam fought through the snow to get out of the way, it brought him into the dragon's line of sight.

Despite the numerous bleeding wounds littering Eklos's wings, and the sword through his chest, he moved toward Noam, letting out a plume of flames.

I could do nothing—couldn't move fast enough as Eklos dove for my friend with an ear-shattering roar, sinking his massive teeth into Noam's soft skin. His teeth narrowly missed Noam's head, and instead punctured into his shoulder and chest, before Eklos tossed him through the air like he was made of straw.

"Noam!" I screamed as he landed hard in the snow with a

heartbreaking crunch. His eyes were closed, and the snow beneath him was turning redder by the second. He didn't move, his leg twisted at an awkward angle. I tried to run to him, to help my friend who had taught me so much, had given me hope, but Eklos blocked me again.

I swallowed the lump in my throat, forced down the fear that my friend was dead. The fire in my core cooled, going preternaturally still.

Eklos tutted, turning his head to look at Noam's body bleeding out on the ground. "Look what you've done, you foolish human. His death is on your head." He met my gaze. "All of them are."

My inner beast thrashed at his words.

I closed my eyes for only a heartbeat, feeling the magic I had saved up for this exact moment soar through my veins. The sun was now fully over the horizon, and it hit my scales, infusing power and life into my bones.

When I opened my eyes again, Eklos's smug face dissolved, and he staggered back. Heat hovered over my head as flames and lightning intertwined to form a crown, white flames enveloping my body like I'd done in the forest just days ago.

Tarrin stumbled to my side, blood seeping from a wound on his head. His claws rose into the air as he summoned enormous iron shackles with his World Weaver magic and sent the chains burrowing deep in the ground. They encircled each of Eklos's limbs, and the chain tightened, forcing him down so that he couldn't escape. He fought against them, roaring and flailing around, bloodying his wrists as he clawed at the restraints. He bared his teeth though his eyes were wide.

"You can do this, Kaida," Tarrin's voice rushed into my ears, and I could see the strain on his face as he tried to hold Eklos in place.

I wouldn't let Eklos take another person from me. I wouldn't let him win this war.

And with those final thoughts, I exploded in a collision of lightning and flames, sending the storm of anger, fear, and grief within me, infusing it with my magic, and sent it spiraling for Eklos.

Brilliant light flashed, followed by a deafening thunderclap.

When the lightning and flames dissipated, my ears ringing from the thunder, cold wind blew the smoke away, revealing Eklos… with hundreds of black holes all over his body. They were so large that I could see the landscape behind him *through* his body. Surprised, he looked down at himself before he toppled backward, the ground rumbling beneath the weight. Smoke billowed from all the holes, all the places my magic had scorched and devoured.

With measured footsteps, I stalked to his side. Each of his breaths were rasping, horrid things. He opened his mouth to speak, but no sound came out.

Good. I didn't want to hear his pleas for mercy.

I sheathed one of my swords on my back, then shifted into human form.

His eyes shone with nothing but hate as he stared at my human face.

I gripped the sword between my hands, hesitating.

"Do it," he spit, goading me.

I tightened my grip on the sword. The resolution I made back in Belharnt suddenly came to mind. I'd promised myself that I would not be like Eklos; I would not let the pain of the past decide my future. I would not be ruled by hatred but choose to rise above it. For a better Elysia. Yet as long as Eklos lived, he would never stop until all shape-shifters and humans were destroyed.

A laugh bubbled out of his throat as his red eyes pierced into me. "I knew you couldn't do it," he rasped. "You humans are too weak."

"Silence!" my inner beast snarled. "I am not the one who's weak, Eklos. Only a coward would take pleasure in using and abusing another living being. Only a weak person would enjoy slaughtering innocents and spreading hate like a poison." I leaned over him. "I am not weak. It takes strength and courage to face what you put me through my entire life. It takes strength to face the darkness and hang on long enough to see the light again. It takes *strength* to no longer want to walk this world but to push on despite the ache in your heart.

"Everything you've put me through, Eklos, every year in Belharnt, every day at The Den… I am strong because of it. You tried to break me—to take everything from me. And maybe at times, you did. But look at me now, *Master.*" I spread my arms to the side, letting the crown of magic over my head flare. "Everything I am, I am because of your cruelty. And guess what?"

His eyes narrowed as he gasped for air.

"*I win.*" I raised the weapon, sunlight glinting off the sharp metal.

I remembered what I'd told Noam during our sword training months ago back in Mistwick. *A sword will not bring down Eklos, with scales hard as stone and smoke capable of killing me with hardly a thought. Learning to fight with a sword will not save me. Or Elysia.*

"This is for Noam," I bit out before thrusting the sword deep into his chest, relishing the thud as it went all the way through, slamming into the snow beneath. I slid it free with a metallic, squelching sound.

"This is for every human you've ever killed, touched, or harmed," I continued, stabbing him deep in another part of his chest. His eyes bulged, blood spilling between his teeth.

"This is for my mother," I cried between ragged sobs, forcing the sword into his heart.

Hot tears streaked down my cheeks like little fires on my skin.

Eklos's gasps for air, for me to stop, as he clung to life had me closing my eyes for a moment.

When I opened them, Eklos's red eyes were fixed on me. Every memory of life as a slave, every nightmare of Belharnt, every cruel day in The Den… they all passed between us in that moment. I didn't know if here, on the brink of death, if he regretted any of it.

Either way it didn't matter.

I adjusted my grip on the sword and held it above my head.

"And this, Eklos…" My arms shook, and a sob ripped free of my throat. "This is for me." I screamed and plunged the blade into his skull, directly between those red eyes that would haunt me forever.

CHAPTER 55

TARRIN

I KNEW THE MOMENT that Eklos was dead because everything on the battlefield instantly stilled as though there were a lifeline connecting him to every single one of the army dragons.

It would have been convenient if the remaining dragons *had* keeled over dead as soon as Eklos's heart ceased, but unfortunately that didn't happen.

Before the war began, Kaida and I had talked about what would happen once we won the battle—*if* we won—and what we would do with any dragons that managed to survive. We knew that if allowed to remain alive, there was a chance that someday they would try to spread their poison again, and try to rise against us, though neither of us relished the thought of taking even more lives.

Z had presented an alternative that, in the end, we all agreed to. If any of the surviving army dragons surrendered, we would spare their lives. Any who didn't… Z's rebels would take care of them.

Kaida and I didn't want to begin our reign or start building a new Elysia by slaughtering those who genuinely wanted a second chance. If they proved they wanted things to be different, that they wouldn't spread the poison that ran through Eklos's veins, then we would give them that chance.

And Z was all too willing to deal with the rest.

Bodies littered the snow in every direction, the smell of carrion and death filling the frigid winter air like a suffocating cloud.

Kaida stood over Eklos's body, staring at him, her arms hanging limply at her sides. I expected to feel relief or the last remnants of anger toward her former Master… anything. But what concerned me was that I felt absolutely nothing. Kaida's thoughts were quiet, her magic dormant. It was utterly silent as she stood there shaking in the winter wind.

I needed to go to her. Help her. Whatever storm was quietly brewing inside, I needed to help her weather it.

I shifted into human form, and before I could even call for him, Z was at my side.

"My King?" he asked, and for the first time I thought I saw a glimpse of respect in his eyes. I didn't know if Z and I would ever get along or fully see eye-to-eye, but in this moment, he looked to me as his ruler, and not like a spoiled prince who didn't know what he was doing.

I wished I knew how to explain how badly I needed that; to know that someone as powerful and old as him could see me as his King. But somehow Z knew.

I opened my mouth to ask him to take care of things, to handle the rest of the army, to check on Metta and my parents, but the only sound that came out was a strangled gasp.

That familiar smirk contorted his snout. "Consider it done, my King. Go take care of her."

How he knew what I was asking, I didn't know, but I gave a single nod, hoping that it conveyed my gratitude for him in this moment, and for all he had done to fight for us.

A genuine smile spread across his snout before he bowed and

headed back toward the line of enemy dragons that the rebels had lined up.

I didn't look back as I turned and sprinted across the snow toward Kaida.

Not even when the screams of the dragons began.

CHAPTER 56

ELDRIN

"NOAM!"

I crashed into the snow next to him, shifting into human form, blood seeping between my fingers as I tried to staunch the bleeding on his chest. I knew it before I had even touched him… it was no use. The wounds were too deep. Eklos's teeth had barely missed piercing Noam's heart.

A jagged line of teeth holes punctured in a diagonal row from his shoulder down his chest and ending at the ribs on the opposite side of his body.

Noam fought to open his eyes, his brows furrowing at the effort. Every breath was a shuddering wheeze out of his mouth.

"Noam," I repeated, my voice breaking at the word. I brushed the sweat-drenched hair out of his eyes, grimacing when blood smeared his forehead. "Hold on, you're going to be okay."

A small smile curved his lips. "My friend," he wheezed. "Is it over? Did we win?"

I choked on a sob. "Yes, Noam. Eklos is dead."

Blood dripped from his mouth as he smiled again.

"Hold on," I repeated. He couldn't die. After everything we had been through, he couldn't leave. "I told you to be careful, not for you to put yourself in Eklos's path," I scolded, though it was halfhearted.

He barely managed to shake his head side to side. "Eldrin, it was an honor to fight by your side… one last time. I am grateful that I got to see the end of Eklos's reign before…" Another cough worked its way up, halting his words.

"Stop," I pleaded, hot tears streaming down my cheeks. "Stop saying such things. You're going to be all right."

I looked around, searching. "Rythos!" I shouted. "Help! Rythos!" If he could mend Noam's wounds long enough for us to stitch them closed, maybe there was a chance.

A moment later, heavy footsteps sounded behind me.

"Please, Rythos. Help him," I cried.

The gray dragon kneeled at my side, studying Noam before shaking his head.

"I can't, Eldrin. His wounds are too great, and he's already lost too much blood." He put a clawed hand on my shoulder. "I'm sorry."

"Please," I begged, a sob breaking from my throat.

"I'm sorry," he repeated before leaving me with my dying friend.

Noam tried to smile, but more blood spilled from his mouth, coating his cracked lips. "It's all right, Eldrin. T-tell Kaida… I'm sorry, and that… she will be a great Queen. The Ancient Magic… was meant for her."

He moved his hand so that his palm was facing up and I clasped it in both of mine. His breaths were rattling, each full of pain. It was only a matter of time. I squeezed his hand tighter as if that would keep him here longer.

"You should be… so proud, my old friend. Look at what you all have done." Noam's eyes left mine for a moment to glance at the sky. Annion's dragons soared through the air, helping to transport the wounded farther into Metta where they could receive care.

"You didn't quit, though everything was against you. You didn't give up hope despite all signs pointing to utter defeat." He paused, struggling to take another breath. "You kept fighting, kept going. You didn't cripple under pressure or bow to your fears." Noam's lips spread into a bigger smile. "And look at what the result was." His grin ripped my heart into pieces. "Victory."

I swallowed back the strangled sob that threatened to escape. "You told Kaida that you weren't like your ancestors, that you weren't brave and valiant like them. You were wrong. Your name will be passed down with theirs, and humans and dragons alike will tell their children the story of *Noam* the Great."

Silver lined his eyes as he squeezed my hand, his throat bobbing as he swallowed. "Farewell, my friend. I'll tell Aela you said hello," he whispered, and my heart halted in my chest. The light faded from his eyes, like sand down a hole, and Noam's hand went slack within my own.

The cold air clouded above his face as he exhaled…

And then he was gone.

CHAPTER 57

KAIDA

Y INNER BEAST went silent.

It retreated into a deep part of me, satisfied.

I watched as the smoke stopped flowing out of Eklos's snout, as the light left his eyes and he passed from Elysia into the afterlife.

What would he find there? Would he have the peace he didn't deserve? Or would he suffer for the remainder of whatever eternity awaited us after we died? As much as he deserved pain and retribution for all he had done in his life, the human part of me also hated the idea of anyone suffering indefinitely, even if it was him.

I closed my eyes, rubbing my frozen fingers over my face.

It was over.

Eklos was dead.

So why didn't I feel better? I expected to feel relief, to cry tears of joy, or jump into the air with exhilaration that the war was over and that the evil in Elysia would finally come to an end.

But instead, I felt… nothing.

The clouds were finally peeling away, revealing a gorgeous blue sky that should have felt like a new beginning, but my insides were heavy, like a dark storm.

Eklos's red eyes were dull as they peered unseeing at the sky.

His scales had faded to a light-gray color, blood still dripping from his various wounds though his heart no longer beat. My sword still stood horrifyingly straight out of his skull, the amethyst jewel at the center of the hilt flashing in the sun while the blade still pinned his head to the ground. I couldn't stop staring at it.

Trembling arms wrapped around my waist from behind and Tarrin's familiar scent filled my nose as he buried his face into my neck.

"We did it," Tarrin said, over and over, pressing his hot lips to my skin. "Kaida, my love, you did it. It's over."

I didn't know if his words were simply to reassure me or to convince himself of the fact. Probably both.

He spun me around to face him, taking my face in his hands. His emerald eyes pierced into mine, holding so much pride and love that I struggled to hold his stare. With the amount of killing I had done today, how could he still love me? How could he look at me like I was the most amazing thing in this world?

I was a killer. A murderer.

"Stop, Kaida," Tarrin's lips murmured, his brows lowering over his eyes. "You are not a monster. You did what had to be done, my love. You saved us—saved Elysia."

I shook my head against his words. Something began writhing in my core, hot and electric, frantically looking for a way to escape. My fingers tingled, arms trembling at the force of it.

"Kaida?" Tarrin asked, studying my face, likely feeling the onslaught of whatever this was down the shifter bond.

Nausea swirled in me. I spun away, out of Tarrin's arms and crashed to my knees.

Tarrin said something, tried to reassure or comfort me, but I didn't hear the words. It was just a burbled noise in the back of my head.

I couldn't concentrate on anything but this burning, writhing pit in my core that had bile rising in my throat. I clenched snow between my fingers as I dry heaved, desperately trying to calm down, but to no avail. Mighty tremors shook my body. Thunder rumbled somewhere above us.

Eklos's corpse was sprawled mere feet away from me. The moment my eyes fixed on him, I erupted.

Every piece of fear, every sliver of a nightmare, every ounce of grief and fury poured out of me as I threw my head to the sky and let out the mightiest blast of fire I had ever created, never mind that I was in human form. At the same time my arms lifted, lightning forked from the single cloud remaining in the sky, and with a deafening scream, my arms crashed to the snow, the lightning following, striking the ground with the force of a tidal wave that knocked everyone outside to the ground. The following clap of thunder was unlike anything I had ever heard.

And yet in its wake, I heard silence. True silence—not a building fury within me. My well of magic deep in my core felt empty, cool, as if I had emptied every last bit out of me, all the poisonous bits that my beast had fed on. It was gone.

All that was left was a cool, soothing peace spreading through my bones.

And when I finally looked at what I had done, I couldn't help but laugh, though there was nothing truly funny about it.

Eklos's body was gone—the dragon of ash and smoke reduced to ashes and dirt. My sword was still standing in the snow, the amethyst glittering in the sunlight.

It really was over.

Eklos was gone.

The army was defeated; the Remnant reduced to rubble.

We had won.

Through heavy limbs, I pushed myself to my feet, Tarrin's hands instantly finding my shoulders to steady me.

His eyes were narrowed, studying me.

"We won," I whispered.

My favorite half smile curled his lips. "We did."

It was a time to celebrate. We should've been joining our families, rejoicing that the war was over, our enemies vanquished.

But instead, I buried my head in Tarrin's chest and cried.

CHAPTER 58

ELDRIN

I DUG NOAM'S GRAVE by hand, splinters from the wood handle digging into my skin as I forced the shovel beneath layers of snow and frozen earth.

It would have been easier to have used the strength of my dragon form to dig, but I couldn't bring myself to enter that body quite yet. The emotions were still too strong, like a pummeling fist straight to my heart.

When the hole was finally big enough, I dropped the shovel to the snow, and looked at my old friend, lying utterly still on the ground. The blood had been cleaned from him; his torn clothes replaced with some of the finest garments a human could wear.

I couldn't help but marvel at him. Against all odds, he had befriended a dragon, though he had every right to distrust and hate me. Then he stuck by my side for decades. And when it mattered most, he risked his life to go on a journey that had a great chance of failure and death and managed to not only find an army of shape-shifters and humans, but brought them back to fight in a war that wasn't their own.

It was a rare thing—to find so much goodness, such strength, in a person.

Noam was the best of them all.

Charred snow in the distance caught my eye. The place where Eklos, my cousin whom I had run from for centuries, had finally met his end. It was a strange feeling—finally being free. I no longer had to look over my shoulder, wondering if those red eyes would appear, or find a new place to hide.

Eklos was dead. And I was free.

I wasn't quite sure how to feel. I only wished that Aela and Noam were still here to witness the rebirth of Elysia—one void of slavery where they could have finally lived in peace.

A sniffle broke through my thoughts, and I found Kaida standing to my right, swiping at her red nose. Her brown hair was tucked back into a leather band, though wisps of it still escaped, fluttering in the cold breeze. The battle had ended hours ago, but dried blood was still caked over her skin, dirt smeared across her face. She had yet to change clothes.

She sniffled again before clearing her throat. "He did it." Her gaze was firmly fixed on Noam's peaceful face.

I nodded, swallowing the lump rising in my throat. "If not for his bravery, this battle may have ended differently."

Kaida's lips pressed into a thin line. "I miss him, Eldrin."

I held my breath to choke off the sob that tried to rip its way up my throat. "I do, too." I clenched my hands into fists, wincing at the splinters in my palms.

"But he wouldn't want us to be crying over him," I said after a moment. "He's likely rolling his eyes and scolding us in the after-life at this very moment."

A sad smile curled at the corners of Kaida's lips. "That sounds like Noam."

I gave a nod. "His spirit was as bright and hope-filled as the sun. And, like the sun, though we might not be able to always see him, Noam will always be with us. His spirit lives on in Elysia."

Steady tears leaked from her eyes as she kneeled next to Noam, running shaking fingers across his forehead.

"Thank you, Noam," she whispered, her chin trembling. "For everything."

When my daughter pulled herself together enough to stand, she fixed those startling turquoise eyes on me, so much like Aela's.

"Can I help you bury him?" she asked.

I could almost feel Noam smiling from wherever in the afterlife he was, and I had to swallow multiple times, trying to stuff my sob down deep enough where I could respond.

Finally, with a wobbling smile, I replied, "I'd like that."

⚃

When dusk had fallen and the cold of another winter's night descended over the village, I found Rythos waiting in front of Gendon's home. Ever since he had saved me during the battle, mending my wounds enough until Lita could stitch them up, I hadn't seen him. Part of me expected him to be dead.

His orange eyes studied me as I approached.

"You're still here?" I asked, stopping in front of him, ignoring the twang of pain in my chest.

"I just wanted to say goodbye," he said, his rumbling voice quiet.

"Goodbye?"

Rythos nodded. "I'm leaving. There's nothing left for me here."

I opened my mouth to speak, but to say what, I wasn't sure.

It's not like we had a friendship that would convince him to stay. He had spared my life in the battle, but I didn't know if he had forgiven me for leaving him all those centuries ago, or if he was capable of doing so now.

It didn't surprise me that he'd want to leave. Now that we knew there were other continents, other worlds beyond Elysia, I didn't blame him for wanting to leave all this pain behind and start somewhere new, somewhere fresh.

I nodded. "When?"

"Now," he answered, lowering his gaze to the snow. "I don't expect to ever see you again, Eldrin…" He paused, rubbing at his neck. "But I wanted you to know that I regret every piece I played in the war; all the pain and heartache I caused you and your family. My anger at you blinded me, and Eklos knew how to take advantage of that. He made me believe that you left after you promised not to because you thought you were superior to me. That you could never deign to be friends with the likes of me once you became *mutator formarum*." He met my gaze. "I know now that it was all a lie. I'm sorry."

It was more than I ever expected to get out of him, so a stunned nod was all I could give.

He pushed off his perch against Gendon's house and began walking down the path that led out of Metta.

"You could stay, Rythos." The words blurted out of me, though I wasn't sure where they had come from. Not once had the thought of Rythos joining our little family crossed my mind. But seeing his dejected face, so full of sadness and regret… He had no one. Everyone needed somebody.

"Stay. Heal with us."

For a moment, he appeared as though he were considering my offer.

A sad smile spread across his snout. "No, Eldrin," he replied, though his eyes softened. "Now that we know for sure there are lands outside of Elysia, I think it's time for me to discover what other worlds are out there." He looked up at the night sky. "What else I can offer the world besides…" He trailed off, gesturing at the snowy field where the battle had taken place. "This."

I expected his words, but his reason took me by surprise. Rythos wanted to be better, to discover who he was without the hatred of his past, and the fuel that Eklos used to stoke it into an inferno.

I understood his drive to find a new purpose. The need for it.

Seeing the understanding on my face, Rythos gave a final nod and turned to walk away.

"Goodbye, Eldrin."

It wasn't until he was well out of earshot that I was able to whisper, "Goodbye, old friend."

CHAPTER 59

TARRIN

MY MOTHER BUSTLED around the temporary tent that had been erected to treat the wounded. Along with many other women from Metta, she washed, stitched, and bandaged humans and dragons alike to the best of her ability. The scent of Flamaria flowers, used for their medicinal properties, mixed with the tang of blood and set my stomach to churning. This was the second time I had dared to visit the makeshift infirmary, after vomiting up my guts up the first time. Some of the wounds were untreatable, and the sight of people lying on blankets in pain, waiting for the afterlife to claim them… it was too much.

But as the new King of Elysia, I wanted to show my gratitude to them for all they had sacrificed. Even though it caused nausea to swirl in my stomach, I swallowed it down, lingering between each human and dragon, silently thanking them.

Both of my parents had somehow made it through the battle unscathed, despite being in human form. They each had a peppering of shallow wounds, but nothing life-threatening, and though my father had lost his ability to shift into dragon form forever, he seemed to be in much better spirits than my mother had when the same happened to her.

After the battle ended, he had explained that when he was a youngling, being a shape-shifter was frowned upon. He didn't grow up in Shegora where it was embraced and accepted. So, as a young dragon, he hid his ability away, never telling anyone. He forced himself to accept that he was only a dragon—nothing more.

And then when he met my mother, he wanted to share his deepest secret, but when he saw the dragons' reaction to Lita, a shape-shifter, becoming Queen... he knew he had to continue keeping it hidden, if only to keep her and their reign safe.

He didn't want to risk any backlash or bring further scrutiny on our family. He claimed that after so long keeping it hidden, he no longer missed shifting between forms, and the magic had gone dormant to the point where once he tried to shift again, it wouldn't come to the surface.

My father had apologized, too, as he wrapped me in an embrace for not protecting the humans. For not taking a stand. He had explained why he remained complicit with the Council's decisions. The treason had run too deep, and it was the only way to stay their hand.

In the end, we put it behind us—there was no use dwelling on something we couldn't change—and decided to move forward, promising no more secrets.

I glanced across the tent, finding him carrying a heavy bowl of water over to my mother, pressing a kiss to her temple.

It was still strange to see my father, with his pale skin and blue eyes, graying hair cropped short. For now, I was just immensely grateful that they both were alive, and that we had made it through a war with their hearts still beating.

Others were not so lucky.

I winced as I thought of Noam, of Gendon, and half the population of Metta that had been slaughtered, including a number of Z's rebels. I shuddered to think of what may have happened had the shifters from Almyra not shown up to help.

Alathar had survived too, and was somewhere in Metta, helping the effort to rebuild. I was thankful he had made it through the battle, though I wasn't surprised by it. He was the one who had taught me how to fight, after all. I looked forward to sitting down with him when everything was back to normal, whatever normal was, and listening to his stories of traveling to Almyra. I still marveled that both him and Noam were sent to the same place, albeit unknowingly, and both returned to Elysia just when we needed them most.

Needing to breathe fresh air, I gave a small wave to my parents and left the tent, relishing the clean, crisp air seeping into my lungs as I stepped outside. I bit the inside of my cheek as I walked back through the remainder of Metta.

Much of the village had been destroyed, burned down to cinders. The dragons that survived the battle were helping to lift and move large pieces of debris, while the humans swept away the ashes, creating a blank slate for something new. It would take months to rebuild, but Kaida and I had promised Gendon that it would be our first priority once the war was over. Even though he was no longer with us, we would follow through on our word. Phelix had returned with those who'd been evacuated. He was the new leader of Metta, but he was taking time to mourn the loss of his father.

An ocean-blue dragon was helping lift a burned log that used to be part of someone's house. When he caught sight of me, he carefully lowered it to the ground and made his way over.

As he arrived, he lowered into a bow and said, "Your Majesty."

I couldn't contain my eyeroll. "Z, after everything we've been through, I think you can call me Tarrin."

That infernal smirk twisted his snout. "As you wish… Your Majestic Tarrin-ness."

I snorted once before dissolving into a fit of laughter.

Though our relationship had always been strained, I felt as

though we had finally come to an understanding, one that allowed for mutual respect. He still got under my skin, but that surge of jealousy, of hate, was no longer there.

"Anything new, Z?" I asked once I got control of myself.

Z sobered. "My rebels have taken care of the remaining army dragons who refused to surrender."

My stomach dropped, but I fought the urge to close my eyes. All those lives, gone, just because their hearts were so full of hatred, and they wouldn't let it go.

"And the others?"

Z turned his snout to the blue sky, thoughtful. "I've absorbed them into the rebels and tasked some of my most trusted dragons with training and helping them. I'm confident the dragons that surrendered will make a full recovery—of both body and heart."

"That's good to hear," I replied, my thoughts spinning. An idea formed in my mind, and I spoke before thinking it through. "Z?"

"Hmm?"

"Now that Eklos is gone, and there's no threat of war, or a need to fight anymore, what use for your rebels is there?"

Z scratched at the scales on his head. "I suppose there isn't much of a need, but they're my family, Tarrin. I won't just send them away. Many of them… this is all they have."

I nodded, expecting as much. "Well, then I have a proposition for you."

He arched a scaled brow. "And what might that be?"

I waited a moment, letting the idea fill me like my magic, knowing in my gut that this was the best thing for Elysia.

"It's possible that in the coming days and months, when we disband slavery and free every human, that there may be backlash. There will need to be protective measures in place, dragons to help keep order, who fully believe in our mission to make Elysia a better world."

"What are you saying?"

For the first time, I gave a full smile to Z. "How would you feel about resurrecting the King's Guard, with you as its captain?"

His eyes widened, surprise causing his snout to fall open. His eyes narrowed after a moment as he studied me, checking to see if it was a serious offer.

Finally, he straightened before dropping to a knee before me, bowing his head.

"My King, it would be an honor."

⋆

My mother thought that the people of Metta, Z's rebels, and the Almyra shifters could use a reason to celebrate.

Not that defeating Eklos's army wasn't reason enough, but it was tainted with grief and pain.

She wanted something that had no association with pain or loss or anything negative. Somehow that celebration translated to a coronation party for me and Kaida. Though we had already been married, it hadn't been a public thing as it normally was. So, my mother had the bright idea of having a party where those gathered in Metta could celebrate with us—the coming of a new King and Queen. A new Elysia.

Even though Gendon hadn't made it through the battle, he had left a will of sorts, stating that we were welcome to use his house as often as we needed, and of course, Phelix had been more than happy to have the company now that his father was gone.

It didn't feel right though—being here when he wasn't, using his bedrooms, eating the food left in the kitchen.

I think I spoke for all of us when I said that we all missed his smiling snout, his positive personality that kept hope alive among us all.

Kaida slipped out in the early hours of the morning. It had been only a couple days since the war ended, and she hadn't been sleeping well, waking at odd hours of the night. She often left to walk the streets of Metta, carefully avoiding the snowy field at the end of the road where remnants of the battle remained, though countless dragons and humans had worked hard to clean it up.

I closed my eyes, searching for her through our bond, relief flooding me as I found her safe and unharmed, though her emotions were full of sadness. The place where we had chosen to bury the dead… she had visited it multiple times—walking through it, thanking them for their sacrifice, for their help in bringing about a better world.

She was there now, and I forced my mind away from hers, letting her have privacy. We were all feeling the grief of losing people we loved, of struggling to move on after such a violent war. We all needed to process, to work through it without outside judgement. After everything she had given, it was the least I could do—give her the time and space she needed, even if all I wanted to do was run to her and wrap her in my arms.

I paced the length of our bedroom in Gendon's cave-home, skirting around the bed frame to avoid stubbing my toes. I was dressed in my coronation clothes, the tightness, the luxury of them feeling all wrong in the face of everything around us. I had wanted to wear black to honor those that didn't make it through the war, but my mother insisted that this was a time to celebrate and was not the time for mourning. According to tradition, I was supposed to wear turquoise clothes to match the color of my scales, but I was able to negotiate with her to wear something a little more subdued.

Instead, I wore a fitted blue jacket that reminded me of the color of Z's scales, with gold buttons lining the front, and strange tassel things that I thought were absurd dangling from my shoulders. Matching pants adorned my bottom half and shining leather boots were shoved on my feet.

My wavy hair was tucked back into a leather band, though

loose strands managed to still flutter in my eyes. Perhaps I should change it up, chop it all off.

Don't you dare, Kaida scolded through our bond, though amusement laced each word.

It's just hair, I offered back.

If you cut it off, then I'd have nothing to run my hands through.

I arched a brow even though she couldn't see it. *Okay, you convinced me.*

I felt her smile before she went silent again.

Something shiny caught my eye in the mirror, and I turned to find the silver box that held my crown. Sitting next to it, in a slightly smaller rose gold box, sat Kaida's crown.

I chuckled to myself, remembering the crown of flames and lightning she had worn during the battle. She didn't need a physical crown at all, but it would make me the happiest male in all of Elysia to see this one upon her brow.

I lifted the lid, peering at the piece of metal inside. Sapphire stones lined the front of it, little gold spires shooting up to the sky until, at the center of the crown, a large amethyst stone sat, so pure you could almost see through it, and so vibrant it flickered purple lights on the wall. Woven in amongst the jewels were pieces of metal shaped into flames and vines.

It was beautiful, just like her.

A knock on the door interrupted my admiring before it opened, and my mother popped her head in.

"Ready, Tarrin?"

I couldn't help but chuckle. "You realize that most of Metta is still sleeping right, Mother?"

A smile twitched at the corners of her lips. "It never hurts to be early."

I glanced outside where dawn was just beginning to spread its fingers through the sky. "The coronation isn't until midday," I replied, arching a brow.

We both stared at each other with serious faces for another moment before we burst out laughing in tandem.

When we finally quieted, she waved toward the door. "Come have breakfast with your father and me. Kaida is welcome join us too, if she'd like."

The smile was quick to slip off my face. "She's out at the graves."

My mother only nodded. "You can still invite her. She's your wife and a part of this family. Now that this mess with Eklos is over, we have all the time in the world to get to know each other." She winked before disappearing out the door.

A sensation like cool water covering my skin on a hot day ran through me.

Time.

That was something we never had before.

It was always against us.

But now... now we had every minute... every second of the rest of our lives to be together, to grow and heal.

I hadn't known quite what the future would look like when we got to the other side of this war.

But *that*... that seemed like a great place to start.

CHAPTER 60

KAIDA

IT WAS THE third time I had visited the spot where Noam was buried.

The fabric of my pants grew wet from kneeling in the snow as I pushed the last of the dirt into place above a second grave.

It was Jinna's.

It had taken hours to find her. Her lifeless body had been pinned beneath the carcass of a dragon. My heart had ripped into two at the sight of her, a small smile on her face even in death as though she had finally found peace—finally reunited with her brother, Tal.

Hot tears steamed against the cold air on my cheeks.

I truthfully didn't know how I had any tears left at all.

Though we had won the battle, defeated Eklos and the Remnant, and subsequently the army, I still fought against the crushing grief of losing so many.

Jinna hadn't deserved to die, nor did Noam.

So many innocent people slaughtered by the dragons.

I squeezed my eyes closed, more tears leaking out.

Footsteps crunched through the snow behind me, and I knew who it was before the scent even hit my nose.

"We shouldn't be celebrating," I murmured, feeling Tarrin's heat wrap around me as he kneeled by my side.

"On the contrary, my love. This is exactly the time to celebrate."

I snapped my gaze to his, hating the look of pity on his face.

"Our friends are dead, Tarrin. How can we celebrate that?"

"The people we lost… They knew there was a chance they wouldn't make it to the other side of the battle. And they accepted that and fought anyway. Don't cast aside everything they gave with their sacrifice by wishing they were still here. It was because of that sacrifice, that bravery, that we stand here now; that Elysia has a chance to prosper and grow into a world worth living in. Though, yes, it is sad… they wouldn't want you to be torn up over their loss. They'd want us to *live*." Tarrin wiped the streaks from my cheeks.

"Yes, we mourn them and miss them, but we also thank them for all they gave, and now we turn and make their sacrifice worth it by creating that better world that they dreamed of with us. The best way to do that is to stop looking back, to stop thinking of the what-ifs, and simply move forward."

He was right, of course. Even Jinna bravely mourned the loss of her brother, Tal, while making an effort to move forward. *I won't let his sacrifice go to waste.* Her words echoed in my mind, bringing fresh tears to my eyes. I didn't know how to turn these feelings off, to shove them away.

He shook his head, hearing my internal thoughts. "You don't have to shove them away or ignore them, Kaida. Feel what you're feeling. Fully, completely. It's okay to be sad. It's okay to feel grief and loss over our friends. But *don't stay there*. You accept those feelings, but you keep moving, continue forward. It's not easy, I know. But out of these ashes of death and loss, we rise, and we create something even more beautiful than we ever dreamed."

Tarrin wiped the wetness from my face once more. "No matter how long it takes, no matter how many tears I have to wipe from your cheeks, I will be here, and we will weather the storm of grief and victory together. You're not alone, my love." He pecked a kiss on my forehead.

A small smile curled my lips, but it was all I could muster. My breath shook as I exhaled. "What now?"

My favorite half-smile lit up his face. "Oh, many things," he said with a wink. "But first, we've been invited to breakfast with my parents."

I resisted glancing at the graves. "I'm not very hungry."

Tarrin sensed my mood through our shifter bond. "No? I heard they have a large assortment of cheese." We locked eyes and his grin grew, recalling our first meal together when I had stupidly asked if he liked cheese.

I couldn't stop my lips from curving into a smile. "I do enjoy cheese."

"I thought you might," he winked again. "And after that, we must attend a coronation."

I wrinkled my nose. "Sounds like a stuffy affair."

"Wait until you see the King and Queen. Quite stuffy indeed," he replied through a wry grin, and I couldn't help the chuckle that slipped through my lips.

His resulting smile was full of wonder and love and my cheeks warmed beneath his gaze.

I pressed a kiss to each of my palms and pressed them into the cold dirt over both Noam's and Jinna's graves.

"Goodbye, my friends."

I wanted to say more, but the words wouldn't come. Perhaps someday I could return and thank them properly for all they gave. Tell them of the Elysia that they helped bring about.

But today wasn't that day.

So, instead, I grabbed Tarrin's hand in mine and said, "Let's go get crowned."

ℭℬ

The sun was high overhead, the day warmer than those before it. Dripping icicles hung from the roofs of the remaining houses in Metta, the snow sloshy and wet beneath our feet as we walked the long street that led into the heart of the town.

Normally, a coronation would take place in the throne room at the Royal Palace but seeing as none of us were ready to leave Metta just yet, we made do with the courtyard in the very center of the village. Somehow, despite the heavy damage to many of the homes and shops, the village center remained relatively unscathed.

The people of Metta lined the street as far as the eye could see, crowds of them pressed together in the distance where the courtyard was. Tarrin and I walked hand-in-hand, our boots sinking into the snow beneath us. We had decided that we would stay in human form until the end of the ceremony, when it required us to be in our dragon bodies.

We wanted to start our reign with the humans knowing they had an ally in us.

Endless smiles, shouts of joy and gratitude, and bundles of snowflowers pelted us as we walked the long street, my grip on Tarrin's hand growing tighter with each step. A sparkling amethyst gown adorned my body, the same color of my scales. The bodice was tight, with silky skirts flaring to the ground. Long sleeves clasped around my wrists, though the fabric on the upper arms was loose and flowing, blowing in the light breeze. I should have been dreadfully cold in the winter air but found myself comfortable and warm.

The entirety of the fabric shimmered like iridescent scales in the sunlight. It was breathtaking, perfectly complimenting Tarrin's coronation outfit. Though it was expected of him to wear a suit that matched the color of his scales, he asked to remain in dark-blue garments. He wanted me to shine, he had told me, for I was the reason we had defeated Eklos, defeated the reign of evil in Elysia.

I had told him he was being silly, but he remained firm in his decision.

Even though the color of his suit was more subdued, the tailors that made it had created it to shimmer just like mine. He looked like the midnight sky with all its stars; I looked like the first signs of dawn after an endless night.

We reached the end of the street that led to the courtyard and paused for a moment as people swept out of the way to make room for us. It wasn't very large, but arches of snowflowers were strung between the rooftops, stark white against the cloudless blue sky. The scent of crisp winter air and cotton filled my nose, and I inhaled deeply, letting it calm the roiling in my stomach.

Martik and Lita stood on the dais that had been built out of wood, in garments that matched the turquoise and ruby colors of their former scales, two wooden thrones reaching toward the sky behind them.

Though it had been days since the battle, and Martik had explained to us repeatedly why he had never told anyone about him being a shape-shifter, it was still a strange sight to see his tall, lanky form, standing there hand-in-hand with Lita. I guess that was the good thing about the future—we had all the time in the world now to get to know this new Martik, to understand him.

And now him and Lita had another chance at life, at loving each other.

If that didn't show the victory we had won, I didn't know what did.

Tarrin's mother was beaming, her eyes bright as they flickered between the two of us. In unison, the former King and Queen of Elysia reached their outside hand toward us, their inside hands intertwined.

"Come, Tarrin and Kaida of Elysia," Lita called across the courtyard and everything went silent. "Your future awaits you."

Tarrin led us forward, down the narrow path the villagers had opened for us. Many reached out, though they didn't touch us, murmuring their thanks and well-wishes for the future.

Are you ready? Tarrin's voice filtered down the bond.

What kind of a question is that? I replied. I was born and raised a slave, thrust into a new world as a shape-shifter, battled an army of dragons, and now I was about to be officially crowned the Queen of Elysia. Was *anyone* ever ready for that?

He smirked, though his eyes never strayed from the end of the path where his parents stood.

All those things you believe disqualify you… those are what make you the perfect candidate to be Queen. You understand this world we live in better than anyone.

I gave an imperceptible shake of my head. *I'm no ruler.*

Tarrin's hands caressed my mind through the shifter bond. *Sometimes, Kaida, it's our biggest trials, struggles, and imperfections that create exactly the right combination to do what is needed. Maybe you're not what people expect as a ruler, but you're a lover of people, of justice, of making things right. And* that *makes you the perfect person to do this.*

A tear slipped out of the corner of my eye at his words, just as we arrived in front of his parents. Lita reached forward, her warm fingers brushing it away. She cradled my cheek in her palm for a moment before she cleared her throat.

"Good people of Metta," she called, her voice echoing between the buildings. A hush fell over the crowd, every eye fixed on the former Queen.

"Today, we celebrate. Not only Elysia's victory over evil." She paused as the people erupted into cheers, many raising their hands to the sky. "But we celebrate the crowning of a new monarchy, one that will usher in an era that Elysia has not experienced in millenniums." Another deafening roar rocked through the people.

"In every season there is a time of destruction and a time for growth and rebuilding. We have all fought hard to end the era of evil in our world. And now…" Lita paused once more, looking at Tarrin and I with a smile. "And now, we get to experience a glorious rebuilding of Elysia, one built on justice, peace, but most importantly, love.

"I have witnessed these two face the most horrifying and horrendous evil, and yet they stand before you, ready to do what is right. They do not wish for revenge or retribution, but peace and unity." Lita smiled, looking out at the crowd as they cheered before fixing her attention on us.

"Tarrin," she said, taking hold of his hands. "Do you hereby swear to protect Elysia, to do everything in your power to prosper and help its people, and to serve faithfully from now until your last breath?"

Tarrin gave a firm nod. "I swear."

At this, his mother smiled, and Martik reached across their clasped hands, extending his own to me. I slipped my hands into his, all our arms creating an X, the old rulers and the new linked together.

"Kaida," his voice rumbled, his turquoise eyes bright in the light of the sun. "Do you hereby swear to protect Elysia, to do everything in your power to prosper and help its people, and to serve faithfully from now until your last breath? And love my son with all your heart?" He added the last question quietly so no one else could hear but us.

Despite my doubts and fears of being the Queen that Elysia needed, there was one thing I knew for certain.

I loved Tarrin with every fiber of my being, dragon or not, and I loved the people of Elysia. I would face countless wars if it meant keeping them safe.

My lips spread into a grin as I glanced at Tarrin, then Lita, and lastly Martik.

"I swear."

Z appeared next to Martik, Eldrin appearing next to Lita, each holding a metal box. Z handed the silver one to Martik, and the former King opened it, slipping the crown from its velvet bed.

He lifted it into the air, hovering over Tarrin's head.

"Then I hereby declare you, my beloved son, King Tarrin of Elysia."

Martik set the crown onto Tarrin's head and the crowd erupted into a rumble of praise and adoration.

In the time it took for them to settle and quiet, Eldrin gave me a big smile, and handed the rose gold box to Lita. As soon as the lid opened, I couldn't hold back a gasp. It was delicate, perfect, all the way to the amethyst stone at the center.

Lita lifted it above my head, meeting my gaze.

"I hereby declare you, my beloved daughter…" She paused and tears filled my eyes at the title I had missed so much since the death of my own mother. "Queen Kaida of Elysia!" She settled the crown into my hair and my magic awoke, lightning and flames intertwining amongst the metal. I glanced at Tarrin and found flickering flames ascending from the tips of his own.

Absolute pride shone on Lita's face as she stared at me. The crowd was deafening, some cheering, some crying from joy.

"People of Metta, of Elysia, I proudly introduce you to your new King and Queen!"

In unison, Tarrin and I turned to face them, simultaneously shifting into dragon form.

I love you, Kaida.

I grinned at him. *I love you, Tarrin.*

And with a mighty inhale, we linked claws, and each sent a plume of white-hot flames into the sky, thus signaling the start of the reign of King Tarrin and Queen Kaida. The reign of a better world.

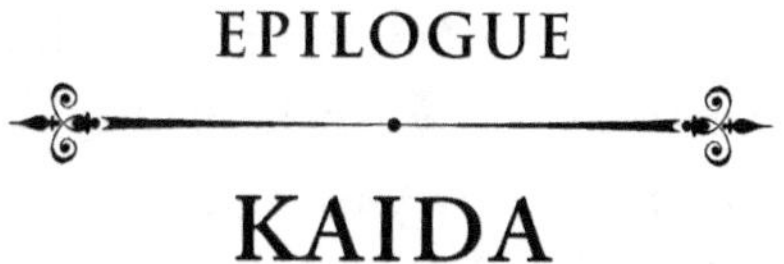

KAIDA

Six Months Later

"MY LOVE, DON'T you think it would be better to wait until later to mess with your hair?" Tarrin's voice came from the doorway of our room at the Royal Palace.

Meara, the girl who had been assigned as my slave when I first arrived at the Royal Palace over a year ago, let out a chuckle and I stared at his reflection in the mirror before me. Though it had taken some time to work through her massive betrayal when she had delivered me to Eklos and I was subsequently taken back to Belharnt all those months ago, we had managed to work things out, slowly rebuilding trust, and she had become one of my closest friends.

"Well, I have to look my best, don't I?" I said through a smile. "A proper Solstice hasn't been celebrated in centuries."

The Summer Solstice had finally arrived, and for the first time since before Xalerion, Elysia would be celebrating. Unlike the Winter Solstice where gifts were exchanged and time was spent with family, the Summer Solstice was a vibrant celebration of life. Full of music, food, and dancing. After everything we had fought through, it was important to me and Tarrin to celebrate life, and what better time to do that?

A fond smile tilted his lips. "I'll tell them you'll just be a few moments then." He disappeared back into the hallway.

As soon as he slipped through the door, Meara moved away, preparing my dress as I went to look out the window.

When Tarrin and I left Metta to travel home, his parents and Z had accompanied us. When he had told me that he was going to bring back the King's Guard and have Z's rebels take it over, my heart had swelled. Despite all their disagreements, they finally figured out how to work together, and I was relieved that I wouldn't have to say goodbye to yet another friend by leaving Z behind. My father decided to stay in Metta, continuing the effort to rebuild on our behalf, intending to join us for the Solstice.

I blinked against the bright sunlight as I took in the view. It was a strange thing, looking out at Elysia from the highest level of the Royal Palace. Visually, it appeared the same as it always did. The same gardens and countryside around the palace, the Ilgathor Mountains far in the distance, followed by all the other towns and villages my eye couldn't see. It was all the same… but the heart was different.

Shortly after we returned to the palace, Tarrin and I signed our first decree—banning the use of human slaves. They were to be seen as equals, living side-by-side with the dragons. With their newfound freedom, and the spreading knowledge that there were other lands beside our own, many chose to sail away from here, searching for new places to live, for new beginnings.

And as expected, there were a number of dragons all over Elysia that didn't agree with that decision. Thankfully, Z and the new King's Guard were able to quell any disturbance or uprisings the dragons attempted.

It took a few months, but everything finally quieted down,

and for the first time in a millennium, there was true peace in Elysia.

The thought made my heart swell.

I lived seventeen years as a slave, being tortured and abused. But now, on the verge of turning nineteen, I was free, as were the rest of the humans. It was a day I had never expected to see.

"Are you ready, miss?" Meara called from the side of the bed where she held up my dress.

It was a stunning piece in ruby red with flowing, gauzy skirts and loose sleeves that cinched at each wrist. It shimmered like dragon scales. Despite the beauty of it, I scowled.

"What did I say about calling me that?"

Her cheeks reddened. "Old habits," she murmured with a shrug, and I smiled, crossing the room, and slipping into the dress.

"Thank you, Meara," I said, and she buttoned up the back of the dress, adjusting the stray hairs that had already fallen out of its updo.

"Shall we?" I asked her, and a genuine smile lit her face.

"After you, my Queen."

Instead of going first, I linked arms with her, and led us through the halls of the palace. The humid air swallowed me like water as we wandered through the gardens, and the same familiar fountain, from so long ago when Tarrin had first brought me here, loomed in the center of the celebration. Thousands of different blooming flowers surrounded us, filling the summer air with fragrance. Tiny torches were strung together between trees and bushes, creating a twinkling affect like stars even in broad daylight. A wooden table was off to the side with a plethora of different meats, fruits, and pastries, including a large mango pie I'd requested Lita make for Tarrin.

We kept the party small, just our close friends. After the war, we simply wanted to enjoy each other's company without fear perched on our shoulders. Perhaps next year we'd invite the rest of Elysia, but this time… it was just for us.

Martik, Lita, and Tarrin were seated in a few chairs set before the fountain, while Z was filling his mug with ale at the table.

I couldn't hold back a snort. "Already drinking, my friend?" I said to him as we arrived.

He winced, turning to face me. "I don't do parties."

A giggle spilled out of me, but I let him be.

"Where's Eldrin?" I asked, noticing my father was absent.

Lita waved a hand. "He said he'd be here."

Right on cue, the shadow of a dragon flew overhead, circled us a few times, then landed with a thud in the gravel.

"You're late," I drawled.

Eldrin's eyes softened. It had been six months since I had last seen him—the longest we had been apart since we were reunited all those months ago. I hurried over to him, throwing my arms around him as he shifted into human form.

His chuckle brushed my hair. "I missed you too, daughter."

I pulled back with a grin and led him over to everyone else. In a matter of moments, there were hugs and laughter and crude jokes, but all I could do was stare.

I couldn't help but marvel at my friends. Dragons *and* humans. We were safe and together… And there was peace—true peace— in Elysia for the first time since the Order of the Magus walked these lands. A pang went through my stomach at the thought, my mind drifting back to Noam who was deep beneath the earth back in Metta.

Eldrin met my gaze. I knew he missed Noam too. I wasn't sure how he stayed in Metta with the reminders of the ghosts of the past around every corner.

But from the day the battle ended, to the day I breathed my last breath, Noam's sacrifice, and all the others who died in the name of freedom, would not be in vain.

I would be grateful, celebrate their lives with each breath I continued living.

And as I sat in this garden with all these people I loved, with Z dozing off to the side with a mug hanging precariously from his claws, Martik and Lita and their hands intertwined talking with Eldrin, or even Tarrin as he gazed at me with eyes full of love...

Everything we had been through, all the things we had fought through. In the end it was all a gift. And I didn't think I would ever stop being grateful for it.

Tarrin cleared his throat, lifting his glass into the air, the bubbles fizzing over the rim. Z jolted awake.

"To a lifetime of peace, happiness, and love."

"Well, that sounds boring," Z remarked, in his typical snarky fashion.

We all burst out laughing.

"How about to new beginnings," I amended Tarrin's toast.

Z looked thoughtful for a moment, glancing around at everyone before offering me his signature smirk.

"Now, *that* I'll toast to."

THE END

ACKNOWLEDGEMENTS

Is this real life? *Scales of Ash & Smoke* started as a measly little chapter in a high school creative writing class…and now it's become an entire trilogy. What? Never in my wildest dreams did I ever imagine I'd be here, and though it hasn't been easy, it's been worth every moment of joy and stress. *Scales of Sun & Storm* was the easiest of the three to write (not that writing a book is ever easy) mostly because I was so desperate (or my characters were) to finally have that happy ending. The end battle has been playing like a movie in my mind for over a decade and being able to put those words onto paper was a dream. I love this book with all my heart. *insert happy tear emoji here*

I hope, more than anything, that when you finish this book, you feel hope; that it felt like coming home. Life can be so dark and challenging, but there is always hope, even if it's only a glimmer. Keep fighting, keep going. Don't give up.

And never ever quit dreaming.

I hope you loved Kaida and Tarrin's story as much as I do.

Writing and publishing a book can be a lonely journey, but it really takes a village to make the magic happen. There are a few people I could not have done this without:

Thanks be to God—for His never-ending faithfulness throughout this entire process. Whether I needed peace or provision, He always came through. He never failed. I'm so thankful for this gift that He has given me, and may He get all the glory from these books. I would not be where I am without Him.

To my husband, Cody—you are the biggest dreamer I know, and I'm so thankful that you've continued to push me to reach for the stars. You never once doubted my ability to write and publish these books, and that has meant everything. Thank you for pushing me to continue to dream and reminding me that the doubts and fears in my heads are all lies to keep my stories away from those who need it. I love you, honey bunches of oats.

To Brittany Cox—you will never know how much you truly helped me as I finished this book. You helped keep me sane, never failed to encourage me, and gave me that kick in the butt right when I needed it. I am extraordinarily thankful that you started bugging me (LOL) on IG and that we became such good friends. You've made this journey a lot less lonely and helped to pull me out of some very dark moments. Love you, friend! Now get to writing!

To The 3 Authorteers—I am so blessed to have found writer buddies like you. You've made this very lonely journey of being an author so much better, and I love that we can talk about anything and everything. You guys are my writer besties and I'm so grateful for your constant encouragement and your friendship! I'm always cheering you on!

To my Beta Readers—thank you for reading the scary draft of my book, for all your constructive criticism, as well as your encouragement. It's terrifying having readers see my story for the first time, but your feedback has been invaluable, and has lit a fire under me to push to the finish line. Y'all are the best!

To all my author/bookstagram friends—I'm so thankful for each of you! Your excitement, encouragement, and every like, comment, and share mean so much to me. I feel so blessed every day to have found a community of people who are so supportive and that cheer me on, and that I can cheer on as well.

To Elizabeth Hitchcock—Thank you for being my biggest fan that never expected to be a fan LOL. Your excitement and enthusiasm have given me so much life over the past year and has helped to keep me going. Thank you for being my biggest cheerleader and for starting the tradition of coffee & cannons for my book releases. Love you, friend!

To Andrea Hurst and Lucia Ferrara—thank you for all the work you put into editing my book and encouraging me along the way. You helped me make this story what it is, and it never would have been possible without both of you.

And to my readers—I am beyond honored that you chose to pick up these books that have been such a treasure to me. All I've ever wanted was to write stories that provide an escape from reality for a while. Stories that have light and hope in what often feels like a dark world. Books are keepers of magic that can transport us out of anything we're facing and into something greater. I hope when you pick up this book, you feel uplifted, hopeful, and have a big old grin on your face. Thank you for reading the finale of Kaida and Tarrin's story. It means the absolute world.

ABOUT THE AUTHOR

Emily Schneider is an award-winning author who grew up in Minnesota where she spent most of her life studying music and singing, which ironically has nothing to do with writing fantasy novels. While music had always been a passion, Emily could never get away from her love of reading and writing books full of dragons, Fae, monsters, magic, and romance. When she is not writing about dragons  and magic, you can find Emily chasing around her two dogs, Pixel and Frodo, playing Mario Kart with her husband, or watching The Lord of the Rings for the one-hundred-and-eleventh time.

Emily is the author of *Scales of Ash & Smoke*, fantasy winner of the 2021 Best Indie Book Award.

emilyschneiderwrites.com

IG: @emilyschneiderwrites

TT: @emilyschneiderwrites

www.ingramcontent.com/pod-product-compliance
Lightning Source LLC
Chambersburg PA
CBHW050855210726
48290CB00004B/1243